The Broken Shore

Catriona King

Copyright © 2013 by Catriona King
Photography: Andrey Yurlov
Design: Crooked Cat
All rights reserved.

The Broken Shore: 978-1-909841-35-2
No part of this book may be used or reproduced in any manner whatsoever without written permission of the author or Crooked Cat Publishing except for brief quotations used for promotion or in reviews. This is a work of fiction. Names, characters, places, and incidents are used fictitiously. Any resemblance to actual persons living or dead, business establishments, events, or locales, is entirely coincidental.

First Black Line Edition, Crooked Cat Publishing Ltd. 2013

Discover us online:
www.crookedcatpublishing.com

Join us on facebook:
www.facebook.com/crookedcatpublishing

For my mother.

About the Author

Catriona King trained as a Doctor and a police Forensic Medical examiner in London, where she worked for many years. She worked closely with the Metropolitan Police on several occasions. In recent years, she has returned to live in Belfast.

She has written since childhood; fiction, fact and reporting.

'The Broken Shore' is the fifth novel in the Craig Modern Thriller Series. It follows Marc Craig and his team through the streets of Northern Ireland in their hunt for a young woman's killer and sees them uncover links to a terrorist from the past.

'The Slowest Cut', a sixth novel in the Craig series, is nearing completion.

Acknowledgements

Huge thanks to my friends for always being there.

Thanks to Crooked Cat publishing for being so unfailingly supportive and cheerful.

And I would like to thank all the police officers that I have ever worked with anywhere, for their unfailing professionalism, wit and compassion.

Catriona King
Belfast, December 2013

The Craig Modern Thriller Series

A Limited Justice

The Grass Tattoo

The Visitor

The Waiting Room

The Broken Shore

The Broken Shore

Chapter One

Tuesday 29th October 2013: Portstewart.

The woman's hand lay palm-up on the ice-cold sand and the grey Atlantic water filtered between her fingers, wrinkling each pale tip. The hand was delicate, with slender fingers, each one with its nail broken and torn. The smoothness of its skin said youth, just as its pallor indicated death.

The man dug the grave deeper, tiring from the task, until finally he gathered his detritus and strolled away. He inhaled the sea air deeply and smiled, enjoying the final rays of the evening sun. A couple jogged gently in the distance, listening to the noisy, breaking waves. They completely missed the mound of sand, covered in a moment by the coming tide, and they missed the man who had made it. The sun set behind the cliffs as the lone figure entered the high grass, all signs that he'd ever been there erased by the night.

***

Friday 1st November 4 p.m. Docklands Coordinated Crime Unit.

Craig threw the file down hard on his desk, swearing in frustration at his wasted time. The sudden thud caught Nicky's ear and she stood up outside at her desk, peering through his frosted-glass office door. She thought for a moment then sat down again, choosing discretion as valour's better part, then she pressed her percolator's button and beckoned Liam Cullen over with a wave.

He was glad of the interruption. Studying for his Chief Inspector board had been bad enough, but now that he'd passed it they wanted him to read more crap to 'bring him up to speed'. He pictured unseen senior officers making the parentheses with their hands and shuddered. Paperwork bored him to death, but they hadn't had a good case in weeks to give him an excuse to stop.

He stood at Nicky's desk listening to the coffee boil, until Craig's swearing finally died down and she tapped gently at his door. She gauged the tone of his 'come in' then entered, pushing Liam in front of her as she did.

Liam kicked a pile of papers from his path and gazed at his boss. His tie was loosened halfway down his neck and his dark hair was standing on end, indicating he'd been raking it hard. He looked like an advert for hair wax. Liam grinned and then risked an old joke, pointing at the word Superintendent on the door.

"You asked for it, now you've got it, boss."

Nicky braced herself for the tirade that never came. Instead, Craig gave a rueful grin and beckoned them in. He smiled gratefully at the coffee and nodded them both to a seat. Liam normally stood, arguing it was better for his back, but now was no time to insist.

They'd barely sat down when Craig started to complain in a voice so pitiful that Liam mimed playing a violin. Craig laughed, acknowledging that he wouldn't get any sympathy for taking higher rank. He'd known what the job entailed when he'd taken it on and anything was better than having Terry Harrison as his D.C.S. They sipped their coffee in amiable silence for a moment then Craig had a thought.

"Nicky. Do you remember that sergeant, Jake McLean; the one who helped us on the Ackerman case?"

She thought for a moment then nodded, setting her newly

auburn pony-tail bouncing.

"What about him?

"He wanted to come back and work with us, didn't he?"

"Yes. He was really disappointed when he had to go back to Stranmillis. He definitely wanted to stay."

Craig turned to Liam for confirmation. He was fishing a piece of soggy biscuit from his cup. Each time he reached for it, it slipped from his grasp and he muttered under his breath. Nicky sighed heavily then slipped two red-nailed fingers straight into his tea, grabbing the biscuit and depositing it deftly on his saucer without skipping a beat. Liam went to object but he was stopped by an arched eyebrow. Craig laughed at the exchange, then turned Liam's attention back to McLean.

"What do you think of him, Liam?"

Liam shrugged. "Aye he was good, right enough." He smiled knowingly, reading Craig's mind. "And he's good with the old paperwork as well."

"That's not what I…"

Liam shot him a sceptical look and Craig stopped mid-sentence and smiled, knowing he'd been caught out. Liam crammed another biscuit into his mouth then started speaking again, much to Nicky's disgust.

"I think he enjoys it myself. Some people are weird like that, aren't they?"

Craig laughed again, his navy eyes crinkling up.

"Check if he wants to come back, Liam, would you? But do it on the Q.T. or Chief Inspector Nugent will moan that I'm poaching his staff. I'll talk to him if McLean says yes." He waved at the files on his desk. "We need him. If I don't get rid of some of this paperwork soon, you'll have to dig me out of here one day."

They drank their coffee in silence for a moment until Nicky broke it.

"I probably shouldn't say this until I'm sure, but Portstewart Station was on the phone."

The two men leaned forward simultaneously, like synchronised swimmers about to enter a dive. Nicky laughed at their eagerness and waved them back.

"Don't get excited. I'm sure it'll turn out to be nothing, but..."

Craig sprang to his feet and grabbed the phone, dialling the small station on the North coast. The call was answered with a yawn.

"Hello. Portstewart Station."

"Hello, is that D.C.I. White's office? It's Superintendent Craig from Docklands C.C.U.. Is he free?"

Jim O'Neill jerked upright. He'd been the sergeant at Portstewart for five years and nothing much ever happened. Well, not unless you counted cows on the beach as a crime. He'd expected the call to be a routine query about meetings or court reports, not a Superintendent from the big smoke.

"Sorry sir, he's at Headquarters this afternoon, meeting with the Chief Constable. Can I take a message?"

"Thanks. Just ask him to call me when he gets back." Craig hazarded at guess at why White had called the C.C.U.. No-one dialled them just to ask directions. "I believe you had a murder recently?"

"Yes, sir. A very nasty case. That's what the D.C.I's meeting is about."

"Excellent."

The word was out of Craig's mouth before Nicky's expression told him it was the wrong choice. He backtracked quickly. "Excellent that he's meeting the Chief Constable, I mean. Terrible about the case."

The man at the other end smiled, knowing exactly what Craig had meant.

"I'll get him to call you when he comes in, sir."

The line clicked off softly and Craig glanced at his watch. Four-thirty. It was Friday and they were all tired. He crossed to the door and scanned the open-plan office outside. It was like the Marie Celeste. Then he remembered. Annette was on a course for new Inspectors and Davy was spending the day with his girlfriend Maggie. He made up his mind quickly.

"Give Jake McLean a call, Liam. Nicky, re-direct the phones to my mobile. I've made an executive decision."

Liam smiled, knowing exactly what it was.

"We're heading for the pub."

Chapter Two

Portstewart.

The young man watched for days as the police vans appeared and left; their flashing lights incongruous on the sunny beach. He lit a cigarette and blew the smoke out in a stream, watching as it wafted away on the afternoon breeze. They'd found the body quickly and moved even quicker after that. He was glad, not from any sense of concern, but it saved him from having to camp there for too long. They'd be finished the forensics soon then he could up sticks and go home, to wait for the report on the local news.

He squinted at the sun then peered at the white-suited shapes, moving within their taped-off square like figures in a boxing ring. Suddenly a car appeared and he sat upright, craning his neck to see who disembarked. He smiled as he recognised the driver. Dr John Winter; Head of Forensic Pathology for Northern Ireland. He'd been hoping that he would come. That was only left one man missing and he would soon appear. He poured out more tea and lit another cigarette, lounging back in his deckchair to watch the rest of the show.

***

Craig clicked on the light and headed for the fridge, pulling out a cold beer. He ran it across his forehead then slumped down on the settee and flicked on the seven p.m. news. He just had time for a shower before he headed to his folks for the traditional Friday dinner his mother insisted on. He gulped down half the bottle then glanced ruefully at a picture on the coffee table, lifting it for a closer look. The woman in the frame was pretty, with long red hair that twisted and curled down her back. She was smiling, but not with her eyes. Julia McNulty. She was an Inspector working in Limavady and they'd been seeing each other for nearly a year, mostly at weekends.. It made for a long distance relationship and yet another Friday night spent apart. It wasn't ideal and it was growing even less so by the week.

It didn't help that his ex-D.C.S, Terry Harrison, had taken over as her boss and refused her transfer request to Belfast. He was deliberately obstructing it just to cause them grief. It left them with two options. Either he left Belfast and transferred to the North-West, or Julia quit the force and moved to Belfast to be with him. A third option shouted for attention, forcing him to look at it: they could split up. He shook his head hard, as if he was trying to convince someone else. It wasn't what either of them wanted and it would be a last resort. A failure; and a reward for Harrison's jealousy.

Terry Harrison was a self-seeking bastard who abused his power and hated Craig, most recently for saving his ass in the Ackerman case and 'making him look like a fool'. Some people just couldn't say thanks. Harrison had resented him since he'd come home in 2008 after fifteen years in London at The Met. Now he was getting his revenge.

There had to be some way to thwart him. Even as Craig asked himself the question the answer was 'what?' He'd returned to Belfast because his parents were getting old. His father's heart attack in April had reminded him again of their age and how much they needed their children nearby. At the moment he only lived seven miles away, but if he moved to Limavady to be with Julia it would take him nearly as long to reach them as when he'd lived in London. And leave his sister Lucia with all the responsibility for their care. She'd held the fort for years, and he couldn't, wouldn't, do it to her again.

Julia understood, but she loved being in the police and he couldn't ask her to leave. Even if he did he doubted that she ever would. He took a long drink of his beer then stood up and headed for the shower, still thinking as the water ran down his muscled back. His mind drifted back to the third option, afraid that there was no escape. It felt as inevitable as tomorrow and he knew they'd have to have the conversation soon. He towelled himself dry and shook the sad thoughts from his mind. Tonight he'd be the dutiful son and eat a home-cooked meal. When Julia arrived tomorrow they would talk.

***

John Winter stared at the girl on the table. She was around twenty years old and petite, and she looked so peaceful that he was tempted to tuck her in and turn off the light. Only the pale blue tinge to her lips and the coolness of her skin said that she wasn't dreaming; she would never wake up from this nap. He sighed loudly, knowing that no-one would hear him and then lifted a scalpel, resigned to his work.

It wasn't often he was called to the north coast for a case but they'd been insistent that he came, without telling him why. 'Didn't want to prejudice his findings' was Andy White's excuse. As if they ever could. He shrugged and turned back to his task, keen to complete the post-mortem as swiftly as he could. Not from any sense of impatience, but because he knew that somewhere there was a parent about to hear a painful truth. The sooner he was finished, the sooner they could. Could what?

Stop hoping and praying their daughter was staying with friends, and soon they would hear her key in the door? Get past the horror of identification and get on with mourning their loss? Start healing and accepting the future without their child? That was all his speed could provide, but perhaps it was something. As he made the first cut he already knew that it was nothing at all.

***

"Marco, where is pretty Julia this evening?"

Craig pulled himself from his thoughts at the question and glanced curiously at his Italian mother, Mirella. She never asked about his girlfriends, not since Camille, his ex-fiancée. He was convinced they were invisible to her unless they wore a ring. He was about to ask why she was inquiring when he saw the concern in her eyes. She knew! She knew about his problems with Julia. He glanced accusingly at his sister Lucia, her tawny hair hiding her face as she slipped some spaghetti to Murphy the dog. No, Lucia couldn't have told her, he hadn't said a word. It convinced him again that his mother was a witch, albeit a white one in every way. He smiled, knowing that she wouldn't stop asking until he gave her a plausible reply.

"She's working, Mum. Up in Limavady. She's coming down tomorrow."

Mirella Craig tutted so loudly that even Craig's laid-back father turned to look. Tom Craig lived inside his own head most of the time, dreaming of scientific inventions and books he was about to read. His main connection with the world was through his vivacious wife. Other than that he let it pass by undisturbed. He raised an eyebrow and they all sat waiting to see what followed Mirella's tut.

"This work is no good. Not for you and definitely not for a girl."

Craig smiled at the thirty-something Julia being called a girl and waited for Lucia's feminist hackles to rise. Instead she just smiled, still loved-up from her boyfriend Richard's recent visit and giving her mother a pardon every time.

"She should be pretty and sing and dance, not carry guns and chase across the fields. You also. All this death is bad."

Craig laughed out loud at the image. It made their lives

sound like an episode of '24'. He couldn't entirely disagree with her, there was easier work they could do and it would make life a lot simpler if they were both in different jobs. But it wasn't an option for either of them. Julia had left the army to join the police and she wasn't going to leave the police to sing and dance for anyone. He was rescued by his mobile ringing. He answered it gratefully, mouthing an apology to his Mum.

"D.C.I. Craig."

The laugh on the other end made him smile and the voice that followed was instantly recognisable.

"You really need to get used to saying Superintendent, Marc. Otherwise they might take it back."

"Hi John, what can I do for you on a Friday night?"

Craig walked out of the kitchen as he talked, feeling his mother's daggers in his back.

"Where are you?"

"At my folks."

"Oh yes. Sorry, I forgot. Is Julia up?"

"Not until tomorrow. Don't worry, I'm glad you called. You've just saved me from being tortured to death by Mum. What can I do for you?"

"Well... it might be something, or it might be nothing at all."

"A new case?" Craig didn't try to keep the eagerness from his voice. After three weeks of paperwork he thought he deserved a break.

"Yes and no. It's a strange one... I'm up on the North Coast."

Craig knew immediately where he was.

"Portstewart?"

"How did you know?"

"I'll tell you in a minute when I call you back."

He ended the call unceremoniously and checked his missed calls, pressing the latest to redial. It was answered immediately by a familiar voice. Andy White. He'd headed up the Drugs Squad in the C.C.U. until recently, now he was a D.C.I. up the coast, inching closer to Dungiven by the year as he made his way home.

"Hey, Andy. You called me?"

"Marc Craig, as I live and breathe. I did indeed. Fancy a wee trip to the seaside, hey?"

Craig smiled at Andy's Dungiven accent. Liam mimicked it perfectly, never omitting his tendency to say 'hey' after every other phrase.

"Who and where?"

"A young girl on Portstewart Strand. It's a strange one in more ways than I can count. I've cleared it with the Chief and he says you're good to go, hey. Can you come up on Monday?"

"I can do better than that, I'll come up tonight." He glanced at his watch: nine p.m. "How does an hour sound?"

"It sounds like you're driving a Lamborghini these days! Don't kill yourself rushing, hey. I'll have the kettle on when you arrive."

Craig clicked off the call and quickly re-dialled John.

"Where are you staying, John?"

"Brewster's."

"Right, I'm meeting with Andy White around ten o'clock. I'll see you in the hotel bar afterwards?"

"You'll see me in the mortuary before that."

***

The easy late-night drive almost made Craig forget what he was driving to. A life ended before its time and parents weeping and mourning their loss, certain that it was somehow their fault. He wondered why parents always blamed themselves for whatever ills befell their child, as if they could form a shield at birth and protect them from the world. The world had a habit of getting in, whether you shielded people or not.

He pulled into Portstewart town and caught sight of its famous beach. The Strand was one of Northern Ireland's Blue

Flag beaches, and one of the few where cars were still allowed to drive. Its smooth beauty looked peaceful, undamaged by hands or wheels, all traces wiped clean by the North Atlantic tides. It looked too peaceful; perhaps the rough water pushing at its shore was a truer sign of what awaited him.

Craig shook his head at his maudlin thoughts and flicked on the CD in the deck. It was one of Julia's, Adele's '19', a departure from his usual Snow Patrol. He let the melodies wash over him as he drove, wondering what to do about their romance. The miles between Belfast and Limavady were sapping the life from the relationship and the only two options he could think of wouldn't fly. That only left the third way.

The phrase made him smile, despite the darkness of his mood. It reminded him of Cool Britannia and songs by D Ream. The 1990s in London and everyone caught up in the buzz; before it had all fallen flat on Iraq. So much had happened to him since then.

An image of his father in the cardiac ward reminded him why he'd moved back to Belfast and strengthened his resolve. His parents needed him now, far more than anyone else. In that moment his decision was finally made. The third way it would have to be. He wasn't leaving Belfast and Julia would have to make her choice, even if it meant them splitting up. He allowed himself a moment's grief then turned up the volume and drove towards someone else's pain.

Chapter Three

The dark-haired man smiled to himself and he pulled back the tent flap until his view of the Strand was clear. The forensic tape and uniforms had diminished by the hour and now only a lone police officer stood guard. Guarding what? The body was gone and all useful traces had long been erased by the tide. Yet still he stood, like some monument to grief; honouring the dead.

Anger filled the man suddenly and he slammed his fist into the tent-pole, shaking his temporary home. Where was the grief for him? Where were the kind words and caring hands when he'd been left alone? Nowhere. It had made him what he was. Cruel and lost. He smiled. He had no self-delusion left. He *was* cruel. But had he been born that way, or had life moulded him and made him hard?

He shook his head hard, trying to force the answers loose. Only one appeared: the image of a child, loving and gentle, happy with his own games. Defenceless and left alone, to meet with what? Harsh words and harsher hands. Dark spaces and little food. Every word greeted by silence or blame or God's word, until he'd learned. Learned to keep it all inside. Learned to be cruel and cold. Learned to do onto others before they did it to him. He'd learned well.

***

Craig smiled as he crossed the station reception, extending his hand to his friend. Andy looked just the same. The same upright, energetic stance and the same blue shirt. He always wore one, every day, come rain or shine. The colour matched his eyes. The rumour was that his wife had bought a job lot, coaxing him into wearing them with promises of delight at home. Whatever the reason, Andy's shirts were as constant as the Atlantic Ocean. Craig found it strangely comforting.

Andy White was an easy-going man, until he got a villain in his sights. Then his affable Dungiven ways morphed into cool precision and his blue eyes grew steely to match. He'd headed up Drugs in Belfast for years, seeking a transfer home with every promotion round. Craig was glad he'd finally managed the move north, even though he did miss the sound of his Dungiven 'heys' echoing across Dockland's canteen.

"Hello Andy. How's life on the wild Atlantic coast?"

Andy smiled and led the way to the staff room. He knocked-on the kettle and nodded Craig to a chair, grabbing one from across the room. Craig was surprised.

"I don't think I've ever seen you sitting down!"

"Special measures, hey. This is a bad case and it's about to get worse. We've just got the victim's I.D."

The look in his eyes said that there was something very wrong. Not that someone's death could ever be right, but something was compounding it this time.

"It's Lissy Trainor."

Craig looked at him blankly so Andy said the name again. It still rang no bells.

"Assistant Chief Constable Trainor's girl."

Craig's mouth fell open as the penny dropped. Melanie Trainor's daughter was their dead girl!

"You're positive?"

The question was out before he could even think, even though no-one would ever make the mistake.

Andy nodded. He poured Craig a coffee then took a deep draught of his tea.

Craig shook his head. "Does she know yet?"

"Not yet, I'm on my way to the mortuary now." Andy

nodded at his drink. "This should be whisky, for Dutch courage, hey. The body was found on Thursday morning but there was no I.D. or match on her prints. We've just got her name."

"How?"

He gave a rueful smile. "Your mate John. She had an unusual tattoo on her inner thigh; a number. He recognised what it was."

"A phone number?"

Andy shook his head and took another sip. "No. A hospital case number. "

He laughed grimly. "Only John would have recognised that, hey. He checked it and the girl's name and photo came up. Seems she had a kidney transplant when she was fifteen. She must have got the tattoo as a souvenir."

"God, hadn't she been through enough in life already, without this happening?"

It was rhetorical. They fell into silence and Craig broke it first.

"How old was she?"

"Twenty-one. Just finished law at the University of Ulster. A bright wee girl with her whole life ahead."

"How did she die?"

Andy shook his head and stood up, grabbing his jacket and heading for the door.

"Let's go and find out."

***

The morgue was small and cold with faint traces of formaldehyde scenting the air, a legacy from someone passed. The cosy red-brick of the entrance gave way to lines of white corridors, all leading to one place. John Winter stood at the end of one, his pleasure at seeing his friends tempered by decorum and respect for the dead. He greeted them in a subdued voice.

"Hello Marc, nice to see you. Hi again, Andy."

They nodded in return, all urge to banter dampened by the building's name. John turned and they followed him in silence into a bright, steel-coloured room where the air was cool and their footsteps made the only sound. He walked to a table and lifted the white sheet on it back from a young woman's face. Craig gazed at her small, round countenance, the first hints of cheekbone just starting to show through the puppy fat. Thick dark lashes swept down to her cheeks, their colour matched by the tendrils of hair that fell across her brow. She was a child in all but years. She was Melanie Trainor's child.

Trainor had been Craig's Superintendent for four weeks when he'd first come back from The Met. She'd been OK. He corrected himself immediately, knowing that his assessment was being made kinder by the pain about to overwhelm her life. She'd been OK-ish, if ruthless ambition and barking orders were your definition of OK. He shrugged; she had it in common with a lot of the higher ranks. Perhaps it was something you acquired, or perhaps it was what had got them there. He'd probably never know.

He stared intently at the girl and saw the strong resemblance to her Mum. It made the macabre coincidence too real and he turned away quickly, not envying John and Andy the task they had ahead. John covered the girl's face respectfully and ushered them into an office where he'd managed to find coffee and some mugs. They drank in silence for a minute until Andy's clear voice cut through the air.

"Does she know yet, John?"

Winter shook his head and glanced involuntarily at the clock. It was almost midnight. Craig knew what he was thinking. Did he let the mother have a good night's sleep before he plunged her into a nightmare that she would never escape, or tell her now and ruin her sleep for years to come?

Craig voiced his opinion. "Let her sleep, John and tell her first thing. Andy and I can start the work tomorrow and by the look of you, you need a good rest."

They fell into silence again then Andy asked the one thing they needed to know. "How did she die, John?"

"Strangulation." That one word conjured up a hundred methods and images too gruesome to entertain. He continued. "Approximately three days ago."

"Tuesday?"

"Around then. The cold water affected Rigor so it's hard to be accurate. The strangulation was manual and before you ask, no, I don't think she wasn't raped. She was still dressed when she was buried."

Craig nodded, grateful for the little things, then he stood up to go. John stilled him with a hand. There was something else. He swallowed hard then pulled a file from the drawer, laying it face-down. The cardboard cover was faded and badly frayed at the edge, as if it had been read and read again. Craig hazarded a guess at its age; 1970s or '80s. But what did it have to do with Lissy Trainor's death? John sighed heavily then answered Craig's silent question.

"Do either of you remember a case in '83, at the height of The Troubles?"

"We were still at school, John, and so were you!"

Winter smiled. He and Craig had known each other since they were twelve, over thirty years before. They'd gone to the same integrated grammar in Belfast. They'd been thirteen-years-old in 1983 and Andy would only have been ten.

"I didn't mean did you work it! I meant did you remember hearing about it on the news."

Craig shook his head, thinking back. The deaths and murders in the eighties were too many to recall, especially for a sports mad boy who never watched TV. Andy looked as puzzled as he felt.

"I doubt it, John, but give us some more detail. Was it one that Melanie Trainor worked?"

John stared at him, astonished. "How did you guess?"

"I'm a genius, hey. Listen, I don't mean to be rude, but it's after midnight and some of us need our sleep. Could you hurry up?"

John startled and glanced at the clock. He forgot everything when he was fascinated by a case.

"Quickly then. Not only did Melanie Trainor work this case as a young Inspector but the M.O. is almost identical to her daughter's death. Young woman, strangled and buried at exactly the same spot on Portstewart beach. No signs of sexual assault."

"Who was she?"

"Her name was Veronica Jarvis. Her family called her Ronni. She was suspected of being an informer for MI5. They pinned her death on the IRA."

"Pinned it?"

"Well, the IRA didn't actually claim it, but they convicted one of their commanders for the death and he was sentenced to twenty years inside. He did fifteen. Got early release under the Good Friday agreement in 1998."

Andy interrupted eagerly. "Didn't the IRA always claim the things they did?"

"Mostly, except for some of the people they disappeared. That's one of the things that makes me suspicious."

Craig nodded. John definitely had something. For Melanie Trainor's daughter to die in the same way as a murder she'd investigated was way beyond coincidence. His mind filled with questions. Two dominated. Why? And why now, thirty years after the fact? Was it straight forward revenge? Every police officer knew that some cases put them and their families more at risk than others. Thankfully it was rare and rarely this extreme, but they spent their days dealing with dangerous criminals not boy scouts.

Craig stood up again and Andy stood as well, signalling the close of discussions for the night. John reluctantly locked up and then they made their way to the hotel, all of them dreading what tomorrow morning would bring.

Chapter Four

Saturday 7 a.m.

Julia pulled the brush through her curls without any mercy then wound her hair into a tight chignon. She was going to see the Chief Constable to beg him to arrange her transfer so she needed to look smart. He'd agreed to see her at Headquarters in Belfast but she wasn't telling Marc she'd be in town until afterwards. It was her last chance of a transfer, and the last chance at making their relationship work. She didn't need any more pressure today.

She pulled her jacket down sharply and stared at her reflection in her polished shoes, years of military training in every glint. Perhaps if she hadn't already had one career change she wouldn't be clinging so tightly to the police. But from the army to the police had been a hard enough shift, leaving the police for Civvie Street would be a step too far.

She loved Marc with all her heart, except she mustn't do, or her giving up the police and moving to Belfast would be a done deal. There was something holding her back. Was it really as simple as her desire to stay in the police, or did she simply not love him enough? She shook her head, rejecting the idea. She loved him desperately. She wanted to have his children and be his wife. Dear God, she'd even started trying out recipes for food he liked. But…

She needed her own career. It made her feel safe. The future could bring anything but she would always have the job. It wasn't that she didn't love him; she just didn't trust life enough not to throw her a curve. She lifted her bag and stood up straight then turned and left her flat; praying that Sean Flanagan would take her side and she could tell Terry 'Teflon' Harrison where to stick his Limavady job.

***

Craig woke when the first shards of daylight hit his eyes and lay in bed thinking. If someone had killed Melanie Trainor's child in the same way as a case she'd led, it was an obvious link. But to what? Was someone trying to tell them something, or was it just simple revenge? He thought for a moment longer and then thrust himself out of bed in one smooth leap. As he stood in the shower with warm water running down his back his thoughts moved to other things. Julia was going to see the Chief Constable today to request a transfer. She hadn't told him, Nicky had found out. Her secrecy told him something, but what?

He admired her drive but he felt guilty at the same time. She'd never ask him to use his credit with the Chief to get her moved, but he knew that she thought he should have tried. Why hadn't he? He didn't know why. He shook his head beneath the shower, trying to clear it. Was he worried about his own career? No, that wasn't it. He didn't give a damn about promotion; he hadn't even wanted the one he had. Was he getting cold feet about her moving down? Or was part of him secretly hoping that she wouldn't come, so the decision to end their relationship would be taken out of his hands? No. Even as he thought it he knew the 'no' was weaker than before. Did he want to end their relationship but he simply didn't have the guts? And if so, why? Was he happier single? No. The 'no' was surer this time. That wasn't it. He wanted a relationship, and marriage and children someday. What then?

The water ran through his hair and into his ears, shutting out all sounds but the rushing in his head. He focused as it flowed down his body, thinking of the last question he'd asked. He knew he wanted marriage and kids, so what was wrong? Did he want them with someone else? The image of a woman flashed through his mind and he reeled back against the shower's wall in shock. It wasn't Julia! He tried to focus on the face. Was it Camille? No, definitely not. Then who the hell was it? Someone he'd already met or some fantasy?

He shook the urge away quickly, filled with guilt. He'd never been unfaithful and he wasn't about to start now but he knew in that split second that if Julia and he broke up, someone else was already waiting in his heart.

***

9 a.m.

"OK Andy, what would you like me to do? We've nothing on in Belfast that Liam can't handle, so I'm all yours for a few days."

Andy smiled slyly at him and Craig knew that he was about to ask for something more. "Well now. Since you've mentioned the shiny new Chief Inspector Cullen, hey, how would you feel about him joining us for a few days?"

An image of Liam grinning immediately filled Craig's mind. He would jump at the chance of a trip to the coast, especially if it meant a few nights sleep in a hotel. Liam loved his children dearly but with a toddler and baby under a year, sleep was a luxury that he would pay anything for. Even better if it was on the State.

"OK, you're on. Annette can step up if needed. And she may have a new sergeant this week, depending on how persuasive Liam's managed to be. I'll give him a call."

Two minutes later Liam was ready to rock and roll.

"Here, should I bring my bucket and spade? I hear Portstewart Strand's lovely this time of year."

"Don't bother; the sand's already given us more grief than we need. Did you manage to get hold of Jake McLean?"

Liam pulled his pen from his mouth and inspected it, peering at it for a moment before popping it back in. Nicky screwed up her nose in distaste and threw a packet of baby-wipes at his desk. He ignored her and talked on.

"Aye, I did indeed. He didn't take much persuading, I can tell you that. He seems to like it down here. Said Stranmillis was a bit too quiet for his liking and he fancied some action."

"Is D.C.I. Nugent OK with the move?"

"Right as rain. I promised him a year's supply of wine gums and he caved right in."

He guffawed loudly and Craig pulled the receiver from his ear in pain. No-one could ever have accused Liam of having dulcet tones. He heard Annette and Nicky joining in, in the background and gave them a minute to enjoy the joke. When the laughter subsided he tried again.

"Seriously, Liam. Did you check with him?"

Liam gave a heavy sigh at being brought back to earth then spoke in a mock-reverent tone. "Yes, Superintendent, sir. I did, sir. Detective Chief Inspector Nugent said he's happy to second Sergeant McLean for six months and see how it goes from there. Seems he thinks a stint in murder is good for the soul."

"What did he want in return?" Ronnie Nugent never did anything for nothing.

Liam was silent for a moment then he sighed again. "He wants me to run some workshops for his new recruits. 'Detecting techniques for the Noughties' or some other crap like that. I hope you appreciate the sacrifices I make for this team."

Craig laughed so loudly at the image of Liam standing in front of a class that Andy motioned him to turn on his speakerphone. Liam heard the echo immediately.

"Oh aye, now I bet 'Dungiven Hey' is listening in! Morning, Andy."

"Morning Liam, hey. And that's D.C.I. Dungiven Hey to you."

Craig interrupted.

"Seriously though, thanks for doing that, Liam. Jake will be a great addition to the team. And look on the bright side."

"There is one?"

"Yes. All those workshops will look great on your CV. Boards love things like that. See you by noon."

He cut the line quickly before Liam could reply then glanced at Andy and laughed again, then they set off for the mortuary and a more sombre start to the day.

***

Andy parked outside the single-storey building and they walked across the car-park, neither of them eager to reach their goal. Craig ran his fingers under the over-starched collar of his new shirt, bought in the local shopping centre that morning. He'd left Belfast without packing and he'd nip back when he had time, but for now it would just have to do. Neither of them spoke; just fell into step as they walked, reluctance in every pace.

They saw the high-end limousine simultaneously, knowing immediately who its passenger had been, and hurried towards the entrance, reluctant to leave John to deal with everything alone. Their progress was halted by a wail that ripped the clear morning air, freezing them both to the core. They listened as it grew, so high and relentless that for a moment nothing moved. Not the uniformed guard standing confused by the car and not the still air that neither of them breathed in. Even the birds seemed to slow and turn, searching for the origin of the sound. They glanced at each other and forgot their reticence, running towards the morgue. To the room that held a dead daughter, and a mother who had just died as well.

***

John sipped at his coffee, gathering his thoughts, then he turned towards Craig with a look that said he was dreading what came next.

"You don't need me there to talk to her, Marc."

Craig half-smiled 'yes we do' as Andy translated their shorthand in his head. John had been chilled by Melanie Trainor's reaction, more chilled that he liked to admit. In fact, he wouldn't admit it, hiding behind 'you don't need me there' instead. But he knew why Craig was insisting. None of them had seen a reaction that bad, not in all the years they'd been on the force, more than three score between them. Craig was afraid of how the ACC might react once the questions had to start.

John gazed at his friend pleadingly, fatigue written all over his face. Craig's voice cut through the air.

"I'm not a doctor, John. You are. Have you ever seen someone take it that hard? She might collapse."

John shook his head and sighed, knowing that Craig was right. Melanie Trainor might have made it to the top in a world of men but she was here as a mother today. One who had loved her child if her tears were anything to go by. She could collapse, or worse, when they started to talk, and whether his patients were usually dead or not, he was a doctor first of all. He needed to be there.

He took a deep draught of his coffee and made a face. It was cold. He walked to the kettle in silence and stood in silence until it boiled. Then he put a fresh pot on a tray and they walked into the relatives' room together, bracing themselves for the pain.

***

"Nicky, here's a list of everything Annette needs to do while I'm away."

Nicky glanced up from her screen then leaned back in her chair and threw Liam a questioning look. He was standing arms-folded in front of her, his newest tie and jacket saying that this was an important day. She couldn't be sure but she thought he'd actually combed his hair, although it was hard to tell from the sandy fuzz on top of his head.

"Have you got a mistress or something, Liam? Only the last time you combed your hair was on your wedding day. Danni told me."

Liam's guffaw was so loud they probably heard it on the thirteenth floor. When it stopped he wagged a thick finger in her face.

"Let's have a little respect for your acting boss, madam. I'll have you know I'm off up north to help out on an important case."

"So the fact that it involves the ACC has nothing to do with your hair, I suppose?"

A stifled laugh behind him made Liam turn, just in time to see Davy Walsh, their young analyst, drop down behind his desk. He wagged his finger again.

"Now there's a man who could do with a comb. I thought you had the weekend off, Davy?"

Davy stood-up and wandered over, tossing his black Emo locks back dramatically from his face. He looked like an Armani model and Nicky said so. When he'd first joined the squad eighteen months before he'd been so shy that he'd stuttered relentlessly. Now he teased Liam with the rest of them, his stutter now only occasional, on 's' and 'w', and often used to best effect.

"I could lend you s…some of my hair wax, Liam. It would smooth out that frizz."

Liam looked genuinely shocked. "What frizz? I'll have you know they're my family curls. I was born with bright red ringlets according to my Mum and this is what's left."

"That's something to be thankful for, then."

Liam threw Nicky a look so pained that they all laughed again.

"W…what's the boss up to in Portstewart, Liam?"

"Dead girl, found on the beach. Nasty business. Anyway, it's not your problem. Didn't you and Maggie have plans for the weekend?"

"No, just for yesterday. She's gone to her Mum's in Scotland for a few days, so I'm going to catch up on my computer games."

Nicky leaned in conspiratorially. "Her mother is ACC Trainor. That's why Liam's combed his hair."

"W…whose mother? Maggie's?"

"Keep up, Davy. The victim's mother is ACC Trainor."

"S…seriously? I didn't think she was married."

Nicky smiled at him in a way that said she wanted to pat him on the head. "You sweet old fashioned thing, Davy Walsh. Lots of parents don't get married nowadays." She pursed her lips disapprovingly. "Although they should. Selfish, thoughtless…"

Liam interrupted before she launched into a moral lecture. "She's married to Hugh Trainor, the politician. He's an MLA with the Energy Party."

Davy whistled. "He's richer than God too. His family own all those pubs up the Lisburn Road."

"Then she should work for free."

Nicky had her arms folded now and Liam could tell she was winding herself up for a rant. The boss could handle her when she started but he always got flustered and gave in for a quiet life. Time to leave. He walked across the office throwing a wave back over his head.

"Tell Annette I'll call her later and be sure to give her that list."

Nicky yelled at his back. "I hadn't finished, Liam Cullen."

He kept on walking, saving his riskiest comment for when he reached the exit to the lift.

"That's why I'm leaving. I was afraid you never would."

He slipped through the glass doors expecting something to hit him, then jumped into the lift and prayed it moved faster than Nicky did.

***

Craig sat opposite Melanie Trainor while Andy stood, almost to attention, by the door. John had hovered for a moment then chosen a spot at the end of the sofa where she sat. It was a challenging situation for all of them, although it shouldn't have been. She was a victim's mother first and foremost, and they should treat her that way. Her job didn't provide a shield from the pain of loss, so why did they have to keep reminding themselves of that?

Craig stared at her, watching as her hands curled and uncurled as if they were searching for something to hold. They stretched into activity until her loss hit her again and made them limp, then the cycle started again.

The ACC was a pretty woman, somewhere in her fifties but looking two decades younger. She was small and dark, with large brown eyes that gazed out sadly from her face. Her hair was black and long, how long was hard to tell when it was wrapped in a chignon every day, but she still caught admiring glances wherever she walked. Craig remembered her from years before, always driven and working hard, but not loathe to using her pretty smile to get her way. He remembered her words from back then.

"Whatever works, Craig. Whatever works."

He'd wondered then if she was hard or merely smart. She'd done whatever it had taken to succeed in a man's world and found her own way of evening-up the scales. Some called her a pioneer, carving the way for the women who came in her wake. Others, manipulative and cold, Machiavellian in the extreme. He didn't know. His jury was still out. But today she was none of that; today she was simply a woman who'd lost her child.

The thoughts took less than a minute to race through his mind, a minute in which John watched her like a hawk. He'd never seen him so shaken by carrying out an I.D. but Melanie Trainor's wails had chilled them all. Finally Craig broke the silence, his voice soft and kind. It reached across the table while his body remained upright, showing respect.

"Ma'am. Is there anything we can do to help?"

She raised her head and gazed at him, her eyes dry and her thoughts a million miles away. She didn't answer for so long he wondered if she'd heard him, then she sighed. It was a deep soft sigh, a breath exhaled so slowly that it lingered, revealing everything and nothing and most of all despair. Her eyes were blank with the shock and he saw John nod, knowing that she wasn't there. She sighed once more then stood and walked silently past them to the door, not seeing anyone but her daughter as her chauffeured car drove away.

Chapter Five

1 p.m.

Liam picked up a lettuce leaf in disgust then set it down at the side of his plate, taking a bite of burger.

"I don't know why they have to ruin a perfectly good burger with bits of grass."

"They're trying to make it healthier."

Liam snorted and Craig laughed then cut into his steak. No matter how dark the case was or how depressing the mood, Liam could bring them back to earth. Craig glanced at Andy and John, nodding them on to eat, then started talking while they did.

"OK. It's clear we're going to get nothing from ACC Trainor, at least for today. So let's concentrate on other things. John, can you chase up the post-mortem results? Davy's checking to see if anything similar has showed up before."

"You mean other than the case in '83?"

"Yes."

John nodded and turned his attention to his sausage. He was trying to go vegetarian with little success, but today wasn't the day to beat himself up about it. Craig was still talking.

"Andy, we need to re-interview anyone major from the case in '83."

"Except ACC Trainor."

Craig nodded ruefully. "Except her. Let's defer that experience for as long as we can." He turned towards Liam then noticed something. He'd combed his hair!

"Did you comb your hair, Liam?"

Three pairs of eyes fixed on Liam's head and he blushed under their scrutiny.

"I did not comb my hair. Have you ever known me to comb my hair? Ever?"

Craig watched as a patina of red covered Liam's face. Andy joined in.

"Boyso yes, you have too combed your hair. What did you use, hey? A combine harvester?"

Craig and John laughed so loudly they nearly choked on their food. Liam stood up indignantly.

"I'll have you know I had red curls when I was a boy! Everyone admired them."

They laughed for so long that Craig saw a waiter approach. He waved Liam to sit down and forced his face into a serious look.

"It looks good Liam, and I'm sure the ACC would have appreciated it."

"Aye, if she'd ever seen it, hey."

After a few more jokey comments they fell silent again. The only sound was four men eating and drinking until they'd finished their meal. As coffee was served, Craig started again.

"Liam, find out Lissy Trainor's movements in the last few days. Does she have a boyfriend? Who does she mix with? Who saw her last and where? You know the form. Ask Davy to chase up background when you have something for him to research. And her e-mail and phone accounts."

Andy interjected. "You and I can start with the '83 case, Marc. I'll get a copy of the file."

Craig glanced at his watch. "OK, let's meet at the hotel at five o'clock for a debrief. I'll be on my mobile till then. And if Melanie Trainor contacts any of you let me know right away. The sooner we can speak to her, the sooner we can find out why someone might have wanted her daughter dead."

***

Annette looked around the open plan office and smiled. She was in charge and she liked it. Well, not really in charge, but it was a pleasant illusion until Craig or Liam's phone call shattered it. She yawned, tired of the file in front of her and strolled over to Nicky's desk, indicating the percolator and switching it on at her nod. She arranged three cups and saucers as she waited for it to boil. Saucers; how long had it been since they'd used them, except for guests? Mugs had become the default when Liam was around. Nicky smiled in approval and reached into her bottom drawer, withdrawing a packet of special biscuits and arranging them daintily on a plate.

Davy smiled at the girly ritual. While the cat's away, the mice will use napkins. He looked up from his horseshoe of computers and shut down the report he was working on, loping over to join them. Just then a fair-haired young man pushed his way quietly through the floor's double-doors. Annette recognised him immediately and waved, beckoning him over to Nicky's desk.

"Hello Jake, you must be psychic, the kettle's just boiled."

The others smiled in greeting then Davy pulled up another chair and Jake McLean joined his new team for Saturday afternoon tea.

***

"It was a nasty case in '83, all right. Veronica Jarvis was beaten and strangled, then buried up to her neck in sand. In exactly the same place as Lissy Trainor."

"The similarities are hard to ignore."

Andy leaned back against the desk and turned a page in the file. "There are some differences, though."

"Such as?"

"Lissy Trainor wasn't beaten and she was completely covered

in sand, whereas Jarvis' head was left exposed. Nothing showed of Lissy until the sand got eroded, and her hand was nearest the surface."

Craig shook his head. "The Atlantic could have eroded the sand in both cases. I'll get Davy to check the tides now and in '83. But the beating might be significant."

"The lack of it you mean."

Craig nodded in acknowledgement then frowned. "Beatings were more usual back then, especially in punishment killings."

"You mean because Veronica Jarvis was suspected of being an informer she would have been treated worse?"

"Yes. The paramilitaries weren't known for their gentle ways. But that's another thing. The IRA didn't claim it."

Andy shrugged, puzzled. "Maybe because it was a girl? They thought it would make them look bad?"

Craig smiled at his naiveté. The IRA had killed plenty of women; there was no chivalry in terrorism.

"They weren't gentlemen, Andy. They killed women as well. No, Ronni Jarvis might have been beaten but I don't think the IRA committed her murder, no matter what the records say."

"Who then?"

Craig shook his head. "That's what we need to find out. But first of all we need to talk to the man the jury blamed."

***

Melanie Trainor stared unseeing into the fire, lit earlier than usual in an attempt to drive the cold from her bones. It didn't work so she pulled the heavy mohair throw around her, huddling in further as she blinked back the tears. She stared at the happy picture in her hand, trying to burn the image of Lissy into her mind to replace the one she'd seen earlier that day.

The Lissy in the photograph smiled up at her, her eyes as brown and large as her own, her long dark hair shining and tumbling down her back. Her arms were full. A certificate in one hand, a bouquet in the other; newly degree-ed and ready to take on the world of law. She'd wanted to be a barrister, full of the oratory and wigs inspired by 'take your daughter to work day'. Watching her from the gallery while she testified in court.

A tear rolled down Melanie Trainor's cheek and she let it fall, watching as it splashed on the costly slate hearth. The room was full of expensive things paid for by hours of study and work. All meaningless now. She would give them all to hear Lissy's voice again. She listened, trying to recall her youthful tones. They came through loud and clear, but how long would she hear them for? How long before she couldn't recall her voice or hear her laugh at all? She gulped down her brandy and made herself a vow. Whoever had done this would pay with the rest of their life. It was no comfort at all.

***

Craig raked his hand through his hair in exasperation then closed the file in front of him. He couldn't believe the sparseness of its contents, but who was he to judge? At a time when there'd been tens of murders each week and a police force under siege, he could understand that things might have been forgotten, and handwritten memos misfiled. It was difficult to imagine a world without computers, but he remembered using an old typewriter in London, twenty years before. Things hadn't been so efficient then, even there, and they hadn't been dodging petrol bombs every day. It had been a dark time in Northern Ireland's history. He glanced again at the thin file in his hand. But even so...

He turned to see where Andy was and found him in a corner of the records room. They were at Headquarters in Belfast and they'd been lucky, the records sergeant had heard of the ACC's loss and been willing to throw open his archive doors at the weekend. There were plenty who wouldn't have been so cooperative, especially at half-term.

He watched as Andy's eyebrows rose as he perused a buff file with a red stripe on the front, signifying it was probably a terrorist offence. Andy had studied law before he'd joined the force, just like he had, and he was fascinated by court reports. It was probably why they were both so hard on Barristers; it felt like they'd sold the law out for the highest price.

Andy had been in fraud and vice before drugs, so the details of terrorist atrocities had been through the spin cycle of the evening news before either of them had heard. The men on the ground through the worst of it had different stories to tell. An image of Liam in uniform flashed into Craig's mind and he gave him a mental salute.

"What have you got, Andy?"

Andy shook his head and screwed up his face. "Nothing you'd like to read. There were some real bastards running around back then, hey."

"You'll get no argument from Liam on that one. Any particular bastard leap out at you?"

"Aye. The one convicted on Ronni Jarvis' murder. Jonno Mulvenna, a really nasty bit of work."

"Mmm..."

Andy stared at Craig questioningly. "Was that mmm...yes, or mmm...no?"

"Yes, he's a nasty bastard, but no, I don't like him for Jarvis' death."

"Why not?"

"Mulvenna's one of the few from back then that I remember. He targeted the police and army but he wasn't part of a punishment squad."

He pulled out his mobile and pressed dial. A moment later the call was answered by a laughing Nicky and he smiled at the sound of her voice.

"Docklands Murder Squad, can I help you?"

Craig smiled again. She hadn't noticed his number coming up so he decided to have some fun. He made his voice as gruff as possible. "Mrs Morris, it's ACC Murphy here, what's so amusing?"

Nicky gave the phone a look of panic and the laughter stopped dead as the others caught the look on her face.

"Good afternoon, ACC Murphy. I'm sorry, sir. One of the men was just cracking a joke."

"You don't get paid to tell jokes. Where's Superintendent Craig?"

She was about to reply when something about the voice seemed familiar. Craig's mix of Italian and Northern Irish gave his voice a warm quality that was hard to disguise, even behind his mock anger. Nicky squinted at the phone and then spoke.

"Oh him. He's off gallivanting again, sir. Or in the pub. It's impossible to get him to do any work at all."

The others stared at her aghast until she laughed.

Craig joined in. "OK, you've caught me, Nick. Glad to hear someone's having fun. Is Davy there?"

"I'll transfer you now." She'd barely covered the handset before she yelled. "Davy, pick up your line. It's the chief." Craig pulled the phone back from his ear in pain. Nicky might only be five-feet-three but she had a voice a town crier would envy.

Five seconds later Davy's softer voice came through. "What can I help with, boss?"

"Davy, could you go back through the archived files on The Troubles and search out everything you can find on a Jonno Mulvenna, please? He might be under John or Jonathan as well, but Jonno was what he was known by."

"IRA?"

"Yes. Provisionals. His usual targets were police and army officers, but he was probably involved in other things as well. There was a murder case in '83 that put him inside until the Good Friday Agreement in 1998. See what you can find on that."

"Is it linked with your case up north, s...sir?"

"Yes, unfortunately. I'll let you know more when I do." Craig paused then continued with a note of envy in his voice. "You sound like you're having fun."

Davy glanced over at the small group he'd just left. Jake was amusing Nicky and Annette with card tricks. He was good at them but Davy thought he'd better not give Craig the details when they were working so hard up north.

"Jake just told us a joke."

Craig smiled wryly. "Oh, I thought he might be showing off his magic skills. He's a champion magician you know, I saw him perform last year. "

Davy said nothing and Craig smiled again.

"Enjoy yourselves. It's a Saturday, even though we are on call. And tell Annette to send everyone home anytime she likes. There's no point all your weekends being spoiled as well."

"Thanks, boss. I'll check Mulvenna right now and s...send you what I find."

The phone clicked off and Craig turned back to Andy, tapping the folder in his hand.

"This is the investigation of Veronica Jarvis' death."

Andy peered at it; it was thinner than any murder file he'd seen. Craig walked to a table and laid the contents out. Apart from a charge sheet there was only a summary sheet containing details of Mulvenna's conviction and sentence, and one page from forensics. Andy turned it over. It matched Mulvenna to a partial print from the tape covering Ronni Jarvis' mouth. His mouth fell open.

"They convicted Mulvenna on that? I know they were under pressure to clear things up quickly back then, but hey!"

Craig nodded. It was exactly what he was thinking but something else was nagging at the back of his mind. He closed the file and sat down, then he put his phone on speaker and dialled Liam.

"Hello, boss. What can I do for you?"

"We'll meet later for an update, Liam, but I've a quick question. You policed during The Troubles, didn't you?"

"Man and boy. So?"

"In your opinion, how often were ordinary crimes labelled as terrorist offences?"

Liam let out a low whistle before he spoke. "Plenty of times. And vice versa. A lot of unmarked weapons were 'signed out' from terrorists on loan to ordinary citizens for a few hundred quid. They'd be dumped after the crime, whatever it was, and they were impossible to trace. We used to joke that The Troubles saved the divorce courts a lot of work. But we were so busy with the bombs and bullets that some things were let slip."

"OK, thanks. And how easy would it have been back then to frame a terrorist for something they hadn't done?"

Liam gave a loud laugh. "You mean one of them got banged-up for someone they didn't kill? Happy days."

Craig raised his eyes to heaven and smiled. Liam's political incorrectness was legendary. It had been dialled down considerably in the run up to his recent promotion board but it was back now, alive and kicking hard.

"Seriously, Liam. Would it really have been that easy to frame someone for murder?"

Liam swallowed another laugh and attempted a serious voice. "I'd be lying if I said it hadn't been tried, boss. There was a lot of frustration back then and the pressure was on to get these bastards off the streets. But…"

"Yes?"

"Unless there was some evidence, it would have been thrown out at trial. They'd never have been sent down if the evidence hadn't been there. Who do you think was framed?"

"A Provo called Jonno Mulvenna."

Liam's tone changed to anger. "A cop-killer like Mulvenna was fair game. He would have been lifted as often as we could. What do you think he was framed for?"

Craig sighed. The more Liam said the more he became convinced that Mulvenna had been a dupe.

"The murder of Veronica Jarvis, back in 1983. I'll update you later, Liam. Thanks for your help."

Before Liam could say any more Craig cut the call and turned to see the objection on Andy's face.

"No, Marc. We can't do this, hey. We can't re-open an old case. If Mulvenna didn't kill Ronni Jarvis he killed plenty more. If we start questioning his conviction it will open a can of worms that will go on for years."

Craig stared at the file and turned to a black and white photo of a twenty-something man staring unsmiling at the camera. They could see the naked hatred in his eyes. He was a killer without a doubt, but was he Veronica Jarvis' killer? And if he wasn't then why had he been convicted for her death? Was it just exhausted police work or had he really been framed?

He shook his head, trying to push away his doubts. The last thing he wanted was to defend a terrorist, but if he was innocent of this it had ramifications far beyond this case. If Mulvenna had been framed for Ronni Jarvis' murder then Lissy Trainor's murder mightn't just be a copycat, the same man might have committed both. He could have been out there, running free for thirty years.. But if he had been free all that time then why hadn't he killed between 1983 and now?

He looked at Andy and nodded, ignoring his objections. He didn't have the answers but he knew that the questions had to be asked, whether people wanted him to ask them or not.

Chapter Six

The man watched from a distance as the woman in uniform climbed into the car and her husband indicated left at the end of the street. He knew where they were going, by the grave expressions their faces wore. To choose a way to remember their beloved child. Bury her or burn her, it didn't matter. She was still dead. He smiled at the woman wearing her uniform. Nothing would get in the way of her career, not even her daughter's death. Good to know that she hadn't changed. She was still a cold, hard bitch.

He cast a glance around the street and then crossed it stealthily, slipping down the house's driveway to push open the garden gate. The flowers stood upright in neat borders, the hedges cut back to within an inch of their lives. She even controlled her garden. No sentiment, disposing of anything that wasn't of use.

He slipped a knife between the patio doors then entered the suburban house, wandering casually from room to room. A single picture of Lissy sat on a dark-wood desk in the study. Her husband's desk. A smaller pine desk sat alongside, with only a book on top. The bitch didn't even display a picture of her child. He wasn't shocked; he just wondered how long it would take her to forget that she'd ever had her at all.

He lifted the photo and stroked the glass, half-smiling at the dark-haired girl beneath. He'd been sorry when she'd begged him to let her go and he was sorry about her death. She'd seemed nice, very nice, her whole life just waiting to be lived. But she'd had to die, or the truth would never come out.

***

Hugh Trainor fingered the pink silk interior then stroked his hand down the side of the coffin's pale wood. Lissy would have liked it, it was pretty. Even in death she would have wanted style. He thought of her wide impish smile and her habit of calling him 'Pops', too old now for Daddy and always too much fun for 'Father' to pass her lips. He choked back a sob at the memory and pictured her when she was young. Dancing along the street and holding his hand. Gazing up at him as he if had every answer in the world. The sob became a tear joined by others and he turned his back hastily on his wife. She wouldn't approve. An elected official crying in public, an MLA with genuine emotion. Whatever next?

He sniffed hard and wiped his face then turned back to the anteroom and nodded to the man behind the desk, ignoring the disapproval in his wife's eyes. He wondered how long their marriage would last now that the glue between them had gone. Not long, if he had his way. He'd always known Melanie hadn't loved him, she'd just thought him a 'suitable' match, an asset to her career. God forbid anything should get in the way of that. He would be no great loss to her; even less than Lissy was.

He pulled out a chair and sat down, as far from his wife as he could, then he filled in the forms to arrange the last party his pretty daughter would ever attend.

***

"I've s...sent you everything I can find, so far, boss. There'll be more on Monday when everything's open again. I found some stuff on the case in '83, but there isn't a lot. Record keeping back then s...seemed to be pretty thin."

Craig nodded. "I know. Thanks Davy, that's great. Now go home. It's the weekend."

"I'm happy to come back in if you need me."

"Be careful of what you offer..."

Craig shut his phone and tapped the computer keyboard, pulling up the files Davy had sent. He pressed print and then sat back to read. He was halfway through the Jarvis notes when his phone rang again. It was John.

"Hi John, what can I do for you?"

He glanced at his watch. It was four-ten. They were meeting in under an hour. What couldn't wait?

"Marc, I know we're meeting soon but I just thought I'd let you know that the Trainors visited the morgue thirty minutes ago. I asked if they would speak to you but they said tomorrow would have to do."

"How were they?"

"The father was as you'd expect. Really cut-up. But she barely blinked. There was none of yesterday's emotion at all." He paused, shocked by what he'd seen. "She was in uniform and he was driving her into work when they left. Can you believe that?"

Craig nodded. He wasn't surprised. Melanie Trainor was very cool. He corrected himself. No, she wasn't cool, she was cold and everyone knew it. She was bright but not that bright and there'd been questions many times about how she'd made it to the top. Especially from cleverer women who'd fallen along the way. Some of the complaints could be dismissed as jealousy, or chauvinism in a country where women spent too much time chained to the kitchen sink. But unfortunately he knew that the rumours were true. Melanie Trainor had used her pretty smile to take her places her brain couldn't reach. She was promiscuous and strategically so; a strategic shagger, in the parlance of the day, targeting men of power who could take her to the top.

He'd worked opposite her on a case three years before, and watched as she'd spent late nights 'in conference' with businessmen and politicians. She'd dismissed any man that she didn't consider useful and disappeared upstairs with the lucky lad, only to reappear with him at breakfast the next day. She was open about it, arguing that she was playing men at their own game. Perhaps she was, but she was already married to Hugh Trainor, a well-respected politician tipped for the First Minister's post someday. How much higher did she need to go in Northern Ireland's small pond?

"That's not a shock, John. She's very driven. She wants to be Chief Constable someday and she may well get there."

"Her husband seemed like a nice man. He looked like he really loved Lissy. I have to say, they weren't the warmest couple I've ever seen. Frozen waste as Natalie would say."

Natalie Ingrams was John's long term partner and Craig's money was on her soon being his wife. She was lovely girl and a brilliant surgeon, but subtlety had never been her strong point. She and Liam had both gone to the JCB School of diplomacy.

"OK, thanks John. I'll try to speak to them tomorrow." He glanced at his watch again. "Listen, we're debriefing at five. Fancy meeting before then for a quick drink?"

"Good idea. See you in the bar in twenty."

Craig read for five more minutes then rolled up the Jarvis file and put it in his pocket. Then he headed for the hotel bar and a well-earned beer.

***

Annette wandered through Victoria Square's House of Fraser and rifled through rails of clothes, searching for an outfit for her sister's wedding in four weeks' time. It was her second time round and she was holding it on the pitch at her husband-to-be's rugby club, where they seemed to spend every Friday nights. Annette couldn't see the attraction herself, but live and let live.

She was wondering idly whether she could persuade her to change the dress code to jeans and trainers when her phone rang, disturbing her thoughts. It was a number she didn't recognise but then that wasn't new. People from cases gone by often called her, long after she'd forgotten she'd handed them her card. She wandered into the lift area and pressed answer, giving plain 'Annette McElroy' as her name. The voice on the other end surprised her and for a moment she wasn't sure it was who she thought. It seemed so unlikely that she would call.

"Lucia?"

Lucia was Craig's younger sister by almost eleven years and they'd met many times at post-case drinks and family 'do's. They hadn't spoken for months, not since the Britt Ackerman case had wrapped up. The quiet voice answered 'yes', confirming Annette's guess. It was Lucia. She spoke in a nervous almost-whisper as if she was afraid that someone else might hear and Annette heard something in her voice that she'd never heard before. Fear.

She shook her head. It couldn't be. Lucia was absolutely fearless, fighting for every underdog in the world. She was paid to do it nine to five in her work with a charity, but practically every weekend was spent marching for another good cause, much to the amusement of the uniforms and Craig's red face. She remembered the time she'd had to be cut off the gates of Stormont and smiled, recalling his shocked look. He'd been purple with embarrassment but beneath it they could see his unmistakable pride.

"Annette, I…"

Annette heard the fear again. It was clearer this time. She stopped being plain Mrs McElroy, out shopping on a Saturday afternoon, and became an Inspector again, taking control.

"Where are you? I'll come to you."

Twenty minutes later she was clear about the reason that Lucia had called, and even more clear why she hadn't dialled her big brother's phone.

***

"Marc, where are you?"

Craig stared at his mobile wondering what Julia meant. "What do you mean? I'm at work."

"But I called the office ten minutes ago and there's no-one there."

John watched as a look of horror suddenly covered his friend's face. He mouthed 'what's up?' and watched as Craig drew his finger across his throat, mimicking a knife. The look on his face said he was in deep shit.

"Where are you, pet?"

Julia gazed around Craig's living room then stirred the pot on the cooker again.

"I'm in your flat. I'm cooking dinner and I just wanted to know what time you'll be home." She paused and sighed. "I met with the Chief Constable today and I need to tell you what he said."

Craig didn't know what to say, so he said nothing. He'd got so carried away with the case that he'd completely forgotten she was coming to Belfast that weekend. He could either tell the truth and be hanged for it, or drive home now and let Andy down. He chose the job.

John could hear Julia yelling from ten feet away as Craig left the bar quickly to continue the call. Five minutes later he returned, looking the worse for wear. He grabbed at his beer, downed it in one then ordered another. John said nothing, just waited until the storm had passed then shot him a questioning look.

Craig shook his head. "Don't ask, John. Suffice to say I'll be in the bad books from now until Christmas. Let's change the subject."

John did as he was told, grateful they weren't going to have a deep and meaningful talk. They could both do without it. He took a drink and brightened his tone, even though the subject matter didn't fit.

"You know Melanie Trainor?"

Craig nodded vaguely. "Not well, but maybe as well as

anyone ever does."

John raised his eyebrows and waved him on.

"I worked a case with her on a case three years ago. She was a Superintendent then and headed for the top."

"And now she's there. From Superintendent to ACC in three years. There's hope for you yet."

Craig shook his head, disagreeing. "She won't be happy until she's the Chief. Don't get me wrong, that's not a bad thing. Ambition's fine, but…"

"But?"

"Well let's just say Andy nailed it when he said she could cause a fight in an empty room."

John laughed loudly. He hadn't heard the Derry expression in years. Craig was still talking.

"She's aggressive. With suspects, people under her, with life probably. That's not the sort of person I would choose to run the force."

"Any reason *why* she's that way?"

Craig shrugged. "I suppose it can't have been easy fighting her way through a man's world. The old boys' network is pretty dense."

"So are most of the old boys. But you think there's more to it?"

"I'm not sure, but sometimes it was as if she thought she was being chased. Like she was somehow waiting to be found out and told to leave."

John nodded. "Imposter Syndrome. Waiting to be tapped on the shoulder and told that you don't deserve to be here. It's pretty common in people who lead the vanguard, and let's face it; she's one of the first female ACCs here."

Craig shrugged again, conceding. "You're probably right."

"But…"

He laughed at John's knowledge of him and his laughter was renewed by Liam and Andy wandering into the bar, already laughing about something else.

"Share the joke, lads."

Liam shook his head. "Can't. It's far too rude for your sensitive ears. "He glanced quickly at Craig's beer then beckoned the barman across.

"Another round of whatever they're having, a pint of bitter and…"

He turned to Andy. He was perusing the cocktail menu, turning it over in his hand as if trying to make a choice. Liam grabbed it and pointed to the rudest name on the list. "And one of those for my young friend. He doesn't get out much."

Andy blustered not to bother and added another order for beer, but not before the waitress had laughed at Liam's joke and he was satisfied the evening's banter had begun. Craig motioned them to a table in the corner of the bar.

"OK, it's a Saturday night and we're stag, so we all know how this is going to go. But before we get too drunk to speak let's get the business out of the way."

Liam raised his beer glass. "Here, here. There's nothing like a realist to tell it like it is."

"John, do you want to start?"

John turned at the sound of his name, dragging his eyes away from the pretty barmaid carrying drinks across the bar.

"OK. Lissy Trainor definitely wasn't raped. She was killed quickly by manual strangulation and there are signs that she struggled. Her finger nails were broken and there are scratch marks on her throat, my money's on them matching where she tried to prise his fingers off. There was latex under her nails as well."

"He wore gloves."

John nodded. "Unless we're very lucky her skin will be all we'll find. There was very little blood, just around the scratches. The tide washed away everything else. The crime scene investigators collected everything they could find at the scene, but I wouldn't hold out much hope."

"Did her parents come in today, Doc?"

"Yes, and it was very odd. " He turned to Craig. "Although it does fit with what you said earlier, about Melanie Trainor's personality."

Liam leaned forward eagerly. He had a white ring of foam around his mouth and Craig was tempted to tell him. A quick glance from Andy said they'd have more craic if they left it alone.

"What about her, boss?"

Craig repeated his earlier comments and Andy nodded. "Tough lady and not adverse to a bit of bed-hopping if it helps her get her way, hey."

"Is that the voice of experience, Andy?"

Andy threw Craig a wise-up look. "Nah, not my cup of tea. She's good looking but scary as get-out. I don't fancy having my performance appraised in bed."

Liam was about to drag the conversation down even further when John continued reporting about the Trainor's viewing earlier that day.

"The father was very cut up, really badly. But Mrs Trainor's reaction was nothing like yesterday's. She just stood and watched him without a tear."

"Maybe she wore herself out crying last night?"

John shook his head. "She didn't look as if she'd been crying that much, but that's no indicator of grief, plenty of people just shut down and don't say a word. It was the way they interacted that surprised me most."

"How so, Doc?"

"She just watched him cry. No attempt to comfort him, not crying with him, nothing. She just stood across the room and watched him break his heart." He shrugged, dismissing his own report. "It probably means nothing. It takes all sorts."

"He's an MLA, isn't he?"

"Yes, the Energy party, And independently wealthy too. His family own the Sandbank group of bars and hotels."

Liam let out a low whistle. "If I owned that lot you'd never get me out of them."

Craig smiled wryly at Liam's nearly empty glass and beckoned the barmaid over to order another round.

"Does anyone know any more about him?"

Andy nodded and Crag smiled at him. Andy was a lightweight when it came to getting drunk and he could see the signs already. His tie was loosened halfway down his neck and his blue shirt had two buttons undone. It wouldn't be long before he started singing. Craig had been out drinking with him before.

"He's an MLA for East Dungiven and the surrounds, and not bad one I have to say. My Mum likes him and she's wild hard to please. Says he's a nice man too, she often sees him in the town and he'll stop and have a yarn. His daughter was usually with him. They were very close."

"Did they ever see the ACC out in town?"

He made a face. "Nope. Too posh. Well, that's what my Mum says and she's always right. So she tells me anyway."

"OK. So ACC Trainor's not exactly wife and mother of the year and we know she's ambitious in the extreme."

Liam wiped his mouth and interjected. "I hear that she only married him for his contacts."

"And the money?"

Liam shook his head. "Actually no. Everyone pretty much agrees she wants power more than anything else. And she's a stickler for the rules, on the job and off it."

John smiled as the barmaid brought over their drinks and Craig raised an eyebrow as she flirted back. None of his business. John was a big boy.

"Do you have an example, Liam?"

"Just general things. Prissy about uniform – she put a mate of mine on complaint for wearing the wrong shirt one day. She goes to the opening of an envelope, always at church on Sundays, you know the craic."

Buttoned-up. It was hardly a crime in Northern Ireland, even if it ought to be.

"It hardly fits with her promiscuity, does it?"

Liam sniffed and looked at them meaningfully, as if his next words would be the wisest they'd ever heard.

"Well, it's obvious, isn't it? It's all about the front. She wants to look whiter than white because otherwise it might affect her career, but what happens behind closed doors…"

Andy leaned in eagerly. "And she's strategic, hey. She only sleeps with men who can help her career. They won't talk because they're in senior positions and they'd have something to lose as well if it came out. Everyone's keeping up the front."

Liam nodded sagely and sipped at his beer. Craig gazed across the table at the two men, struggling to keep a straight face. They were like police Jedi, imparting wisdom to their Padawans. Andy was still on a roll.

"Mind you, good on her, that's what I say. Men have been doing it for years." He raised his glass. "Here's to feminism, hey."

Craig agreed with the conversation's general gist. Melanie Trainor was all about status and power and she would do anything to gain it, and keep it. It explained the coolness John had witnessed between husband and wife. It was a status marriage, not a love one, at least not on her part.

"OK, let me tell you what we've got on the case in '83. Veronica Jarvis was found in exactly the same spot on the beach as Lissy Trainor. She was badly beaten, strangled and buried in the sand. Perhaps only up to her neck or perhaps completely and the tide washed the sand away. There was no apparent sexual assault, so in every way except the beating, Lissy Trainor's murder is identical. A known IRA terrorist was charged and convicted for Veronica Jarvis' murder. John, 'Jonno', Mulvenna. He went down for twenty years but because it was charged as a terrorist offence he was released after fifteen under the Good Friday Agreement."

Craig sipped at his beer and Liam leapt into the gap.

"Was that why you asked about people being framed, boss? You think Mulvenna was?"

"Perhaps."

Liam shook his head slowly and Craig knew he was on delicate ground. Liam had policed in Northern Ireland for almost thirty years, including during The Troubles, while the rest of them had been at university and working, either in Vice like Andy or like him, in London with The Met. Liam had buried scores of his colleagues and picked pieces of them off the ground after bombs. Mulvenna had probably killed some of them. Craig spoke quickly.

"Let me say something here, straight out. Mulvenna is a killer and he deserved to be put away. He should have served a lot longer than he did. I have no sympathy for the man, and Liam, I know this is too close to home."

Liam face was reddening and his fist was clenched snow-white. Craig had never heard anger like it in his voice before.

"Mulvenna blew up one of my mates. Shuggy Nolan. Young lad with a baby under two. the bastard ran the squad targeting police and army in Belfast, and his only regret was probably that he didn't kill more of us. They should have hung him for the things he did." He glared at Craig. "And now you're trying to get him off. Well you can count me out."

He was standing now, looming over them all, six-feet-six of pissed-off cop. John and Andy froze, watching the exchange. It would have been comical if it hadn't been so sad. Craig shook his head tiredly and waved Liam back to his seat. He couldn't imagine how he felt, he'd only lost one friend to a shooting, on the North End Road in Fulham, but Liam had lost one practically every week. Craig spoke so quietly that the others strained to hear.

"Liam, I'm *not* trying to get him off. Be clear on that. But if Mulvenna *did* kill Ronni Jarvis then we have to interview him for this death as well. It's too similar to be coincidence. If he did it then I'll be happy to lock him up and throw away the key for killing Lissy, and every other death he caused. But if he didn't…"

The look on Liam's face said that he suddenly understood. He finished Craig's sentence for him. "Then there's a murderer on the loose who's killed two women thirty years apart, and he'll kill again."

Craig nodded and updated them on what he'd found then he closed the case for the night and they tied on a well-earned drunk.

Chapter Seven

Lucia nursed her glass for so long that the ice inside it melted and her cold white wine became a lukewarm mess. Annette ordered her a fresh one then sat back in the booth in Ivory, the restaurant at the top of the House of Fraser, and waited for her to talk. After a few more minutes' silence, Lucia reached into her pocket and withdrew a sheaf of papers, pushing them gently across the table.

Annette started to read the top sheet. It was a print-out of a long text sent from someone called 'Watchin' U'. Her eyes widened as she read it and her mouth fell open when she reached the sexually explicit description at the bottom of the page. The author was unambiguous about what he'd like to do to Lucia, but coy about his identity. She glanced at Lucia, taking in her tawny hair and pretty oval face and thanked God that she'd always had average looks. Beauty was a double-edged sword.

Lucia pointed at the page, speaking for the first time since they'd met. Her voice was a female version of Craig's and Annette smiled at how alike they were.

"I've been getting them for four weeks now. This is just a sample. The latest ones are much worse."

"Worse than this? Lucia, why didn't you tell Marc?"

She shook her head and Annette saw tears brightening her dark-blue eyes.

"You know what he would have done, Annette. He'd have gone mad and then he'd have told the folks. The last thing they need after Dad's heart attack is to have to worry about me." She gave a wet smile. "Besides, you don't know Marc's temper like I do. If he found the man who sent them he'd kill him with his bare hands."

Annette stared at her, her eyes widening in surprise. "Is this the same Marc Craig we're talking about? Kind, rational and given to the occasional rant? Killing someone bare-handed?"

Lucia's face was solemn.

"Annette, he may seem calm at work but he's a typical Italian male behind it all. If someone hurts someone he loves ..." She sipped at her wine then went on. "There was a man once, when I was about six and Marco was seventeen. I was playing in the front garden and he tried to open the gate lock. Marco was upstairs listening to music and Mum and Dad were out shopping in town."

She hesitated, as if what she was about to say was a betrayal somehow.

"He got the gate open and came in. I didn't know what to do so I started to cry and Marc heard the noise. He came running downstairs, just as the man picked me up and was starting to run away."

She stopped speaking, gazing into Annette's eyes as if she was eliciting her promise not to repeat what she said next. Annette nodded.

"Marco...he completely lost it. He pulled me out of the man's arms and told me to go inside, but I didn't, I hid behind the front door and watched. Marc started punching the man and he started to fight back but Marc was stronger and he won. He... he really hurt him Annette. There was blood everywhere. He broke his nose and arm and he was in hospital for a week. Dad took Marc to the police station and he was given a lecture, but when the circumstances were explained no charges were brought."

Lucia paused and Annette filled the gap with a question, on automatic pilot while she thought about what she'd said. "What about the man?" Lucia stared at her blankly. "Was he charged?"

Lucia nodded. "Yes. It turned out he was a known sex-offender. They locked him up for years, although he's probably out again now." She looked pleadingly at Annette. "So do you see why I can't tell Marc about these e-mails? If he lost his temper that way again it would ruin his career.

Annette nodded, thinking about what she'd just heard. It made sense. There'd been times over the years when she'd seen Craig holding something back. Keeping his emotions just a bit too tightly under control, almost as if he let go he'd never get the genie back into the bottle. Or the beast back into its cage... It was a side of him that they'd never seen, but now she knew about it she wasn't at all surprised.

She nodded at the pages, back in Inspector mode. "Do you have any idea who might have sent them?"

Lucia shook her head, throwing her long hair across her face. She pushed it back with a half-smile, relieved that Annette was going to help, without Marc or her parents being told. She was a thirty-two-year-old woman but they still treated her as if she was five.

"None. I called the phone provider but the number's an unregistered pay-as-you-go. I've racked my brains for old boyfriends, or men who've made me feel creepy, but there's no-one who stands out."

"Has anyone been hanging around your work or outside your flat?"

"I haven't noticed anyone, but I'll keep a look out."

"I need to see the rest of the texts."

"There have been letters as well."

"Posted to your home?"

"Yes."

"Any e-mails?"

Lucia shook her head. "They probably think they'd be too easy to trace."

Annette thought quickly. "Right, I need to see everything you've received and I want you to take taxis or drive everywhere until we sort this out. Develop a leak in the ceiling of your bedroom, bad enough so that you have to stay with your folks for a week or so while it's repaired."

"But, I…"

"But nothing, Lucia. Those are my terms for keeping this under the radar. Tell me now if you can't go along with them and I'll hand the case over to Marc."

Annette folded her arms stubbornly and Lucia could see from her expression that she wasn't playing games. She nodded reluctantly.

"Meanwhile, I'll get Davy to do his thing with the texts and letters and get patrols to drive past your flat and see what they pick up. Don't tell anyone at your work about this, or that you're staying with your folks."

Lucia smiled, relieved. Annette made a good Inspector and she trusted her. She just hoped that Marc didn't find out. Keeping this from him could put them both in his bad books for a long, long time.

Chapter Eight

Sunday Morning.

Craig slumped down to breakfast nursing the hangover from hell, to see three other men feeling exactly the same. The only comfort was that Andy looked worse than all of them and he'd had the least to drink. They'd poured him into bed at three a.m. and continued their session in Liam's room, trying to persuade John that he wasn't in love with the barmaid and that death at Natalie's hands would be far more painful than his imagined loss.

"How come none of you look as rough as me, hey? You drank the Bann dry last night."

Liam nodded sagely. "Aye well, that'll explain it then. We're used to drinking the Lagan and it's powerful stuff. The Bann's like diet soda to us."

Andy made a weak attempt at laughter then held his head and stared out at the sea. The hotel had views of the Donegal Peninsula and glimpses of Scotland as well. The whole area was stunning, including the beach where they'd found Lissy. It was known locally as the Strand, but whatever you called it, it was beautiful. Miles of pale clean sand dotted with people taking an early morning stroll. In the distance a few adventurous surfers were braving the North Atlantic's unpredictable moods.

John was staring out the window as well, but he wasn't admiring the shoreline. He was thinking of any forensics the C.S.I.s might have missed. Craig contrasted his focus with Liam and Andy's morning craic, wondering who had it right. After ten minutes of coffee, toast and banter, he pulled them all back to work.

"OK. Liam, did you get anywhere with Lissy Trainor's movements yesterday."

Liam pulled a small notebook from his pocket and flicked to a page near the back. He shook his head slowly as he spoke.

"Saturday was a hard one to pin people down. All her classmates went home after they graduated from Uni in July, so that only left the local ones. I also went to the street where she lives with her Mum and Dad."

He gave a long whistle and Andy covered his ears, wincing. "It's up on the cliff near the convent, and man, you should see the house. Big as a barracks. That cost a fortune, you can bet on it. There was a boat in the drive and all."

Craig interjected. "Did you knock at the Trainor's house or just the neighbours?"

He already knew the answer. Liam was too long in the tooth to foul the path this soon.

Liam shot him a wry look. "Neighbours. I'll leave the Mr and Mrs for another day. Anyway... the girl next door is called Billy Munroe, and..."

"Billy?" Andy was staring at him confused.

"God, you're as old fashioned as Davy." He ignored their questioning looks and carried on with a superior tone. "Billy's her nickname. It's cool for girls to take boys name these days, apparently. Mind you, her real name is Wilhelmina so you can understand why."

Craig waved him on, as amused as Andy now. Liam could turn a simple report into an episode of Have I Got News For You. Sometimes it drove him mad but it was just what they needed today in their hung-over haze.

"Well, Billy says that Lissy hated her Mum but loved her dad and he was the only reason she stayed living at home. But she was planning to move in with her boyfriend in a couple of weeks. Excited about it too, then all of a sudden it was all off and there were tears every day. Billy had no idea why but she did say the boyfriend had been a bit of player at school."

"Isn't everyone a player at sixteen?"

They turned towards the question and saw John with a smile on his face. Craig had been to school with him and John was the sort who'd worshipped girls from afar, but if he wanted to pretend he'd been a player, who was he to 'out' him? Andy was staring wistfully into space, remembering.

Liam sniffed and moved on. He'd been too busy working on his parent's farm at sixteen to play around, then he'd put on the suit and started getting shot at, met Danni and that was the end of that. Although he liked to practice flirting with Nicky to prevent rusting up.

Craig interjected. "OK Liam, keep going with the friends and get the boyfriend in for a chat. Let's have him in at the station, it'll focus his mind. John, anything more on the '83 case?"

John shook his head. "The M.O. was slightly different. Ronni Jarvis was beaten then strangled before she was buried in the sand. I've a call out for any hair and sand fibres they had back then, but as you said yesterday, the case was thin. The bruises led them towards a punishment killing, but if they hadn't been there it could have been put down as an ordinary murder. She wasn't a small woman and she was fit. She used to play camogie for Antrim, and that's not a game for the weak. There were no blows to her head and she wasn't knocked out, so the strength required to bruise and then strangle her could only have been a pretty strong man."

"Or men?"

John nodded. "Maybe. But there was only one set of hand prints on her throat. As you know, the IRA never claimed it and they usually did, unless they 'disappeared' the person. And leaving her on Strand knowing the tide was going to come in was never going to disappear her for long."

He looked thoughtfully at Liam. He had the most experience

of them all of The Troubles. "Liam, what's your feel on this: terrorism or domestic murder?"

"By domestic you don't necessarily mean husband or partner Doc, do you?"

John shook his head. "No. I mean anything non-terrorist. An 'ordinary' murder, if there is such a thing."

Liam rubbed his chin and paused. He liked being asked for his opinion.

"Ordinary, definitely. The IRA claimed their kills. That was the whole point. 'Look at what we can do and be very scared.' Especially with people they thought might be informers. And they used bullets, not strangulation. With people they wanted to kill, like women, who they knew there might be a backlash against, they usually 'disappeared' them. My money's on this being nothing to do with the 'RA, but it made for a quick answer back then."

"Or a handy cover."

They looked at Craig questioningly. He took a sip of coffee and started to explain.

"OK. Let's say that someone wanted to kill a woman, any woman." He suddenly thought of something and turned to John. "John, Ronni Jarvis wasn't sexually assaulted, was she?"

John shook his head, but it wasn't a firm 'no'. "The report says not, but…"

"What?"

"Forensics back then weren't what they are now. Unless there was obvious semen a lot of rapes were missed. Add to that the fact she was given a bath every time the tide came in. Well, let's just say that I wouldn't be sure that she wasn't sexually assaulted, no matter what forensics they couldn't find. I'd like to go back and take another look."

"At the samples or the body?"

"Samples and reports first, but body if I'm not convinced. We might be looking at an exhumation."

Craig rubbed his eyes tiredly. "OK. Let's just say that she

might have been raped. If we add that in with Liam's feelings about the IRA, then it makes Ronni Jarvis's death much more likely to have been a sexually motivated killing than a terrorist punishment murder. That leads me on to my next question."

He turned to Liam and Andy. "Jonno Mulvenna?"

Andy answered first. "What about him, hey? He's a nasty bastard, have no illusions about that, Marc. If he wasn't guilty of this, he just paid for something else." His voice rose agitatedly and Liam reinforced his sentiments with a nod. "Overturning his conviction will do no-one any favours."

"Except maybe Lissy Trainor." John nodded in agreement and Craig waved Andy down.

"Look, as I said before I have no sympathy for Mulvenna but if he was framed for Ronni Jarvis' murder, then why? And if someone wanted him banged up and out the way, why again? It might just have been because they thought he deserved it. OK, that's the simple explanation. But what if it served another end? To get the real killer off? And if there is someone else out there who killed Ronni Jarvis, then did they kill Lissy Trainor? And if they did, then why her? Is it linked to her mother in some way? Or even her father's job? There are a lot of unanswered questions here."

John nodded more furiously with each question Craig asked and gradually Liam and Andy joined in.

"OK. Was there anyone else in '83 who was a suspect in Ronni Jarvis' death? And if so why were they just a suspect; why did they drop out of the loop? Did someone want them protected who also wanted Jonno Mulvenna banged up? If we find the answers to those questions then we'll be halfway there."

Liam tapped his chin thoughtfully with his pen. "Of course there are two other things to consider."

"What?"

"If it is the same killer then why not kill for over thirty years?"

"Yes, and?"

"If it's a straight copycat, then why no beating this time? And you're definite Lissy wasn't raped, aren't you Doc?"

"Yes. Positive."

"OK, then why copy the strangulation and burial, but not the beating and possible rape, if it's the same man? And if it's not the same man then why just copy the most dramatic bits?"

Of course…

"To ensure the crime caught our attention."

"And the media's, boss."

"The fact that it's Lissy Trainor would catch the force's attention at the highest level too, Marc."

"And ACC Trainor's in particular."

Craig nodded thoughtfully. Liam was right, there were dimensions to this case way beyond the obvious. He smiled at the newly minted D.C.I. and tipped him a small salute.

"Well done, Liam. Now everyone knows how you passed the board."

Liam blushed faintly and covered his embarrassment with a deep gulp of tea.

"OK. That leaves us with a lot of interviews. John, dig as deep as you can on the forensics on both cases."

"Even if it means exhuming Ronni Jarvis' body?"

Craig winced then nodded. It might have to be done.

"Andy, you and I are going to pay Mr Mulvenna a visit. I need to speak to the Chief Constable at some point as well. I don't think Melanie Trainor will talk to us, unless she's instructed to."

"That's interesting, hey. You'd think she'd be desperate to find out who killed her daughter."

"Yes, you would. But remember the Jarvis case was hers and she can't have missed the similarities. She may not want anyone digging around too much." He shrugged his shoulders. "Tough. We'll do what we have to do." He turned to Liam. "Liam, chase up those interviews and ask Davy to find out anything he can about Ronni Jarvis' life and if there were any other viable suspects on the case. If there were, then who had a vested interest in keeping them out of the nick?"

He beckoned over the waitress but instead of asking for the bill as expected he ordered them all another round of drinks and scones.

"This is going to be a long day. We need coffee and fortification before we start." He scanned their pale faces. "And more than one of us needs our blood-alcohol to drop before we go anywhere near the street."

Chapter Nine

Annette put down the phone to Davy and glanced at the file. It was Sunday and even though she was on duty, making the phone calls about Lucia's case from home seemed more appropriate somehow. This wasn't a murder, and going behind Craig's back was one thing, going behind it in full view of his glass office, even when he wasn't in there, felt like quite another.

Davy was on board to help Lucia, and Nicky too. She'd felt bad about asking them but she'd explained Lucia's reasons for by-passing Craig under the heading of 'over-protective big brother' leaving out all mention of the assault when Craig was seventeen. That was Lucia's business. They'd been eager to help and Davy had started tracing the texts and letters already. Meanwhile Lucia had kept her part of the deal, telling her parents a small white lie and moving back home. The unmarked patrols would keep an eye on her apartment for a few days and report back. Now she just had to come up with a list of possible suspects and they could start to eliminate them one by one.

A cup of hot tea was placed in her hand, breaking into her thoughts. She looked up at her benefactor and smiled. Pete was making a real effort nowadays; he had been since they'd had their traumatic almost-split five months before. The jury was still out on whether they could make their marriage work, but he was trying hard and she was willing to let him. Whether it worked or not she knew she would survive now, with or without him. She loved her job and making Inspector wasn't bad but she wasn't stopping there. After all, if Melanie Trainor could be an ACC then there was nothing to stop her from reaching the top. She smiled across the room at her husband, grateful that he couldn't read her thoughts. Inspector was high enough at the moment, but whatever she decided in the future, Pete wouldn't be allowed to stand in her way.

***

Craig parked his black Audi in front of a row of modern terraced houses near the Coleraine Road. They looked about five years old. Children's toys and bikes were scattered in front of two of them, indicating that they were family homes. A battered car and a gleaming BMW motor bike were parked in front of another. Even if he hadn't known which number Jonno Mulvenna lived at, the bike would have given it away. Once an adrenalin junkie, always one. Anyone who'd taken planted bombs to kill high value targets like the army and police wouldn't have any problem with a bit of speed.

Craig climbed out and joined Andy beside the boot, holding the file photo of their interviewee in his hand. They'd called in advance and instead of Mulvenna being reluctant to speak to them as they'd feared, he'd been positively welcoming. Craig had no idea why but they'd soon find out. He glanced at the black and white headshot and grudgingly admitted Mulvenna had been good looking in his youth. Or a 'big honey' as Nicky had described him.

With his jet-black hair and bright blue eyes he had the 'black Irish' look of many born in the North-West. Some said it was a legacy of the Spanish Armada's sailors washing up on the West coast, others of the American's stationed in Derry during the war. Wherever it came from it was the stuff of matinee idols and the favoured portrayal of terrorists by Hollywood, romanticising their murderers to make the reality more palatable.

But there was nothing palatable about Jonno Mulvenna's record. Four successful car bombs planted in six years with the deaths of sixteen police and soldiers to his name, not to mention the prison officers he'd picked off through his sights. Only fifteen years prison for all those deaths. Mulvenna was a bad, bad man and Craig could understand why someone had thought framing him for Jarvis' murder was justice. But it was a rough justice that had just come back to bite them on the ass.

Andy slipped on his jacket and they walked to the door of number fourteen, then knocked and waited, their reflection warping back at them in the BMW's shining chrome. The door was opened a minute later by a man whose only concession to the years was some greying at his temples that made Craig think of Richard Gere. He was shocked. If this man's evil was written anywhere it wasn't on his face. Dorian Gray must be missing a portrait. Mulvenna was in his fifties but he looked almost as young and fit as he had in '83. He smiled at them and Craig stared back unyieldingly. He flashed his badge and Mulvenna shrugged, waving them into a neat front room with a series of oil paintings on the walls.

The paintings subjects were varied. A bird, a man who resembled Mulvenna and a stunning woman caught Craig's eye. He glanced at Mulvenna's hand but there was no ring. That meant nothing nowadays. Men like him didn't wear them, always free in their minds. He turned to look at the other wall where a painting of Portstewart Strand held pride of place. An aide-mémoire of Jarvis' murder? No, he doubted it; there was nothing dark about the image. The painting was just like the others: beautiful. Whoever had painted them had real talent, and Craig said so. He was surprised by the faint blush that coloured Mulvenna's face.

"I did them. I'd always drawn, but prison art classes taught me to paint. I'm getting my Masters at the moment."

It figured. It suited the Hollywood romance. Any minute now Mulvenna would try to justify his past as a war, seeing himself as a warrior of some kind. Something about the scene bothered Craig and then he worked out what it was. Mulvenna was a romantic. The murder of Ronni Jarvis didn't fit his approach to life. Mulvenna waved them to a seat and poured them a waiting coffee as Craig reluctantly drew closer to the conclusion he didn't want to reach. Mulvenna started talking before he had a chance to speak.

"I know why you're here and before you even ask, the answer's no. No, I didn't kill Ronni Jarvis, no matter what the courts decided. And no, I had nothing to do with the death of the girl on the beach last week."

Andy went to interject and Mulvenna stilled him with a look. Craig saw its steel and nodded inwardly. This was the menace he'd expected to see. He was shocked by Mulvenna's next words.

"I deserved to be put away in '83, and for a lot longer than I was."

He paused, not as if he was expecting an argument but in thought. "I killed a lot of your lads and army as well, but…" He stared at them earnestly, as if challenging them to disagree. "Whether you believed it was or not, we saw it as a war. We didn't have the guns and tanks and uniforms you had so we did what we could, how we could, to get the British out."

Craig interrupted angrily. "You're trying to justify what you did?"

Mulvenna shook his head slowly. "No. Not justify. Explain."

He stared Craig straight in the eyes, as if begging him to understand but knowing he never would. After a moment he sighed and shook his head. "I don't feel guilty about killing them but I regret every man that I killed. Every one of them. I'm sorry they're dead and I'm sorry for their families, but I can't turn back the clock."

Andy leaned forward, spotting a gap. "And what about every woman?"

They were surprised by the strength of Mulvenna's next words. "NO! I've never harmed a woman, never."

Andy went to continue but Craig quietened him

imperceptibly, wanting to hear what Mulvenna had to say. Their coffees sat untouched, as if to drink them would be a betrayal of their dead colleagues. If Mulvenna noticed he didn't say, he was long past sticks and stones in the pain stakes.

He sipped at his drink and dropped his eyes to the floor as if remembering the women he had known. When he spoke again it was falteringly, his voice quieter than it had been since they'd arrived.

"I didn't even know Veronica Jarvis, and I know what you're going to say. Lots of men kill women randomly, women that they don't know, so why not me? Well here's why not. I was in love, really in love for the first time in my life. I was happy. Why would I kill some woman I'd never even met?"

His eyes were hidden, but Craig knew what they would hold. Tears. He could hear them in his voice. The romance hadn't ended well, that much was clear and Craig thought that it wasn't just because he'd been sent to prison. Andy shot him a puzzled look. This was totally unexpected. They sat in silence waiting for Mulvenna to restart. Finally he did, in clearer tones. His voice was curious, a mixture of soft country tones and hard Belfast picked up from his colleagues in jail. Craig could imagine some women finding the contrast attractive.

"If Ronni Jarvis was an informer then the IRA could have been to blame, but we usually claimed our kills." He looked at them defiantly. "And rape wasn't our weapon of choice. Ronni Jarvis was killed by someone who had nothing to do with the IRA, mark my words. And if they could have got their hands on him in '83 he would have been dead for getting them and me the blame."

His eyes dropped to the floor and he sat in silence for so long that Craig wondered if he would restart. He finally did. "Before you ask, the person I loved left me around the time I was charged and no, I won't give you their name. I owe them that much for all the hurt." Craig gazed at him and saw the last glisten of tears. Mulvenna sniffed. "Ronni Jarvis's murder is thirty years old. What is it you want from me?"

"There are strong similarities between her death and the woman found this week. And other links that I can't tell you about."

Mulvenna bristled. "I had nothing to do with either death."

Craig raised a hand, stilling him mid-defence. "I believe you. But we still need to know your movements last week." He did believe him and a glance at Andy said that he believed him as well.

"I don't want to complain about my sentence for Jarvis. Like I said, I deserved it, for all the others I killed." He shuddered as if remembering the things that he'd done then stared straight at Craig.

"When was the woman killed?"

Craig thought for a moment, calculating the benefit of telling him.

"Sometime between last weekend and Thursday."

Mulvenna nodded. "I've an alibi for that whole time." He half-smiled to himself, as if having an alibi was a novelty for him. "I was on a residential art course up in Ballymena with forty other painters. It ran from Friday 25th for a week. I only got back two days ago. You can check."

"We'll do that."

Craig paused, calculating how to use the man's faux-chivalry to best effect.

"Trying to overturn your conviction would take years and you don't seem to want it. But if it wasn't you who killed Ronni Jarvis then it could have been the man who killed this latest victim, so we need your help with a few questions. OK?"

Mulvenna nodded. "I'll give you anything I can."

"I know it was a long time ago but tell me what you remember about the period around your arrest."

Mulvenna cut across him. "It was yesterday to me. I remember where I was when the news came in that Ronni Jarvis had been found. In Whiterock, off the Falls Road. I didn't know her so it wasn't that that made me listen, it was the burying in the sand. That caught everyone's attention. When the news said the IRA had claimed it there was uproar." He gave them a wry look. "Not that I would have put it past some of the bastards I knew. Every organisation has its psychopaths, men who take pleasure in the kill. We had our fair share of those."

"Anyone stand out as capable of doing this to a woman?"

Craig knew as soon as he asked that the answer was yes. The look in Mulvenna's eyes said he only had one name in mind. Mulvenna nodded.

"A bastard called Declan Wasson. Evil little fucker. I couldn't stand him. He lorded it over the young recruits like he thought he was God and we all knew that he beat his wife. The word was that he was protected, but it only after he died in '89 that we found out who by."

"Who?"

Mulvenna's stare gave them the answer immediately. The Police or MI5. Craig looked at Andy and nodded. It was impossible to fight a war without information, and informants were highly prized assets. They were hated by their own side and often despised by their handlers, but their information saved lives.

Mulvenna read their minds and shook his head. "Wasson didn't inform out of any sense of integrity, if that's what you're thinking. This was about power and money for him, pure and simple."

"How sure are you that he killed Jarvis?"

"One hundred percent. He bragged about it once because he thought he was flameproof. I think he thought he was immune to prosecution because of who he knew, but who he knew got him killed."

"He's dead?"

Mulvenna nodded. "Found shot in the head in '89. You didn't get the IRA blamed for something they didn't do and walk away from it for long."

Craig's heart sank as he realised what it meant. If Wasson had killed Ronni Jarvis and been shot in '89, it would explain why there'd been no similar murders since then. Lissy Trainor's murder was a copycat. But by whom?

Mulvenna read his train of thought. "Someone's fucking with you, lads. I'd lay my life that someone just copied the murder because the method was so dramatic they knew it would get in the press. Was it the same in every detail, or just in the obvious ones?"

Craig didn't answer but his glance told Mulvenna everything he needed to know.

"Well, it's just my amateur sleuthing but I'd say, look at what the two cases have in common apart from the way she was killed. Someone's telling you something. And look at why Wasson was protected and I was framed. "

Something in Mulvenna's eyes told Craig he already knew the answer to the last part, but he needed more information before he was sure. Craig nodded and stood. Andy followed and Mulvenna walked them to the front door. Craig turned before they left.

"We may need to talk to you again."

Mulvenna nodded. "That's fine. Just don't waste your time asking me anything about the IRA. Old loyalties die hard."

***

Craig drove along Strand Road then pulled up outside a café. They drank their coffee in the car, each man mulling over his thoughts. Finally Andy spoke.

"Mulvenna basically said he was framed by one of us."

"Yes."

"But why *then*? And why for a case he was likely to be acquitted on? If they'd wanted to frame him successfully a shooting or bombing would have been a much better bet. Much more his style."

"Why then was probably because Wasson did it and they wanted to keep him out of jail. Why choose Mulvenna to frame is the interesting bit."

Craig reached into the back seat and lifted Mulvenna's file, opening it to the charge sheet.

"They charged him with every shooting and bombing they suspected him of when they convicted him for Jarvis."

"So?"

"Well, the last one before her death had been two years before in '81. Mulvenna was low profile in '83, so why suddenly pull his name out of the hat to cover Wasson's crime?"

"Why was he low profile for two years?"

Craig flicked through the pages until he found a reference in the file to the United States. Mulvenna had been over there fund-raising for the IRA from '81 to '83, on and off.

"That's why he was keeping his head down. He was raising money for 'the war'. It wouldn't have done to have him all over the papers here for killing policemen while he was busy glad-handing the yanks."

"OK, so then why frame him in '83? They could have framed him in '81 before he left."

Craig closed the file before he spoke. "Because someone wanted him out of the way in 1983 for a specific reason and we need to find out who and what that reason was."

Chapter Ten

Monday 8 a.m.

"Do you need some money, love? Is that what it is?"

Lucia smiled at her father. He looked so healthy that no-one would ever have believed he'd had a heart attack just seven months before. They were in the kitchen at her parent's home in Holywood, sitting at the worn trestle table where they'd eaten breakfast since before her feet could reach the floor. Mirella was fussing around her, getting to spoil her baby again and loving it.

Tom Craig smiled at his wife then raised an eyebrow at his daughter. She was as pretty as ever, her face scrubbed clean of make-up and her tawny hair falling heavily down her back, with the year round tan she and her brother had inherited from their Mum. But she looked exhausted, as if she was carrying a heavy weight. She'd spent an hour on the phone the night before with Richard, so that could be part of it, but she looked more tired now than when she'd gone to sleep. He shook his head in sympathy.

Richard was a concert pianist with the prestigious London City Orchestra and that entailed touring for eight months of the year. He knew from experience what that meant for the partner left at home. Mirella had been a pianist when they'd met in Venice over forty years before, and she'd always toured. Less after the children were born, but still… She wasn't selfish, she just needed to perform the way the rest of the world needed to breathe. He'd been the Lucia left at home, except with two small children to care for.

Mirella had toured for part of every year until she'd retired. It had been lonely and tiring and more than once he'd wondered if it had been worth it for him and the kids. Evenings had been spent on long calls before her concerts, with her nervous and fraught in case her one wrong note spoiled the performance of the whole team. Then late night calls afterwards, on a high if it had gone well, or a low on the rare occasion it fell flat. They'd talked for hours because she needed to, leaving him exhausted at work the next day. Then there were the hours and hours of practice, even when she was home.

He smiled across the kitchen at his vivacious wife, watching as she piled eggs on a plate and placed them in front of her daughter, chiding her to eat. If he hadn't managed to get through those years he wouldn't have Mirella now, and he couldn't imagine life without her. But he sympathised with Lucia; no, more than that, he empathised. Richard wasn't being deliberately selfish, any more than Mirella had been, music was just his life and there was little room for anything else.

He repeated his question and smiled at his daughter, awaiting her reply. He already knew that whatever emerged from her mouth wouldn't be the truth, he just hadn't worked out yet why she was going to lie. They'd been thrilled when she'd asked if she could come home for a few days while a leak in her bedroom ceiling was being repaired. Mirella had started baking immediately. But he knew the ceiling wasn't the truth. He'd always been able to tell when Lucia was lying, even when she was very young. Her nose wrinkled-up in a particular way, just like it was doing now.

And there was something more. The old Lucia would have camped out in her living room while her bedroom ceiling was being repaired. Anything rather than give up her independence and move home. There were only two reasons she wasn't doing that. She was broke, or worse, something was frightening her. He prayed it was the first and waited for her reply.

"No, Dad. I'm fine honestly. In fact I got a pay-rise last

week."

He nodded, knowing it was the second reason. She was afraid of something. He thought about how to frame his next question without making her bolt. Lucia had been independent since she was three, or had thought she was. He remembered her stomping around the front garden, railing about not being allowed out into the street. Passers-by had laughed at the angelic looking toddler ranting about the injustice of it all. It explained her urge to march every weekend, righting the wrongs of the world. Marc did it too, but in a different way. He shook his head, wondering how they'd bred two such strong-minded kids. A glance at his fiery wife gave him a clue.

Mirella walked over to the trestle carrying a pile of toast. He knew that his plate of bacon sat on the sideboard, but she knew better than to uncover it while their vegetarian daughter was sitting in the room.

"Lucia, why you not eating?"

She stared at her daughter's small hand pointedly. "Look how thin you are. Richard will not find you when he returns."

Lucia laughed at the image and quickly lifted a piece of toast. "Look, Mum, I'm eating. I promise you that by the time I move back to my apartment I'll be fat. OK?"

Mirella threw her a sceptical look and laughed. Tom Craig watched as his daughter continued to neatly avoid his eyes, confirming his conclusion that something was worrying her. He just couldn't work out what it was.

***

Craig gazed at the two files in front of him, his eyes shooting back and forth between them as he jotted things down on a list. It was headed 'similarities 1983/2013' and so far it was five items long. Woman, strangled, buried, Portstewart beach and Melanie Trainor, first as the senior investigating officer and now as a parent mourning her child's loss. No matter how he cut it, it was too big a connection to dismiss. He yawned, then took another sip of coffee and glanced at his watch, startled by the time. Eight-fifteen, he promised to meet the others at breakfast fifteen minutes before, although he reckoned Saturday night's hangover followed by a day's work might have slowed them down a bit.

He grabbed his jacket and headed for the door then stopped and turned back, lifting the page. It was a working breakfast and it was time to gauge their reactions to a few things. Two minutes later he was in the dining room gazing at two bleary faces. John hadn't arrived yet and when did he'd probably look as rough as the rest. Liam was holding his head moaning.

"Now I know what weekends are for. You don't notice the benefit until you don't have one."

Craig shot him a rueful look. "Sorry Liam. We'll take time off when this is over, I promise."

"As long as I can spend my time here. Sleeping. That way I'll get some rest. I swear our Rory has the best pair of lungs this side of the Irish Sea and he seems to think our bedtime is the signal to try to them out!"

Liam had a three-year-old daughter and a ten-month-old son, so two days sleep in a bed sixty miles from home was a holiday for him.

Andy laughed and slapped him on the back. "We're planning our first, hey."

"Well, keep practicing and pray you don't succeed, that's my suggestion. 'Cos when you do your bed will never be your own again."

Liam gave a martyred look that made them all laugh just as John wandered in with a folder in his hand. He dropped it on the table without preamble and grabbed a seat, turning it round so that his arms were hanging over the back. His hangover seemed to have worn off quicker than theirs had.

"Good morning, gentlemen. I've just been for a walk on the Strand." He cast a look at their grey faces. "By the looks of you,

you should all try it. It's a lovely day out there."

He took a deep breath as if demonstrating calisthenics and Liam leaped into the gap.

"There's nothing worse than a preacher, religious or otherwise. Don't rub it in, Doc."

John laughed and glanced at the page sitting at Craig's elbow, pouring a cup of coffee as he talked.

"I see you've been making a list, Marc. Well, let me update you first before you start reading it out."

He opened the folder and turned quickly to the back page, searching for the thing he wanted to report.

"Right. Lissy Trainor wasn't raped. I said so yesterday but they rushed the forensics for me and it's confirmed. No bruising, semen or anything. "

"Couldn't the semen have been washed away by the tide, John?"

"Normally I'd say yes but she was wearing plastic leggings. They were waterproof so that would have stopped the water washing it away. The swabs have confirmed that there was nothing."

"Pleather."

They turned to look at Andy. He was nodding knowledgeably. Liam took the bait.

"What?"

"Pleather. It's a form of fake leather, made of plastic. It's very fashionable with young girls. Makes the leggings tight."

Liam gawped at him, astounded. His knowledge of women's fashion amounted to two things, sexy or his Mum. He was suspicious of men who knew more.

"Here, are you one of those cross-dressers then, Andy?"

Andy coughed so hard that he spat out his toast. "No, I am not! But I have three sisters and a wife; it'd be hard not to pick up some things."

"Well I managed it and I had sisters too."

John interjected dryly. "I don't imagine there was much call for PVC on the farm, Liam."

"Aye, you're right, not unless it could be used for growing potatoes." He gave a loud guffaw. Craig shook his head in mock despair.

"Very funny, Liam, but you can rein in the cracks about cross-dressing. If anyone hears that at work you'll be in trouble."

Liam sniffed grudgingly and nodded. "Aye, aye, you're right, boss." He turned to Andy with a solemn look on his face. "Andy, if you want to wear PVC leggings, then you go right ahead. It's perfectly OK with me."

Andy started to laugh again and Craig tried to stop himself joining in, but Liam's droll delivery defeated them all. He nodded John on.

"OK, well. Lissy wasn't raped or beaten, and she was strangled and drowned with all her clothing still intact."

"So that rules sex out as a motive, unusual in the death of a young woman."

John nodded, yes it was. "I've only seen a handful of cases where it wasn't a cause. Evie Murray-Hill is the most recent."

He was referring to the murder of a young pregnant woman they'd investigated seven months before. Thankfully the baby had survived the crime.

"It's very unusual, and it points to a different motive than the usual rape or robbing. There's nothing to suggest past violence or domestic abuse. Lissy x-rays are clean for old fractures."

"So she was targeted and killed for a specific reason?"

John nodded. "Probably. What that reason was is over to you." He turned to a loose page at the front of the file and started reading. It bore the header of a post-mortem and Craig could read Veronica Jarvis' name upside down.

"Veronica Jarvis on the other hand was beaten badly and most probably raped before she was strangled and buried on the beach. Although there was no semen found, she did have extensive genital bruising and tears, so I don't know why rape wasn't listed as probable on her P.M. They seem to have dismissed it completely, but then forensics weren't as advanced back then." He looked at Craig. "If rape had been included they would have ruled it out as a punishment killing immediately."

Craig nodded. He was right. Most of the reason it had been labelled a punishment killing had been the lack of rape. And because Veronica Jarvis had been friendly to the police who'd patrolled her Catholic street, wanting to keep things peaceful for the sake of her three sons. When she'd been found dead it had been assumed she must have been passing them information as well as cups of tea and that the IRA had killed her in revenge.

The IRA had always denied involvement in her death but Jonno Mulvenna had still been quickly convicted and put away. What if he hadn't been involved and she'd been the victim of a sadistic rapist instead? A rapist that someone had wanted protected? And Mulvenna had just been a useful stooge? Mulvenna had told them as much.

John continued. "I don't think we need an exhumation, Marc. There's enough physical evidence for me to be convinced Veronica Jarvis was raped. So that's another major difference between your cases."

Craig nodded then started to outline his thoughts. He saw Liam's coming objection and raised his hand quickly, stilling him before he jumped in. "Let me finish first, Liam, then everyone can tell me why I'm wrong." He tapped the list in front of him, reading out the similarities between the cases.

"Two women killed thirty years apart, strangled and buried at the same spot on the same beach. One was raped and beaten but the other wasn't. OK. It could be a straight copycat for dramatic effect but there's another major similarity. Melanie Trainor, or Melanie Rogers as she was back in 1983."

Liam sat back and nodded. He would tell them what he'd found out when Craig finished.

"What if Veronica Jarvis was killed by someone else? A man

who someone wanted to protect for some reason, say an informant? A man who might have been supplying Melanie Trainor with information that could help her crack cases and advance her career?"

"God, we know she's ambitious, Marc, but ambitious enough to let a murderer go free?"

"Let's say she thought that she could control him, offer him incentives to stop him killing again?" He turned to Liam. "Liam, can you get Davy to widen the search for murders with a similar M.O. to anywhere in Ireland, and get him to search for any and all crimes linked to a man called Declan Wasson."

Liam's mouth dropped open.

"You recognise the name?"

"I do indeed. Nasty wee scrote was lifted every other month back in the eighties. We covered his cases at college."

"Lifted for what?"

"Domestic battery. He used to beat the hell out of his wife, but she wouldn't press charges, and back then they had to let things drop unless she would."

"Mulvenna said he was an informant. If he was feeding Trainor useful tips it could explain why she covered his back when Ronni Jarvis' body was found. I want to know if she succeeded in keeping him clean after that, or if there are any un-attributed rapes or rape-murders after '83. If Wasson continued to rape until his death in '89 then someone might have believed that was Melanie Trainor's fault because she failed to put him away in '83. It might have gained her enemies who could have gone after her daughter."

Liam interjected. "Here, boss. If Lissy Trainor wasn't sexually assaulted then her killer could have been a woman. What if Wasson raped again after '83 and Trainor covered it up to keep him as an informant? This could be one of his female rape victims taking revenge on the ACC?"

Craig nodded slowly, it was good point and he hadn't thought of it. But the options didn't stop there. Andy leaned forward.

"Aren't we forgetting something obvious, hey? "

Three pairs of eyes stared at him.

"What about Veronica Jarvis' kids? She had three boys who she adored by all accounts, and they probably adored her back. If they thought Trainor had let their mother's killer go free there's no telling how long they might have been bearing a grudge."

"Andy's right, boss. The Jarvis boys were still at primary school when she died. I remember hearing about it on the news. That would make them in their late thirties now, still plenty strong and fit enough to kill a young girl."

John interrupted. "They'd have had to hate Melanie Trainor a lot to wait this long and then kill her child. And how would they have known that Mulvenna hadn't been a righteous rap?"

"Righteous rap? Have you been watching those American crime series again, Doc?"

John blushed and nodded.

"Well, don't. You sound like Jay-Z."

Craig raked his hair in thought for a moment before he spoke.

"OK. They're all good points. Liam, chase up the Jarvis kids and find out if they have alibis for Lissy Trainor's murder. John will give you the exact time frame."

John nodded. "Right, well. It would be nice if I could be exact, Marc, but Lissy had been dead for several hours before she was buried and we don't know what day that was on. We know she was found on Thursday morning at seven o'clock, by a horse-rider out for a gallop."

Craig turned to Andy. "Do we have their statement, Andy?"

"Yes, and I've had men on the beach interviewing people for days, but no-one saw anything. It was Halloween this week so a lot of people were away, and it rained on Thursday and was blowing a gale. The Strand would have been deserted, except for the hardy annuals. I've had men there every day interviewing but there's been nothing yet."

John restarted. "It's hard to get timings from Rigor because it had resolved by the time she was found, but she has two types of Lividity; primary and secondary. The primary Lividity is on her back. It indicates she was killed and left on her back for some time, but definitely less than six hours because there's secondary Lividity as well. It's on her feet, ankles and hands where the blood pooled when she was buried upright in the sand."

"So she was moved less than six hours after death and buried on the beach?"

"Yes. There are some patches in the Lividity on her back which give us a clue to what sort of surface she was lying on after death. It looks like they were made by small twigs or sticks. Her clothes are being examined for spores and remnants now."

"Was she undressed at any time, John?"

He shook his head. "I don't think so. The twig marks are very faint, indicating that the pressure was through clothes, and there are creases in the Lividity on her back from what looks like the folds from her clothing. We're checking her top for a match. There was nothing on the lower half because of her leggings."

He paused, inviting questions.

"So she definitely wasn't killed at the beach, Doc?"

"Definitely not. It may have been nearby but it's hard to tell. Portstewart Strand is one of the last beaches that you can drive a car onto, so she was probably brought there by car. And before you ask, the C.S.I.s did their best with the tyre tracks but there were hundreds of them all over that stretch of beach so you're looking at a dead end there." John paused then restarted.

"OK. Lissy was killed somewhere where there were twigs, so maybe a garden or a wood, left on her back for less than six hours then brought to the beach to be buried in the sand. She was found on Thursday morning at seven o'clock but she could have been buried there days before. Her hand was visible when she was found so the sand protecting it had been washed away and it bore the marks of having been exposed to water for less than ten hours. I'd say if she was found on Thursday morning then the sand that was covering her had been worn away by the tide the night before."

"OK, so uncovered overnight on Wednesday by the tide, but buried God knows when?"

John nodded. "That's about the size of it, sorry. We're trying to narrow time of death now, but the sand protected her from the water and she was cold the whole time. She would have been almost frozen and that throws T.O.D. off. Your best bet to narrowing things quickly is finding out who saw her last, or catching a break from someone who saw her abduction."

Craig nodded. They needed to trace her last movements and interview her friends.

"We'll come back to that in a minute. Andy, if you chase Davy on possible past victims of Wasson between '83 and '89, then we can see if Liam's theory of a female killer might run true, although she'd have to be a strong woman to strangle Lissy with her hands. Liam, check any male relatives of the rape victims as well as Veronica Jarvis' sons. I'll chase up the informant side with MI5 and speak to the Chief Constable. Liam, tell us what you found with Lissy Trainor's friends and then Andy and I will update you on Jonno Mulvenna. I also have a slightly different theory of the crime."

They all looked at him curiously but he waved Liam on.

"Aye well. I interviewed the girl next door, Billy Munroe but she hadn't seen Lissy for two weeks - she was away with her mates in Greece for a fortnight. Then I interviewed her ex-university flatmate, Mary-Ann Eakin, but she's been living in Dublin since the start of October and they only keep in touch by e-mail now. I canvassed the neighbours on both sides of the street but no-one remembers seeing Lissy since last Friday week when she was out in the front garden playing with her dog.

That only leaves the boyfriend."

"What have you got on him?"

"His name's Conor Ryland. He lives with his dad. Like I said before, they knew each other at school but it seems they've only been dating since their first year at Uni. He was a well-known player at school, and both girls, Billy and Mary-Ann Eakin, said that he'd been getting up to his old tricks again and two-timing Lissy behind her back. Mary-Ann says Lissy dumped him three weeks ago and he'd been hassling her to give it another try, including waiting outside the place where she works part-time. He wasn't home when I called last night, so I'll chase him up today."

"Where did she work?"

"A boutique along the front called 'The Magic Box'. It sells those scented candles and girly stuff."

"I like scented candles, hey."

"Aye well, that figures. You probably light them on the nights you wear your pleather."

A loud laugh ran through the group attracting the glance of a waitress nearby. She'd overheard and was stifling a laugh. Liam restarted, gratified by her amusement.

"Lissy worked there on Thursday and Friday evenings and all day Saturday. It closes at six o'clock on Saturdays. The twenty-seventh would have been her last day working there before she died."

"Who else works there?"

"Don't know yet. It's shut on Sundays. I'll call there today and canvas the promenade, but my guess is it's mostly tourists down there during the week, although maybe some locals shop there on Saturdays."

"I'll help Liam with that, hey."

Craig nodded, thinking. "Has Davy had any joy on her phone and e-mail accounts yet, Liam? We need to know is she was meeting anyone last weekend."

Liam shook his head and dropped a piece of bacon into his

mouth, chewing as he talked. "Give him a chance, boss. The lad's good, but even he needs time off on a Sunday."

Craig startled suddenly, realising that it was only Monday morning. "God, you're right. Sorry. I've lost track of the days."

Liam sniffed. "You need to watch that, boss. Next thing you'll be wearing odd socks like the Doc."

They all stared down at John's feet, including him. Liam was right! He was wearing one brown sock and one black.

"Do I do that often, Marc?"

"Ask Liam, I hadn't even noticed."

"Once a week at least and more often on a Monday. Anyway, I'll chase Davy today and hopefully Lissy had some phone calls that tell us where she was between the Friday the neighbours saw her and the Thursday she was found. I'll see if she socialised with anyone from the shop that weekend."

"Good. Anything else, anyone? Before I start?"

There was silence while Craig took a drink of cold coffee, screwing up his face. John beckoned the waitress over to top them up and Craig started. He updated them on their meeting with Mulvenna while Andy chipped in, then he stared at them all so intently they knew that whatever he was going to say next would rattle everyone's cage.

"OK. Here's my take on the murder in '83. Jonno Mulvenna didn't do it." Liam went to interject but Craig stilled him with a glance. "Don't get me wrong, he's a murdering bastard no matter how he tries to hide it behind 'the cause'. And strangely he's not complaining about being banged-up, says he deserved the years he did, and more. But there was something that didn't fit."

Andy nodded in agreement.

"I've seen men like him before, they're lovers not fighters and if they do fight it's always for some romantic cause. Their own personal crusade. Mulvenna justifies what he did in The Troubles by saying that it was a war. Now we might think that's crap but it's his take on life. And it's a take that doesn't allow for him killing a woman." He turned to Liam.

"Liam, were any of the police or army he killed, female?"

Liam thought for a moment and then shook his head. "But that was by good luck, not judgement, boss."

"I'm not so sure. You should have seen his house. Paintings all over the walls, and every one of them something of beauty."

"He probably nicked them."

Craig laughed, conceding it would have been true of many criminals he knew, but it wasn't true this time. "He painted them himself and they're bloody good. He has an exhibition coming up."

Andy looked surprised. "He didn't say anything about that."

"No, he didn't, but I noticed a flyer on the coffee table. It's tomorrow night, at a gallery on the Lisburn Road."

"He must be good, Marc. Those galleries are pretty fussy."

"He is. But that's irrelevant except that it underlines his approach to life. He says he didn't kill Veronica Jarvis and I believe him. He told us about Wasson informing on the IRA and it made sense that someone was protecting him. He implied it was MI5 or us, but I need to find out more from MI5 on that. What doesn't make sense is why Mulvenna was chosen for the frame-up when he hadn't been active here for nearly two years. He'd been in America, so what brought his name to the fore just at that time, for a type of crime he'd never committed?"

Craig stared at the ground and John recognised the signs. He was about to say something completely left of field. He didn't disappoint him.

"What if Mulvenna's frame-up had a personal motive?"

Liam and Andy frowned and John smiled. It was just what he'd been thinking.

"You mean someone who hated him, hey?"

"Well, there were plenty back then who fitted that description. He'd killed sixteen of us."

"Had he killed anyone else, Liam?"

"Who do you mean? Civilians?"

"Yes."

Liam thought for a minute and then slowly shook his head. "Nope. All his kills wore a uniform. He probably regarded them as fair game." He drew his hand despairingly down his face. "Oh hell. That opens the door to all the peelers' kids taking revenge. It'll be like looking for a needle in a haystack!"

"I agree. If Mulvenna was framed because of hatred we could have a list of suspects a mile long, but…"

"But now you don't think he was framed, Marc? Make your mind up. I'm getting wild confused here, hey."

"He was framed all right, but maybe not because someone hated him."

"Expedience, Marc?" Then John saw where he was heading. "Love? You think he was framed because someone loved him?"

"Andy, you've seen him. Even as a man I could tell that he was handsome, couldn't you?"

Andy shot Liam a wary glance and then nodded. "At the risk of Cullen here starting on about cross-dressing and scented candles again, yes, I could. He looked like that actor, Richard Gere, when he was young." He took Mulvenna's photograph out of the file so they could all see what he meant. "He looks the same now, only a bit greyer around the gills."

Liam grinned and Andy put the photo away hastily as Craig restarted.

"And if charm could be bottled he'd make a fortune. I think he was framed in 1983 by someone who loved him."

"Because he'd rejected them?"

"Possibly, or because they wanted rid of him and he wouldn't let go."

"Male or female?"

Craig was momentarily surprised by John's question. He hadn't thought any further than women but John was right. In the Northern Ireland of 1983 being gay would have been seen as something to hide. A weakness in a chauvinistic country full of hard men. Maybe Mulvenna was gay. He hadn't specified if the person he'd been in love with had been a man or woman, just referred to 'them'. What if he'd been having a gay relationship with someone who didn't want to be found out? Homosexual acts had been illegal in the province until 1982 so it made sense. But so did his other theory.

"Maybe gay, or maybe a woman who had too much to lose."

"Married? An angry husband who caught her out?"

"Anything's possible. But what if whoever it was saw an opportunity to get Mulvenna out of their life and frame a terrorist at the same time. It's a win, win all round and no-one was going to cry for Mulvenna. Let's take the simple route and say he was framed by a man or woman who was his lover in '83. That should narrow the field for us as bit. Add in that it's someone with a vested interest in protecting an MI5 informant and what does that leave us?"

He looked at them all expectantly, knowing that John had leapfrogged his train of thought and hit the answer in one. Craig shook his head imperceptibly at him; he wanted to see what conclusion Liam and Andy reached on their own. Liam gawped openly as realisation dawned and he blurted it out.

"A cop! You're saying that Mulvenna was shagging one of us, or one of our wives? No way, boss, not back in '83. He was a wanted terrorist who specialised in killing police officers. No-one linked to the force would have been stupid enough to go near him. It would have been career suicide if it had ever come out." He paused and a look of anger crossed his face. "It would have been suicide, literally."

Andy nodded rigorously. "I agree with Liam, Marc. You're wrong. You went away to London to work so you missed the worse of the hatred back here then. Any peeler who'd been found fraternising with the enemy would have been ostracised by their own. Like those women in France after the war. Tarred and feathered. How many Catholic girls had that done to them during The Troubles for sleeping with army lads? That's how it was back then."

"I agree. But that's even more reason someone might try to hide it."

"But if Mulvenna knew he was being framed then why didn't he say? He could have named and shamed his lover and taken them down with him. They were taking a hell of a risk that he'd keep quiet."

"Maybe he did say it in the interviews when he was arrested, but it was ignored." He glanced at Andy, remembering what Mulvenna had said. "Or maybe he kept quiet because he really loved them and he thought he'd hurt them enough. Who knows?" He paused and took a drink of his espresso. "OK, if not the police, then who? Army? Someone working with them? Someone who also knew about Wasson being an informant?"

"Maybe, but not a cop. Army. Or an MI5 handler maybe, they were twisted enough bastards to think sex with a terrorist was a thrill. Or maybe someone on the legal side."

Craig glanced at John and he knew they were both thinking the same thing, but it would fall on deaf ears so he played it Liam's way. It didn't matter, they would get there eventually and he needed to do some digging behind the scenes before he was sure. He shrugged, conceding.

"OK, let's add MI5 handlers and crown solicitors to the list to be ruled out for framing Mulvenna. I'll ask around and see if I can find out if he's straight or gay; at least that would narrow the field a bit. We already have a list of people to speak to on Lissy Trainor's murder, including her boyfriend and the people who could have hated her Mum. The Jarvis' kids, the women Wasson might have abused and the men who loved them. That's plenty to be getting on with for now."

He stood up to leave. "Right, I'm heading upstairs to make a few calls then I'm going back to see Mulvenna. Liam, make a list of everyone we need to interview and Andy will OK the interview rooms with the station sergeant, for anyone we need to bring in. We'll split your list in three and use today to eliminate anyone we can."

"What about the ACC, boss?"

"I'm going to speak to the Chief Constable now about the best way to deal with her. He may want to speak to her himself initially, given the sensitivity of the case. I'll let you know. John, unless you need to be up here, I would go back to Belfast and get on with your life. I'll pick up your hotel tab. I'll call you tonight."

John nodded his thanks and Craig left, making the list of the calls he had to make. Number One was the Chief Constable and not just to ask for his help on diplomacy with a grieving Mum.

Chapter Eleven

Melanie Trainor sat on Lissy's bed and lifted her small blue jumper. She held it to her face, inhaling deeply to smell her daughter's perfume. It was a floral one she'd first given her on her eighteenth birthday. She always wore it, that and the small silver heart pendant her father had given her when she was ten. She'd lengthened the chain many times through the years, determined not to consign it to 'things that used to fit' until finally he'd had it made into a bracelet and it never left her wrist. They'd bury it with her now that she was dead.

She inhaled again, her tears soaking into the soft angora wool. Dead. It was such an old word, reminiscent of grey hair and fragile skin, not the vibrant dark waves and healthy tanned plumpness of her child. It felt wrong, more wrong that it had ever felt before. She'd seen too much death through the years. Quiet deaths and noisy deaths. Tidy, and messy beyond belief. All different but they shared one thing; the loss of the sound and touch and look of someone who was loved. And now it was her turn, her child. Her child.

She howled with a suddenness that tore the air and made Lissy's small dog bolt to cower in the corner, unable to escape through the closed bedroom door. It went on and on sounding like a wild thing caught in a trap, clawing and biting to escape the pain. Finally hoarseness forced her into silence and she curled up on the bed, clutching the jumper so close that it became a misshapen mass, not to be worn by anyone now. That was what she wanted. It was all she wanted now. Not revenge, not conviction, not punishment, just this. The peace to mourn her child and count the things she'd done to bring this about.

***

Craig took the seat that he was waved to and glanced quickly around the large study. It was dark and wood-lined, warm with the smoke from the cigars its owner puffed, hiding them from his wife by declaring the room off bounds. His empire and his alone. The furnishings were old and frayed, chairs worn from the long debates of age and chess games played until their bitter end. Hard-backed books were piled on dark oak shelves and stacked precariously around them in towers of random height, some of them so high that they were angled, frozen pre-teeter in mid-air.

The Chief Constable smiled and took the armchair across from Craig. It was leather and old and cracked, worn into comfort just like his Dad's at home. When Craig had phoned he'd expected a brief chat by phone or an office appointment at best, not this. But the CC had been insistent he visit him at his Portrush home. It was near the famous Royal Portrush Golf Course and every bit as grand as the proximity implied.

"We bought the place years ago for weekends. I like to play a bit of golf when I can. Now we spend most of our time there, when I can get away from the press. Come up. We'll have an informal chat. It will be better in my study, away from my staff officer's prying eyes, and I can have a cigar as well!"

He's laughed as he'd said it. A loud, round laugh that suited his personality and his shape. Craig gazed at the man opposite and smiled to himself. Sean Flanagan was definitely larger than life. At six-feet-five, the only man taller than him on the force was Liam and they had more in common than their height. Flanagan had been a GAA and Rugby star in his youth and Liam had been the same. He could imagine them both shunting their way around the pitch, brute force the order of the day, then into the bar at night full of songs and bonhomie.

Larger than life in every way.

Flanagan tapped a cigar from its holder and glanced surreptitiously at the door, then snipped its end defiantly.

"She'll be here in a minute, once she smells the smoke, but with an open window and a good west wind I can get five minutes out of it at least. Five minutes of smoke for the hour long lecture from hell about my health." He gave a wide grin. "It'll be worth it."

He puffed at the corona until its end glowed then he waved Craig to pour the coffee and sat back, waiting to hear what he had to say. Craig took a deep breath and started the update. After a five minute monologue he stopped and waited for Flanagan to speak.

Flanagan puffed his cigar thoughtfully and Craig saw a fleeting look of sadness cross his face. He seen it before but it had never lasted long enough for him to work out what it was. It passed again as quickly as it came. Flanagan's cigar was nearly at its end and his glance at the door said that he knew he was pushing his luck; even Craig's presence wouldn't protect him much longer. He stubbed it out and carried the ashtray to the window, tipping it into the flower bed below. He answered Craig's raised eyebrow casually.

"It's good for them"

Whether it was or not, he'd done it and they were safe from Mrs Flanagan's angry raid. Unless they were her flowers he'd just killed. Flanagan sat back down and linked his hands against his chest, deep in thought. Then he spoke. He had a deep, sonorous voice, its strength and volume softened by a Derry drawl.

"The question is... do we believe that ACC Trainor is the link between these cases? That has yet to be proved. At the moment she's first and foremost a grieving mother and our hearts must go out to her."

He paused and looked at Craig, nodding. Craig nodded in return and they fell silent for a moment, thinking of her daughter, then Flanagan spoke again.

"Let's take it that our respect for her loss is a given, then if or when we rule out other links, or when her lack of cooperation obstructs that process of ruling out, she must be treated like everyone else. A crime has been committed and our role is to solve it. Agreed?"

"Agreed, sir."

Flanagan stared into the unlit fireplace for a moment, deep in thought and Craig knew what was coming next. *However*. He was right.

"However, Marc, I'd like to hear what your feelings are. Tell me what your gut says, not the evidence."

Craig hesitated for a moment. He liked the Sean Flanagan, but he was still the Chief Constable. He was the sort of man he'd like to meet for a drink someday when they'd both left rank behind. But no matter how informal the setting he knew that whatever he said now would be heard through his boss' ears. He thought for a moment and then shrugged. He'd never played political games before and he was too damn old to start them now. He wasn't going to sugar-coat it.

"I think the murders of Lissy Trainor and Veronica Jarvis are inextricably linked. I think Jonno Mulvenna was framed to protect a police informer in 1983, probably by his handler."

Flanagan raised his hand to pause him. "Mulvenna was innocent of the murder? You're sure?"

Craig nodded. "You said to give you my instinct and it says yes. He was set-up to protect Declan Wasson."

Flanagan nodded slowly and waved him on.

"But it's more than that. I think Mulvenna was chosen to be framed for a reason. He'd been out of the country most of the previous two years, fund-raising for the IRA, then suddenly his name's picked out of the hat for a type of crime he'd never committed before? No. I'm not buying it. This was personal. Whoever framed him did so for a reason."

Flanagan interrupted.

"You won't remember, Marc, but he was enemy number one

back then for the police. He killed a lot of our lads. Plenty of people wanted him put away."

Craig nodded. "Yes, sir, I agree. But with all due respect, why then? Why not when he was most active? Why wait until two years later when he was essentially a politician to do it? It doesn't make sense."

He took a deep drink of coffee and watched as Flanagan's thoughts ran across his face. He was taking what he'd said seriously! Craig felt relieved. He hoped he'd listen as easily to the next part. He restarted tentatively, outlining their theory about a romantic relationship between Mulvenna and someone in the police.

Flanagan's eyebrows shot up in surprise and he shook his head, but not with a no. It was a nod of disbelief that someone could be so foolish. He believed him. Flanagan sipped his coffee for a moment then started to speak. His tone was confiding, as if he was afraid someone would overhear his words; perhaps himself.

"It's not as far-fetched as you might think, Marc." He stared into the distance and Craig thought he caught a wistful look. "Back then feelings were running high. People were dying all around us; civilians, police, the terrorists themselves. People were young and it felt like wartime, when no-one knew how long they had to live."

War; there was that word again. He'd thought Mulvenna was using it in self-justification, now Flanagan was using it as well. He was still talking.

"We were under siege and everyone was afraid." He caught Craig's quick glance. "Yes, me as well. No-one wanted to die, but we all knew that we could any day. It heightened people's feelings." He looked at him pointedly. "All sorts of feelings."

Craig nodded, trying to imagine Sean Flanagan thirty years before. He'd have only been in his thirties, leaving home for work each day, never knowing if he was coming back. Northern Ireland was a powder keg in more ways than one.

"The police and army socialised together, drank together... sometimes even slept together. It wasn't behaviour to be proud of but it happened all the same. Affairs were rife between officers, but divorces were few and far between, because of the traditional times. There were unexpected shootings in Northern Ireland that had nothing to do with The Troubles but were probably labelled that way just the same."

"Amongst the police?"

Flanagan shook his head. "Not that I know of, but then I don't know everything. I do know that there were a lot of babies produced that maybe shouldn't have been. Or weren't wanted" He smiled. "But I'm old fashioned, I think every baby was meant to be here whether people asked it to come or not."

Craig swallowed, pushing forward with his idea. "Relationships between police and terrorists? MI5? Army as well? How likely was that?"

Flanagan shrugged. "Who knows and who's to judge? Not me, I'll tell you that. Love is love." He looked at Craig wisely. "Have you ever heard of a coup de foudre, Craig?"

It was French for 'a stroke of lightening', an unexpected event. It was usually applied to love at first sight.

Craig nodded. He'd felt it when he'd first seen Camille.

"When you see someone who takes your breath away so much that you fall in love at once. Where you can't imagine life without them and you have to have them." Flanagan gazed into the distance again and smiled. "That's how I felt when I met my wife. Still do." He grinned. "Even when she stubs out my cigar." He turned to Craig seriously. "Now imagine that feeling in wartime, when you don't know if you'll ever see them again. Imagine the heightened tension. Add in the Romeo and Juliet effect of being on opposite sides of the fence, and, well..."

Craig nodded. It could happen. Jew and Muslim, Sunni and Shi'a, Police and terrorist. Some loves would last beyond the war and some were only ever that, a love just for that time. He took it one step further.

"And what if they were gay, sir? What about two men? Mulvenna and someone in the police, army or MI5? Someone hurt or rejected who wanted to take revenge?"

Flanagan paused in his reverie, frowning in thought. There'd been plenty of gay officers in the force, even back then. They'd kept it quiet but everyone had known. So what? People were people and love was love, but in 1983 it could have added another reason into the frame.

"If they'd thought Mulvenna was going to make their relationship public you mean? But what was to stop him saying it in interrogation anyway? Death might have stopped him talking but not an arrest."

"Would anyone have listened if he'd said it in an interview, sir? His word against a serving officer's? Even now that could be treated as revenge for being arrested."

Flanagan nodded slowly. It was possible. Everything they'd discussed was possible.

"OK. Every hypothesis you've mentioned could be fact, Marc. What do you need from me to rule them out?"

Craig leaned forward eagerly, glad that they were speaking face to face after all. He could never have said all this on the phone.

"Let me see the full archives of Mulvenna's arrest, interviews and trial. We'll pursue all the other lines of enquiry we spoke about as well. Liam and Andy White are leading on those and my team in Belfast is backing them up. But I'm certain the two murders are linked and I need to find out how."

"You'll leave ACC Trainor out of it until you've ruled out everything else? And come to me before you interview her formally?"

"Absolutely. Do I have your support, sir?"

There was silence for a moment then Flanagan nodded. Craig knew he was thinking the same thing he was. They needed to do this quickly before someone sabotaged their case.

Chapter Twelve

Liam had left The Magic Box shaking his head. The strange stuff they sold he could cope with; Ouija boards and crystals were old hat even when he was young. It was the girl behind the counter that had really freaked him out. Grey-white hair in a teenager was odd enough but he'd seen it in one of Danni's magazines so he knew it was some new trend. It was her full body tattoo that had really made him stare. Hardly an inch of her five-feet-six had been left un-inked, including her face. She was a pretty girl, what he could see of her beneath the black and red, but why would anyone cover their body with other people's art?

He shuddered as he remembered the piercings on her face and rapped hard on Conor Ryland's frosted-glass front door. A dark shape appeared in the hallway and stood immobile, as if deciding whether to answer his knock or not. Liam rapped again, adding. "Police, open up please" to his introduction, wondering if it would make them bolt. He sincerely hoped it wouldn't; he needed to run after someone like a hole in the head. He wasn't as fit as he used to be and the ten pounds around his middle meant he was definitely no Usain Bolt.

The shape moved hesitantly towards him and Liam smiled to himself, satisfied that the 'police' bit had done the trick. In his experience people fell into two groups. Those who ran away at the sound of the word, and those who walked slowly towards it terrified and thinking of all the things they'd done wrong. The shape belonged to the second type. As it solidified through the glass Liam could see it belonged to someone young and slim.

Beyond that he couldn't tell.

The door creaked open and he held up his badge, flashing it in the face of a boy no older than twenty-one. He was thin and pale and his dark blonde hair stood on end, in a style Liam thought was more bed-head than design. He stared up at him through bleary eyes that Liam recognised were swollen from tears. His hands were raw and red and his fingernails were bitten down to the quick. The boy looked rough; there was no doubt about it.

"D.C.I. Cullen, son." He still wasn't used to the D.C.I. title. It would probably start to sound right about the time he retired. "Who might you be?"

The boy sniffed and rubbed his hand across his eyes, unashamed of his tears. The younger generation had one thing right at least. He'd been so buttoned up when he was young he couldn't even cry at funerals and he'd been to plenty of those. By the time his son was grown they'd probably be crying at the drop of a hat.

"Conor Ryland. Are you here about Lissy?"

The sadness in his tone was added to by the unexpected lightness of his voice. He might be a player but he was still a kid. A promiscuous one but a kid nonetheless. Liam nodded and the boy showed him into a small front room. It was sparsely furnished with worn out things and Liam contrasted it with Lissy Trainor's luxurious home. He bet the MLA and police chief hadn't been too happy about their daughter's choice of boyfriend. He was half-wrong.

"Lissy's dad's been round to see me. He's a really good bloke. Wants me to do a reading at the funeral and say something."

He let out a harsh sob and his whole frame shook as he dissolved in tears. Liam scrutinised him carefully. His t-shirt was days old and his bare feet needed a wash. He needed caring for and Liam made up his mind to do the caring.

"Where's your father, Conor?"

"He works on a cruise liner out of Belfast, one month on,

one month off. This is his month on. He'll be back at the end of November."

"Right, son. Where's your kitchen? "

The boy pointed down the hall.

"Have you eaten? No, don't answer that, I can see you haven't. Right then." Liam turned the boy by the shoulders to face the stairs. "Go and have a shower and change your clothes, while I cook breakfast. When you're clean and you've eaten we're going to have a little chat."

***

What was taking the cops so bloody long? He'd left them a trail of clues a mile wide. Even someone as thick as they were couldn't have missed the story they told. All they had to do was follow them, so why had they gone to speak to the boy instead of arresting the one who was responsible for everything?

The man shook his head and stared through the shop window, idly rearranging books on a shelf. A customer walked past him down the aisle, picking her way between more books stacked on the floor. He smiled absentmindedly at her in greeting, his mind five hundred metres away on the Strand. He couldn't understand it. He'd left the girl where she would definitely be found and he'd strangled and buried her just like the other one. Surely they couldn't have missed the similarities? They must have made the link by now, so why hadn't they arrested them?

He muttered 'fucking idiots' under his breath and the elderly woman turned and stared as he continued the conversation. He threw his arms out wide then curled his hand in a fist as he talked, as if he was fighting someone who wasn't there. She put down her items quietly and left the way she'd entered to the street. The man didn't even notice, too busy muttering to himself.

Perhaps he should have raped her? No. His face contorted in

disgust and he felt bile shoot into his mouth. He spat it on the floor and shook his head. Rape was for animals and he wasn't one of those. It was dirty, brutal and obscene. Her death had been quick and gentle, like he was disposing of a pet. He hadn't hated her, she was a child; older than he'd been when he'd been hurt but a child nevertheless. He was sorry he'd had to do it, but it was the only way. They had to pay for what they'd done.

He jerked himself from his reverie and glanced around the store. It was empty, his solitary customer nowhere to be seen. He shrugged, there'd be another one and he'd be there every day, watching until they were caught and suffered for what they'd done.

***

Nicky tidied the pile of letters and left them on Craig's desk, ready for him to sign. She gazed out through his window at the sky, peppered with seagulls practicing their swoops. The place felt empty without him. She smiled to herself and blushed, admitting it felt even emptier with Liam gone. She missed him although she knew she shouldn't; they were both happily married. But in a different life…She left the office briskly trying to hide the admission from herself and bumped into Davy. She stared up at his angular face and smiled. She could swear he'd grown in the past year, even though he was twenty-six.

"The boss is on the phone, Nicky. S…says he needs a word. Put him back to me when you're done."

She nodded haughtily, not sure that she liked him telling her what to do. She retook her seat and pressed to divert the call. The sound of her husky voice made Craig smile instantly and he pictured her ruling the roost while he was away. Annette might be nominally in charge but the C.C.U. was Nicky's kingdom and no-one had any illusions about that.

"Hello, sir. How's the North coast? Are you and Liam working on your tans?"

Craig smiled. He'd known she would mention Liam with her opening breath.

"Not unless you count wind-burn. How are things there? You keeping them all in line?"

She sniffed and put him on speakerphone, then recounted a list of everyone's misdemeanours five minutes long, ending with the worst one in her eyes.

"And Liam left his coffee cup unwashed on Saturday. There was blue mould in it this morning!"

Craig smiled. "Did you wash it for him?"

He already knew that her answer would be no, but he just wanted to hear her indignation. He was homesick.

"Did I wash it, indeed! It will be waiting here for him when he gets back, even if there are plants growing in it. And you can tell him that."

"It'll be my first priority."

She laughed then asked him what he needed her to do.

"It's a long list, mostly for Davy and Annette. Annette can delegate as she likes. Before I start, did any new cases come in at the weekend?"

She went to answer then caught Annette and Davy's warning looks and swallowed what she was going to say. Lucia wouldn't thank her for giving things away.

"Nothing, sir. We're all yours."

"Right then. Hand me over to Davy then he can pass me to Annette. And Nicky."

"Yes?"

"Liam's mould will be there for another few days yet, so I would chuck in a few seeds and see what you can grow."

***

Liam watched the boy wolfing down the eggs and bacon as if it was a death row meal. He'd been eating for twenty minutes non-stop and there was no sign of it ending, so he poured them a fresh cup of tea and started to talk. Ryland could answer his questions between bites.

"How long had you and Lissy Trainor been dating, son?"

Conor stopped mid-bite and gazed at Liam as if he was going to cry. Liam shook his head gently, halting his tears before they started. and waited for his answer. It came in two quiet words.

"Three years."

Liam nodded; it fitted with what Lissy's next door neighbour had said. Since their first year at university.

"Did you study law as well?"

The boy shook his head. "Politics, philosophy and economics at Queens. I want to be a politician like Lissy's Dad. He's been helping me get my first job."

Liam stared at him gravely, wondering if he'd be so forgiving if someone broke his daughter's heart.

"Did he know that you'd broken up?"

The young man shook his head furiously. "We hadn't broken up. Where did you get that from?"

"Lissy's flatmate and the girl next door. Are you saying that they're wrong?"

"I'm saying they're silly gossips who should have kept their nose out of our relationship. Billy and Mary-Ann have never even had a date! They were jealous of Lissy. They wanted to split us up."

He sobbed suddenly, taking Liam aback. Fresh tears trickled down his cheek, landing on his clean t-shirt. Liam handed him a sheet of kitchen roll and gently urged him on.

"Surely Lissy must have told them? Where else would they have got the impression from?"

Conor wiped his nose, smearing a blob of brown sauce across his face. Liam let it sit there. If he wiped it away another would only take its place. His voice softened. "Tell me, son."

He swallowed and then started telling Liam a tale that he'd heard and been part of a hundred times before. He'd loved Lissy but he'd felt tied. Three years of dating had made everyone see marriage as the logical next step and he'd buckled under their expectations and done what a million men had done before. He'd run away.

"I went to Turkey with my classmates for two weeks. There were some girls in the crowd that Lissy didn't know and she got upset." He paused, sniffing harshly. "We had a fight. But they were just girls who were friends, honestly. Not girlfriends. I'd loved Lissy since school; none of them could ever have taken her place." His face screwed up in anger. "Those cows Billy and Mary-Ann were just waiting to stir the pot while I was away. I came round to see Lissy as soon as I came back and she screamed at me that we were done and dumped me."

Liam shook his head slowly. If he'd five pence for every time he'd seen that storyline played out amongst his friends he'd be able to afford a fortnight in Turkey himself. His voice was gentle.

"She'd have come round, son."

Conor looked at him and nodded. "She already had. She phoned me on Saturday. We talked things through and she asked me to meet her on the South Pier at Portrush Harbour, on Sunday night at eight-thirty. I was there but she never came. I waited for nearly two hours and I called her mobile loads of times, but she never called me back. I phoned her for days." He stared at the table. "I thought she'd changed her mind and dumped me. And then…"

Then she was found dead. Liam's heart went out to the lad and he'd no doubt Lissy's phone logs would confirm the calls, but he'd only been five miles from the place she'd been found so he had to ask the question.

"Did anyone see you there that Sunday night?"

Conor gazed blankly into space, and then nodded once. "There were people in the guesthouse opposite, they saw me. Probably thought 'poor bugger, he's been stood up.'" His lip curled. "And then of course there was the lovely Mary-Ann.

She'd been tailing me all evening hoping to catch me out doing something wrong."

Liam's eyebrows shot up. Mary-Ann Eakin had said she was in Dublin that weekend. He repeated his thoughts out loud.

Conor shook his head. "She started her new job down there weeks ago but she was always back, visiting her folks in Coleraine. I saw her in Portstewart on Sunday afternoon. Ask her. And ask her if she saw me at the pier that night as well, although she'll probably lie. Bitch."

Liam wagged a finger in remonstration. "Here now, son. That's no way for a gentleman to talk."

"And she's no lady." His face crumpled. "Lissy was. She was the gentlest person I ever knew. Kind to everyone. And now she's dead and I don't know what I'm going to do."

His shoulders heaved with sobs so harsh that Liam could feel them in his bones. Liam handed him a hanky and let him cry, for the girl he'd loved and would never see again.

***

"Is that everything, chief? Chase Lissy Trainor's e-mails and phone logs and see if there were any s...similar murders in Ireland anywhere, or any rape cases between '83 and '89 that fitted Declan Wasson's M.O.? Liam already called me about those."

Davy waited for Craig's answer, knowing that there was something more. He tapped his pen annoyingly against Nicky's partition as he listened until she grabbed it from his hand, only relenting when he gestured wildly at the phone, indicating that Craig was giving him something to write down.

"*All* the details?"

"Sorry, Davy, but yes. I need Mulvenna's arrest, interview trail and conviction transcripts and when you get them, give them to Annette. I'll tell her why next. Andy and Liam are interviewing people at the moment so they may come back to you with some queries on those as well. Thank God we don't have a case in Belfast right now."

Davy put his tongue firmly in his cheek. "True."

"Transfer me to Annette please."

Something moved in Davy's peripheral vision and he turned to see Nicky frantically waving a fax and pointing at her phone. He transferred the call back to her, strolling back to his horseshoe of computers to get started on his list.

"Hello again, sir."

Craig was surprised to hear her voice instead of Annette's.

"I thought Davy was transferring me to Annette?"

"I took back the call. I've just had a fax in from Dr Winter's office that you need to hear about."

"What's it about?"

"It's the toxicology report for Lissy Trainor. She was full of Morphine when she died."

Morphine. What the heck was that doing there? There'd been no sign that she was an addict, unless...

"OK, Nicky. I'll call John after I speak to Annette. Is she there?"

Annette was at her desk running through the printouts of Lucia's texts that Davy had given her first thing. They read like the one Lucia had showed her on Saturday, but there was nothing to identify the sender. Jake was at the desk beside her doing the same with Lucia's phone-calls; home, mobile and work. The home phone-calls were ten pages long. Annette smiled; Lucia talked nearly as much as her Mum. Nicky waved to catch their attention then transferred Craig to Annette's phone.

"Good morning, sir. What can I do to help?"

Craig laughed. She'd just said his six favourite words after sex and beer.

"Thanks Annette, but you might regret asking. Is Jake with us full time now?"

Annette glanced at the fair-haired sergeant and grinned.

"Yes, and raring to go."

"Good. OK, Davy's digging out the files of Jonno Mulvenna's arrest and trial in '83, for the murder of Veronica Jarvis. Briefly, it has a lot of similarities to the murder we're working on up here and the lead officer back then was ACC Trainor. She's our current victim's mother."

Annette's gasp told him that the grapevine gossip hadn't extended that far. It wouldn't take long.

"This is sensitive and confidential, Annette, but I know I can trust you with that." He had no idea just how true that was. "When the files come in, give me a call and I'll tell you what I want you to look for. Use my personal mobile please. I'll explain why when we talk." His voice changed to a cheerful tone. "How's life at the ranch without us? Quiet? Nicky's been telling me all about Liam's cup."

Annette laughed. "That's only her way of saying that she misses him. But for God's sake don't tell him that, he'll be unbearable if he thinks we care. It's quiet here thankfully, I spoke to D.C.I. McKenzie and he's rearranged the rota to make sure we're not on call again until next week."

"Good. We'll be back before then, not that you need us. Right. I'm off to phone John. I'll be in touch."

The line clicked off and Annette shot the pile of paper in front of her a baleful stare then she called early elevenses and put the kettle on.

***

Craig was surprised by his phone ringing while he was mid-dial to John. He was even more surprised by the voice on the other end. Melanie Trainor's imperious tones echoed down the line.

"Superintendent Craig? It's ACC Trainor."

He stared at the receiver for a moment remembering the Chief Constable's warning three hours before. But he hadn't called her in for interview, she'd contacted him. A conversation couldn't hurt. He swallowed hard.

"Yes, Ma'am."

"I'd like to see you, Craig. Do you have some time now? I believe you're still in Portstewart?"

"Yes. At the station."

"Good, I'll meet you there and save us both a trip to my office. Ten minutes?"

She didn't wait for a reply, just cut the line and left him staring at his phone. He thought for a moment and then made the call to John.

"Hi, John. Nicky's just told me you sent a fax through to the C.C.U.?"

"Ah, hello. Yes, it was Lissy's toxicology. I have her stomach contents too if you're interested."

"Just the highlights please, ACC Trainor wants to see me stat."

John went to ask and Craig halted him mid-stream. "I'll tell you when I know what it's about. At the moment I haven't a clue."

"Right. OK then. Lissy's stomach contents show that she had an ice-cream about an hour before she died, washed down with cola of some sort. I can be more specific about the flavour when we've run a few more tests, but at least we know whoever took her was feeding her well. It's her blood work that's really interesting."

"Morphine." As soon as the word was out Craig knew he'd stolen his thunder. He apologised. "Sorry, John, I'm just in a rush. What can you tell me?"

John's voice held a brief huff then returned to its normal cultured self. "Yes, Morphine. Injected not swallowed. Before you ask, she wasn't prescribed any morphine and there are no track-marks to suggest addiction."

"So you think the killer gave it to her?"

"Yes. The levels indicate she received a massive bolus. Given her size and the amount she had in her blood I'd say she only survived about five minutes after the injection. Death was from respiratory failure. I thought at first that the strangulation had been the cause, but it was definitely the Morphine."

"Where was it?"

"Injected into her jugular vein in her neck. It would have been a painless death. She'd have been asleep before she started to have trouble breathing. She was strangled as she died from the morphine but she wouldn't have felt a thing. It was definitely done before she was dead. She had the typical bruising and petechiae from strangulation and she would only have got those if she'd been alive when it was done."

"Tricky injection site."

"No, not really. Anyone who goes to the movies would have seen it done before."

"You're sure she was unconscious when she was strangled? But how does that fit with the scratch marks on her neck?"

There was silence for a moment before John spoke.

"God, you're right! If the Morphine had put her out completely she couldn't have struggled and caused those. Poor girl. She must have woken up at some point after she was injected." He paused then restarted "There's another thing, Marc. There were traces of a benzodiazepine in her bloodstream and stomach."

"She was sedated?"

"Yes. Digestion shows she was given it the same time as her ice-cream and drink, then they injected her with the Morphine. I think they meant her to die without feeling a thing. The last thing she was supposed to experience was drinking cola and eating ice-cream but unfortunately she must have woken up."

"Nice way to go, if there is such a thing."

"It tells us a lot about her killer."

Craig nodded. "They staged her death to match the case in '83 but they took no pleasure in it. They didn't beat her or rape her and her death was basically intended to be falling asleep."

"If they took no pleasure in it then what was the point?"

"To draw our attention to the case in '83. This whole thing is to make us see something that happened then." He paused. "I met with the Chief; Sean Flanagan."

"And?"

"He's on our side and he didn't seem to think my theory was too left of field." He thought for a moment. "Are you busy this evening?"

John thought quickly. Natalie was on call from home and he normally kept her company at her place. He shrugged. She would understand him disappearing for a few hours.

"What time were you thinking?"

"Seven. We could meet somewhere halfway? It would help to talk things through."

"OK, let me think of a venue and call you back. In the meantime, I'm going over Lissy's post-mortem again with a microscope, in case there's something else that I've missed."

***

The Chief Constable had been sympathetic and she knew he would do his best, but Julia didn't hold out much hope of a transfer. Terry Harrison had got there before her, explaining why he really needed her to stay in the North-West. He'd actively start looking for her replacement, of course he would, sir, but all of them, including the Chief Constable, knew it could take years for Harrison to find someone qualified who wanted to move to Limavady. Especially if he dragged his heels. People in Northern Ireland stayed close to their roots and nothing short of a natural disaster would shift them. There were Belfast people, Derry people and people from Fermanagh and Newry, with little in between. Everywhere else was just a commute.

She tapped her slim fingers against her desk and stared down ruefully at her dun brown suit. It was her least attractive outfit but it was getting a lot of wear nowadays, anything to avoid the lecherous attention of Terry Harrison. She heard the kettle boiling down the corridor and pulled open her half-glass door, wandering down to see who was there.

Gerry Shaw, her sergeant, was standing in the coffee room with his back to her, pushing a handful of biscuits into his mouth. She called his name and he spluttered in surprise. He spun towards her with crumbs trailing down his tie.

"You scared the life out of me, boss. I thought you were Harrison. You shouldn't creep up on people like that. It's dangerous."

She stared pointedly at her high heels before she spoke. "It's pretty hard to creep up on anyone in these bad boys. And what do you mean dangerous? I've just saved you from a carbohydrate overdose."

"Don't joke about it, I'm eating for two." He pointed at his stomach and she was surprised. She hadn't noticed it before but he was getting a paunch. "Our Linda is pregnant again and I'm eating in sympathy."

She grinned broadly. Babies were always good news.

"Congrats."

Something occurred to her and when she spoke again it was in a wheedling tone.

"With another baby on the way you'll need to earn more money, won't you?"

"Maybe, but Linda's parents are helping us out."

"That can't go on forever. You have to think of the future."

He saw where she was heading and held his hand up. "Whoa. If you're thinking of putting me up for the Inspector's Board, forget it. I've enough of my plate without burning the midnight oil studying P.A.C.E. Besides, you've already got the job."

She shook her head sadly and picked at a biscuit while he made the tea.

"I can't keep commuting to Belfast for much longer and

Teflon won't let me have a transfer."

He was shocked. She never referred to Harrison by his nickname, not even in private, although everyone else in the station did. She must be really pissed.

"He says it would leave him an Inspector short and until he can find someone to replace me he won't let me go."

Gerry was surprised to see a tear forming in her eye. She was genuinely upset.

"Can't the Chief Constable intervene?"

Julia shook her head and red tendrils escaped her fierce chignon and fell across her face. She looked vulnerable. It was a side of her he never saw. She'd joined them from an army captain's post and she ran a very tight ship, but he supposed everyone was vulnerable when they were in love.

"He says he can't really. Marc had already spoken to him, and he was very kind, but he said that Harrison has the right to insist." She pushed her hair back angrily. "I could resign and move to Belfast then try to find a job, but..."

"You've already changed your life once by leaving the army and you don't want to do it again."

She was shocked by his perception. She nodded and Gerry thought again.

"Look, let me speak to Linda. If she agrees then I'll put in for the exam in 2014, but there's no way that I'd be ready before then."

Her heart soared for a moment then fell again, knowing the distance was killing their romance already, in another year it would be beyond life support. She pushed her doubts to one side and smiled at her deputy gratefully. If his wife agreed then he would try and that was all she had any right to expect. She already knew it would be too little too late.

Chapter Thirteen

When Craig walked into the staff room, Jim O'Neill's hushed tones told him the ACC was already there. His raised eyebrow said that she wasn't in the mood for delays. Craig turned towards the corridor housing the relatives' room and was stopped by an apologetic "Sorry, sir. Other way" as the sergeant's finger indicated an interview room. Craig knew right then that this wasn't going to be an informal exchange. He walked down the short, grey corridor and halted outside interview room two. Half of him wondered whether he should knock, then the grown-up half pushed firmly at the door and stepped inside. What he saw next said that Melanie Trainor stood on ceremony no matter what was happening in her life.

She was seated at the room's small Formica table dressed in full uniform, her hat sitting by her side. But it was where she was sitting that amused Craig. In the interviewer's position. He wondered how he could ever have imagined anything else.

She glanced up as he entered and nodded him briskly to a seat. It felt like a job interview, at best. He resisted her nod and stood across from her, hands in his pockets like a defiant teenager up in front of the beak. She stared pointedly at him and started to speak without any preamble.

"I'm here against my better judgement, Superintendent Craig, and I won't be answering any questions about my daughter or her mode of death."

Having satisfied herself that she'd excluded anything personal from their talk, she reached inside a polished document case and pulled out a sheaf of paper. The 'Dear' at the top of each page said that they were letters. The differing size and colour of paper said that they'd been written at different times. Some were scrawled on A4 sheets of file paper and others more neatly written, on watermarked sheets from a writing pad. He remembered his mother giving the same paper to him and Lucia after Christmas each year, to write thank-you letters for their gifts. Basildon Bond. It was her 'good' writing paper; thick and elegant. He could still remember the excitement of using it. Terrified in case he got a word wrong and had to use another sheet, but secretly hoping that he would so that he could get to start again.

All the pages were handwritten, covered in letters of differing sizes, and exclamation marks, with words underlined. She laid them on the desk with a look of distaste and spoke again.

"If you're looking for a motive for my daughter's murder, these may give you one."

Craig could see she was going to keep talking, and he knew that if he didn't take charge of the conversation soon he would never get a chance. He interrupted briskly.

"When did you start receiving them?"

"In 1984. At first they were hand delivered, when I was living in the centre of Portstewart. When I moved in '85 they were posted; the postmark is Coleraine. I had it examined, and the handwriting. They were all from the same person. A woman, the graphologist said, which makes sense given the content."

"Do you have any idea who sent them?"

He pulled out a seat and sat down facing her, equalising their position, height wise at least. She stared at the notes saying nothing for a moment. Finally she shrugged as if to say 'why should I protect her?' Craig watched her silent debate with interest. No-one asked themselves that question unless they felt they'd had a reason to protect someone in the first place. No, maybe not a reason. A duty?

"They're from a woman called Bronagh O'Carolan. She was

the victim of a rape investigated back in 1984."

"I take it that it was never solved?"

The letters' evident unhappiness was testament to that. Trainor nodded.

"She blamed me."

"You were the investigating officer?" He asked the question with surprise. Melanie Trainor had been in murder in 1984. What was she doing investigating a rape?

She shook her head, confirming he was right. "No. I was nowhere near the case."

"So why…"

She cut across his question saving his breath. As she stared at him he noticed her eyes were a warm dark brown and behind the formal disguise she looked very like her daughter. He couldn't imagine how hard it must be seeing your dead child's reflection every time you looked in the glass.

She answered his query. "The Senior Investigating Officer, Superintendent Murtagh, was pretty sure a man called Declan Wasson was to blame, but the forensics were weak and he couldn't get a conclusive match so he was set free." She dropped her eyes. "He lived in the same estate as Mrs O'Carolan so she had to see him every day. Finally it got too much for her and she killed herself in 1986. The letters ended then."

She fingered a sheet of pale blue paper then turned it face-down on the table-top. "This was her last note to me. She posted it three hours before she died."

The small room fell silent and Craig listened as the wall-clock marked the time. After more than a minute he asked another question.

"Why did she blame you?"

Trainor lifted her eyes to look at him. They held a mixture of anger and disdain but he wasn't sure who they held it for. Him, herself, or the woman she thought had taken the coward's way from this world? Because if he was sure of one thing it was that Melanie Trainor would have viewed Bronagh O'Carolan's suicide as the act of a coward. When her voice came it was strong and clear.

"Because I convicted Jonno Mulvenna of a crime."

Craig knew what she expected his next question to be. "What has that got to do with Wasson?" But instead he surprised her.

"Was he innocent?"

Her shock was visceral and she jerked back in her chair. She gathered herself hurriedly to disguise it but it was too late, they both knew he'd seen it and there was no way to bluff. She tidied the letters into a pile and rested her hands on top, using the time to compose her face into a mask of indignation and untruth. Then she let him have it in an icy voice.

"Who do you think you're talking to, Superintendent? I'm your senior officer, remember that. I came here to assist your investigation, not be questioned like some petty crook."

Craig gazed at her unflinching. "Yes Ma'am, I'm well aware of that. But my question remains. Why would Bronagh O'Carolan blame you for a rape you didn't investigate, that occurred the year after another crime in which a woman was killed? A crime for which you convicted Jonno Mulvenna? Unless there are other links between the two cases? She must have felt that you'd convicted the wrong man. Did she believe that Declan Wasson, her accused rapist, was guilty in the Veronica Jarvis murder? Not John Mulvenna?"

It was the question he'd been asking himself and everyone else for the past three days. He hadn't intended to get there this quickly with her but she'd opened the door and it seemed rude not to walk through.

He watched as her hands clenched, throwing her knuckles into white relief against her tan. He could almost hear her mind racing, wondering whether to lie, or perhaps to continue a lie that had already been told for thirty years. Instead she relaxed suddenly and drew herself upright in her seat, showing the metal that had taken her to the top. She smiled at him. It was a cold half-smile that didn't reach her eyes and it was calculated to generate fear. It had probably worked on her subordinates for years. Well she could think again. He might not have her elevated rank but he was subordinate to no-one and he was going to get an answer to his question, either here or under oath.

She finally spoke, her mime not enough to break his nerve.

"She believed Declan Wasson had committed the crime that Jonno Mulvenna was convicted of. And that if Wasson had been put away in 1983 for the murder of Veronica Jarvis he could never have attacked her in 1984."

Her voice was calm and cool and she lifted a small piece of lint from her jacket as she spoke, casting it away into mid-air. Craig wasn't fooled; he'd seen displacement activities plenty of time before with interviewees. From kicking the table to tapping their fingers annoyingly on the desk, or glancing up and down and all around the room. Her lint was just an elegant version of the same. He knew right then that she was lying and he was on the right track. She was still talking but he knew her words would all be lies. Instead he listened to the message in the gaps between them and the real truth, in her tone of voice and posture shifts. They confirmed the story from the lint.

"Wasson was looked at briefly for the Jarvis murder but it didn't stack up, Mulvenna was a much better suspect and all the evidence pointed his way."

Really? All what evidence?

"Mrs O'Carolan wanted the murder case re-opened, to convict Wasson and put him away, but there was nothing I could do." Again, really?

Trainor slipped her hand inside the document case and pulled out another file. It held a series of typed letters much more orderly than the last. Her gaze said this was the last answer Craig was getting and she expected him to be satisfied with it and stop looking elsewhere. He raised a questioning eyebrow.

"These are from Bronagh O'Carolan's eldest son. James. He's thirty-three now. He was six when she died."

"What age were her other children?"

She glanced at him as if she was confused.

"You said he was the eldest, what age were the other ones?"

She dropped her eyes and Craig thought that at least she had the good grace to do that. Her voice was quiet. "Three and one year. Two little girls."

On the last word her voice broke. She regained her composure quickly and tapped the pile. "He's been writing to me since he was at Queens." She sighed. "Each letter is the same. Blaming me for letting Wasson go and asking for the Mulvenna conviction to be examined." She shook her head. "Wasson's dead and it won't bring his mother back. Why doesn't he just leave it alone?"

The question was rhetorical but her tone was a mixture of pleading and despair and Craig knew she was afraid of what might be found if the case was examined again. He framed his next question in such a way that she couldn't attempt to pull rank. He wanted the mother, not the ACC.

"Do you believe James O'Carolan had something to do with your daughter's death?"

She glanced at him quickly, her mouth ready with a defiant word. What she saw in Craig's eyes was sympathy for her loss. It disarmed her for a moment and she nodded, then shook her head quickly as if she couldn't decide whether to answer yes or no.

Craig saw something else behind her confusion. She was afraid, and… there was guilt as well. The guilt could have been for Lissy, for her being murdered for her career. But the fear? He parked it for future analysis and waited for her reply.

"I think…perhaps…" She shook her head despairingly, settling on "I don't know. It's why I brought the letters for you to see."

It wasn't the only reason, Craig was sure of that. He reached out his hand and she gave him both files. He pushed back his chair and stood, looking down briefly at the top of her head, then he turned and left the room. Leaving her to mourn her daughter alone, without trying to maintain the façade of rank.

Chapter Fourteen

"What have you got, Liam?"

Craig thought again then amended his question. "Look, it's twelve-thirty, do you fancy an early lunch? I've just spent an hour with the ACC and I need a break."

Liam grinned to himself imagining their exchange. She was a fierce one, right enough, but his money was still on Craig. He said as much.

"Craig five, ACC Trainor, nil points."

Craig smiled at the reference to the Eurovision. "Isn't that usually Luxembourg? Anyway, lunch?"

"Aye. That'll do. I'll give Andy a bell. He's off pulling the rape files, he'll need a break from that. See you there in twenty."

Craig knocked off his phone and sat back in his car seat, thinking. He gazed at the Brewster Hotel's impressive façade, not seeing anything but Lissy Trainor's young face. It wasn't much comfort that he was heading in the right direction. It might lead to the Jarvis murder being re-opened and Mulvenna's conviction being overturned and no-one wanted that, including Jonno Mulvenna. And what comfort would it offer the Jarvis kids? Their mother was dead and if Declan Wasson was the guilty man he was dead as well and well beyond the law. What good would proving it do now?

He corrected himself. This was about catching Lissy Trainor's murderer. They mightn't need to actually reopen Ronni Jarvis' case, just look as if they were. That might bring the person who'd framed Mulvenna out of the weeds. It was going to get dirty, corruption cases always did, but if someone in MI5 or the force had framed Jonno Mulvenna, no matter what their reasons, then they had to be caught. They might have caused Lissy Trainor's death, even if they hadn't killed her with their own hands.

He glanced at his watch. He had ten minutes until Liam arrived so he lifted his mobile and called the C.C.U.. It was answered by a voice that Craig didn't recognise.

"C.C.U.."

"Hello. It's Superintendent Craig. Is Nicky there?"

"No. I mean yes, but she's gone to buy a sandwich, sir. It's Jake McLean. Can I help?"

"Ah, hello, Jake. Sorry, I didn't recognise your voice. Nice to have you join us. Are you settling in OK?"

"Yes, sir. Annette's showing me the ropes."

"Good. We'll get a chance to chat later in the week, but for now could you give Nicky a message for me, please?"

"Sure."

"Tell her I need to find out who Declan Wasson's handler was in 1983. She's to use all her diplomacy on this one. They could have been someone in the British Army, MI5 or the police, and no-one of them will want to give her the name."

He heard Jake scribbling furiously and gave him second to take it all down.

"OK?"

"Fine, sir."

"Right. Tell her to call me with any queries. I'm meeting Liam and Andy for lunch then I'll try to see Jonno Mulvenna again."

"*The* Jonno Mulvenna?"

Craig was surprised. The Troubles had ended when Jake was still at school.

"Yes, how do you know about him?"

"I did Criminology at Uni, sir. One of my assignments was on Terrorists and their reform. Mulvenna's a successful artist now, isn't he?"

"Seems to be." Craig thought of something. "He has an exhibition in the Morena Gallery on the Lisburn Road tomorrow night. I'm going to see what I can find out. Do you want to come?"

"That would be great. Like seeing the theory in action. I'll give Nicky your message."

"OK, bye."

Craig cut the line, smiling. McLean's enthusiasm would make him a good addition to the team. He re-dialled, giving the Chief Constable an update on his meeting with the ACC and then headed into the hotel for lunch.

***

Lunch was a quiet affair, with Andy red-eyed and bleary from a morning spent reading dusty files and making a short list of people to interview. Craig updated them on what he knew of Bronagh O'Carolan's case and Liam shook his head sadly.

"Six, three and one. My God, that's young to lose your Mum. Who brought them up?"

Craig shook his head. "I don't know. Their Dad I presume. The eldest, James, went to Queens I know that, so he must have done OK." He turned to Andy. "I know it's not strictly part of the case, but it would be good to know what happened to the other kids, Andy. And James will definitely need looking at. He's been writing to Melanie Trainor for years asking her to re-examine Mulvenna's conviction. I've got his letters here."

He indicated the two files by his side then turned back to Liam.

"Liam, do you want to tell us about Conor Ryland? Then Andy can tell us about his list. I'll update you my meeting with the Chief and John's toxicology on Lissy, then I'll come back to the letters."

Liam swallowed hastily then talked as he ate. "Aye well. First,

I went to that hippy shop, The Magic Box. Weird wasn't the word for it. It was full of Tarot Cards and incense, all that sort of stuff. Anyway, there's nothing there. Lissy was fine when she left there on Saturday evening and no-one met up with her after that. No crime, just weirdo central. There's nothing there with Ryland either, boss. He loved her and they hadn't split up, it was just a bit of malicious gossip spread by Lissy's friends. Particularly Mary-Ann Eakin. She seems to have had a real thing about them."

He gave them a knowing look and sniffed. "She lied. She wasn't in Dublin this weekend; she was here, following them. Or rather she was following Ryland. He'd arranged to meet Lissy on Sunday night at Portrush Harbour at eight-thirty, but she never turned up. He says plenty of people saw him there. I'll get uniform to check it out but I'm pretty sure it'll be true. He said he saw Mary-Ann Eakin following him, so I'm going to have a go at her again."

"Jealously? Or love?"

"No idea, but both have been a motive for murder plenty of times before. I'll do a spot of cherchez la femme after lunch."

"That's two French expressions in one day, Liam. Is there something you'd like to tell us?"

Liam guffawed loudly then grinned. "Well spotted, Hercule. Danni's got me learning it for our camping holiday next year. We're driving down through France and Italy."

Craig laughed. "Keep it up. I can't wait till you start on the Italian. Andy?"

He turned to see Andy fighting a losing battle with a plate of spaghetti. He had tomato sauce on his shirt but Craig knew it would be replaced with an identical one after lunch. He shook his head.

"A morning buried in paper, hey. But at least I've got all the files now. I should have a list of possibles by close of play today. Davy's being a great help."

"He always is. I don't know what we'll do if he decides to

move on."

"Here, is that likely, boss? I've just managed to break him in and I was hoping to teach him to swear in French."

Craig laughed. He thought Davy probably already knew all the swear words there were to know. "I hope he doesn't go, but he's very bright and we can't pay him what he's worth." He took a drink and restarted. "OK. First of all, I updated the CC this morning and he's aware of where this case might lead."

"He's OK with it?"

"He didn't exactly do a happy dance, but yes, he's OK. Just as long as I keep him up to date."

Andy dipped a napkin in his water and rubbed at his shirt as Craig talked on. "John got back to me. Lissy Trainor died from a Morphine overdose."

Liam gasped. "But I thought she was strangled?"

"It turns out the strangulation was carried out peri-mortem, to produce the bruising and petechiae, probably to mimic the Jarvis case. She was given a sedative of some sort orally in some ice-cream and cola, about an hour before death, judging by its digestion. Then she was injected with Morphine. A big enough dose to kill her quickly, within five minutes John said, judging by the blood level. She was strangled in those five minutes before death. John said she was probably given the Morphine when she was still asleep from the sedative, so she wouldn't have known anything."

"That's something at least."

Liam shook his head. "That doesn't work, boss."

Craig nodded. He'd spotted John's rookie mistake as well.

"She fought him at some stage. She had scratches on her neck and that's how her nails got broken, remember? She must have woken up while she was being strangled."

"You're right Liam. I spotted that earlier. She woke up while she was being strangled. Poor girl, she must have been terrified."

An image of Lissy Trainor struggling flashed through Craig's mind. He pushed it away.

"OK. We know she was killed somewhere where there were twigs on the ground and moved less than six hours after death, to be buried vertically in the sand. From Conor Ryland we know she didn't meet him on Sunday night, so we can assume that she was kidnapped then. Liam, check if her outgoing calls and texts stopped then, just to confirm that she didn't deliberately stand Ryland up. We know her body was found on Thursday so that leaves us four days from kidnap to discovery with her buried less than six hours after she was killed. What we don't know is which day she was actually killed. At the moment it could have been anytime between Sunday and say Wednesday night, depending on how deeply she was buried in the sand."

"Davy's working on the tides to see if that will help."

"It was definitely set up to mimic Ronni Jarvis' death, then, boss?"

Craig nodded. "We can't rule out that this was just about Mrs Jarvis, but my conversation with the ACC…"

Andy cut in. "I thought you were leaving that for a while, like you said to the Chief."

"I was. She contacted me this morning." He indicated the piles of letters under his hand. "She wanted to give me these and set me running in the direction of James O'Carolan."

He handed Andy the two files.

"Letters written by Bronagh O'Carolan to ACC Trainor from her rape in '84 to '86 when she died, including one posted three hours before she killed herself. The second file contains letters from her eldest son James, asking for the Jarvis case to be re-opened."

"On what basis, hey?"

"On the basis that Bronagh O'Carolan believed that her rapist Declan Wasson should have been put away for Veronica Jarvis' murder. If he had been then she would never have been raped."

"And three children wouldn't have lost their Mum. "

Craig nodded as Andy flicked through the piles. "This puts

him top of the list for revenge-killing Lissy."

"Sadly, you're right. If not at the top, then near it. But keep an open mind, Andy. This all feels just a bit too neat, especially the way Melanie Trainor basically handed them to me like she'd solved the case."

"Sometimes the most obvious things are true, boss."

"Yes they are, Liam."

"But…?"

Craig laughed. Liam knew him too well.

"But, we need to look at the rape victims' revenge angle, just as we need to look at Ronni Jarvis' kids and Mary-Ann Eakin. But, I think this is a nasty can of worms and until I get to the bottom of it…"

"It'll be burger, chips and a good night's sleep by the seaside. Happy days!"

Chapter Fifteen

By three p.m. Andy had seven women's names in front of him and a second list of members of their immediate families. He spilt his first list into two columns. Women in whose rapes Declan Wasson was the prime suspect but no-one was charged, and those where they'd managed to get him as far as court, only to have the case thrown out on one flimsy pretext or another. There were two in the second list and five in the first, but it didn't matter whether they'd got to court or not, Craig was right. Someone had been watching Wasson's back, someone with a lot of power. He shook his head. There may have been police involvement in framing Jonno Mulvenna, if he was framed, but Wasson had been Teflon coated by someone higher up. It had MI5 and government written all over it.

He read the women's names aloud, trying to imagine their pain. Bad enough to be raped and brutalised, but to know who had done it and for them to walk free; how did anyone get past that? He imagined what he would do if it happened to a woman that he loved. He would want to kill to get revenge, but he would have directed it at Wasson, not the family of a police officer, even if they were somehow involved in getting him off. But then that was him and the police were his own, he could only speculate on what other people thought.

It wasn't even as if Melanie Trainor had led one of the rape investigations and engineered Wasson going free, she'd led a murder case. Yes, Wasson might have been suspected of Veronica Jarvis' murder, but without forensics they were on a hiding to nothing in putting him away. He shook his head, convinced that Lissy Trainor could have been murdered as revenge against her Mum, but not that it was revenge for one of Wasson's subsequent rapes.

He'd say as much to Craig, but interview them anyway to rule them out. He picked up the phone and called the C.C.U.. Nicky answered cheerfully.

"Hello, Docklands C.C.U.."

"Hi Nicky, it's Andy White here, hey. Is the boy there?"

Nicky laughed, wondering when Davy would be seen as anything else. "I'll transfer you now."

Davy was sorting through reams of print-outs of Lissy Trainor's e-mails and calls, arranging them in two neat lines. The phone rang from somewhere beneath the papers and he rummaged for it, pushing them to one side in his hurry then staring balefully at the disarray. Now he'd have to start again. The annoyance showed in his voice.

"Yes."

"Boyso, who hit you with the angry stick? It can't be Liam; he's up here making my life hell."

Davy laughed then apologised "S...sorry, D.C.I. White. I've just knocked my filing system all over the floor."

Andy stared at the files in front of him in empathy. "Aye, well, I have another wee burden to give you."

"Fire ahead."

"You know those rape cases Marc wanted us to look at?"

"Yes."

"Well I've got a list of names for you to check. If I send them through could you pull up the summary sheets and e-mail them back to me. Just the summaries, not the whole file."

Davy sighed, it would take him hours and he'd arranged to meet Maggie at five. They were going to the flicks to see Asa Butterfield's new release, Enders Game.

"W...would tomorrow afternoon be soon enough? It's just; I've a load of other things to do before I leave tonight."

Andy heard his pleading tone and laughed.

"Tomorrow afternoon is fine for most of them, but I'll be interviewing someone tomorrow morning so it would be helpful if you could send theirs through before then."

"S…sure. Which one?"

"The woman's name is Bronagh O'Carolan. She was raped in 1984 and she died in 1986."

"Oh."

"Yes, it's a sad case. I need anything you can find on her children as well, especially her eldest son James. And Davy, could you transfer me to Annette?"

"That's fine. I'll get the O'Carolan information to you by close of play. I'll transfer you now."

He mouthed at Annette to pick up the call and turned back to his work. He knelt on the floor to sort out his files and swore under his breath, while Nicky put on the percolator, preparing for a busy few hours.

"Hello. Annette McElroy."

"Hey Annette, how are you?"

"Grand, sir. It's lovely and quiet here without Liam, and you can tell him I said that. What can I do for you?"

"Davy's getting some summary sheets for me and background on about twenty people. I don't want to have to interview them all so I wonder if you could find out if they were in the country between last Sunday the 27th and Thursday the 31st when Lissy Trainor was found. And check their alibis for me? Anyone without a strong one I need to see."

"No problem. I'll get on to it tomorrow. Look, it's just a suggestion and I'll need to check it with the boss, but Jake and I are happy to help with interviews or anything we can. We can do it from here or go to you."

"That's very kind of you, but check with Marc before you go offering yourself. He may have other plans. Mr Craig works in mysterious ways."

She laughed, knowing it was true, and signed off.

Andy stared at his list of victims' relatives and then lifted the phone again, this time to Jim O'Neill.

"Jim, do we have anything on a local lad called James O'Carolan. Son of Bronagh O'Carolan who committed suicide in '86."

"I'll check and get back to you."

While he waited Andy read the last letter James O'Carolan had sent Melanie Trainor. It was dated the 6th of October that year and it was unambiguous in its tone. He hated her and the final paragraph of the neatly typed page said just how much.

"I hope that someday you get to feel the pain we've felt for years, and I hope that it's soon."

Three weeks later her only daughter was dead. Wish, threat or promise? When he interviewed James O'Carolan tomorrow he'd find out.

***

"The uniforms have found someone who saw Conor Ryland, boss, or someone very like him, at the pier on Sunday night. They were in the bar of a nearby guesthouse and they said half the bar was watching him 'cos he was sitting there for so long they were sure he'd been stood up."

"Good. Any sightings of Mary-Ann Eakin?"

Liam smiled. Once Craig had ticked one box, he was onto the next thing.

"Not yet, but they'll keep asking. But here, there's another thing."

"Yes."

Craig picked absentmindedly at the edge of the desk they allocated him in the station, waiting to hear what else Liam had found. Whatever it was it would be useful to the case. Liam wouldn't mention it otherwise.

"Someone called the tip line and they transferred the call to me." Craig could hear him flicking a page of his notebook. "A Mrs Jenna Farrelly. She says she saw Lissy on Sunday night standing in front of a shop on the promenade, talking to a dark-haired man. It was about seven-forty-five, which would make sense if she was on her way to meet Ryland at eight-thirty."

Craig sat forward urgently. "Description?"

"Around thirty, tall with thick dark hair."

"Were they talking or arguing?"

"Talking. She didn't think anything of it until she saw Lissy's picture on the news and remembered."

Craig's could feel himself tense. This was something, he was sure of it. But what? Would a killer who'd mocked up such an elaborate crime-scene really be stupid enough to stand on a crowded street with his victim just before he took her? He didn't think so, but there were a lot of stupid criminals out there. It was something that surprised most cops who'd been weaned on the criminal masterminds portrayed on TV.

Something else occurred to him. Arrogance. Arrogance could have made their killer want to be seen with Lissy, especially if he'd thought they'd never find him. Or if he wanted them to.

"OK, Liam. This is important. I'm sure of it. I want you to interview Mrs Farrelly now. Get everything you can from her, you know what to ask. I've a couple of calls to make then let's meet back at the hotel at six."

He cut the call then dialled Nicky at the C.C.U..

"Any joy with Wasson's handler, Nick?"

Nicky raised her eyes to heaven at Craig's expectations of her speed. Just as well he was right.

"Yes, sir. Declan Wasson was a big fish apparently."

It would explain why he'd been so protected.

"He'd been a paid confidential informant since 1975, and by all accounts he passed tips on the IRA as often as every other week. Helped crack a lot of crime."

At what cost?

"Who ran him, Nicky?"

"Well it was hard to get through the usual secrecy and

muttering about sealed files."

"But you did."

"Yes I did but I don't want it taken for granted. You owe me big time, sir. I had to call in several favours on this one. Seems it was mainly MI5 who ran him, but the army and police both borrowed him occasionally as well."

"How about in '83? Who was his main handler then?"

"A spook called Roger Lowry out of Thames House in London. He was over here between 1980 and '89."

"Wasson died in '89."

"So maybe that's why Lowry went back to London. If Wasson was his main man, then perhaps he chose that time to transfer."

"That's if MI5 had nothing to do with Wasson's death."

Nicky smiled at his suspicious mind, it was exactly what she'd thought. Craig continued.

"OK. So Lowry was handling Wasson for MI5 in '83. Where is he now?"

"Retired. He's living in a place called Lowestoft up the Suffolk coast. Do you know it?"

Craig smiled to himself. It was a place that he and Camille had week-ended many times. A beautiful port town whose recorded history went back as far as the Doomsday survey of 1086. Not that they'd seen much of the local history, bed had had much more to offer them back then.

"Yes. It's very pretty. Worth a trip. Who's in charge of that section at Thames House now? "

"Someone called Peter Guthrie. I called but they insisted he needed to speak to you on a secure line. I've arranged it for tomorrow morning at ten o'clock."

She'd anticipated everything.

"Nicky, you're a wonder."

"I am. I'm glad you noticed, I have to remind Gary once a week at least."

She laughed her loud navvy's laugh and Craig started to

laugh as well. Craig imagined her husband Gary doing exactly what he was told, and knowing just how lucky he was to have her. The noise drew Annette over to Nicky's desk and she signalled that she wanted to speak to Craig.

"Where would you like me to take the call with Guthrie, Nick?"

"Portstewart station please, in a meeting room. It'll be the most secure."

"Fine. Thanks for that."

"You're welcome. Before you go, Annette's hovering. She'd like a word."

She handed the phone to Annette and shooed her as far from her desk as the line would stretch. She had work to do and she didn't need people cluttering up her space.

"Hi Annette. What's up?"

"We're not busy here, sir, apart from doing background stuff for you and D.C.I. White. So I suggested that Jake and I could help him with his interviews, once he's sure who he'd like them with. He said to check with you."

"Good idea. Andy will have all the rape case interviews and Liam will generate a fair few as well. They're mostly going to be to rule people out, but unfortunately they still have to be done. We have uniforms out canvassing the locals at the moment so if you could start interviewing it would be a great help."

"Great. There or here?"

"Base it on where the interviewees live. You can get Nicky to arrange rooms in the local stations or interview them in their homes, whichever suits the mood. You'll know when you speak to them whether they need a formal setting or not."

"Great. I hear you and Jake are doing your art critic bit at Mulvenna's show tomorrow night?"

Craig startled, realising the time. "Yes, thanks for mentioning that. I have to go. I want to catch Mulvenna again if I can. Bye."

He dropped the call suddenly, leaving Annette staring at the line. She turned back to her desk and lifted the pile of paper Davy had handed her an hour before. Lucia's e-mail traffic and phone dumps. Lucia'd said she hadn't had any e-mails from 'Watching U', but there could be clues in there nevertheless.

She'd drawn a blank trying to think up a shortlist of men who could possibly be stalking her, but Annette had never held out much hope there. Lucia liked everyone; she wouldn't spot a pervert unless he hit her over the head.

She glanced at the clock. Four p.m. She would give herself two hours to see if there were any patterns, then tomorrow she'd turn her full attention to Lissy Trainor's case.

***

Lucia pulled down the shop's shutter hurriedly and cast a glance around the deserted Belfast street. There was nothing to be seen except for the undercover police car parked on the corner, with a female officer at the wheel. She shuddered. Was this how some people lived their whole lives, followed and watched? Protected for their own good? She'd only had it for two days and already the lack of freedom made her want to scream, or jump on a plane and run away. No wonder some famous people went mad.

She shook herself for being selfish, knowing that she was very lucky someone cared. How many women had to deal with stalking alone? The small charity shop stood impassively, as if it was listening to her mental rant. Its cancer logo reminded her not to be such a child. That was real suffering; not this.

She turned and walked towards the city centre, with the car following close behind. Annette had told her to drive door-to-door, but it was a lovely autumn day so she'd parked a mile away. She smiled at the scene. It must have looked ridiculous, a woman with a car crawling after her down the early evening street. She felt like the star of some bad hooker movie.

She reached her car and threw her baggage into the boot,

gunning its elderly engine and heading for the M3 and home. Not home now, but home back when she was a child. Whoever her stalker was had succeeded in making her one again.

***

Craig was driving to Mulvenna's for another chat when a tearful call from Julia stopped him in his tracks. He sat in the car deciding what to do, then turned back towards the hotel. His heart had gone out to her as she'd sobbed down the line. She wasn't a crier so he knew how badly it meant she felt. The Chief Constable had been kind, she'd said, but there was nothing that he could do, not without giving Harrison a direct order. That would guarantee ruining all their careers if it got out, and they all knew that Harrison would make sure it would.

Craig had leapt in then, saying "Sod our careers. I can't bear to see you this unhappy."

He'd meant it. If a job was making you miserable then no matter how much you loved it, it had to go. They could both start again. There were plenty of other things they could do. Her reply had been more sensible. "In Northern Ireland, Marc? Really?"

As soon as she'd said it he'd known that she was right. Jobs were few and far between in such a small place. Jobs you loved even fewer. They could go to London, but the whole reason he'd left there was to be close to his parents as they grew old; well, most of the reason anyhow. The fact that his and Camille's relationship had ended messily had helped him decide as well. But he still loved London and Julia's mother lived there so it was a definite option. Perhaps they could both transfer to The Met? Julia had been mollified by the suggestion and it had stopped her sobbing at least, but even as Craig said it he knew he was lying, not to her but to himself.

A vision of his father's face when he'd suffered his heart attack filled his mind. He'd recovered well from it, but how could he leave them after that? He restarted the conversation slowly, meandering back to her moving to Belfast and changing jobs, at least for a while, just until something came up in the force down there. Her tone had changed from sad to angry and defiant; reminding him of when he'd first met her, during the Jessica Adams case. She'd been hostile and prickly then, with a wall around her fifty-feet thick. He could hear it being rebuilt.

"So it's OK for me to give up my job, Marc, but not you? God forbid that you should ever make a sacrifice."

"I didn't mean that, it's just, my parents live here and they're elderly. They're the reason I moved back from London. To be close-by to help. And I can't move anywhere without a job."

"But I can? That's what you mean, isn't it? I'm the little woman so I can. My career doesn't matter! I made a big change when I left the army, Marc. I'm not making another to be unemployed."

She'd slammed down the phone and he'd been left staring into space, knowing that she'd be crying at the other end, but not knowing what to say to stem her tears.

***

At six-thirty Liam and Andy were waiting in the bar, bantering and competing to see who could catch the most peanuts in their mouths. Liam glanced at the clock, the boss was late. It wasn't like him, he would normally phone. He'd give him another five minutes and then send out the dogs. Just then Craig walked in and one glance at him told Liam everything he needed to know. He beckoned the waiter over.

"Three beers, please. And make them big ones."

Craig slumped down at the table and threw his jacket onto an empty chair. His tie was halfway down his chest and his top two buttons were undone, it was as close to out of uniform as Liam had seen him in a while. There were only two things that could have caused it; too much beer or a woman. He dismissed the first because of the time of day and pondered the second for a moment, arriving at girlfriend, sister or Mum in order of descending grief. He plumped for the first. Detective Inspector Julia McNulty; she could generate enough grief for ten men.

He'd met her before Craig had and while he'd thought she was bonny, even beautiful, she was headstrong and brittle; not his type at all. He thought of his tiny wife Danni at home with their two kids and smiled to himself. She gave him hell plenty of times, but there was nothing brittle about her, no matter how hard she tried. McNulty lived up to every fiery stereotype her red hair implied and she tried to keep Craig on a short leash. Tried, being the operative word.

He glanced at his boss sympathetically. Even he had to admit that when good looks and brains had been handed out Craig had been top of the queue. If he'd been born with that combination he'd have broken a new heart every week but Craig was a one woman romantic and his heart was playing havoc with his brain.

"Rough day, boss?"

Craig nodded at the waiter as he set down their drinks, then nodded again at Liam when he left.

"You could say that."

He slipped into silence for a moment, listening while Liam and Andy bantered their way through the gap. Finally after ten minutes of beer and craic he started to join in. They talked about nothing serious for almost an hour while Craig listened as Liam and Andy recalled the outrageous exploits they'd got up to during The Troubles to let off steam.

"Do you mind that time we hung the Chief Constable's bed out the window by its legs after the Rugby match? He was looking for it for hours."

He gave a loud guffaw.

"I'm not as old as you Liam, but I heard about it during training, hey. Plenty of people had done it before but never to the Chief. Did he ever find out who it was?"

Liam shook his head slowly. "Suspected, but never charged."

They entered the restaurant and started of a dinner of jokes and drinks, until finally after two hours they retired to Craig's room for a debrief of the day's work. By eleven o'clock they all knew the plan for the next day.

"Andy. Annette and Jake McLean, our new sergeant, will help you and Liam with any interviews you need. The big ones and anything that uniform can't do. They're keen to get involved, so call Annette when you have them arranged and they'll go to whichever station is closest to the interviewee."

"That's grand. We should get through them in no time at that rate."

"Aye. Andy's taking James O'Carolan tomorrow morning and I've the eye witness, Mrs Farrelly, and the Eakin girl."

"I've a call with MI5 at ten in the morning then I'm all yours until five. Whoever you want me to interview just say."

"MI5? You really think the spooks will tell you the time of day?"

"Yes, I think they will. It's not every day a senior officer's child gets killed. It terrible that Lissy matters to them more than anyone else's daughter, but if it gets us our killer I'll work with whatever I can get."

He paused then restarted, waiting for Liam to make a crack. "Can you let Jake go at five tomorrow please, Andy. Mulvenna's having an exhibition of his paintings in Belfast and Jake's coming along with me."

"Art lover is he? I knew that from his floppy hair. I bet he has a black polo-neck in his cupboard just dying to be worn."

Craig laughed despite himself. "Hardly. He wrote part of his degree about the reform of terrorists and Mulvenna was one of his case studies. He knows a lot about him and I'd like his help."

He glanced at the clock, it was nearly midnight. He stood, signalling he was heading for bed and grinned at the other men, feeling much better than he had five hours before.

"I'm not your Dad so raid your mini-bars and stay up as late as you like. But there'll be no sympathy for hangovers tomorrow morning, that's all I'm going to say."

***

Tuesday. 9.30 a.m.

Breakfast came and went in a flurry of moans about sore heads, and phone calls arranging interviews. By nine-thirty Craig was on his way to the station. Jim O'Neill showed him into a small board room, with a screen at one end and a conference-call spider sitting in the centre of the table. He'd expected the call to be audio alone so he was surprised when at ten o'clock exactly the screen flickered into life and the faint image of a man appeared. For a moment he thought that an outline was all he was going to get, like in cold-war spy movies, then a cheerful round face smiled out at him and motioned him to hit the speakerphone. Craig was impressed. They didn't have this in the C.C.U., something that he'd rectify soon.

"Hello, Superintendent Craig. Peter Guthrie here. Good morning."

"Good morning Mr Guthrie. Thanks for agreeing to this call; I know this was Roger Lowry's case. Are you up to speed on it?"

Guthrie grinned and nodded, wobbling the ample fat around his neck. He wasn't like any spook Craig had ever met. They always looked thin and pale, as if they'd spent too many years hiding in darkened rooms. Maybe today's terrorists did their business in restaurants instead.

"Ah ha, I can tell what you're thinking, Craig. That man looks too healthy to be a spy."

Craig laughed. "You've got it in one."

"Yes well, I'm mostly Whitehall based." He patted his ample stomach. "Most of my spying is done in gentlemen's clubs."

They both laughed then Guthrie turned over a page of the

file in front of him and nodded.

"Declan Wasson, mmm…"

"Nasty bit of work by everything I've heard."

Guthrie nodded while he read. "Yes. I can see nothing here to contradict you. OK, I'll tell you what I can, although even my file has whole paragraphs redacted. Wasson approached the police in 1975 offering his services as a C.I. It was purely financial on his part, no altruism involved."

"Is that normal?"

"No, not really. To be fair, most of the people who offered to inform on the IRA or loyalist paramilitaries back then were doing it because they wanted the bloodshed to end." He gazed at Craig solemnly. "And a lot of them lost their lives when they were found out. It was a thankless task, informing. Yes, they got a small amount of money, but for the risks they took… Well, let's just say there were a lot of brave people around who weren't wearing uniforms back then, and we wouldn't have peace now without them."

Craig was surprised. He'd never heard an MI5 officer sound so sympathetic about The Troubles and he said so.

"Ah well, yes. You're right. Some of my colleagues were a bit jaded, as you'd expect after thirty years of listening to the same old guff. But we know there were some brave people amongst the chaff like Wasson. Pity they'll never be recognised."

Recognition would mean exposure and even now, fifteen years after The Troubles had ended, there were people who would reward informants with death.

"Anyway, Declan Wasson. Petty thief, ABH, domestic battery; all in all a real charmer. But he was well known in west Belfast circles. He grew up there and drank with all of them. IRA of all sorts; Officials, Provos, Real IRA, the 'I can't believe it's not butter, IRA.' His contacts were invaluable to us and he gave us a lot of good leads. Saved quite a few lives through the years, not that that mattered to him. As long as he got his fifty quid a week he was happy."

Craig let out a low whistle. Fifty pounds in the seventies was worth around three hundred now. It was a fortune back then and it must have been noticed.

"How come the IRA didn't twig if he was flashing all that money about?"

Guthrie shook his head, smiling. "He only got ten pounds of it in cash. The rest went into a bank account. We'd lost C.I.s before when they'd flashed too much money around. Anyway, because Wasson was so well positioned he was a valuable asset."

Craig cut in. "And that meant you covered his ass on other things." He paused and Guthrie saw the look of disgust on his face. He knew what was coming next. "You let Wasson rape and kill women, to keep him as a C.I."

Guthrie sighed and closed the file, staring at Craig. Craig stared back and for a moment nothing was said. Then Guthrie spoke again, his cultured tones reverberating around the room.

"It was a dirty business, there's no question about that, but you have to understand something, Superintendent Craig. Back then we were fighting a war and information was sometimes all we had. Wasson didn't get off scot-free. Each time he was suspected of a rape some of our men took him away and beat him to a pulp, to warn him to stop. Sometimes we let him go as far as a trial, to scare the living daylights out of him, but we had to let him off at the last minute. He'd have been no use to us locked up in Crumlin Road Jail."

"Your tactics didn't work. He wasn't scared enough to stop."

He shook his head sadly. "No, they didn't. You're right. It happened and it happened far too often, but it was a strategic decision, taken right at the top. There was nothing MI5 on the ground could have done except shoot him, and then we'd have lost his information."

"And Veronica Jarvis? Was her murder covered up by a strategic decision too?"

Guthrie re-opened the file and flicked to the middle then he ran his finger silently down a page. He read for a moment then looked at Craig, swallowing hard.

"Wasson confessed to his handler that he'd killed her and asked for help covering it up. His handler refused so Wasson appealed higher up and they sanctioned it."

"Why frame John Mulvenna?"

Guthrie said nothing and stared out of the screen. His face contorted, as if he was struggling with a decision. Finally he leaned forward confidingly.

"I didn't tell you this and if it comes out then I'll deny it. Do you understand?"

Craig gave a terse nod.

"We didn't."

Craig was confused. "You didn't what? Frame Mulvenna?"

"Yes. We didn't frame John Mulvenna. He'd been out of the front line for two years, off in America pressing the flesh. There were others much higher on the list of who we wanted off the streets in 1983."

"So who did frame him?"

"I can't give you their name, but I can tell you that it was a local decision. *Very* local."

He closed the file and straightened up, preparing to end the call. When he spoke again there was no mistaking the sincerity in his voice.

"I've no sympathy for Mulvenna, Superintendent, but I hope you get the person who framed him, I really do. For all sorts of reasons, of which Lissy Trainor is only the latest one."

"Can you give me something, anything, to point me in the right direction? Please."

Guthrie nodded. "An English expression then. What goes around comes around, Mr Craig. Goodbye."

The screen darkened and the line went dead, leaving Craig staring into space, knowing that he'd been right from the start. What goes around comes around. He knew the expression well. Revenge.

Lissy Trainor's death was revenge for Mulvenna being

framed, but revenge by whom? Not Mulvenna that was for sure. Who else had a score to even over Ronni Jarvis' death? He was thinking on the right path but it wasn't going to lead him where he thought.

Chapter Sixteen

P.C. Ian Flood pushed back his cap and stared along the promenade, shielding his eyes from the late autumn sun. He'd only interviewed six shopkeepers so far, and his reception had ranged from 'do you think I've nothing better to do than stand here and watch who comes and goes?' through to 'I've a business to run' and 'would you like a cup of tea, constable?' from the lady running the tourist shop.

He'd been so tired asking the same questions by then that he'd taken her up on the offer, and spent ten minutes drinking tea and eating cake while she turned every man in Portstewart into a possible suspect for the crime. He'd smiled as she'd delved into particular detail about the man in the bookshop three doors down; saying he never spoke to the rest of them and had a shifty look. If looking shifty was all it took to be a criminal then half of his mates would be locked up in the nick.

He laughed then pulled his cap back down and turned towards the south end of the parade of shops, plastering on a smile and ignoring his aching feet. He couldn't imagine the Chief Constable ever pounding the beat like this, but he supposed he must have done, back when there were horses and carts. He laughed again more loudly and a young woman walking past shot him a shy smile, putting a fresh spring into his step. He pushed open the door of the butcher's shop with renewed energy and got ready to ask his questions again.

***

Andy was waiting in the interview room when they showed in James O'Carolan. He stood up, extending his hand to shake. After a few seconds pause O'Carolan took it suspiciously, as if it was some sort of trick. Suddenly Andy thought of something.

"Excuse me for one minute, Mr O'Carolan."

He walked into the corridor looking quickly up and down then lifted the wall phone to the front desk.

"Is Superintendent Craig still here?"

"Yes, sir. He was on a video call. It ended ten minutes ago but his car's still outside."

"Could you find him and ask him to join me in interview room two. I've someone he might like to meet."

He re-entered the room and poured water into two paper cups then he took the seat across from O'Carolan and scrutinised him. He was in his early thirties; thirty-three to be precise. They knew he'd graduated from Queens with first in Physics and IT, now he was climbing the greasy pole. Judging by his air of confidence he was doing well. A discrete Armani symbol on his jeans said he was doing better than that.

Andy scanned his face while O'Carolan scanned his in return. He was dark-haired and handsome in an open, healthy way. No matinee idol, but Andy couldn't imagine him being short of dates. It was hard to picture him as the bereaved six-year-old standing by the grave in Bronagh O'Carolan's funeral photograph. He'd stood there solemnly holding his little sister's hand, while their father had sobbed and buried his face in the blanket covering the baby in his arms. It was a pitiful image and hard to reconcile with the confident man opposite. Maybe he had nothing to do with Lissy Trainor's death but he fitted the description of the man Jenna Farrelly had seen her with on the promenade, and he'd written threatening letters to her Mum.

They sat in silence waiting for Craig until O'Carolan broke the vacuum.

"What is it you want from me, Chief Inspector? "

"I'll get to that in a moment, Mr O'Carolan. I'm just waiting for my colleague Superintendent Craig to join us."

At that moment the door opened and Craig entered. He shook hands with O'Carolan then pulled a chair from the wall and sat at an angle at the table's end, waiting for Andy to start.

Andy nodded towards the tape recorder and O'Carolan shrugged his assent. He switched it on and started speaking.

"This is an informal interview on Tuesday the 5th of November at eleven-ten a.m., with Mr James O'Carolan of Mountsandel Road, Coleraine. Also present are Superintendent Marc Craig and D.C.I. Andy White. Mr O'Carolan has refused council or companion. Could you confirm that for the tape please, Mr O'Carolan."

"Confirmed."

Andy reached into his briefcase and removed the typed letters spreading them out. O'Carolan didn't blink and Craig already thought they were dealing with an innocent man. An arrogant one, but an innocent one nonetheless.

"Do you know what these are, Mr O'Carolan?"

"Let's cut through the bullshit. These are letters I wrote to Assistant Chief Constable Melanie Trainor blaming her for my mother's death and asking her to re-open the Mulvenna case."

"And threatening her."

O'Carolan shrugged. "That's one interpretation. I prefer to think of it as making my feelings known."

"And those feelings were that you wished her harm."

O'Carolan shook his head. "Not physically. I wanted her to suffer the way we had suffered from my mother's loss, emotionally. Nowhere in those letters did I ever threaten her with physical harm."

"And yet her only daughter is now dead."

He nodded assent. "Yes, she is. And I'm very sad for the girl, but not for her mother. Trainor had the power to put Declan Wasson away in 1983 and if she had done he would never have been free to rape my mother one year later."

He leaned forward angrily and Craig could see Andy tense.

He didn't move, sure that O'Carolan wouldn't raise a hand.

"My mother was a gentle, kind woman, D.C.I. White. A writer and musician, a sensitive soul, and what Wasson did to her completely destroyed her. He may not have put a bullet in her but he killed her just the same, and that bitch Melanie Trainor is responsible."

He stared at Craig and then back at Andy, his eyes full of hate. "So am I sorry that she's lost her daughter? No. Not one iota. Now she'll have to feel what we've felt for years, knowing every day that she could have prevented our mother's death."

He banged his fist hard on the desk then leaned into the tape, saying sarcastically. "For the benefit of the tape than was James O'Carolan banging his fucking fist against the table. OK?"

He lounged back in his chair and Andy leaned forward until he was nearly in his face.

"Did you kill Lissy Trainor?"

O'Carolan half-laughed then shook his head. "No, but I'll tell you this, I bet she was killed because of something her mother did to someone. I bet some other poor bastard out there had their life ruined by your precious ACC Trainor and they took their revenge."

"Where were you on Sunday the 27th of October?"

O'Carolan stared at them both in turn then he reached into his jacket and pulled out a phone, starting to read out some numbers and names. After each one he listed the time he'd been with them from the 27th to that day. He finished and then stood to go. "You know where you can find me."

Andy stood to stop him but Craig shook his head, waving O'Carolan on. When he'd left the room Andy pressed off the tape and paced around the room muttering, until he managed to irritate Craig.

"Sit down, Andy. You're giving me a sore head."

Andy sat down but kept muttering until Craig stilled him with a look. Then he raked his hand through his hair and laughed.

"Well, that has to rank up there with one of the most interesting interviews I've ever heard."

"Controlling bastard."

"As opposed to us? Because of course we're never controlling, are we?" He laughed and Andy joined in. "He's lying about something, for sure. But he didn't do it, Andy, you do know that?"

"How can you be so certain?"

"Telling he was lying was easy. He didn't blink but his feet were tapping like Fred Astaire's when you asked him about Sunday the 27th. He saw Lissy then, I'm sure of it. But he doesn't feel right for murder. Too 'in your face'. Our man's going to be a much darker proposition. Quieter."

Andy nodded grudgingly. "There's not much love around for the ACC, is there?"

Instead of answering him Craig thought for a moment. "I wonder if that lack of love extends as far as her husband?"

"The MLA? Do you think he'd talk to us?"

"Perhaps not in front of the ACC, but if I kept it informal, maybe..." He stood up quickly, formulating a plan.

"Andy, you keep going with the rape victims' families and work with Liam on the Jarvis' kids. You've got Annette and Jake to help you, don't forget. I'm going to see what I can get from Hugh Trainor.

***

"Davy, have you finished looking at Lucia's phone dump and e-mails yet? I've been through them, but most of them seem to be work, or her boyfriend, Richard."

Davy looked up from his computer and peered across the office at Annette. She was slightly blurred. He was getting short-sighted from staring at his screens. It was only a matter of time before he would need glasses. He didn't mind, he quite liked the way they looked. Maggie wore a blue Elvis Costello pair and they made her look sexy. Maybe they would do the same for him.

He grabbed the papers he'd set on one side and loped across to Annette's desk.

"There's nothing in her e-mails, Annette. Her pervy texts we already know about, but it's a dead end there as w...well. Unless a pay-as-you-go phone is registered there's no way of tracing who it belongs to, beyond hoping they bought it using a credit card."

"Did they?"

He shook his head. "No s...such luck. It was bought in Royal Avenue with cash, six weeks ago."

"Any chance the store kept its CCTV?"

He shook his head again. "Already asked. It's a small shop. They wipe their tapes after a week."

Annette frowned. Whoever 'Watching U' was, he was lucky. Or clever. He might have shopped in a small store deliberately, guessing they would try to keep costs down by re-using their tapes. Davy was still talking.

"Her incoming calls check out, except for the number I've highlighted." He pointed at a number starting in 001212. It was an unusual prefix and Annette said so.

"That's because the call's been routed through another line. In New York"

"How does that work?"

Davy pulled over a chair and sat down, glad to have a chance to display his expertise. Computer forensics were a special interest of his and he wanted to specialise in them someday. He pulled up a website offering virtual phone numbers.

"For a fee you can arrange for your calls to be routed as if they're coming from anywhere in the w...world. It's basically a marketing ploy. Companies use it to make it look like they have offices in lots of cities. But there's nothing to stop someone doing it to hide who they are."

"Ah, I understand." She didn't of course, she didn't have a clue, but it never did to show your ignorance to someone half your age. "Is it deliberate, do you think?"

Davy nodded and his silky hair fell across his face, reminding Annette of an elegant horse. She reached over and pushed it back so she could see his face and he smiled at the maternal gesture.

"For s…sure. This could be our mystery man."

"So they were calling her at home as well as using the pay-as-you-go?"

"The pay-as-you-go was for the texts, because you can't hide a number on a text and you can't re-route them. But they obviously needed more cover for phone-calls. What did Lucia say they'd said?"

"Nothing. She said they'd texted and written letters but she didn't say anything about any calls. I don't think she knows."

He gave her a knowing look. "Or she's too embarrassed to tell you about them because of what they said. Leave it with me. I'll dig deeper and see if we can trace them back."

"Great, thanks. I'll see if I can get her to tell me what they said." She made a note to call Lucia then turned back to their murder case. "How are you getting on with Lissy Trainor's stuff?"

"W…well, there's nothing much on her phone so far but I've only done the day she disappeared. It's just the usual girly stuff. She texted reams to her friends about the boyfriend, Conor Ryland. It's mostly nice, although there were a few recent exchanges where she wasn't quite so fond of him. Everything stopped at eight o'clock on Sunday night. The last thing was a text to Ryland saying she'd meet him in thirty minutes, then nothing."

"Ryland told Liam about their recent spat, something to do with a holiday in Turkey that she wasn't on. "

"Lads' trip?"

She nodded. "Something like that, but they'd made it up

when he got back."

"Is Liam s…sure?"

"Positive. He says the boy's clean and I would trust his gut over gossip any day. What does that leave us with?"

"I'm halfway through listening to her phone messages then I'll start on her e-mails."

She glanced at him and her question was clear. He nodded.

"By close of play today, I s…swear."

Just then Nicky's phone rang. It was Craig. They had a brief conversation then she transferred him to Annette, signing that she wanted him back before he cut off.

"Hello, sir. How are things up North?"

"Cold. How are you getting on?"

She updated him on Lissy's last text, then read out the alibi's of some of Andy's suspect list.

"Good, then if you're on top of everything, how do you fancy a road trip to Parliament Buildings this afternoon?"

"To meet Hugh Trainor?"

"Exactly. If he's there today. Has Nicky managed to check on his whereabouts yet? "

Annette smiled. Nicky had had thirty seconds since he'd asked her. She put Craig on hold and went over to her desk. Nicky was on the phone and jotting something on a pad. She said. "Yes, yes, thank you" to someone at the other end then hung up.

She ripped off the page triumphantly and handed it to Annette, then glanced at her watch. "Tell him, one hundred seconds. He'll know what it means."

Annette went back and picked-up Craig's call, giving him the message. He laughed loudly.

"What's that about?"

"Nicky and I are running a competition. Every time I give her a query to deal with she times it. When she gets the answer in under ninety seconds I'll pay for her and Gary to have an evening out."

"All that motivation training worked then. OK, I've got a time for the meeting with Hugh Trainor. Three-fifty this afternoon, at his office in Parliament Buildings. Shall I meet you there?"

Craig glanced at his watch remembering the cryptic clue Guthrie had given him that morning, What comes around … If Lissy had died because of something Melanie Trainor had done then maybe the answer to her death was closer to home than he thought. They needed to ask the questions and if they couldn't ask them of the ACC her husband was the next best thing.

"OK, I'll meet you in the reception of Parliament Buildings at three-thirty. And can you tell Jake that Jonno Mulvenna's exhibition starts at seven o'clock. I'm going home to change and I'll meet him there."

"Art exhibition, eh? I'll tell him to wear a beret and a serious look."

***

"You're sure the man you saw was talking to Elizabeth Trainor?"

Jenna Farrelly screwed up her face in exasperation and repeated what she'd said.

"Yes, for the twentieth time. He was talking to the girl from the photo in the police appeal. She was wearing a pair of black shiny leggings and a woollen top, like some sort of fancy jumper." She waved her hand in the air indicating some invisible fashion. "And before you ask me to describe it, it was just pink and fancy, like young people wear."

Liam stared down at the woman. She was what most people would have called motherly. Small and round with short brown hair, she wore a long skirt and a woollen cardigan that she'd cinched in firmly with a belt. On her feet was a pair of short suede boots that he was sure he'd seen Danni wear a couple years back. That was the extent of his sartorial knowledge but her fashion sense seemed to support her vagueness about Lissy's clothes.

He nodded; satisfied that she was a solid witness. She'd come forward saying that she'd seen Lissy talking to a tall dark man at around seven-forty-five on the Sunday night. Nothing he'd asked her in the past thirty minutes had shaken her from her version of events. He pulled over a line drawing of the promenade and tapped it.

"Can you show me where you saw them on this diagram?"

She reached into her handbag and pulled out a metal case so small that Liam watched with surprise as the contents unfolded into a pair of glasses that she perched on her nose. He'd need some of those soon. Danni was giving him hell about sitting so close to the TV. That would only leave Craig and Davy spec-less on the squad. Maybe he'd get a trendy pair, after all, sex symbols like George Clooney wore them and they still managed to pull the birds. And he still had all his own hair and teeth. He wasn't looking for anyone but Danni but he still liked to attract the odd look.

He pulled his attention back to the map and saw Jenna Farrelly's finger firmly planted on one spot. She was indicating the street outside a small specialist bookshop with a determined look in her eye.

"There, that's where I saw them. They sat down on the bench opposite."

Liam peered at the map and made a note. "You're sure? No doubt at all?"

She shook her head firmly as he marked the map with pencil then folded it up, then she sipped at her coffee and slid a biscuit from the plate, Liam did the same with two of them and they chomped in silence for a moment. He drained his cup in a final gulp and restarted.

"OK, we know you saw Lissy and we know exactly where. Now, can you tell me any more about the man?"

She thought for a moment then closed her eyes for so long

that he thought she'd fallen asleep. Just when he was about to tap her arm she opened them and waved a finger at his pen, instructing him to 'take this down.'

"He was tall, not tall tall like you, but then very few people are I suppose. But he was tall."

"How tall would you say?"

She thought for a moment then nodded, finding a comparator. "Like that young constable who showed me in."

Liam strode to the door and opened it, yelling at the top of his voice. "P.C. Flood, come down here a minute, will you."

At the sound of Liam's booming voice, Ian Flood dropped the file in his hand and rushed into the room. Liam moved him to the middle of the floor and stood beside him. They watched as Jenna Farrelly walked around them for a moment then nodded once. Liam turned to the confused P.C.

"How tall are you son?"

Flood opened his mouth but Liam interrupted him before he could speak. "No, scrap that. Go and measure yourself against the chart in custody and come back."

He nodded him out then turned back to his guest.

"OK, how old would you say?"

Jenna Farrelly scrutinised Liam's face then shrugged. "Forty-seven or forty-eight?"

He looked at her in confusion then realised that she meant him. He was slightly put out that she'd got his age in one.

"Not me, the man you saw with Elizabeth Trainor!"

"Oh, him." She screwed up her face in thought. "Between thirty and thirty five, I'd say. Towards the lower end probably, but he definitely wasn't less than thirty."

"Hair colour, eye colour?"

Flood re-entered and Liam motioned him to stand still while she thought.

"His hair was very dark, almost but not quite black. Not that coal black you see sometimes, but nearly. His eyes were brown."

"You're sure? Because that hair can go with blue or brown

eyes."

She shook her head firmly. "Definitely brown, I noticed because he was wearing a rust coloured jumper that made them flash, you know, when he turned round, and I like brown eyes. They were dark chocolaty brown. And he had a tan."

Liam smiled. She was a gem. It wasn't often you got a witness that would stick to their guns but this one would, he was sure of it. He noticed her glance at the clock behind him and hurried up.

"Constable Flood, how tall are you?"

"Six-feet-one, sir. According to the chart."

Liam turned towards Jenna Farrelly and raised an eyebrow questioningly. She nodded firmly and he waved the P.C. out.

"You say you saw them clearly?"

"Absolutely. They were chatting for at least five minutes."

"Not arguing?"

"No. Talking. As if they knew each other."

"Did the girl seem upset, or afraid in any way?"

She shook her head firmly. "Not at all. But they didn't look like a couple either. There wasn't that affection between them."

"Which direction did they walk in when they turned away?"

"She walked east towards Strand Road and he walked west. He was throwing his car keys in the air, as if he was going to get it. I'm afraid I don't remember any more than that. I was rushing to meet my daughter."

"Did you notice anything about the keys? A logo maybe?"

She shook her head. "Sorry. Nothing stood out."

That only left one thing to do.

"If I put you with a sketch artist, do you think you could tell them what he looked like?"

She looked at her watch pointedly and Liam leaped in. "It'll only take thirty minutes and we'll get you a car home afterwards."

She gazed at him unflinchingly. "A plain one? I don't want my husband seeing me pull up in a police car. He'd have a coronary."

"Whatever colour you want."

She nodded, satisfied, and lifted her cup of tea, draining it. Liam called the sketch artist and then Andy, to find out how tall James O'Carolan was.

Chapter Seventeen

The man watched the police doing their door-to-door enquiries, not knowing whether to be angry or amused. Amused at their ineptitude, or angry that despite him practically leading them to the person responsible for their crime they still couldn't see.

He lifted the heavy boxes one by one, stacking them outside the shop's back door then thought about what he should do next. The police were making some progress, but it was all so bloody slow. Short of writing the culprit's name in the sand he'd left them every possible clue. He thought for a moment about burying Lissy in the sand and shuddered. He wasn't a killer and he'd liked the girl, but how else could he bring home his message, when he knew he'd be blocked by officialdom at every turn?

He pushed the stack of boxes aggressively into a corner and threw another box on top, painstakingly straightening them so they didn't fall. He stared at the column thoughtfully for a moment then realised what he had to do. The little things in life were easy to control, now he had to think big.

***

By the time Craig got to Stormont Estate and parked, Annette was already inside Parliament Buildings, sitting in the high-ceilinged marble reception under the curious eyes of the guards. It wasn't every day they had police there looking for one of their MLAs. They normally visited them at their home or constituency, in an attempt to be more discrete. Craig showed his I.D. and signed in, reading their questioning looks and their minds. He allowed himself a small smile, remembering Annette's last trip there with Liam the year before. It had resulted in a Minister being taken away to 'assist with their enquiries'. The guards' stares said they wondered if they were about to have a repeat show.

They waited patiently for fifteen minutes until finally at four o'clock a young aide came to take them upstairs. They followed her through the maze of corridors until they reached Hugh Trainor's room. The aide knocked quietly then melted away, leaving them outside a heavy oak door, waiting to be summoned. They didn't have long to wait.

Hugh Trainor opened the door and smiled warmly, waving them into a small, bright room. The first thing Craig noticed was how relaxed it felt; the second that there were pictures of Lissy dotted everywhere, but none of his wife.

Trainor waved them to two armchairs beside a coffee table, in a corner that caught the sun. Craig glanced at him quickly, taking in every detail. He was a small man, as small as Annette, and handsome. His face was round and healthy, as if he lived an outdoor life. His hands were large and well-worn, matching. If it wasn't for his bespoke suit and polite urban accent, he could have been a fisherman or a labourer. Craig warmed to him immediately. There was something decent about him.

"Tea or Coffee, Superintendent? Inspector?"

He took their orders and phoned them through, then joined them, sitting on a low settee. Craig spoke first.

"Thank you for seeing us as such short notice, Mr Trainor."

Hugh Trainor shook his head. "I should have come to see you, Superintendent. But to be honest I've been putting it off. It's…hard. You understand?"

Craig nodded and saw more in the man's eyes than grief. A glance from Annette said she'd seen it as well. It was guilt, but guilt for what? They got their answer quickly. The aide brought in the refreshments then disappeared. After a moment of pouring and small talk Trainor started talking without a prompt.

"I loved my daughter, Superintendent, I always will. She was everything good in my life and we were very, very close."

Craig saw Annette's look. It said 'how close?' He understood her suspicion, especially now they'd seen Trainor's guilt, but for some reason it didn't fit. Trainor hadn't abused his daughter, that wasn't what his guilt was about. He was still talking.

"Lissy…" His voice broke as he said her name and he sipped at his tea, struggling to hold back the tears. "She… she didn't get on with her mother. Oh, Melanie loved her, but she couldn't show it. She's a rigid woman." He glanced at them with a wry smile. "I'm sure you've noticed that."

Craig conceded the point with a smile of his own.

"She was very strict with Lissy growing up, Superintendent, overly strict in my opinion. She treated her like one of her men instead of a little girl. Lissy was a gentle child, she needed something more than Melanie could give, so it's no secret that she was closer to me."

He put down his cup. "Melanie has basically forbidden me to speak to you without her present, but I want to. There are things that I need to say and she would try to stop me." He swallowed and guilt filled his eyes again. What he said next surprised Annette but it didn't surprise Craig at all. He'd worked it out the minute they'd entered and he'd seen that there were no photos of his wife.

"I've been having an affair for three years, Superintendent, and as soon as decently possible I'm going to divorce my wife."

Annette gasped and Craig shot her a warning look. An affair; that was the guilt they'd seen. Hugh Trainor had a reputation for being a warm family man, posing for happy pictures in the press. But people were rarely what their public persona portrayed.

"I've been unhappy for years, since soon after we got married. Melanie didn't marry me for love and I knew that. She married me for my power and my family's money. But I wanted her anyway and I hoped that her love would grow." He shook his head. "Sadly that wasn't to be."

He stared at them defiantly. "Don't get me wrong, I don't regret my affair. The lady in question is wonderful and I love her and want to make her my wife, but...."

Craig interjected gently. "You wanted your marriage to work and even when it didn't you stayed for Lissy's sake."

Trainor nodded. "Yes, and I would still be staying if she was alive. But now..."

He fell silent and Craig let him think. After a long moment he restarted.

"I'm going to be very blunt now and you'll be shocked. But it's essential that you know, because I think that it may have led to my daughter being killed. Melanie has been promiscuous most of her adult life. Extremely promiscuous. She targeted several men I knew before we got together in 1988, when she was thirty. She slept with them all and they helped her rise in her career."

Annette's eyes widened but she kept herself in check.

"I knew she had a reputation when I met her but I thought marriage would make her change. Sadly it didn't. Most of the men involved were very powerful. Titled, moneyed, in positions of authority. Men who could be useful to her in some way. But...she's determined to be the first female Chief Constable and nothing will get in the way of that, so she would never divorce me. A scandal might wreck her precious plans. When I threatened to divorce her once, many years ago, she said she would stop me seeing Lissy. That was when I stopped loving her. The idea that she could trade her own child's happiness to achieve her ambition was too much."

He shrugged. "We've been leading separate lives ever since and as long as I didn't rock the boat, Melanie was happy. But recently I needed something more, a relationship. That's when I saw Darlene."

Craig interjected. "We'll need to speak to her."

Trainor nodded. "Of course." He handed him a card. "She's expecting your call. She'll confirm everything that I've said."

Craig slipped the card inside his jacket, continuing. "You've said you believe your wife's behaviour may have led to your daughter's death? May I ask you how?"

Trainor leaned back on the settee and sighed. "The first thing you need to understand is that Melanie will deny everything. Every affair, every argument, she'll admit to none of what I've said. The Belfast Chronicle got hold of something last year and she slapped an injunction on them to keep it under wraps. That's how far she'll go to look whiter than white. Secondly, watch your back. If you bring any of this out she'll try to ruin your career, and she can do it, believe me. Her lovers are well placed in the police, judiciary and the political world, both here and in London. She will destroy you if she can. My advice would be to go straight to your Chief Constable and tell him everything I've said, to protect yourselves. I know Sean Flanagan and he's as straight as they come, so he'll keep you right. But be aware, Melanie has several senior officers here who are loyal to her. In fact she's slept with most of them to make sure they are. And she helps their careers, so they'll circle the wagons when this all comes out. She'll threaten you with legal suits, the works."

Annette interjected. "Aren't you concerned for your own career, sir? She could try to smear you in return."

Trainor smiled then shook his head slowly. "No, Inspector. For several reasons. My family is very powerful. We have a cohort of lawyers on retainer, so any damage that Melanie could do to me personally would be minimal. Lissy's death has hurt me more than anything that she could ever do. And also, because I don't care anymore. I've been an MLA for thirty years and I'm fifty-five now. My career in politics is nearing an end."

Craig interrupted. "I've heard your name mentioned as a possible First Minister."

Trainor laughed. "Yes, I've heard that rumour too but I'm not holding my breath. Look, I hope I've done some good in politics and I'll continue to be involved with charity work, but I've been miserable for long enough. I want to enjoy life now. Let Melanie do her worst." He smiled at Annette warmly. "But thank you for your concern."

Craig smiled then gave Trainor a look that said he hadn't finished his earlier point.

"Ah yes, how could my wife's behaviour have led to my daughter's death? Well, it's very simple Superintendent. She's used a lot of men over the years and they weren't all happy when it ended. In some cases there were also very unhappy wives who'd found out."

"But why not target the ACC herself? Why kill your daughter? She was just a vulnerable girl."

Trainor's eyes filled with tears again and his gaze moved to a picture of his daughter. She was around ten in it, half turned towards the photographer with a wide smile identical to her Dad's. She looked happy and he could imagine Hugh Trainor taking the snap, saying 'Lissy, pet, look at Daddy.' Craig was sorry his words had made Trainor sad but his next words said he'd been right to ask. Hugh Trainor almost spat out his reply.

"Because Melanie was always well guarded, she made certain of that. Nothing was more important to her than her own security. And I was usually here, hard to get at. But Lissy was just a girl, out there in the world living a normal life. She was easy to reach, Superintendent. She was vulnerable. Through the years when things were really bad I begged Melanie to arrange a protection officer for her, but she refused. She said it would look like favouritism. Bloody favouritism, for her own child."

He voice rose angrily. "Her job made Lissy a target for anyone who wanted revenge and then she stood back and let it happen."

Suddenly he dropped his head and started sobbing. Annette's eyes filled with sympathy as she watched his shoulders heave.

Craig stood, motioning her to join him, then he laid his hand briefly on Hugh Trainor's shoulder and they let themselves out. What Trainor had said had expanded their suspect pool hugely; now it was his job to narrow it down.

***

Andy wanted to chuck the files against the wall in frustration. He visualised their spines splitting open and sheets of paper floating to the floor. The image wasn't half as satisfying as the reality would have been but it would have to do. He topped up his coffee and stared again at the list of Wasson's victims that Davy had sent through. There were five names on it. Bronagh O'Carolan was one of them. Of the other four cases, all between fifty and seventy-five years old, two were dead and one was in a home suffering from dementia. That only left one woman he could even talk to.

He stared at the names, wondering how to approach the relatives of women who were long gone, or whether he even should. Was if fair to open their wounds again? And where did you stop? Were only their immediate families suspects in Lissy's death, or was it wider than that? Did he rule out the husbands and grown-up children and stop there, or go digging deeper, into friends, work colleagues and more? He sighed in frustration. It was never-ending.

He took a deep draft of his coffee, tutting in irritation as a drop fell onto his shirt, then he dabbed it off and started again. Turning over the pages of each file in turn and making a longer list.

***

The man watched them tiredly as they went door-to-door, street to street, carrying photographs of the girl hopefully, as if people ever registered any face but their own. They had to do it of course, even if it was only to be seen to. To tick a box and strike out the name of another perfect stranger who'd never known Lissy Trainor at all. Unlike him. He felt as if he'd known her all her life.

He'd watched her play in her garden with her expensive toys since she was small and then at her posh private school. Every fashion fad and techy trend was satisfied as soon as she mentioned the word. And yet…he couldn't say that she'd been spoiled. He'd seen her stop by each tramp in the street, giving them coins and even notes. He'd watched her volunteer with charities and carry shopping for the lady next door. Saint Lissy, destined for great things, a better human being than both her parents, especially her Mum. Mum, Mother, Mammy, Mom, he spat the words out at the thought of Melanie Trainor wearing them like a badge.

Her trophy child, the girl who'd had the misfortune to be born to such a bitch. He nodded in acknowledgement. It hadn't been Lissy's fault, or her choice, she was just an accident of birth like they all were. He had to give her credit for one thing. As soon as she could think clearly she'd chosen her Dad. Just in little ways at first, like who she ran to when she cried; always him. Then when she was older, always standing closer to him in photos and in life, except when the bitch trotted her out for photo-ops for her career. Here is my perfect daughter and my perfect life, aren't I wonderful, see what I did. Melanie Trainor, the perfect working mother. I work so hard, I have so much, now give me more. Make me the boss, make me supreme.

He watched the police for a moment longer then turned away from the window and rearranged some shelves, counting in his head how long they had left. Lissy had died on Tuesday and they'd found her two days after that. Now it was Tuesday again. He would give them one more day to work out the answer then he would dispense justice himself.

***

Craig rang the doorbell and took a step back, scanning the small terraced house for signs of life. The faint shift of an upstairs blind tannoyed them loud and clear. Annette stared down the quiet street off Belfast's Lisburn Road and then back at the modest two-storied home. It had a small Victorian garden at the front, divided by the narrow, pebbled path they stood on now. Algerian Iris and winter roses in violet, pink and white bloomed and wound themselves together as they embraced. Ivy rambled around a blue front door set against the snowy pebble-dash of the house's wall. It was all so quaint and pretty that it made her smile. She couldn't wait to see the woman who lived inside.

They heard light footsteps descend the stairs then stop behind the door. Annette could imagine their owner drawing breath for the conversation she knew was coming and she composed her face in a smile. Her sympathy was with Darlene McKenna, whether she was a mistress or not. The door pulled back and Annette's smile widened even more.

Darlene McKenna stood in front them, small and thin, with a wary look that said she was waiting to be chastised. She was in her forties somewhere, pale and fair-haired, with an ethereal quality that made Annette wonder if she would blow away. When her voice came it was almost frail, with a tremor behind her words. "Please come in, Superintendent."

Craig extended his hand and she stared at it blankly for a moment then slipped her own inside, grasping it as if he was a life belt. Her eyes flicked to Annette and Annette saw that they were beautiful; large and soft, a pure, clear grey. "Inspector."

She waved them forward into a small, warm room furnished in a floral Victorian style, as if it was an extension of the garden. Annette gazed around her and smiled. This was no predatory woman, no mistress that every married woman who'd been betrayed like her could hate. This was a quiet soul, a woman from a different time, trying to cope with modern life the only way that she knew how, by retreat. She was no killer, not unless snipping a rose was murder.

Craig imagined Hugh Trainor here and understood why. Darlene McKenna was the complete opposite of the ACC. Gentleness versus aggression, light versus shade, and he knew who Hugh Trainor thought was the light.

"You were expecting us, Ms McKenna?"

She nodded. "Hugh said you would come. I'm happy to answer anything you ask. But first…" She turned towards a ready prepared tray of tea and poured them each a cup. Annette smiled at the delicate china and imagined Liam sitting there, drinking from dainty cups in a grown-up doll's house. Darlene McKenna took a deep breath and started to speak unprompted.

"I know what you must think of me, Superintendent."

Craig went to contradict her but she'd already moved on.

"And I'll answer all your questions as honestly as I can, but first I must tell you what Lissy told me."

"You met her?"

She smiled and her face lit up. "Many times. I was Hugh's personal assistant for twenty years. I watched her growing up."

Realisation dawned on Craig. Hugh Trainor hadn't said that he'd met his mistress recently; he said he'd *'seen'* her. He'd known Darlene McKenna for years but it was only when his love for Melanie Trainor had died that he'd noticed his P.A. and fallen in love.

McKenna's face darkened as she talked on. "Lissy used to talk to me when she was waiting for her father and a few weeks ago she told me that she'd been contacted by some man. He'd asked to meet her, saying that they had something important to discuss."

Craig interrupted. "Did she ever mention his name?"

She shook her head. "I'm sorry, no. Just that he was young and it was something to do with the law." She smiled proudly, as if Lissy had been her child. "She was a very clever girl. She'd finished her law degree and was due to start a Masters in Human Rights Law next term."

She screwed up her face trying to remember. "I think she said it was something to do with her dissertation topic." She shook her head. "I'm sorry, but that's all I know. But I do know that she didn't tell her parents about the man. She said her mother wouldn't be pleased if she met him."

At that she stopped talking, everything she'd needed to say done. Craig turned the discussion to other questions and asked her everything he had to ask, until the conversation wound down to what a lovely summer they'd had and how it had affected the flowers. Finally they stood and left the haven Darlene McKenna had created, knowing that she would have someone to share it with very soon. As they left Craig struck another name off their suspect list.

***

Liam had had enough of the girl's antics and he thumped the table hard, making her jump up and back all at once. He watched the movement, wondering how she'd achieved it and whether she could manage a repeat. He was tempted to thump again and find out, but Ian Flood's face said it would be gratuitous and he'd already achieved the effect he desired.

Liam squinted hard across the table and watched as Mary-Ann Eakin crumbled. Her face flushed and her bottom lip wobbled, threatening tears, but he was stone. Her friend had been murdered and she'd tried to wreak havoc in her romantic life before she had. He had no sympathy for her.

"Now Ms Eakin, tell me again about the events in the week before Lissy's death, particularly about her relationship with her boyfriend Conor Ryland."

He stressed the word 'boyfriend' knowing that it would hurt. The girl in front of him might only be twenty-two but her type was as old as time. He remembered them from when he and Danni were courting. Lovely word 'courting', it was a pity people didn't use it more often, replacing it with unromantic expressions like 'doing a line' or worse. Paying court seemed like a much finer thing.

There had been girls back then like Mary-Ann Eakin, girls who'd tried to split them up. Some who were jealous because they wanted him for themselves, not that he fooled himself that there were many of those. But at least he'd understood the logic there; it was the ones like the girl in front of him that he couldn't comprehend. Girls who didn't want the man, but wanted to keep their friend all to themselves, or for them to be single and miserable too. That was Mary-Ann Eakin and millions like her, before and since.

Her next words confirmed he was right. "He wasn't her boyfriend, he was a two-timing scumbag who went off to Turkey with his mates on a shag-fest. Lissy deserved better."

"And you decided that she was going to get it?"

She sniffed and folded her arms across her chest. Liam noticed a tattooed bracelet around her wrist and shuddered. He couldn't abide tattoos on anyone but even less on girls. He added it to the mental list of things his toddler daughter was never going to do and turned his thoughts back to their guest.

"Did you decide Conor Ryland wasn't good enough for her?"

She nodded defiantly. "Yes. I knew he was playing around. He'd been the same since school. I was going to get the evidence and show her."

A penny dropped in the back of Liam's brain and he smirked. "Dump you, did he? When you were at school?"

Her instant blush told him he'd got it in one.

"It hurts, doesn't it? And you wanted to make sure you hurt him back."

He suddenly leaned across the desk, watching as she jerked back in her chair. "Were you following Conor Ryland to try to catch him out?"

She nodded in reflex then tried to take it back, but it was too late, he'd seen it.

"Was that a yes?"

"Yes." It was a grudging sound but still a yes.

"Were you following him on Sunday evening? And did you see him on the pier at Portrush Harbour at eight o'clock?"

She nodded reluctantly, each movement of her head as small as it could be.

"Say it please, for the tape."

Her round face twisted up defiantly and Liam leaned forward again, squinting her into answering.

"OK, then. Yes. Yes I saw him."

"How long did you watch him for?"

"Two hours."

Liam leaned back and stared at her until her face flushed again, then he shook his head slowly, tutting with each move. Finally he sighed and stood, looming over her for a moment.

"Constable Flood here will take your statement, because he's a nice sympathetic young copper and I've seen your type of jealous, malicious behaviour too often before. It's boring, and so are you, young lady. Take my advice. Go and get yourself a life and stop trying to hijack one that belongs to someone else."

***

Craig showered and shaved and changed into his best suit, one that befitted an evening spent perusing art. He cast a quick look around his apartment then grabbed a bag packed with spare clothes for Portstewart and headed for the door. It was six p.m. and he was meeting Jake at the gallery at half-eight, plenty of time to meet John for dinner and forget he was a policeman for a few hours.

That was the problem with working away from home, every waking hour became about the case. When you were at home at least you could get on with your life; meet your mates, have a drink, even tidy the house if you had nothing better to do. Hotel life was different, all cable TV and different food and over-heated rooms where you never quite slept.

He knew he shouldn't complain. Lots of the guys he'd done law with at Queens were corporate lawyers now, flying all over the world and crossing every time-zone between San Francisco and Sydney. They buggered up their body clocks and spent their days baring their teeth at bigger sharks than themselves. Airports, flights, hotels and meetings; travelling for business was just one long commute no matter how glamorous they tried to make it sound.

He gunned the Audi down the Stranmillis Road and headed towards town, parking on Oxford Street outside John's latest restaurant find, 'OX'. The décor was elegant and after a meal of Antrim beef and red wine they were well relaxed, and John thought it was safe to raise the thorny subject that Natalie had been bending his ear about all week. He swallowed hard, knowing his friend wasn't the most forthcoming of men where relationships were concerned. Craig could see it coming and gave him a resigned look, raising a hand.

"OK, so this is where you meander around the subject of my relationship with Julia, until you finally ask the question Natalie has briefed you to ask. Where it is going?"

John's mouth dropped open then he nodded in relief. "How did you know?"

Craig stared at him sceptically. "Because it's been written all over your face for the past twenty minutes. Don't ever join MI5, John, you'd make a terrible spy." He sipped at his beer and shrugged. "The honest answer is, I don't know."

He outlined the conversations they'd each had with Sean Flanagan and Terry Harrison's attempt to block Julia's transfer at every turn, ending with.

"If Harrison wants to be a complete bastard there's nothing we can do to stop him. There are no vacancies for Inspectors in Belfast, or nearby. Even if he advertises Julia's post and manages to recruit to it, that still leaves her with nowhere to go."

"Can't she take a sabbatical and move down anyway, until an opening comes up here? She could live with you."

Craig shook his head tiredly and John could see they'd already had the discussion many times. Craig fell quiet for a moment and when he spoke again his warm voice held defeat.

"I've told her a millions times, John. I earn enough for both of us. But she won't listen. It's about her independence, which I respect, but not when it's wrecking our relationship."

John scrutinised his empty wineglass for a moment, thinking, then he filled it up and hesitantly started again.

"Let's just say, just for the sake of an argument, that you were in her shoes. Would you do what you're asking her to do, Marc?"

Craig stared at him coolly then shook his head. "Julia's asked me the same question, and to be honest, no, I wouldn't. Even if my parents weren't here and getting older, which is one of the main reasons I moved back, I couldn't move to live with her in Limavady and be a kept man."

John gawped at him and then laughed. "Wow! Kept man! Way-to-go for the un-reconstructed male. Macho Craig or what."

Craig stared at him sceptically. "Be honest, John. Would you? Really? If Natalie worked in Limavady and said 'I can earn enough for both of us, come and live with me and I'll take care of you until you can get a job here', which may be never?"

John went to say yes, then thought for a moment and slowly shook his head. He was as bad a case as Craig. They said nothing for a moment then Craig spoke.

"Are we chauvinists?"

John nodded. "Yes, maybe. I don't know. Is it personal pride that won't let us live off someone else? Or is it specifically women we won't live off, in which case it's chauvinism?" He rubbed his forehead as if it would help him make more sense, then he smiled. "I'll tell you what, I'm bloody glad Julia and Natalie can't hear this conversation, or we'd be dead men."

Craig laughed, then he thought of something that made him laugh again. "We could ask advice from an enlightened man."

"Do you know any?"

"How about Liam?"

They laughed so hard that the man at the next table smiled. His wife joined in. If she'd known what they were laughing about she might not done.

***

P.C. Aine Bailey scratched her neck and frowned. That made twenty-two passers-by she'd stopped and not one of them had known Lissy Trainor, never mind seen her on the Sunday before she'd died. She glanced at her watch and then at her list again. All the shopkeepers had been interviewed twice, except the man at the bookshop and he was nowhere to be found. Some of them had said they'd known Lissy since she was little and everyone was sad, but no-one could remember her calling in that day. No-one except Jenna Farrelly remembered her speaking to anyone at all.

She shrugged and put her notebook in her pocket, taking of her hat and pushing back her hair. Time for a cup of tea. As she entered the nearest coffee shop and radioed Ian Flood to join her there, she didn't see the tall man watching her from the beach. She stirred her tea and bit into a donut, staring through the window into space, when thirty degrees further to her right would have brought her eye to eye with her prey. The man smiled to himself and shook his head, renewing his earlier vow. The cops had one more day to expose the guilty one, then he would give them a clue they really wouldn't like.

***

Craig lifted a brochure at the door of the gallery and flicked through it while he waited for Jake. He didn't have long to wait. Five minutes later a sports car pulled up and he watched through the plate-glass window as Jake kissed the driver's cheek and climbed out. Craig smiled as the car drove away. Gone were the days when gay police officers didn't tell. He was glad of it; he didn't care about anyone's private life, just as long as they did their job.

He nodded as Jake approached and made up his mind to ask his advice about one of his theories on the case.

"Hello, sir." He glanced quickly at his watch. "Am I late?"

Craig shook his head. "I was early. Do you mind if I ask? Was that your partner?"

Jake blushed. "Yes. That's Aaron. We've been together since Uni."

"You should have introduced us. Next time?"

Jake nodded, pleased, then Craig turned the discussion back to the case. He outlined a number of theories, including his theory that Jonno Mulvenna had been framed by someone he'd been having a relationship with in 1983, female or male.

"Would you like me to tell you if I think he's gay, sir?"

Craig shook his head. "I can probably tell myself, thanks, although your opinion would be a help. But it's more the whole theory that he was framed by an ex-partner I'd welcome your opinion on. You studied his case at Uni, so if you could try to engage him in conversation and suss him out about the Jarvis case and his road to Damascus conversion to being artist, it would be useful. He doesn't know you, so he might give you something in casual conversation."

Jake nodded. "Happy to try. I'd better not stand too long with you then or he'll know I'm a cop."

Craig waved him on and turned back to his brochure. He flicked through the pages thoughtfully, wandering over to look at the paintings. They were good. Oils mostly, urban landscapes and people from afar. There were some charcoal portraits as well and one in particular caught his eye. It was a nude of a young woman in her twenties. She had long hair and wide apart eyes and she reminded him of someone he'd met. Before he could put a name to her his attention was caught by a woman standing in front of a landscape to his left. He gazed at the curve of her back and her long blonde hair then caught his breath. It was Camille! He looked more closely and shook his head. It wasn't Camille. Camille was thousands of miles away in L.A. but he knew the woman, he was sure he did.

As he watched her she strolled towards a bronze in the corner and her profile came into view. Her nose was small and fine and her skin was a natural honeyed tan. Then she turned and he glimpsed her eyes, they were large and petrol blue, set wide apart in a heart-shaped face. It was Katy Stevens. She was a doctor who worked with Natalie at St Mary's Healthcare Trust and he'd interviewed her in April about a case.

As the thoughts raced through Craig's mind the woman turned towards the door and caught him staring. She stared back and they stood facing each other across the gallery. For a moment neither of them made a move. Craig had been attracted to her when they'd met but he'd been seeing Julia so he'd done nothing about it. Before he knew it he was standing in front of her. She spoke first.

"D.C.I. Craig. How nice to see you."

She extended her hand and he took it, remembering its delicacy from before, but what his memories hadn't done justice to were her eyes. They were huge and tilted slightly upwards and their colour was dark and light blue all at once. He could feel himself blushing and he saw she was starting to do the same. He stopped a passing waiter and lifted them both a glass of wine while he scrambled for the right words.

"Are you an art lover, Dr Stevens?"

She smiled. "Katy. And yes, I am." She waved towards the wall. "Some of these are very good, aren't they?"

"To be honest I've just arrived and …"

Realisation hit her and her blush deepened. He was on a case. She turned to go and Craig's hand was on her arm to stop her before he realised what he'd done.

"Please don't leave on my account. I'd love us to have a chat."

She blushed again and he saw that he'd embarrassed her. Natalie had hinted that she'd found him attractive but he'd never really noticed it before. It pleased him and made him feel guilty as well. He thought of Julia and dropped his hand then indulged himself by convincing himself they could be friends.

"Look…I'm working tonight, but perhaps we could have coffee as friends sometime? It would be nice to catch up outside a station." He saw the doubt on her face and leapt in. "That's if you'd like to. Please don't feel pressured."

She smiled and he knew he was rambling. She nodded and pulled out her card, placing it in his hand, then she glanced quickly at her watch and said she had somewhere else to be. Craig was still staring at the card when Jake sidled up, tapping the side of his nose like he was a police snout.

"I've just been speaking to Mulvenna about his paintings. They aren't half bad. I really like number twenty-three, Inishowen lighthouse In Donegal, but it's out of my price range I'm afraid. Anyway, I mentioned I'd studied his case at Uni and he was happy to chat. Said he learned how to paint when he was inside and it was the best thing that had ever happened to him. Mind you, he was quick to deny he killed her."

Craig shot him a questioning look.

"Veronica Jarvis, he said he didn't do it straight out, but that he deserved to be locked up anyway for the things he actually had done." He sniffed, in an imitation of a seasoned detective. Craig was just waiting for him to say 'stone me' or 'it's a fair cop' then they'd be back in an episode of Minder.

What Jake said next surprised him. "He's definitely not gay, sir. I'm pretty good at spotting it and he's not. If he was framed by a lover my money's on some woman or a husband who found out. Or he could just have been framed by anyone who wanted him sent down."

He could have been but Craig was sure he hadn't. He nodded Jake to keep looking around and turned his attention back to the walls, returning to the charcoal of the girl and racking his brains. He'd definitely seen her before, but where? He couldn't think so he folded back the page in the brochure and wandered over to Mulvenna to ask.

He was leaning against a white wall, a vision in all black. With his nape length greying hair and swarthy skin he looked just like an artist. No-one would have imagined that the hands that painted such beautiful things had killed sixteen men. Mulvenna stood upright and smiled as he approached and Craig gestured towards the crowd. "Good turn-out."

Mulvenna nodded, obviously uncomfortable with the praise. "Half of them are friends and half are people who want to meet a murderer in the flesh. I'm under no illusions."

Craig scrutinised his face, grudgingly admiring his honesty. Mulvenna wasn't like a lot of killers, trying to deny it had ever happened, or even letting it fade into the past. It was there front and centre in everything he did. If there was such a thing as an honest criminal he thought he'd just met him. He was growing more convinced by the day that Mulvenna had had nothing to do with Lissy Trainor's death.

"Can I ask you about one of your charcoal sketches?"

Mulvenna shrugged as if he didn't care if anyone bought them, just as long as they were seen.

"Which one?"

Craig pointed to his brochure's folded page.

"Ah, number twenty-one. 'Girl being herself'. Do you like it?"

"Yes, very much. Who is she?"

"The clue's in the title. She's a girl who lied to everyone about everything and kept herself hidden. Except I got her to show me her true face the odd time. One of those times I sketched her."

"Does she have a name? I think I've seen her before."

Mulvenna shook his head. "She has a name but it's not for sale. Neither is the charcoal I'm afraid. Sentimental value." He turned away and then glanced back. "I hope you find your murderer, Superintendent Craig, but you won't find anything here."

As he walked away Craig beckoned Jake over and indicated the sketch.

"Find out about that sketch for me Jake. Date, where it was drawn, etc." He walked towards it and peered into the subject's eyes, racking his brains for a moment for her identity. He gave up and added another task to Jake's list.

"Most importantly, I want you to find out who she is."

Chapter Eighteen

Wednesday 8 a.m.

Craig stirred his espresso and waved Liam on with his update. Jenna Farrelly had seen Lissy talking to a man on the parade at seven-forty-five on Sunday night. Four days later she was found dead. It wasn't a stretch to think the man might be connected, so ruling him out or in had to be high on their list of priorities. Darlene McKenna had mentioned a man as well. Perhaps they were one and the same.

Liam pushed the last corner of toast into his mouth and washed it down with a gulp of tea, then he started.

"Aye well, Mrs Farrelly was adamant Lissy was talking to a tall, dark-haired man."

"Were they arguing or just talking?"

Liam shook his head. "Talking animatedly was all she'd say. But he didn't touch her, if that's what you mean. There was no sign of that."

"Any joy identifying him on the door-to-doors?"

Liam shook his head again. "Nothing. My witness is coming in to do a sketch this morning then we'll send the uniforms out again with it."

"And you're certain Conor Ryland's not an option?"

"Definitely not. He was seen by six people up at the pier, just where he said he'd been. He waited there for Lissy from eight to after ten o'clock. Mary-Ann Eakin confirmed it."

Craig raised a hand to halt him. "We'll come back to her in a minute." He turned to Andy. His shirt was just as blue as it always was, but its creases and his pallor were saying that hotel living and his hatred of ironing were taking their toll. He was picking half-heartedly at a piece of potato bread, until the sight of it flopping off his fork persuaded him it was time to give up.

"Tell Liam about your interview."

Andy looked up surprised, unsure whether the question was directed at him. Liam clarified with a wave of his fork. "James O'Carolan. What did he say?"

Andy nodded then placed down his knife and fork, leaving Liam to give his potato bread a new home.

"Aye, well. O'Carolan was a thran one and no mistake. Fits the physical description your witness gave. Around thirty, tall with dark hair. But then that fits a quarter of the men in Northern Ireland, hey." He looked pointedly at Craig. "Including Marc."

Craig smiled. "Except for the thirty part."

Tall with dark hair was a ubiquitous description for a witness, and worse than useless depending on which country you lived in. Andy was still talking.

"He was angry, hey. Hates the ACC."

"It's a challenge finding someone who likes her."

"That seems to be a common theme in this case and it gives us lots of people with motive." Craig raked a hand through his thick hair. "If every suspect has a motive to get back at her then we'll just have to narrow it down on means and opportunity."

"Aye well, anyway. O'Carolan's done well for himself. Works for one the new IT firms based in Derry and seems to spend half his salary on clothes, hey. There's nothing to tie him to Lissy's death except his hatred for the ACC. He blames her on Wasson not being put away in '83 and being free to attack his Mum in '84. He didn't try to hide his hatred."

Craig shook his head. "My feeling's that he's not our man."

Andy shot him a look that said he wasn't so sure. Craig leaned forward urgently.

"What did you find out?"

"His alibi doesn't check out."

"For Lissy's time of death?"

Andy nodded. "And for the whole time period from last weekend, hey."

Liam swallowed his potato bread. "Where did he say he was?"

"In London, at a conference for work."

"And?"

"He was booked on it all right. Anyone who'd been easily fooled would have seen the booking and that would have been that."

Craig smiled. "But not Davy."

Davy's love of detection gave an added dimension to his work.

"What did he find?"

"Aye well, Davy didn't stop at the conference and flight bookings, hey. He checked the passenger manifest and saw that O'Carolan never got on board the plane."

Craig nodded. "Get O'Carolan back in and find out where he was. I want every minute accounted for from Sunday to Thursday. And get his picture to Liam's witness, it might save her having to do a sketch if she can I.D. him from that. Anything else, Andy?"

"Just the rest of the rape cases, but we're narrowing those down and ruling out the victims and their relatives slowly, hey. I reckon we'll know what's what by the end of the day."

Craig turned to Liam. He ran quickly through the witness statement then got to his meeting with Mary-Ann Eakin, Lissy's so-called friend. He let out a low whistle that made the other breakfast diners stare.

"She's a nasty wee girl and that's basically the nicest thing I could say about her."

He shrugged as he said it. There were nasty people everywhere so why should young women be immune? Except that underneath his bluff exterior Liam had a romantic streak.

He put women on a pedestal as being much nicer than men and he was always disappointed when the fair sex proved him wrong.

Craig urged him on. "And?"

Liam sniffed. "Aye well, she wanted either Conor Ryland or Lissy and I haven't managed to work out which one yet."

Andy leaned forward, curious. "She's a lesbian, hey?"

Liam shot him a look that said 'don't rush me' and sat back. "Did I say that?"

He turned to Craig. "Did I?"

Craig waved him on.

"She's jealous, either of Lissy's family and money, or of her relationship with Ryland. Either because she wanted him or she wanted Lissy, and I've no way of knowing which it is." He sniffed. "The answer's irrelevant anyway. Either motive could have led to her killing Lissy. Either she wanted her out of the way to be with Ryland, or Lissy rejected her so she killed her because of that."

Craig held up a hand halting Liam's monologue. "How big is Mary-Ann Eakin?"

Liam thought for a moment. "Five-two, five-three tops." He nodded. "Aye, I see your point. Lissy was five-feet-two but even if she'd been smaller Eakin wouldn't have had the strength to strangle her and bury her on the beach."

"And didn't Ryland say she was stalking him all Sunday night?"

"Aye well, yes she was. But that was only until Ryland went home. She could have had a male accomplice who helped her kidnap Lissy. Lissy was killed using Morphine and Eakin could have injected it then her accomplice could have done the strangulation and burial bits." His pleased expression soon changed to one of defeat. "Nah… that just brings us back to the man the witness saw and why would he have needed to work with Eakin at all?"

Mary-Ann Eakin was just a jealous little girl. Unless they

182

found some connection between her and the man on the parade they were clutching at straws.

"Check her alibi, rattle her cage loudly and then forget her, Liam. But she's to stay in the North. We might need to speak to her again."

Craig gave them brief updates on Hugh Trainor and his visit to the gallery the night before, conveniently forgetting to mention his encounter with Katy Stevens.

"Jake's checking who the girl in the charcoal was." He banged his forehead with the heel of his hand, as if he was trying to knock a memory loose. "I'm certain I've seen her face before but I can't remember where."

"How about Davy running it through facial recognition software, hey? We used that once in a drugs case and it gave us the perp."

"That's not a bad idea, Andy. I'll call Jake when we've finished here."

Liam interjected. "What's your feeling about Hugh Trainor, boss? Any chance he killed his daughter?"

"Not a hope." Craig gave a wry look. "If it had been the ACC that died, then maybe. There's certainly no love lost between husband and wife. But not Lissy. He adored her, no question. She was the reason he stayed in the marriage."

"That and his political career."

Craig shook his head firmly. "No. If anyone wanted him to stay for their career it was Melanie Trainor. He says that she's basically slept with every powerful man in Northern Ireland, anyone who she thinks might help her career."

He took a sip of cold espresso then called over the waiter to bring them fresh drinks before carrying on. He stared hard at Liam, challenging him to make a joke of what he said next.

"Hugh Trainor's been having an affair for three years and he's going to leave the ACC now and marry the lady in question."

Liam opened his mouth to make a crack then saw Craig's look and closed it again, drawing an imaginary zip across his mouth.

"We met the mistress, Darlene McKenna. She was nice, used to be Trainor's P.A. She confirmed that Trainor was with her the whole weekend that Lissy was killed."

"That'll not help his guilty conscience, hey."

"You're right."

"The ACC must have noticed that he was gone, boss."

Craig shook his head. "No, she didn't. They lead separate lives. She was at an Association of Chief Police Officers meeting in Manchester and stayed on for the weekend."

Liam sniffed. "Probably found someone more powerful to sleep with than Northern Ireland could produce."

"Liam…"

Liam sniffed again and fell silent, but Craig could read his thoughts. Melanie Trainor's exemplary reputation in the force wasn't going to last long now.

"Trainor said that the ACC was very strict with Lissy so she turned to him. They were very close." He saw Andy sit forward to interrupt and shook his head. "Not in a bad way, before you go there, Andy. He seemed like a genuinely loving Dad."

He added the phrase that he knew would persuade them both that Hugh Trainor hadn't abused his daughter. "Annette agreed."

Liam nodded and Andy did as well. Annette's people sense was excellent. If she thought Hugh Trainor was kosher then he probably was. Craig smiled and threw in another line.

"She liked the mistress as well."

"Phew, now that's saying something. Danni thinks all mistresses should be shot at dawn."

They fell silent for a moment while Craig and Liam remembered Annette's ordeal five months before when her husband had had an affair. Andy looked at them questioningly but Craig quickly moved on and summed up.

"OK. Liam, chase your witness and show her O'Carolan's photo. If she can't I.D. him then get her to do the sketch. We'll get it out there today with uniform and see if it rings any bells. Set up an I.D. parade for tomorrow, with O'Carolan in the mix please, and get his photo to Davy to see if it fits any open cases."

"Do you think it will, boss?"

"Nope, but it will cross the 'T's. And call O'Carolan on his false alibi please."

He turned to Andy.

"Sorry, Andy, but it looks like another day of you and Davy sorting through the rape victims and their relatives to see what comes up. Can you get in Lissy's next door neighbour as well, please? What was her name?"

"Billy Munroe."

"Fine. Get her in and see if she has anything of use to say. Liam, I need to talk to Melanie Trainor again and get Davy and Jake onto Mulvenna's sketch of the girl, then I'm meeting the Chief again to brief him."

Liam gulped down his tea and raised the question that no-one wanted to ask.

"What if Declan Wasson's victims and their families are a dead end, boss? Who does that leave us with? The Jarvis boys? O'Carolan maybe? Do we throw Mulvenna into the mix for Lissy? He's fit and strong enough to have done it."

"Mulvenna's not our man, although he fits the description of the man your witness saw as well. He has a solid alibi for the time of Lissy's death."

"Can we break it?"

Craig thought for a moment and then shrugged. "Have a try, but it seems pretty tight. He was on a residential painting course up in Ballymena."

"That's only thirty miles from the beach, he could have slipped back, boss."

Craig nodded thoughtfully. "Yes he could... and it wouldn't have taken him long to get there on his motorbike. OK, check it again but my money's on it not being him." He stood up to leave, glancing at his watch. "We all know what we're doing, so let's get on with it."

***

Melanie Trainor knelt by the fireplace in her living room and glanced over her shoulder towards the door, shaking her head ruefully at her nerves. There was no-one coming in. No cleaner; she'd been yesterday and wouldn't be back until Friday. No husband; he was doing important things with important people somewhere else. Hugh was always somewhere else nowadays. It was her fault, she knew that. If she hadn't made it so obvious that she was marrying him for her career and his money then perhaps they would have had a different life together, and a different story to tell now. Except that she had married him for those reasons and by the time she'd realised she really loved him the words were too difficult to say.

She shook her head, remembering the endless dinners she'd spent networking while he'd watched other couples on the dance-floor. Glancing hopefully at her, only to be met with a shake of her head, and then her back, as she turned towards someone who mattered more. She deserved his apathy now and she knew he would leave her soon. The glue that had held them together was gone.

She stared at the elegant parquet floor and saw a five-year-old Lissy running across it with her feet bound in polishing rags. Squealing as she ran into a slide and Hugh caught her at the other end. Then an older and more elegant version, tiptoeing quickly past as she'd sat at the large table and worked, her papers spread out much further than her study desk. She saw herself, barely glancing up and never smiling as her teenage daughter slipped past.

A harsh sob caught in her throat, catching her unawares. She felt the tears on her cheeks and brushed them away ruthlessly. They were no use to her now. Lissy was gone and no amount of crying would bring her back. But she had to know why. Why had they chosen her to kill, and why bury her in the sand where Ronni Jarvis had been found? Were the deaths linked somehow, or was it just some random sadist who thought he'd copy the case to make them chase their tails?

At least Lissy hadn't suffered, not in the way Ronni Jarvis had. She'd just gone to sleep and woken up somewhere else. But why would a sadist give her a peaceful death? Why wouldn't he have raped and beaten her like before? What pleasure had he got from killing her only child?

As she asked herself the questions she lifted the fireside rug and slid back the section of floor beneath it, exposing a small safe. She turned the tumblers quickly to reveal what was inside. Her first answer came as she lifted out a small book. The pleasure hadn't been in hurting Lissy but in hurting her. Leaving her to live with the knowledge that her child had been killed because of something she'd done. Right or wrong, it didn't matter. Something she'd done in the past had taken her beautiful daughter's life.

Guilt overwhelmed her and the tears flowed again as she stared through their fog at the book in her hand. She turned it over, half-smiling at the lurid purple fabric that bound its back. Had people ever really liked that shade? She ran her fingers slowly down the lettering on the front, thinking back to the day she'd bought it in the stationery shop. She smiled as she remembered the twenty-five-year-old she'd been. Already an Inspector and aiming for the top, determined that nothing would get in her way.

But she'd been something else as well then. She'd been in love. Day-dreaming, butterfly-generating love, for the only time in her life. And he'd loved her back. But it had to be their secret, there were too many obstacles to overcome. Romeo and Juliet, but their obstacles were bigger than family on either side.

She turned the small book over and traced the numbers 1983. Her diary. What was written inside was so dangerous that it could have destroyed her life. It had destroyed her lover's. So why hadn't she just thrown it on the fire? Why keep it to be found by accident someday? As she turned the first page a photograph fell out and she had her answer. The lovers, smiling and kissing in front of her eyes. Her heart soared and she knew why she hadn't disposed of it. She was still in love.

***

Craig smiled at the speakerphone as the words came thick and fast from the other end of the line. After a moment of listening he spoke.

"Slow down, Davy. I'm older than you. It takes me a while to process things."

Davy smiled, knowing that Craig was probably already ten paces ahead, but he took a deep breath and started again.

"Lissy Trainor's e-mails."

"OK, what about them?"

"They w…were written in code."

Craig frowned to himself. What had he uncovered? Had the girl been some sort of spy?

"What do you mean code, Davy? Do you mean a kid's code or a real encryption?"

"Half-way between the two. She was s…smart. Beyond smart, she was a genius. Most of her e-mails are normal, just the usual 'what are you doing at the weekend, who's dating who?' stuff that you'd expect from a girl her age."

Craig laughed. Davy sounded like Old Father Time when he was only a few years older than Lissy had been.

"But?"

"Exactly! But her e-mails to one contact were always written in a complex s…substitution code."

"Can you work it out?"

"Yes. She was good but not as good as me. I'll have it cracked by the end of the day."

Craig smiled at his confidence. In anyone else it would have been an arrogant boast but with Davy he knew that it was true. If he said end-of-the-day that meant he'd have cracked it by afternoon tea.

"Who was she writing to?"

"Ah, that's the other thing. It was someone called Commodus_1, but when I contacted the internet provider, they said the address was a front."

"Can they get behind it?"

"They're trying. But they said it was routed through about five servers, across different continents. W...whoever did this knows their stuff."

Craig paused, thinking. If they found out what the messages said then the I.D. of the sender might give itself away. A thought occurred to him.

"Commodus? Wasn't he a Roman Emperor? Is there some clue there?"

"What, apart from the fact he w...was a psychopath?"

Davy paused then restarted as realisation dawned. "You mean, does the choice of the name say something about the person who chose it? Probably not, except that he thinks he's important. Leave it w...with me. I'll call you back if I find something." He paused then remembered he had a message for Craig. "Sorry, boss. Before you go, Nicky says Dr Winter's looking for you."

The phone clicked off and Craig smiled to himself at Davy's confidence. Gone was the shy young graduate who'd first joined them. He was a core member of the team now, although if he was right about his urge to be a detective they might lose him soon. He shuddered at the thought and turned back to the pile of paper spread across the interview room desk. He was just re-reading Lissy's P.M report when the door opened with a bang. Liam strode in and grabbed a seat, sitting down with a smile on his face.

"Well now, guess what I've just heard?"

Craig took the bait. "What?"

"Three little words that made me as happy as hell."

"Don't tell me, Danni called to say she loves you."

Liam spluttered and waved the suggestion away but Craig could see him counting the words in his head.

"No. Try again."

Craig racked his brains for a moment then gave up and nodded him on.

"That's the man."

"What?"

"They're the three words. That's the man. My witness has only gone and I.D.ed the guy seen talking to Lissy Trainor on the Sunday evening!"

Craig leaned forward so quickly that Liam jerked backwards in shock.

"Who was it?"

His money was on someone other than James O'Carolan, but he was prepared to be proved wrong. The grin on Liam's face said he was preparing to string out the reveal, but the look on Craig's said that he'd better not.

"Jonno Mulvenna. I showed her his photo as part of an array and she picked him out. So much for his alibi. Ballymena painting course, my ass."

Craig shook his head and Liam's face fell. He would have loved it to be that easy but it was impossible. The witness had said the man was mid-thirties at most, Mulvenna was fifty-eight. He looked good but there was no way he could past for thirty, not even in a very dim light. The penny dropped on Craig quickly.

"You showed her the photo from Mulvenna's file, didn't you?"

Liam hesitated for a moment then looked at him like it was a trick question. "Aye... so what?"

"Your witness said the man was no older than thirty. Mulvenna was twenty-eight in that photo but he's fifty-eight now. And his alibi's solid as far as we know. You phoned Ballymena yourself. He was never away from the other painters for long enough to get to Portstewart and back. She I.D.ed Mulvenna because you showed her an old photograph."

Liam shook his head hard then, after a pause, he banged his fist on the desk. "Aw, shit. I knew it was too good to be true."

But the way Craig was nodding to himself said perhaps not. Craig stood up quickly and headed for the corridor, talking as he walked. Liam loped after him.

"Where are you going?"

"Is your witness still here?"

"Aye. She's having a cuppa in the canteen until a car comes to take her home."

Craig stopped and Liam could see his brain racing. "Cancel the car and ask her to come back into the interview room, but don't say why. I'll join you there in a minute."

Craig walked swiftly down the corridor and pushed at the fire-exit door. A minute later he was breathing in sea air. He gazed out at the Atlantic Ocean inhaling deeply. Docklands C.C.U. sat beside the river Lagan and he could see all the way to the Irish Sea when he stood outside, but the air here felt different. Cleaner somehow.

The Atlantic's waves were high and grey, crashing loudly against the sand as if they were angry with it. The sea wind blew hard against Craig's face, prickling it with rain and wafting the scent of seaweed and ozone up from the beach. The last of Lissy's crime-scene tape fluttered in the distance and a solitary police car sat alongside it keeping watch. There was nothing else but the sand and the waves to distract his thoughts. Craig stood there for a moment letting the view clear his head and tried to make sense of what he'd just heard.

It couldn't have been Mulvenna that Jenna Farrelly had seen but how many men looked *exactly* the same? So much so that she'd convinced Liam with her I.D.? There were a lot of tall, dark men in Northern Ireland but similarity wouldn't have made her quite that sure. That left them with one possibility. If it wasn't Jonno Mulvenna that she'd seen, it had to have been someone related to him.

He pulled out his phone and gave Davy the task of finding out, then stared at the sea for five more minutes until Davy called back. Craig nodded as he listened, then cut the call and re-entered the red-brick building. Jenna Farrelly was seated in the interview room with a bemused expression on her face. Craig extended his hand to shake and nodded Liam to sit at the table's end while he took up position opposite their guest. He knew that how he asked the next questions was important. He didn't want to sway her but he needed to raise the possibility that she was only half-correct.

"Mrs Farrelly, my name is Superintendent Marc Craig. I'm heading up the investigation into Elizabeth Trainor's death."

She shook her head sadly. "Terrible thing. She looked like a nice wee girl. I used to see her on the beach all the time."

"Yes, it was terrible. " He paused and lightened his tone. "Chief Inspector Cullen tells me that you often shop on the parade."

"Yes. The butcher's. Our Damon loves the sausages they make." She shot him a wry look. "But before you ask, I'm sure I saw the girl that Sunday. I know because it was my daughter's birthday and I was admiring the leggings she wore. Elsa wanted a pair so I asked her where she bought them."

Craig nodded. Good, she was a clear witness and hard to shift. That would help if it ever got to court. He framed his next question carefully, ignoring Liam's puzzled look.

"You said that Lissy was talking to a man that day?"

She folded her arms defiantly, as if daring him to challenge her. "Yes, she was."

"Would you mind describing him again for me?"

She sniffed and glanced at Liam, waiting for his nod. Then she started talking in a bored tone.

"As I told Mr Cullen, he was about six-feet-one tall, around thirty with very dark hair and brown eyes. He was good looking. Like that film star out of Pretty Woman. Whatever you call him."

"Richard Gere?"

She lifted her finger and pointed at Craig triumphantly. "The very one. Mr Cullen showed me a lot of photos and I picked him out."

"You're sure he wasn't going grey?"

She nodded emphatically. "He was dark. He wasn't old enough to be grey."

Craig nodded. Her description fitted Jonno Mulvenna except for three things. Jonno Mulvenna had blue eyes, very blue; he'd noticed them both times they'd met. But the man Jenna Farrelly had seen had brown. Mulvenna also had greying hair and although he was well-preserved he would never pass for thirty. She was describing someone who looked like Mulvenna had when he was young. Davy had checked and viewed every available photograph; there were no younger brothers, cousins, sons or nephews anywhere in the Mulvenna family that fitted the bill. That only left one explanation.

Craig stood and extended his hand again. "Thank you for that, Mrs Farrelly, and I believe you've given us an excellent sketch as well. If you wouldn't mind waiting here, Chief Inspector Cullen has a car arranged to take you home. Liam?"

He nodded Liam to follow and they walked to the end of the corridor in silence, then Liam turned to Craig with a questioning look on his face.

"You're sure it's not Mulvenna, boss?"

"Sorry to rain on your parade, Liam, but not unless he was wearing contact lenses and miraculously became thirty years younger. Mulvenna has blue eyes and greying hair and there's no way he'd pass for that age."

"If it's not Mulvenna then maybe he has a brother or a son?"

Craig shook his head. "I got Davy to check with the DVLA and passports. There are no males in Mulvenna's extended family that fit the bill."

Liam went to moan then he saw a smile in Craig's eyes that said they weren't dead yet. "What? You've thought of something, haven't you?"

Craig nodded but said nothing.

"You have to tell me, boss. Otherwise it's like..." He searched around for an abuse that compared. "Cruelty to animals."

Liam realised what he'd said at the same time Craig did and they laughed simultaneously.

"That ranks up there with your best. Nicky will love it."

Liam shrugged, knowing it would be back at the office before he was, but he wasn't letting go of his theme. "Come on, boss. Tell me what makes sense of Mrs Farrelly's sighting."

"I will, I promise you, but first I need to call John."

He turned on his heel and pushed through the fire-exit again for another phone call and more air, leaving Liam running through the last ten minutes in his head and coming up blank.

Chapter Nineteen

"You're sure, John?"

Craig gripped the phone excitedly and willed his friend to repeat his words.

"Positive. We found a hair under Lissy's nail and it didn't belong to her. I'll start the search once we've got the D.N.A.."

"Do me a favour, add Jonno Mulvenna to your check-list. I'll give him a call and clear it but I don't think he'll object to giving you a sample of D.N.A.."

John voice was shocked. "You really think he did it? But I thought his alibi held up."

"Yes, it did, and no, I don't think he did it, but I need you to compare his D.N.A. to the hair and tell me what you find."

John frowned in concentration. There was only one reason for doing that if he didn't think Mulvenna was their killer. He thought he was related to whoever was.

"Does Mulvenna have a son?"

Craig smiled to himself. He'd known it wouldn't take John long to work it out.

"Not as far as we know, but..."

"But how many men have sons they know nothing about."

"Exactly."

They fell silent for a moment, imagining how many unknown off-spring they both might have. John gulped, thinking of his misspent youth and the endless sperm donation sessions that had paid for his student beer. He continued briskly.

"Right. I'll do that. But what prompted this sudden change

of tack?"

"Liam's witness I.D.ed Mulvenna as the man she saw Lissy with on the Sunday night, only nearly thirty years younger and with brown eyes."

"So you thought, brown-eyed mother and Mulvenna's sperm. Good call. Have you told Liam yet?"

"In outline but I'll give him the detail once you tell me for sure. We'll keep on pursuing other leads in between."

"Leave it with me."

The phone clicked off then Craig thought of something else. He pushed open the fire-door and prepared to give uniform some more work.

***

It had been five days since Lucia had received the last creepy text message and four nights of folding herself into her teenage single bed, instead of stretching out on the king-sized divan that she shared with Richard when he was home. She glanced at the pink floral duvet cover that she'd once loved so much, then up at the 'Take That' poster emblazoned on the ceiling above and made up her mind. She was going home. Not here, the teenager from hell home, but her own grown-up retreat.

Lovely and all as her parents were, there was only so much opera a girl could stand first thing in the morning, especially when accompanied by her mother yelling up the stairs at her to 'come have the breakfast'. She felt as if she was in Groundhog Day with the date somewhere in the '90s, and she missed her quiet time, thinking and reading the papers over an espresso before she went to work.

She cast a last look around the bedroom and then prepared to go downstairs and give her folks the news, bracing herself for their sad looks. Their looks wouldn't be the main obstacle. After that she had to persuade Annette that it was a good idea. If she didn't do it properly then her big brother would get involved, and that, everyone could do without.

***

Craig smiled at the composite photo, pleased with the changes they'd made. Jonno Mulvenna's 1983 mug-shot stared up at him, minus the number beneath his chin and the height markings on the wall behind, but plus a pair of dark brown eyes instead of his own blue. The grey in his hair had been erased and its style had been modified to give it a more noughties cut. Craig remembered some of the seniors at school sporting the shoulder length mullet in Mulvenna's mug-shot and it hadn't been a good look even back then.

He placed the photo beside the sketch Jenna Farrelly had helped work up and gasped. They were identical. This was the man she'd seen. He nodded Ian Flood to run off one hundred copies and picked up the phone to give Liam a call. He was saved the bother by the sound of his booming voice outside in the corridor, telling some unfortunate newbie to 'let the tea stand next time'.

Craig yanked open the door and stuck his head out. "Liam, leave the lad alone and come in here and take a look."

Liam lumbered in, carrying a cup of tea so pale that at first Craig thought it was milk. He could see his point. He lifted a copy of the photo and waved it in front of Liam's face.

"What do you think?"

Liam sniffed and stared at it as if it was some sort of trick. "What do you mean, what do I think? It's Jonno Mulvenna when he was young. You showed me it before."

Craig laughed and shook his head. "No, it's not. Well, not the one I showed you anyway." He tapped the paper. "Look. His eyes and hair have been changed, to bring it up to date and we've given him brown eyes."

Liam stared again and then nodded, humouring Craig. "Aye, aye. Very good boss. Blue Peter would be proud of you." He paused for a moment and then stuck his neck out even further. "What's the point?"

Craig raised his eyes to heaven. Liam was probably right. The changes were subtle, maybe too much so. Or just maybe it might jog the memory of some passer-by who'd seen Lissy Trainor's conversation on the promenade.

"We're going to circulate it to the troops and get a few put up around town and along the sea front. Someone might recognise him, whoever he is. I'm going to run it past her friends and family and see if it rings any bells."

Liam nodded then looked at his tea and abandoned it as a lost cause. Craig wondered if he'd listened to anything he'd just said, then he smiled. He'd heard all right, and if he asked him to repeat it, it would come back rote. Liam lifted a pile of photocopies and went off to distribute them, while Craig braced himself for the call he had to make and the interview that couldn't be delayed any more.

***

The man watched as they stapled a picture of his face to the lamppost across the street, and handed them out randomly to passers-by. Even from where he stood he could see that it was a match, they'd even got his hair almost right. How the hell had they done that without knowing who he was? But they didn't know or they'd have been knocking on his door right now, instead of wasting paper littering the sea front.

He searched around urgently for the things he needed to take, his eyes lighting on the knife and rope that formed the next part of his plan. The Morphine he'd used for Lissy had been kind and eased her way; he wouldn't use it kindly this time. He shook the image of Lissy's clawing hands quickly from his mind. He'd got the dose slightly too low, but she hadn't clawed for long before she'd finally closed her eyes, to open them again in the next world.

He snorted to himself. The next world. It was funny how the concept stuck even though he'd abandoned religion long before. A lost cause, that was what his parents had said, as if Christian Charity could suddenly run out. Only so much Christianity to go around and he'd used up his lot. Finally his father had got tired of trying to show him the light with the back of his hand and thrown him onto the streets at fourteen. Fifty pounds, the address of a hostel and the last set of clothes he'd been bought; so much for God's abundant love. He hadn't stayed away for long. How could he? After all, his parents had made him what he was.

He stared into the mirror at one side of the shop. It curved and distorted everything it saw, its only purpose to observe the aisles for thieves. His face stared back, pulled out of shape by the refracting glass. It made him look odd and plain, except that he wasn't plain, he was handsome. Handsome enough to catch the young church curate's eye and make him come calling at night on school trips. He'd whispered God's will in the darkness as he slid his hands under his clothes and said that no-one would listen if he told. His God-fearing parents would never take the word of a child against a holy man. He'd been right, they hadn't listened, so he'd used his fists on anyone who glanced at him and saw his shame. Until they labelled him hopeless, a lost cause, and finally set him free.

He was handsome alright. Handsome enough to make girls stare in the street and smile to catch his eye. Even Lissy. He shuddered at the image it conjured and smiled at how she'd made him feel. Happy and confused and most of all angry, but not at her.

He gathered his things as he thought, counting them in his head. The rope and knife and the sedatives at home, they were everything he would need. He cast a final glance at the uniforms stopping people on the prom then locked the front door and turned the notice to 'having a ten minute break'. He slipped through the back and into his car then drove to the wood to bide his time.

***

"Annette, honestly. I have to move back home before I take an axe to my Mum's Pavarotti tapes."

Annette laughed despite herself, struggling to maintain her official face.

"It's not safe, Lucia. We haven't got to the bottom of things yet."

Lucia rolled her eyes in exasperation and glared at her. Her voice matched.

"What more is there to find out? I can't think of anyone who would do this to me. The patrols haven't seen anyone outside my place since I moved out, and the texts came from a throwaway phone that was bought with cash. There's nothing more you *can* do."

"You can tell me about the phone-calls."

Lucia screwed up her face trying to work out what she meant.

"What phone-calls? I only got letters and texts."

"Oh yes, I meant to say. The letters were written by a man and posted from Belfast somewhere."

"How do you know a man wrote them?"

"Forensics said the sentence construction was male, whatever that means. Anyway, don't avoid the question. What about the phone-calls? They were on your home line."

"I didn't get any phone-calls, or any messages on my answerphone. Are you sure there were phone-calls?"

"Certain. They were routed through New York to throw us off the scent. Some virtual phone exchange. Davy's in contact with them now, trying to trace the calls back. I want you to stay at your folks until we do."

Lucia's next words held a mixture of stubbornness and anguish. "God, Annette, do I really have to?"

Annette's silence told her the answer was yes.

"Well then, you'd better explain to my Mum why her recording of 'Nessun Dorma' is in the bin. Then run, because she's scary when she's mad."

Annette laughed. "Just one more night, I promise. That should give Davy time to trace it, then we'll catch this pervert and have you back home."

Chapter Twenty

"Boss, it was O'Carolan e-mailing Lissy. It took a w…while, but I've finally got through the fronts to his e-mail account."

Craig stared at the handset trying to catch up. A minute ago he'd been talking to Annette confirming that Darlene McKenna was clear and that Hugh Trainor's bank accounts and other checks were clean. Neither of them had a motive to kill Lissy; he'd never thought that they had but they'd had to check. Now Davy was on the line without Annette even saying that she'd transferred the call.

"Hang on a minute, Davy, can you put me back to Annette?"

Davy paused and gazed around the open-plan floor. Annette was nowhere to be seen.

"S…sorry but she's disappeared. Shall I go on?"

Craig grunted yes and frowned, then listened as Davy ran through the checks he'd used to trace O'Carolan as the man in e-mail correspondence with Lissy. It wasn't like Annette to be so abrupt, and her disappearing off the floor while he was still on the phone wasn't her style at all. There was something going on. Perhaps she'd thought he'd have guessed it if she'd kept talking to him on the phone.

"And then the internet provider managed to track him down. It was James O'Carolan that Lissy had been e-mailing in code."

He paused and Craig knew it was his cue. He dragged himself back to the case and asked a question that he knew Davy would answer at length, giving him more time to think.

"Any joy on breaking their code?"

Davy launched into encryption speak and Craig returned to his thoughts. Annette's home life was better now so she wasn't avoiding him over that, and anything about the case she'd be happy to discuss. It was something else. Something that she specifically didn't want him to know. That meant that it was personal. Davy's voice rose excitedly, interrupting his thoughts.

"And then we managed to find a key w…word."

"Who's we?"

"Me and the encryption team at The Met. We cracked the code this morning. It was a s…simple cypher but Lissy used French instead of English words to set the key. Really clever."

Yes it was, and it relied on the fact that both she and O'Carolan were educated enough to manage it. Craig parked his concerns about Annette and turned one hundred percent back to the case.

"What did they say?"

"Ah now, that's w…where it gets really interesting. Lissy was basically commiserating with O'Carolan about his mother's death. She initiated the contact between them back in June."

"She must have read about the case somewhere and seen that O'Carolan blamed her mother for not putting Wasson away."

Davy's voice grew more excited. "Yes. That's exactly what happened. She'd seen a magazine article he'd w…written, a piece on the victims of crime, and she contacted him. Their correspondence started from there."

"Why encrypt it?"

"If you read some of the things she called her mother, you'd understand, s…sir. They aren't pretty. Lissy seems to have hated her even more than O'Carolan did."

"Forward the decoded versions to me Davy, please. If that's true then it undermines any idea we have that O'Carolan would have wanted Lissy dead."

"Definitely. She seems to have been his main ally in trying to getting an investigation opened into W…Wasson's part in Veronica Jarvis' murder."

"What? How far had they got with it?"

"They were still at the planning stage but Lissy was applying to do her Masters in Human Rights Law and she was planning to use it as her dissertation case. S...She'd got accepted onto the course before she was killed and she'd e-mailed O'Carolan to tell him. They were due to meet up the S...Sunday she was killed, to discuss the case. I don't know w...what time. It wasn't in the e-mails and there's nothing about it in her texts."

The ramifications of what Davy had found could open a huge can of worms. If Lissy had been working with James O'Carolan to investigate a cover-up that her mother might have led, then that would explain their attempts at code. She may have believed Melanie Trainor read her e-mails and it was her attempt at keeping them secure. What if her mother *had* found out what she had planned? Her own daughter investigating the case that made her career! It was dynamite, and it would have stymied her hopes of becoming Chief Constable for sure.

Putting away Jonno Mulvenna had propelled Melanie Trainor into the spotlight and made it impossible for police hierarchy to keep her down because of her sex. If it turned out that Mulvenna had been wrongly convicted, no matter whether she knew about it or not, her career could fold like a house of cards.

But would she really kill her own child to save her job? She was ruthless; anyone who'd ever worked for her could confirm that. And if the rumours were true she'd used whoever she needed to on her way to the top. But murder her daughter? Craig shook his head, but not as hard as he might have done. He wasn't sure, and if he wasn't sure then that meant that somewhere in the back of his mind he thought Melanie Trainor could be involved in her daughter's death. Had she actually done it? Davy was still talking and Craig interrupted him urgently.

"Davy, this is dynamite and it can't go outside the team. Don't forward the e-mails, please, save them in a protected folder and download everything onto a CD then have a car bring it to me. Brief Annette and Jake to be discrete as well please."

"But w…we can't ignore this, boss. It can't be covered up!"

Nicky glanced across the room at the sound of Davy's raised voice and wandered over to see what was up. Craig went to snap his head off then stopped himself. He would never cover something up but he could see how it appeared. Davy would understand what he'd meant in a second. He did.

"God, I'm s…sorry, boss. I didn't mean that. I…"

"Don't worry, Davy. I know what you meant. We're not covering anything up, the very opposite in fact. There are people in the force and MI5 who won't want this to go any further and they may already have killed Lissy to prevent it. If it's just on your computer drive it could be wiped. We need to keep it safe. When we have more facts, I'll go to the CC myself."

"Yes, yes. You're right. Tell me what you w…want me to do."

"Just what I said before and send the disc up now. Can you keep the de-coder at The Met in the dark?"

"Yes, no problem. He only worked on fragments of the code, he never saw the whole thing."

"Fine. Good work, Davy. Very good work. Now I know Nicky will be standing beside you trying to find out what's going on, because she's nosy."

"Can I tell her you said that?"

Craig laughed loudly. "Not if you value your life. Just put her on. I'll talk to you again later."

Davy transferred the call to Nicky and started to tidy his files.

"Well, sir?"

Craig could picture her wry look all the way from Portstewart. Her tone said that she expected to be updated on what he and Davy had been talking about. She was caught on the hop by Craig's next words.

"What's Annette up to, Nicky?"

***

Lucia locked the front door of the shop and turned the 'Gone for lunch. Back in thirty minutes' sign towards the street, then she sat down with a copy of 'Elle Decor' and the tub of pasta that Mirella had forced into her hand at eight a.m. She had to admit living at home had its perks.

She was perusing the living-space pages, wondering which lurid colour her Mum was going to paint the house next, when she heard a noise behind her. A single loud bang was followed by the shop's back door scraping open. She froze for a moment as she heard an unfamiliar voice calling her name, then quickly relaxed at the sight of Ross Devlin, the charity's new regional manager.

"Lucia? Hello, is anyone here?"

He was standing in the doorway of the storage room, wearing a wide smile and carrying a file of papers in his hand.

"God, Ross, you scared the life out of me."

"Sorry. I know I should have phoned, but I was just passing and thought I'd drop in."

He pulled up a stool and sat facing her across the counter, waving her on with her lunch. Lucia nodded towards the coffee pot and poured him a cup.

"Was it me you wanted, or Joan? She's on a day off for her daughter's wedding, so I said I'd cover."

He smiled and a strange expression crossed his face. "Yes, I know. It was you I wanted to talk to."

Lucia handed him the coffee. "OK, shoot. What can I help you with?"

She watched him as he sipped the drink. He was new to the charity and they'd only met a couple of times before at management meetings. He was about forty, slim and pale, but not unattractive. They all wondered why he wasn't married, but then why not? Marc and John were his age and they hadn't tied the knot. Maybe he wanted to do it once and forever, instead of divorcing because he'd married too young. Devlin drank his coffee then opened the file in front of him, turning to a page near the back.

"There's a discrepancy in the shop's inventory, Lucia, and I've been sent to check it out."

She was surprised. It was one of the charity's biggest receiving shops, where people left donations every day. Joan had the system for sorting the goods and selling them on, down pat. She tried to read the page upside down and gave up.

"What sort of discrepancy? Joan Irwin's one of our best shop managers, Ross."

He smiled tightly. "Your defence of her is admirable, and I'm sure you're right. But I still have to do an audit. We need to sort through all the donations brought in this week and check if they've been entered correctly in the book."

"That will take hours! I'm opening again in five minutes."

He shook his head. "Sorry, no. We're closed for the afternoon." He glanced at her pasta. "When you've finished your lunch we'll start. No hurry."

She shrugged and took another drink then got ready to roll up her sleeves.

Chapter Twenty-One

"Right Liam, get the uniforms to lift O'Carolan ASAP and I need to see you and Andy before he arrives."

"It's past lunchtime and my stomach thinks my throat's been cut, boss. Can we meet over a bite to eat?"

The pleading in Liam's voice made Craig laugh and he glanced at the clock. He was right. It was almost two o'clock and he hadn't noticed.

"Fine. But we can eat while we work. Ask the desk to send in some sandwiches and tea and get Andy down to the interview room."

It was on the tip of Liam's tongue to say 'keep your hair on' then he thought of Craig's hair and smiled. It was so thick it stood on end sometimes, especially when he raked his hands through it, like he did nearly every day. Nicky'd bought him some girly hairspray as a joke once to keep it flat. He grinned, remembering. He'd never heard Craig use language quite that bad before.

His thoughts remained private and instead he said. "Give me five" and ordered O'Carolan's lift, then he wandered to the interview corridor to see what was rattling the boss' cage. Five minutes later he and Andy were gawping openly at Craig.

"You can't be serious, hey? You think the ACC took a hit out on her own kid? No way. You've lost it, Marc."

Liam grinned at Andy's turn of phrase. They were both D.C.I.s but Andy had never worked directly for Craig and somehow it gave him a different approach. He might think the boss had lost it as well, but he'd never say it in quite that blunt a way. He watched Craig closely to see how he took the words. He just shrugged and took another drink of tea.

"I didn't say that she did it, Andy. I said that we have to rule her out."

Craig wrapped up the remains of his sandwich and potted it into the bin then turned to face them both.

"Look. Lissy didn't get on with her mother, that much we know. She was also keen on Human Rights Law. Maybe she saw the O'Carolan case as a way to get back at her Mum, or get her attention somehow. God knows it sounds as if she had little enough of that growing up."

"But if she re-opened Mulvenna's conviction she could have ruined her Mum. Surely she couldn't have hated her enough for that, hey?"

Craig shook his head slowly. "Young people have strong feelings about things, Andy. Lissy was obviously passionate enough about Human Rights Law to do a Masters in it, so maybe she wanted to right a wrong and her Mum getting hurt in the process was acceptable damage in her eyes. Who knows?"

Liam wiped his mouth and joined in. "What if someone else, Wasson's handler, found out what Lissy and O'Carolan were about to do and took out a hit on her. MI5 have been known to get their hands dirty before."

Craig squinted in thought. "It's a possibility, I suppose, but Wasson's handler's long retired. The man I spoke to said they sanctioned Wasson getting off for Jarvis' death, although they'd taken a bit of persuading, but they hadn't sanctioned Mulvenna being framed. They said the decision to frame him was local. Very local." He shook his head. "I really doubt they would kill Lissy thirty years later to protect Wasson's memory or Melanie Trainor's career. This doesn't feel like a government hit."

He sat in silence for a moment, half-expecting Liam to jump in with a quip, but nothing came. Andy restarted.

"The other rape cases have drawn a blank. Either the victims and their families have died, moved away or are unable to testify, or they have solid alibis for that week. That leaves us with a short-list of James O'Carolan, the ACC, Jonno Mulvenna or his young doppelgänger."

Liam shook his head.

"Nah. O'Carolan wouldn't have killed Lissy if she was helping re-open his mother's case and why would Mulvenna have bothered killing her? He didn't even object to being convicted. My money's on the ACC or this Mulvenna lookalike, whoever he is. Uniform are saturating the town with his photo now."

Craig nodded and stood up. "Good. I agree. We've narrowed the field to two with one of them in the wind and the other too senior to interview until we've exhausted every other avenue. Now, let's see what O'Carolan has to say about giving a false alibi and what he can tell us about Lissy's last day."

***

James O'Carolan was just as angry as the first time they'd interviewed him. His face was red and he was drumming his fingers on the table so hard that they could hear it through the interview room's wooden door. Craig signalled Andy to watch from the viewing room then he nodded Liam on. He was holding the disc Davy had sent up from Belfast thirty minutes before and Liam set a laptop on the table's Formica top, opening its lid theatrically and booting it up.

O'Carolan thrust his head forward as Craig sat down, stopping an inch from his face. Craig didn't flinch. He'd faced real hard men too often in his career to let a yuppie rattle his cage.

"Hello again, Mr O'Carolan. Do you know why you're here?"

He waited thirty seconds for the reply that didn't come then carried on, turning the disc over in his hand.

"Do you know what this is, Mr O'Carolan?" Silence. "No?

All right then, I'll tell you. But first, would you like a solicitor present? It is your right, although if you've nothing to hide then why would you want one?"

O'Carolan locked eyes with him and Craig stared back, unblinking, with all the confidence of the upper hand. O'Carolan broke the gaze first and Liam silently punched the air. He loved it when prisoners tried that one with Craig, they always lost. He reckoned he'd practiced staring into the mirror when he was a kid.

O'Carolan wasn't a prisoner, he could walk out any time he liked, but he didn't have the wit to work that out. Finally the computer booted up and Craig handed Liam the disc to insert. As he clicked it open O'Carolan finally spoke.

"Why am I here, again?" He spat the last word out as if it somehow underlined their incompetence for not having asked everything the time before. Craig smiled and waved at the computer's back.

"Why were you in e-mail contact with Lissy Trainor? And before you start denying it we have all of your e-mails here, decrypted."

Instead of looking shocked as they'd expected him to do, O'Carolan yawned.

"I wondered how long that would take. Well, if you've got them then you know what we were talking about, without me having to spell it out."

"You were planning to work together on re-opening the Veronica Jarvis case, to show that Declan Wasson had killed her and Jonno Mulvenna was framed."

O'Carolan applauded slowly. "Give that man a prize. Got it in one."

Liam leaned forward angrily. It was all right them taking the piss out of each other but not some scrote who worked in IT.

"Watch your mouth, son."

O'Carolan jerked forward. "Or what? You'll beat me up like you usually do? Is that it?"

Craig motioned Liam back imperceptibly and smiled. "You seem to have a very low opinion of the police, Mr O'Carolan. Is that because of your mother?"

"Amongst other things. I was lifted too often for being drunk as a student as well."

"Weren't we all."

The room fell into tense silence and Craig shifted his body language to a more conciliatory stance. When he felt the atmosphere calm he motioned Liam to turn the screen towards their guest and give him back some control. O'Carolan scrolled quickly through the pages until he reached the last one, then he nodded. The e-mails were all there verbatim, including the one where he'd arranged to meet Lissy the Sunday before she died.

"She didn't turn up."

"Sorry? Who didn't?"

O'Carolan smiled wryly. "You know who. Lissy. We'd arranged to meet on the promenade at six o'clock, but I waited for two hours and she never showed. I got pissed off and left. The first time I knew she was dead was when I heard it on the news."

"How did you communicate six o'clock? It's not in the e-mails."

"Yes it is." He pointed to a sentence. 'Meet you at the front then.' "Six words, six o'clock."

Another code.

"Why didn't you tell us you'd arranged to meet? Why give us a false alibi?"

O'Carolan snorted sceptically. "Same answer to both. Once I'd heard she was dead I knew how it would look for me, and your track record with framing people isn't great."

"Fair enough. Did you ever get to meet her?"

The young man shook his head. "Never. We just e-mailed each other. It was a pity, I was looking forward to it. She sounded like a nice girl. Better than her bitch of a mother."

Craig ignored the comment and motioned Liam to shut

down the computer while he carried on. "Who approached who first?"

"Lissy e-mailed me at work. She'd seen a piece I'd written for a magazine and looked into my mother's case. We e-mailed back and forth a bit and I told her about my suspicions on the Jarvis case in '83. She dug a bit more on Wasson and said she felt there was something there and she wanted to write her Masters on it. Maybe help me get some peace."

And get back at her mother as well... O'Carolan's account fitted with everything Davy had said. Ten more minutes of questions didn't reveal anything that made him a viable suspect in Lissy's death. When they finished questioning him, he looked sad. Nothing like the belligerent man who entered the room an hour before. As Craig walked him to the front door of the station, O'Carolan turned and spoke.

"Lissy was kind and brave. I'm sorry she's dead. My Mum would have liked her."

He was right. The more they discovered about Lissy Trainor the sadder her death became. She'd had a great future ahead until someone had taken it away and Craig knew they were finally closing in on who that someone was.

***

By three o'clock, the shelves in the charity shop's storage room had been emptied onto the floor and the items arranged into four large piles: toys, clothes, household goods and bric-a-brac. Lucia took the list Ross handed her and started to tick off the items in the toy pile one by one, while he did the same with household goods.

The room was stifling hot, despite the fact it was November. Lucia opened the door onto the street and slipped off her heavy jumper, revealing a black t-shirt underneath. If she was this hot, she had no idea how Ross was coping in his suit. She knelt by the door and carried on with her count, completely missing the look in Ross Devlin's eyes. He scanned her slender body slowly, taking in each curve and inch of tanned skin, until his glance finally fell on her legs. Lucia felt his eyes before she felt his touch. She turned just in time to see him reach out to stroke her leg.

She recoiled in shock. "What are you doing, Ross?"

He didn't answer, lunging towards her instead. She went to jump up but he grabbed her ankle and pulled her towards him across the floor. She scrambled for some purchase but the floor was slick and she could feel herself sliding, knowing exactly what she was sliding to. She reached frantically for the edge of the metal shelving and grasped it, then clung on, kicking hard at his face.

She used all her breath to shout a 'No' so loudly that he momentarily lost his grip in shock and she managed to struggle to her feet. She rushed through the open door into the yard pushing her way past the rubbish bins and towards the code-operated gate.

Ross Devlin watched her run, smiling to himself. He'd been watching her for weeks, waiting for the moment he could get her alone. He'd planned it for night time and her flat, but she'd moved to her parents this week and put paid to that. The shop was the natural alternative and Joan Irwin's wedding invitation had given him the perfect chance.

Lucia ran without looking back, afraid to see how close he was. She'd just reached the latticed fence when she felt his hot breath on her neck. Ross wrapped his arms around her lifting her off her feet and she knew that if they re-entered the shop she'd no hope of escape. She pushed her full weight back against him and they toppled together onto the ground. His head cracked the concrete with a sickening thud. He was dazed but he was still gripping her hard, so Lucia did what she'd learned in the self-defence class Marc had insisted she take. She stamped as hard as she could on his instep with her heel and elbowed him in the stomach, winding him. He loosened his grip for a moment and she leaped to her feet and stamped hard on his groin. Then she ran to the gate and punched in the code as fast as she could. Five seconds later she was in the street, free, screaming at the top of her lungs and waving frantically at the patrol car outside to come.

Chapter Twenty-Two

Jake pushed the gallery door open and stood scanning the white walls while he waited for attention from the bored looking girl at the desk. She flicked her eyes over him in a quick up-and-down then smiled, assessing his net worth as worthy of the effort of rising from her seat. She cat-walked her way towards him like an expensive figurine come to life, her grey silk dress and long blonde hair reflecting the gallery's location at the elegant end of the Lisburn Road. She smiled briefly then spoke in an affected voice.

"May I help you, sir?"

Jake smiled to himself, recognising the signs of flirtation in her glance. Good luck with that, it would be a cold day in hell before she got any response from him. He reached into his jacket and withdrew his warrant card.

"Yes, thank you. You can."

The girl took a step back so suddenly that he thought she was going to fall but she righted herself swiftly, regaining her composure and balancing perfectly on her five-inch heels. She spoke again, this time at a higher pitch.

"What can I help you with, officer?"

"I need to view one of your charcoal drawings, please. 'Girl being herself' by John Mulvenna."

She relaxed visibly, realising that the visit was nothing to do with her and Jake wondered what she had to hide. He shrugged, not his problem today; whatever she'd done it would have to wait. She waved him on to the back of the room, past floor-standing bronzes and mounted works of art, until they stood in front of the framed sketch he'd seen the night before. He gazed at it in silence for a moment, taking in its clean lines and smudged shadows, expertly outlining the girl's curves. Mulvenna had captured her mix of strength and fragility perfectly; he was good.

Jake's eyes moved to her face, He looked first at each feature, admiring the slope of the nose and the sweeping angle of the cheeks, and then at the way they melded together, to bring her personality to life. But it was the girl's eyes that really made him stare. They were large and dark and wide apart and they gazed out of the canvas as if she was gazing at someone she loved. Their message was vulnerability and fear in equal part. Why fear? Fear of whoever she was gazing at, or fear of love itself?

He realised he'd been holding his breath and exhaled in a low sigh. The sketch was beautiful, but there was something else. He'd seen the girl before. He called the assistant and watched as she pulled her eyes reluctantly from the door and the search for her next commission.

"I need to ask you some questions about the sketch, Miss..?"

"Murray. Sonya Murray. What can I tell you?"

He glanced behind her at some chairs. "Can we sit down for a moment?"

She seemed surprised at his request, as if only certain people were allowed to sit. He sat and waited until she joined him then flicked open his notebook and gave her a questioning look.

"How much is the charcoal?"

She raised a long slim finger and pointed towards the price tag below the sketch, as if he should walk back and look. He raised an eyebrow and she sighed. "Two thousand five hundred pounds."

"Thank you. And what can you tell me about the artist?"

She energised suddenly, as if someone had flicked a switch, confiding in a low voice that the artist had once been a terrorist and had successfully evaded the police until he'd murdered a woman in cold blood. Jake stared at her, trying to hide his surprise. She'd been a picture of boredom the whole time he'd been there but one mention of blood and she'd sprung into life.

He stared at her trying to gauge her age then realised she was much younger than he'd first thought. She was barely eighteen. Too young to remember The Troubles or the devastation they'd wrought. To her Jonno Mulvenna was a living myth. A walking, talking movie star living in our midst. It didn't hurt that he looked like one too, probably added to the romantic glow. To her Mulvenna was a freedom fighter, no matter what he'd done. He wondered if Mulvenna encouraged the hype.

He watched as she launched into Mulvenna's sad life story and misspent youth. How misunderstood he was and how alone, as if only her love could make him whole. Yes he'd killed people, but in war sometimes people died. War? Was that what he'd said it was? Tell that to his victims. By the time the girl had finished Jake had nearly every detail that he'd hoped to get and every small confidence that had passed between them while they'd stood for hours in the gallery arranging his art. Things Mulvenna had conveniently glossed over in his statement to Craig.

Mulvenna had been in love with a woman once. Really in love. Was it the woman in the sketch? Sonya didn't know. He interrupted her. How old was the sketch? She didn't know that either. The artist hadn't given them a time and charcoals were hard to date. It could be decades old or just sketched the week before. She launched back into Mulvenna's story. Their love was forbidden, made impossible by circumstance, and yet it was real. They'd struggled with it and planned to run away together overseas, away from what divided them.

"What happened? Did they run away together?" Jake asked the question knowing that if the sketch was old the answer was no. Mulvenna had gone to prison. So what had happened to the girl then?

Sonya gazed at the ground as if she could feel Mulvenna's pain. "No. It was very sad. They were pulled apart by something, he didn't tell me what. But…"

Jake leaned forward slowly, not wanting to spook his source. "What?"

She shook her head. "He didn't say, but I had the impression that she left him and broke his heart."

He nodded slowly, it was a familiar tale. He could imagine Mulvenna recounting it to the girl and sucking her into his so-called romantic life. Perhaps it was true and past, a story from his youth, the girl a matron now, surrounded by her kids. Nothing to do with the present day, simply a past love and a broken heart. And yet…

He still couldn't shake the feeling that he knew the girl in the sketch from somewhere. What if the sketch was recent? He watched as Sonya's eyes misted over and closed his notebook, knowing that his next demand would earn him an instant rebuke.

"I need a copy of the sketch, please."

She sprang to her feet in indignation, as if he'd just asked her to betray a friend. "No, absolutely not. Mr Morena won't hear of it."

"Mr Morena, the gallery owner?"

"Yes. He's very specific about things like that. It devalues the art."

Jake nodded but he was undeterred. "You must have publicity material, from the launch last night. Does any of that carry a good photograph of the sketch?"

He could see from the way she quickly glanced towards a corner that it did, and he nodded her to find him some. She walked grudgingly to a pile of ten by tens and returned with one, holding it out at arm's length, displeased.

"They were made for the press. Mr Morena won't be happy that you're taking one."

"And yet, you gave them out to the press."

Jake stared at the print in his hand. The front was a duplicate of the sketch and the back contained details of the launch. It would have to do.

"Thank you, Ms Murray. I'll see what our technicians can get from this. If it's not enough then I'll be back."

He turned on his heel and walked to the door knowing she would be pulling a face behind his back. He didn't care, his mind was already trying to work out where he'd seen the girl before. Davy would give him an answer if there was one to give.

***

Craig pulled his phone from his pocket and flicked it open to answer the call. Withheld number. That meant it was probably work.

"D.C.I. Craig." He realised what he'd said and smiled. It was taking him a while to get used to the Superintendent tag. The soft voice that came down the line was unmistakable and he could hear tears thickening it.

"Hello, Marc. It's Julia."

She was phoning him on a work line, something she never did.

"What's wrong? You sound upset."

She started sobbing so hard that he could only make out every other word. He let her cry for a moment and made soothing noises, until her sobs finally became a gasp and she gulped for air.

"Sweetheart, tell me what's wrong, please. Whatever it is, we'll sort it out together, I promise."

"We can't sort it out, don't you realise that by now? I've tried and it's hopeless. Harrison won't let me go and the Chief Constable won't help. Now Gerry's told me his wife doesn't want him to do his inspector's exams until 2015. He won't be eligible to apply for my job until the year after next." She gasped for breath and Craig stepped in with the words he thought would help. He swallowed hard and then took the plunge.

"Let's get married. Now. This weekend. Then you can move to Belfast and we'll be together."

The howl that answered him wasn't quite the answer he'd been hoping for, but he'd half-expected it all the same.

"NO! No, no, no. That's not the answer. It's a typical man's solution. Marry the little woman and she'll follow you anywhere. Don't you understand that if I'd been prepared to give up my career and move I would have done it when you asked me to before, even without marriage? I don't want to give up my job, Marc. It's my security; it's my life, just as it's yours. Why don't you marry me and you give up your job and move to Limavady? How does that sound?"

Craig didn't know what to say, so he said nothing.

"There, that's your answer. You think your job is more important than mine, because you're a man! I heard it in the army every day and I'm hearing it again from you. You're impossible! This is impossible. It will never work!"

The line went dead and Craig stared at his mobile helplessly. He felt lost about what to do. He knew she was feeling even worse, but he also knew that anything he said at the moment would be useless. Worse than useless, it would be seen as another attempt to undermine her job.

He shook his head. It was Camille all over again, except with Camille it had been her acting career that had made continuing their relationship impossible. Crossing the Atlantic was an impossible commute. But Northern Ireland was a small place, surely there was some way that he and Julia could stay together and both stay on the force.

He racked his brains for a moment then glanced at his watch, making up his mind. Limavady was only seventeen miles away; he could be there in half an hour. He called Liam to say he'd be unavailable until that evening then headed for the car and sped up the Portstewart Road without the slightest idea what to say when he arrived.

Chapter Twenty-Three

"I'm all right, Annette, honestly. Devlin's more hurt than I am."

Annette was gripping the phone so hard that her hand had turned blue. Nicky stared at her questioningly.

"You're positive you're OK, Lucia?"

Lucia smiled at her concern. "Positive. He's been arrested. Unfortunately they've taken him to High Street so Marc's bound to find out. That's where I am now."

Annette shook her head. "Leave it with me. I know Jack Harris, the desk sergeant there. I'll ask him to keep it quiet until I get a chance to tell Marc myself."

"No, I'll tell him Annette. I don't want you getting in trouble."

"We'll argue about it later." Annette glanced at her watch. "I'll be there in thirty minutes; I just need to clear up some stuff here. OK?"

"OK, thanks. And stop worrying. I'm fine."

***

"Davy. What can you do with a sketch and facial recognition?"

Davy looked up from his horseshoe of computers and smiled. Jake's voice held a challenge and he loved one of those. He sat back in his chair and furrowed his brow in a way that he thought made him look like Benedict Cumberbatch's Sherlock.

"A clear s…sketch of a face?"

Jake nodded. "Slightly turned to one side, but clear."

"When was it drawn?"

Jake shrugged. "No idea. It's one of Jonno Mulvenna's. He took up painting in prison but he could have been sketching before that. It could be forty years ago or as recent as last week. The girl in the gallery didn't know."

"OK. W…what do you want it for?"

Jake looked at him surprised, then remembered he would have to put a case number against the work.

"Sorry, I should have thought. It's background for the Lissy Trainor case. The Super asked me to dig around a bit."

The Super. Davy smiled. It was hard for them to think of Craig in that way but Jake had just come on board and he was keen. He stretched out his hand for the sketch then stared at it for a moment with a puzzled frown. Jake saw his look and jumped in.

"That's exactly the feeling I had when saw it. I'm sure I've seen the girl before."

"Mulvenna must have known her well, she's nude."

Nicky heard the word 'nude' and popped her head over her partition.

"Don't you be bringing rude pictures onto this floor, Jake McLean or I'll have words to say." She pursed her lips disapprovingly then Davy saw a twinkle in her eye and he knew what was coming next. "Davy's very young, you know."

She crossed the floor in a few quick steps and stared at the flyer in Davy's hand. He held it above her head playfully.

"I'm only two years younger than Jake. You'll have to stop treating me like the baby soon."

"Not a hope." Nicky jumped up and grabbed the flyer, smiling at the impressed look on his face. "I played volley-ball at school."

She stared at the picture and the frown that crossed her face matched Davy's one minute before. "I know her, I'm sure I do."

"That's what we both said. Davy's going to face-match her and see if she's in the system somewhere."

Nicky smiled smugly then set the flyer on the desk. "No need. I can tell you exactly who she is. That's Lissy Trainor."

Jake's mouth fell open in realisation. She was right, that's exactly who it was. Davy scanned in the flyer and then pulled up Lissy's picture for a match. It was ninety percent; way too high to be random. The ten percent gap fitted with it being a drawing instead of a photograph.

Jake spoke first. "Oh God, you realise what this means."

"Mulvenna knew Lissy Trainor w…well enough to draw her in the nude. He did it. He killed her the same way he killed Ronni Jarvis. Our killer's been staring us in the face all this time!"

Nicky grabbed the desk phone and hit dial, connecting with Craig's answerphone. She handed the receiver to Jake to leave a message while she dialled Liam on the other line. If Jonno Mulvenna had killed Lissy Trainor then he was guilty of Ronni Jarvis' killing as well, despite his denials over the years. They had their man.

***

Liam stared at the phone, then ended the call and slumped back heavily in his seat. His witness had been right all along. It had been Jonno Mulvenna that she'd seen talking to Lissy that Sunday on the parade. He must have skipped out of his art course and sneaked back to Portstewart for long enough to kill her, then returned to Ballymena to get his alibi straight. The fact that the man she'd seen had looked young and had brown eyes could be easily explained with coloured lenses and a trick of the light.

He scribbled down some notes, getting his thoughts in order before Craig phoned, a certainty as soon as Jake gave him the news. He stopped mid-word as a doubt pushed its way through his eagerness to make an arrest. What about Mulvenna's hair? He couldn't have had it cut then grown it back again over night.

He thought for a moment and then shrugged; a wig would cover that. He turned back to his notes but something else nagged at the back of his mind. Mulvenna's alibi. He needed to break it before he interviewed him or said anything to the boss. He glanced at his watch and shoved the page he'd been writing on inside his coat, then he made for the car and Ballymena to run a JCB through a bunch of arty types' lives.

***

Craig had just reached the outskirts of Limavady when his answerphone went. He pulled over and pressed dial. Jake's garbled message made no sense but Nicky's was crystal clear. Something they'd found had made them think Jonno Mulvenna was their man. He shook his head firmly; no. He didn't care what they'd found, Mulvenna wasn't Lissy Trainor's killer, he was sure of that. But something had rattled their cages. He glanced at the clock and then at the darkening sky, knowing that if he started a discussion with Julia he wouldn't make it back to Portstewart until the next day. He mulled over his choices for a moment then hit dial.

"Where are you, Liam?"

The background noise said he was on a road and it wasn't a slow one.

"On my way to check Mulvenna's alibi. You heard then?"

"Only what Nicky left on voicemail. Can you pull over and talk?"

"Aye. Give me a minute and I'll call you back. Where are you by the way?"

Craig thought for a minute and then lied. "On my way to see John, but it can wait. Call me back."

Two minutes later his phone rang and Liam's voice boomed through, loud and clear.

"OK, shoot, Liam. What's happened?"

"Aye well, basically Jake went back to the gallery and got a copy of some sketch for Davy to face-match, then Nicky recognised it. It was Lissy Trainor. A ninety percent computer match said she was right."

Craig immediately shook his head; this was all wrong. He realised Liam couldn't see him and repeated his thoughts.

"There's no way Mulvenna did this, or the Jarvis murder, Liam. They're not his style."

"We have to look at him, boss."

"Yes, we do, and long and hard enough to make sure I'm right. OK. Your witness was pretty sure she'd seen him, and granted, Mulvenna could have changed his eye colour and hair with lenses and a wig. But shedding thirty years is a harder trick."

Liam's tone was insistent.

"But we need to check so I'm heading up to the hippy place to crack his alibi now."

Craig laughed, despite the serious topic. "I don't think all artists are hippies, Liam. Maybe back in the sixties but not now. But crack away. If there's a gap you'll find it, I know that."

"Right. What did the Doc have to say?"

"What?"

"You said you were on your way there."

Craig scrambled quickly for a reason he might be seeing John and came up with an old faithful. "D.N.A.. He was matching the D.N.A. from the scene."

"And?"

Craig frowned. If he hadn't known better he would have thought Liam was trying to catch him out, but his tone said he was just being nosy. His guilt about leaving work during the day was making him paranoid.

"I don't know yet. I'll call you as soon as I do." He wrapped up briskly. "Let me know what the hippies have to say and in the meantime let's get Mulvenna back in."

"Andy's on it now." Liam paused and Craig knew he was glancing at his watch. "See you in a couple of hours. Save the interview until I arrive."

Craig laughed knowing that Liam had visions of popcorn and a ringside seat while they cracked two murders thirty years apart.

"I'll do that. See you there."

He clicked off the phone and stared at the outline of Limavady police station up ahead. He could be there in less than five minutes, but it would be the start of a long discussion that would end up in bed. He shook his head guiltily remembering Julia's tears, then threw his car into a U-turn and headed back the way he'd come. His personal life would have to wait. If Liam was right about Mulvenna it wouldn't be waiting for very long.

Chapter Twenty-Four

Annette stared through the glass at the slumped shape of Ross Devlin. He looked pathetic but she had no sympathy for him. He was a stalker and he'd been going to rape Lucia, there was no doubt about that. They'd found the throwaway phone in his briefcase and Davy would trace the other calls soon; it was an open and shut case.

She smiled at the bandage on his head. Lucia had got away without a scratch and a man six inches bigger than her had had to have stitches in his head. Lucia Craig, one - Ross Devlin, nil.

He would be convicted; there was no doubt of that. The question was how to stop Craig finding out and getting distracted while he had a murder to solve. The even bigger question was how to stop him blowing his stack.

She shrugged. It wasn't her case it was sex-crimes now. Davy would hand the work they'd done over, Lucia would give her statement and they'd get a date for court. If she could keep Jack Harris quiet for a few days they could worry about Craig then.

She turned towards the back of the viewing room and gave Jack her best winning smile. He shook his head.

"I'm not lying to him, Annette."

Annette adopted her best wheedling voice. "You don't have to lie, Jack. Just say nothing."

He looked sceptical. "What'll I do if he asks?"

"He won't ask. Trust me. Lucia came directly to me, Marc doesn't know about any of it. He won't ask."

"I don't..."

She interrupted softly. "I do. I'll do you a favour another

time, I promise. Please."

Jack gave a small smile. He liked Craig but Annette was right. Craig loved his sister and if he knew what had happened he'd get distracted from an important case. He nodded once, conceding the logic.

"OK then. But only if he doesn't ask."

Annette smiled and nodded, then she turned back to the glass and cast a last look at their perp before heading back to the C.C.U..

***

John stared at the D.N.A. result in front of him and rubbed the back of his neck. It was curious, no question about it, but they had what they had and science didn't lie. He turned towards Des Marsham, Head of Forensic Science and watched as he scratched his head, bemused. He took a gulp of coffee and John watched it disappear into his beard, wondering just how much bushier it was going to get.

"Well? What do you think?"

Des sighed and shook his head before he spoke. "Zero point one percent margin of error is hard to argue with, John, but I can run it again if you like."

John shook his head as well. "No. I'm sure you're right, I'm just trying to work out how it fits with Marc's case."

"Sorry to say but I think that's his problem. Much as I know you're dying to solve it first." He grinned. "You're a frustrated cop, Winter."

"Frustrated detective, and you're right. I always wanted to be Sherlock Holmes as a kid, solving the puzzle with my trusty Dr Watson at my side." He laughed. "Except I ended up as Watson and Marc got to be Sherlock instead."

Des smiled, deep in thought. "Well then, how about we try to crack this one? Just for a laugh? We'll give Marc the D.N.A. results but do a bit of sleuthing on the side ourselves. Eh? First one to reach the answer wins a pint at The James."

John stared at him for a moment then extended his hand to shake. Let's see if he could be Sherlock just this once, although his money was still on Craig.

***

Jonno Mulvenna made himself comfortable in the interview room and folded his arms in preparation for the hours of questioning he knew were about to start. Craig gazed though the two-way mirror at the man he was certain was innocent, trying to muster up some enthusiasm for the fight. He had to ask the questions and try to break Mulvenna down, but he didn't hold out much hope. This was a man who'd been on hunger-strike for months when he was interned in '71, defying every effort to make him eat. He'd stonewalled every question until eventually they'd had to let him go without charge. Despite all his crimes his only successful conviction was for Veronica Jarvis' murder; the one crime Craig was sure he hadn't done.

His lack of enthusiasm had been increased by the call he'd had from John ten minutes before. The hair under Lissy Trainor's fingernail had given them her murderer's D.N.A., but instead of him being excited by the story it told, he was more frustrated than before. The D.N.A. was a match to Mulvenna's, but not exact. A familial match. Someone related to him had committed the crime. They already knew he had no male cousins or brothers that looked like him, and that he had no kids. Maybe there were some other relatives who had been working with Mulvenna?

Perhaps it was a female relative? He shook his head as he thought about it. John didn't have the D.N.A.'s sex yet, that required more advanced tests, but a woman wouldn't have had the strength to strangle Lissy, no matter how angry they were at Melanie Trainor for putting Mulvenna away.

And why now, after all these years? Lissy's liaison with James O'Carolan seemed a much likelier cause for her death. Re-opening the Jarvis case would have rattled a lot of cages.

Except that D.N.A. didn't lie. The hair said Lissy had been in contact with a relative of Mulvenna's and they had to follow that trail wherever it led. Just then his phone rang, shattering the room's quiet. It was Liam.

"Shoot, Liam. What have you found?"

"God, it's weird up here, I feel like I've dropped down the rabbit hole and gone back fifty years."

Craig laughed, imagining Liam surrounded by people dressed in cheesecloth and batik. He was still moaning.

"It's a commune, I swear it is, boss. They hold weekends for people who want to get away and navel stare."

"And art courses."

"Aye, those too." It was said grudgingly, as if art and navel staring were closely linked. Liam's idea of art was a free print from the local garage framed on the wall.

"And?"

"Aye well, they're adamant that Mulvenna didn't leave here all weekend. I've checked the activity rota and he'd signed up for every class he could find. Sketching, oils, pottery."

"But he could have slipped out?"

Liam's grudging tone was replaced by one of thwarted gloom. "Much as it pains me to say it, it's unlikely, boss. They took pictures in pretty much every class and he's there front and centre in them all. And in the bar at night. Here, there's one thing that might interest you."

"What?"

"He met a woman. She was with him in the bar photos, holding hands as bold as brass. Her name is Helga, works here as a tutor here, oil painting and the like. I'm interviewing her next."

"Good." Craig thought for a moment. "How far is the venue from Portstewart?"

"It's this side of Ballymena, on the outskirts. Shortest distance is twenty-five miles so if he'd been fast it might only have taken him forty minutes there and back. It's doable."

Craig interrupted. "And if he'd gone cross country he could have shaved off another five miles."

"How could..?"

"On a motorbike. He has a BMW HP4."

"Fast as they come. I didn't even think about a bike."

"I still don't think he did it but have the C.S.I.s check the tyres for soil matches. And find out exactly what he was doing between seven and nine that Sunday night. The time your witness saw Lissy talking to the man on the parade."

Liam thought back through his interviews and realised he hadn't asked. He grabbed at the pile of photos. They were arranged in order of time and he found one that matched. There was no doubt, when Jenna Farrelly said she'd seen Mulvenna standing on the prom talking to Lissy, he'd been in a lecture on Grecian Urns surrounded by the rest of his class. Craig heard him swearing before the words reached the air.

"Aw, shit. He's here, listening to some nerd talk about Greek pots. It wasn't Mulvenna that she saw."

Craig smiled, pleased instead of annoyed. That meant neither O'Carolan nor Mulvenna had been the man Lissy had talked to on the seafront. And the hair they'd found on Lissy's body said Mulvenna hadn't been her killer. But someone had and they were related to Jonno Mulvenna in some way.

"OK. Come back, Liam. I've Mulvenna in the interview room but he can wait until you get here. Someone in his family killed Lissy and he must know who it is. Now he's going to tell us."

Chapter Twenty-Five

Craig gazed through the glass, marvelling at Jonno Mulvenna's calm. He was sitting with his eyes closed and his hands resting calmly on the table, looking for all the world like he was meditating. Maybe he was. After two hours of waiting he was giving no hint of impatience, much less showing signs that he was going to crack and confess all.

With an ordinary criminal the calm might have meant innocence, but from a hardened campaigner like Mulvenna two hours was a walk in the park. It gave them no clue one way or another about his innocence or guilt. Liam had just arrived and he was standing behind him in the viewing room, fed-up and hungry after his wasted trip. Good. It would make him edgy, and Liam edgy in an interview room was an awesome sight, just as long as he could rein his temper in.

Craig turned to Andy. He was sitting on a hard chair with his notebook by his side, ready to jot down any tics or tells that might give Mulvenna away. It was time. Craig led the way and yanked open the interview room door, hoping that the noise would make Mulvenna jump. He didn't move, just kept up his meditative pose. The only thing missing was a drawn out 'Omm....'

They scraped their chairs back deliberately loudly waiting for a flicker of Mulvenna's eyelids to give him away, knowing that it would be caught by Andy's sharp eye. But there was nothing. The only movement in the room was theirs and the only sound the whirr of the station's ancient heater in the corridor outside.

Craig sat in silence for a moment matching Mulvenna's

stance, then he nodded Liam to press the tape and started to speak.

"For the benefit of the tape. Present are Mr John Mulvenna of Mussenden Road, Chief Inspector Liam Cullen and Superintendent Marc Craig."

As soon as Craig opened his mouth Liam could hear that his heart wasn't in it. Mulvenna heard it too. His eyes sprang open showing a blue so bright that Liam wondered if it was real. There'd been too much talk of lenses and wigs for him to believe anything anymore. Before Craig could ask his first question Mulvenna raised his hand palm out, halting anything that they might say. He started to speak before Liam could interject and Craig motioned to give him time. The more a suspect talked the more they gave away even though they thought they were in control.

Liam smiled and folded his arms then sat back waiting for the suicide to commence. He glanced at Craig's face. He was smiling as well, but not at the same thing. He thought Mulvenna was innocent and he was going to give him the chance to tell them why!

Mulvenna stared at them each in turn before he spoke, in a respectful tone.

"Superintendent Craig, Chief Inspector Cullen, I'm going to save you an awful lot of work."

Liam couldn't stop himself. He leaned forward so quickly Craig thought he was going to hit the other man.

"So you're going to confess then, are you? Good stuff. Because we have you dead to rights."

Craig glared at him and Liam sat back and refolded his arms, barely subdued. Craig repeated his warning look then turned back to their guest.

"Please carry on, Mr Mulvenna, but be aware that everything you say will be on tape."

"Of course, I'd expect nothing less. And I'm sure your colleague behind the glass is writing everything down as well."

He leaned back and took his hands off the table, folding his arms in an echo of Liam's stance.

"I was told you wanted to question me again about Lissy Trainor's death, so feel free to ask me anything you like. But I'll tell you now that I didn't do it and I'll tell you why. One, I'd never met the girl so what motive would I have had? Two, I was out of the area when she was killed and three, there is no way you can connect me to the crime, not through witnesses or forensic evidence." He paused and smiled again. "But go ahead and ask me anything you'd like to ask and I promise I'll answer you truthfully where I can."

"Where you can?"

"Yes, where I can. I draw the line at dragging other people into this mess just to cover my own back." He stared intently at Craig then glanced at Liam pointedly as he spoke. "I know you understand that, Mr Craig. I get the impression that you wouldn't do it either."

Craig considered him carefully. Either he was telling the truth or he was a very clever man. Whichever it was he was attempting to divide Liam and him and it wasn't going to get him very far.

"Be very clear, Mr Mulvenna, your opinion of me is irrelevant, so don't get clever. All that matters is that you tell us what you know." Craig indicated the tape. "So go ahead. Speak."

Mulvenna smiled and nodded, recognising a worthy foe. He started to speak.

"I never met Lissy Trainor, which is a pity because she sounds like she was a nice girl. But I did encounter her mother in a previous life. She was a formidable lady and I imagine, no I know, that she's made a lot of enemies through the years. People she put away and the people who loved them. It will be a big suspect pool but I can only suggest that you look there for your motive for killing her daughter, because you're looking in the wrong place with me."

"Convince us."

Mulvenna shrugged. "Why should I? You already know that my alibi for the time of the girl's death is airtight. There are forty people who can vouch for where I was. And if you have any physical evidence then it will have ruled me out. So tell me why I should convince you?"

"Because you want to, that's why you're offering to talk." Craig leaned forward, warming to his theme. "And because you don't want to be labelled as a man who killed a young woman, any more than you wanted the label with Veronica Jarvis' death."

He leaned back and his voice took on a sarcastic tone. Liam glanced at him, surprised. Sarcasm wasn't high on Craig's list of weapons, unless he was goading someone. Realisation hit him. That was exactly what he was doing. He was goading Mulvenna with the one thing he knew he cared about. His self-image. Mulvenna saw himself as chivalrous and romantic and Craig was going to chip that away until he got where he wanted to be.

"You want us to believe that you never touched Veronica Jarvis and you were framed. You want us to believe that you accepted the frame-up because you'd killed so many other people and you deserved to do time. Do you really think we're that gullible? Come off it! You're scum Jonno, terrorist scum, scum that murdered countless people." Craig paused, watching Mulvenna's face. His calm façade was starting to crumble. Craig went in for the kill, his sarcasm thickening. "And you're rapist scum. You raped Ronni Jarvis, the mother of three small boys, then strangled her with your bare hands. Then you did the same to Lissy Trainor to get revenge against her Mum, the woman who successfully convicted you. You took a small, thin, frightened young girl and lured her somewhere. You terrified her, brutalised her, drugged and throttled her, then buried her on the same beach she'd played on as a child and stood back to watch her parents' pain. She was no match for you, why didn't you pick on someone your own size? But she couldn't fight back and that's what you like, isn't it Jonno? That's the sort of romantic hero you are."

Mulvenna moved so quickly that it shocked them both. He was over the table and on top of Craig before he had time to move. Craig's chair toppled backwards and he hit the floor with a bang. Mulvenna straddled him, his hands around his throat, his eyes burning in his head as he tightened his grip. He wasn't there for long. Craig brought his right fist up and cracked him hard on the chin, knocking him back onto the floor. Before Mulvenna could move Liam hauled him to his feet and cuffed him then threw him back roughly in his chair. He glowered down at him as Craig clambered to his feet rubbing his neck. He motioned Liam to take a seat and started again, his sarcasm ten times more brutal than before, but not for the reason Liam thought it was. He wasn't angry at Mulvenna lashing out, it was exactly what he'd been trying to achieve. He was keeping the pressure on.

"You like people to think you're the romantic artist, chivalrous to the end, but that's a crock of shit, isn't it? It's a myth you feed yourself so you can sleep at night. You're a killer of defenceless women, Jonno. Mothers, daughters, wives, none of them are safe from you. Did you strangle Ronni Jarvis like you've just tried to strangle me? Did she struggle and beg and gasp while you ignored her tears? And what about Lissy? She must have been easy meat? Young and fresh; ready to be plucked. Did you rape them both, Jonno, then try to destroy the evidence? We have D.N.A., it's hard to destroy that!"

Liam shot Craig a look then realised his ploy. Lissy hadn't been raped, that wasn't the D.N.A. they'd got. He thought Mulvenna was innocent and he was trying to prove it. He glanced at their suspect and saw that Craig's words were having the desired effect. Any hint of the romantic poet was gone and instead a snarling animal had taken his place. This was the man who'd killed more than a dozen policemen, but had he killed Ronni Jarvis and Lissy Trainor? Mulvenna's blue eyes were bright against his reddening face and white spit was gathering in the corners of his mouth. He yelled across the room at Craig

"NO! I didn't touch them, either of them. I wouldn't. I've never raised a hand to a woman."

"Then why let yourself be banged-up for Veronica Jarvis' death?"

"I deserved it."

"No, that's not enough. If you'd wanted to atone for your crimes you could have given money to the poor. Who were you protecting? Wasson? Was he a friend?"

The next sound they heard was Mulvenna's hysterical laugh. "A friend? He was scum. I would have killed him myself if I'd had a chance. He used his police protection like a shield to do whatever he liked."

"Police? Wasn't he MI5's man?"

The words were out before Mulvenna could stop himself. "He was run by the local plods and they wanted him free to inform. They covered his ass on Jarvis and however many other women he raped."

"And why were you their patsy of choice? Eh? You're really telling me that after two years out of the game raising money in the States you suddenly came to mind? You did it, you killed Jarvis and you're too much of a coward to own up."

"NO! I didn't lay a hand on her. I was framed because they wanted me gone before people found out."

"Found out what? What were they covering up?"

"Plenty. Things that could ruin careers."

Liam froze in his seat, afraid to breathe in case he ruined Craig's flow. Mulvenna had been framed by the police in '83. Set-up to take the fall for Ronni Jarvis' death so that Declan Wasson could keep selling information on the IRA. That much he understood. He even understood a peeler framing Mulvenna; he'd killed enough of them for everyone to be happy with that. There wouldn't have been many questions asked, especially if Mulvenna had been willing to go quietly. But now he was saying that he wasn't framed for the deaths of police, but because someone in the police was covering something up! No way. In the time he's taken to think it Craig had the question asked.

"Who?"

Mulvenna froze and stared into space for a second then he gazed at both of them, fixing Craig's eyes with a fevered look. It was on the tip of his tongue to give them a name and Craig willed him to say the words. He hadn't killed Veronica Jarvis or Lissy Trainor but he'd been willing to stay quiet and carry the label of rapist and murderer of women, knowing what would happen to him in prison for those crimes. For whom? Someone he loved? It had to be. A lover; it was what he'd thought all along. He corrected himself. For someone he'd loved unrequitedly. There was no other explanation. If they'd loved him back then they could never have watched him get put away.

Mulvenna opened his mouth to speak again but no sound came out. After a moment he shook his head. It was a stalemate and they needed to break it. Craig thought for a moment then brought out the sketch of the man Liam's witness had seen and placed it in front of him. Mulvenna shot him a questioning look.

"That looks like me!"

He scanned the sketch reading the statement underneath then he nodded, realising why his alibi for Sunday had been so important.

"I wasn't there." He watched Craig's reaction and then smiled. "But you already know it wasn't me. So who was it, lads? Do I have a look-alike?" He laughed. "Two Jonno Mulvennas, just what Northern Ireland needs."

Craig watched him, wondering if he knew how close he was to the truth. But he wasn't telling him about the D.N.A., he was keeping that little ace up his sleeve.

"What can you tell us about your family?"

Mulvenna shook his head slowly. "Tut, tut, Superintendent Craig. I told you I wouldn't drag anyone else into this. I'll tell you this much, there's no-one in my family that looks like me. Now, take me back to my cell now or call me a brief. Your choice."

His mouth snapped shut and Craig knew that they'd lost their chance. If someone Mulvenna had loved had framed him in 1983 he'd protected them then and he was going to keep on protecting them now. Craig slumped back in his seat and raked his hair. There was nothing they could do to make him give them a name. They would have to solve this some other way. He nodded to Liam to take Mulvenna back to the cell and sat alone with his thoughts.

Someone related to Mulvenna had killed Lissy in revenge for him being framed by the police in a case her mother led. They'd keep digging away at his family tree, but unless he gave them a pointer they'd have to D.N.A. test his whole family and hope they got a match.

What if it wasn't a relative of Mulvenna's and the hair had been a plant? If an old lover of Mulvenna's had been trying to cover things up they could have done it. And they could have been female or male, regardless of what Jake thought. But how the hell did they narrow it down? If it wasn't a lover and just a good friend then that widened the pool even more. What if it *was* a relative, and one of Mulvenna's family had joined the police under a different name and they were afraid of their secret coming out, so they framed him to get him out of the way? No, it was unlikely. Mulvenna hadn't been gagged, just locked-up. He could have told anyone anything he'd wanted.

He thought again. Mulvenna was loyal to his family, he might have kept quiet to protect one of them. There *had* been Catholic officers back then, Liam was only one. Sean Flanagan was Catholic and he'd made it to Chief Constable. If they'd been related to Mulvenna they definitely wouldn't have wanted anyone to know, not when he'd killed their colleagues. But why kill Lissy, unless they thought Melanie Trainor was going to expose them?

He was still thinking when Liam came back. He ran the confused idea past him. Liam rubbed his chin thoughtfully before he spoke.

"Aye. It's possible. There weren't that many Catholic officers back then, but the ones there were definitely wouldn't have wanted it known they were related to a scrote like Mulvenna. They might have wanted him out of the way, right enough. I'll have a dig around and see what I can find."

Liam's grapevine rivalled the windtalkers of World War Two. If it was out there then he'd find it.

"But what about the lover theory, boss? Have we abandoned that? And what would the link to the ACC be if Mulvenna had a relative on the force? Why kill Lissy?"

Craig shook his head. "I don't know Liam. I'm just shooting in the dark. I haven't abandoned the lover theory yet, but I'm not sure how to proceed there. I need to think about it."

As Craig said the words a bizarre idea popped into his head. If Sean Flanagan was out of the way, Melanie Trainor would be next in line for the CC post. What if Flanagan had a secret she was about to expose? What if he was related to Mulvenna? People had killed for less. He shook his head, dismissing the idea as fantasy, then he realised Liam was speaking.

"You were right."

"About what?"

Liam sniffed grudgingly. "You were right about Mulvenna not killing Ronni Jarvis, or Lissy. He didn't do it." He grinned. "If he didn't cave in under your sarcasm it has to be true."

A rueful expression crossed Craig's face. "I'm not exactly proud of it, or of punching him."

"Ah well, needs must. It was either his jaw or your neck and Nicky would have killed us both if you'd ended up dead."

***

"How can one man have so many cousins and aunts? It's like that movie with Steve Martin."

"'Cheaper by the Dozen' you mean? I preferred the 1950's original."

Davy and Jake stared at Nicky as if she was Methuselah.

"I saw it on TV!"

Annette patted her on the shoulder in sympathy.

"It's a sad day when being in your thirties makes you feel old, Nicky, but you've reached it. Time to start listening to rubbish music and dying your hair blue to pretend you're young."

She caught Davy winking at his partner in crime then realised they'd both been had. She pulled herself into an official pose and took back control.

"Right. If you've quite finished teasing Nicky, what have you found?"

Jake started reciting a long list of names in a bored tone. He finally ended with "And Maria McCallion" and sat back with a sigh. Annette joined him. Jonno Mulvenna had fifteen living relatives whose D.N.A. might have resembled his. She looked at the list and divided them the easy way.

"OK. Jake, you take the men and I'll take the women, but let's see if we can narrow it a bit more before we waste our time. Davy, can you check if any of these have emigrated, are in prison or comatose, please. Otherwise they warrant a visit."

Davy smiled and glanced out the window at the torrential November rain then settled back into his chair, smug that he didn't have to venture into the cold. Maybe being an analyst had its upside. He eyed the packet of Rich Tea beside Nicky's percolator and she took the hint, pressing the ever bubbling coffee onto boil while he typed in his search. In the time it took the coffee to perk and a tray of cups and biscuits to land on his desk, he'd finished. He pressed print and handed Annette and Jake each a new list.

"S…seven of the names have gone, that leaves eight. Five men and three women." He popped a biscuit into his mouth and continued to speak, much to Nicky's look of disgust.

"Don't you dare speak with your mouth full, Davy Walsh. You're turning into Liam and one of him around here is quite enough."

He blushed and took a quick gulp of tea, washing away the offending snack. Nicky nodded him to restart.

"S...sorry, Nicky. Anyhow. One of the women is eighty-four-years-old but the rest are between twenty and sixty; siblings, cousins or their kids. There's nothing more I can do to shorten the list, s...sorry."

"Thanks, Davy. Jake, give me one of the men's names."

She lifted a cup of coffee and then glanced at the time. "It's five o'clock now. If Nicky gives us a location map we should be able to do a first sweep by seven."

She drank her coffee quickly, watching as Jake picked at the letters on his mug. He set his cup down.

"Don't you drink coffee?"

He shook his head. "Nope, it gives me a headache. I'm a tea man."

Nicky looked at him as if he'd committed treason then shrugged, making a mental note to add more teabags to her shopping list. She handed them each a map and an address list and waved them off her floor.

***

Jake was halfway through his list when his mobile flashed with a message to ring base. He drew a line through the two names he'd just visited and lifted his phone, thinking. The two men he'd seen had clean alibis and what was more important neither of them looked anything like Jonno Mulvenna. They hadn't been the man Jenna Farrelly had seen talking to Lissy that day. They'd check their D.N.A. to rule them out but he didn't hold out much hope.

The phone was lifted in one ring and Nicky's husky voice

broke through.

"What can I do for you, Nicky?"

"You and Annette can forget the women on the list. Dr Winter's come back with the D.N.A.'s sex. It's male."

Jake nodded. It made sense. Violent murder was usually a man's game. The lack of defensive wounds on Lissy backed up a male attacker too. Lissy hadn't been big but she would have put up more of a fight against a woman, but all they had to say that she'd struggled some scratches she'd made herself and the hair beneath her nail. Her assailant probably didn't have a mark. Nicky was still talking.

"He said the hair was virgin, too."

"Un-dyed? He's sure?"

"Definite. You're looking for a man with naturally dark hair."

It didn't rule anyone in or out and Jake said as much. Mulvenna could have worn a real hair wig to cover his grey and whoever the killer was they could have changed their hair colour since the attack. Nicky sniffed, huffing.

"I'm only passing on the message. Working it out is your bit. I'm going now, to phone Annette."

"Don't worry, I'll do it, thanks. He smiled, mollifying her with his next words. "Thanks for the coffee earlier, Nicky, I'm sure it was very nice. It just gives me terrible migraines, that's all."

It was the right thing to say. He'd remembered Liam saying she got migraines and her immediate change of tone said he'd made a friend for life.

"Oh, they're terrible, aren't they? Do you think coffee makes them worse? Maybe I'd better cut it out and see. Thanks Jake, and thanks for telling Annette."

He cut the call smiling and hit redial, waiting for Annette to pick up.

"Where are you?"

"On the Crumlin Road. Why?"

"Nicky's phoned through. Dr Winter says the hair is

definitely male and un-dyed. The natural colour is dark."

"They could have dyed it since. We've no idea what colour they are now."

"That's what I said. And it's definitely male, the D.N.A. says so. The hair was never grey so doesn't that rule Mulvenna out?"

"No. He still has some naturally dark hairs, she might have just grabbed one of those. Or he could have worn a real-hair wig."

She sighed and Jake knew she'd just wasted an hour visiting the women on her list. He offered a suggestion.

"That leaves us with three men to visit, Annette. Do you want to do them together? If one of them is our man it might be better for you not to question them alone."

Annette smiled at his chivalry.

"Thanks, Jake. Who's next on your list?"

"Mulvenna's uncle. Fergal Muldoon. I'll text you his address and meet you there."

OK, let's see if we can get through them today. It'll give me a chance to update you about Lucia as well."

***

Julia stared through the window of her office at the small car-park, wondering why she was digging in her heels. Limavady was pretty and the surrounding countryside had a lot to offer beauty-wise, but that wasn't what was making her hang onto her job so hard. Not even her brother working as a doctor in the nearby South-West was playing a part. She only saw him once a week and she could easily commute from Belfast to do that, and her Mum was in England so if anything Belfast was closer for seeing her. So if it wasn't her wanting to stay in Limavady what was stopping her from marrying Marc and moving in with him?

Was she really so wedded to the police that a year or so out until a vacancy came up would be such a chore? As soon as the question appeared she answered it, no. It wasn't Limavady and it wasn't the police, it was security. She needed to feel secure. She shook her head. No again. That simply wasn't true. If security was what she needed then marrying Marc would give her that.

Perhaps she didn't really love him? She smiled to herself. Yes, she did. It was the one thing she was sure of in this whole stupid thing. And yet she'd turned his proposal down. Why? Was it because she'd wanted a romantic proposal over dinner with him gazing into her eyes? NO. She wasn't that childish. In the moment she had her answer. She knew why. It was because he'd only been prompted to ask her by having a problem to solve, and the solution had brought his chauvinism to the fore. Marry me, we'll have a baby and you won't need to worry your pretty little head about a career. He hadn't said it in so many words, just in two; marry me.

He was perfect for her, almost perfect, in every way except… She frowned, knowing that a million women would have jumped down the phone and into his arms the moment he'd asked. But she hadn't. Why, again? Was it his assumption that his career would come first? Yes. As soon as she thought it she knew it was only half true. It wasn't just his job he was putting first, but his family. It was a good point, not a bad one. If he did it for them he would do it for her later in life. And yet…

There was something else. When you scratched away the layers of good son and caring man, she knew that deep down Marc believed his job mattered more than hers, and that was something she couldn't have. Maybe he didn't realise it consciously, but it was true and she couldn't live with it.

Years of army macho-men had made her a feminist of the older school. Brittle and overreacting to imagined slights. She knew she did it, but she couldn't stop herself. She knew it was wearing for the men who loved her. Her brother often said it was. But was she really being so unreasonable expecting full equality? It didn't matter if she was. She was who she was, and how can you be anyone else?

She turned away from the window and sat down at her desk, knowing there was no solution within her grasp. She lifted her cigarettes from her handbag and lit one up, knowing she was breaking the law and the building's rules. She didn't care; it would help her think and she needed to do that now. She sucked hard on the slim stick until it glowed then inhaled deeply, feeling the nicotine hit her brain. She felt more relaxed immediately, although she doubted that it worked that quick, then she focused on the problem in hand.

If she challenged Marc to give up his job and live with her, he could legitimately cite his parent's proximity as an excuse. It made even moving midway to live near Lough Neagh nonsense. Plus, they couldn't live on her salary alone, whereas they could live on his. So how could she get to the truth and find out if he was just being practical, or if he really was a chauvinist? And why did it matter to her so much? Was her feminism more important than love?

The only way to find out would be if she was a Superintendent and lived in Belfast, then it would be a straight choice of which of them gave up their career. She smoked until her cigarette burnt down and tried to make sense of things. That *was* the only way it would be an even choice, but it wasn't the life they had. She put her head in her hands and started to sob, defeated. There was no solution that was going to make them both happy.

***

Craig parked his Audi in the allocated space at Headquarters and pushed through the revolving door. When he'd called Sean Flanagan to give him an update he'd suggested it would be better face to face. He was right. Phone conversations were within Melanie Trainor's or MI5's reach, and the more suspects they ruled out the more it pointed towards MI5 and police involvement in '83 coming home to roost.

He nodded at the officer at reception and flashed his badge, waiting until he ran his fingers down a list and found his name.

"Please take a seat, Superintendent. The Chief's staff officer will be down to escort you in a moment."

Craig nodded to himself. This was no informal chat in the study with Mrs Flanagan bringing in the tea. It was getting official now and Craig knew that their meeting would be taped. It might never be used of course, but the Chief was starting to watch his back.

Five minutes later a young officer showed him up and Flanagan's secretary nodded him to knock the door. It was opened quickly and Sean Flanagan stood there with a wide smile on his face. It wasn't the frosty reception Craig had anticipated. He was surprised. Maybe he'd been wrong; maybe the Chief wasn't joining the ranks of people eager to protect their backs.

He waved Craig cheerfully to a chair and Craig scanned his desk for signs of a tape. If there was one it was well hidden.

"Coffee, Marc? I seem to remember you mainline the stuff."

"Yes, thanks, sir."

Two minutes later the coffee was in front of them and Flanagan was munching a biscuit like a man without a care in the world.

"Right. Update me. I've been hearing on the grapevine that the case is turning out to be even more complex than we thought."

Craig nodded. It could get even worse soon. He brought Flanagan up to speed on his conversation with MI5, Liam's witness I.D., Mulvenna's alibi and his complete refusal to speak.

Flanagan nodded. "I'm not surprised at that. I interviewed him once when he was interned. Stubborn bugger. Not the sort to give someone names away." He stared at Craig. "You told me what you thought on Monday, Marc, but it was just theory then. Tell me what you think now you're deeper into the case."

Craig put down his coffee and met his gaze. "I think Mulvenna was framed for Veronica Jarvis' death by someone in the police here who wanted him out of the way."

Flanagan didn't blink.

"Because he was a terrorist, you mean?"

"No. There was a more personal motive, I'm sure of it. Mulvenna had been in the States on and off for two years, fundraising. He wasn't top of the hit list back then. There were ten names before him that would have sprung to mind. He was chosen specifically."

"And the motive was personal?"

"Yes."

"What? Revenge, debt, fear or love?"

Debt hadn't even occurred to him and he said so.

"Look into it then, but your gut says it's one of the others."

Craig nodded. Or a mixture. "I can't shake the feeling that this is a lover taking revenge, sir. Or afraid of being outed."

"Revenge for what? Because Mulvenna was unfaithful to them in the States?"

"Maybe."

Craig watched the older man curiously. There was none of the shock that others had displayed at the idea a police officer could have had an affair with a terrorist. Flanagan read his mind.

"You're thinking, why isn't he more shocked at the suggestion of love across the barbed wire, aren't you? And you were thinking it on Monday."

"Yes, sir. Everyone else seems to be, so why not you?"

Flanagan leaned back in his chair and gazed through the window at the street outside. They were in the city centre but his look said that his mind was somewhere much more romantic. He held his silence for a moment then he spoke.

"I said before that people were young back then too, and feelings were running high. Well, it wasn't just sex, young people fell in love in the seventies and eighties, just the same way they do now. And that was the thing about The Troubles. The people sitting behind desks in Whitehall might have been old men, but the foot soldiers, the men and women on both sides, weren't. We were young and single and foolish and people fell in love with people they shouldn't have done."

Craig asked the question warily, knowing he was crossing the line. "You, sir?"

Flanagan smiled. "Me, the man beside me and the man across the way. None of us were immune to a pair of soft eyes and a winning smile."

"Can I ask, were there many same-sex relationships back then?"

"As many as there are now, Marc, only much more hidden. Remember it was still illegal here until 1982 and the stigma lasted a lot longer than that. Add the macho atmosphere of the forces to the mix and you'll see why if it did happen it would have been kept underground."

"So you think my theory that a lover wanted personal revenge on Mulvenna is possible?"

"More than possible. But you have to ask yourself three things. What could it possibly have to do with the murder you're investigating now? Who was the lover? And how could someone who was young enough to have been Mulvenna's lover back in '83 possibly be linked with the man DCI Cullen's witness saw talking to Lissy Trainor before her death, if he's linked at all?"

"I need to interview the ACC, sir."

"Yes, you do. But I know Melanie Trainor well. You'll only get one shot at her before she clams up.

"She may be able to shed some light on things. She has to be questioned properly."

Flanagan nodded. "Agreed. But with one caveat. I want to be there when you do."

"Of course, but may I ask why?"

"Because I knew Melanie back when she was a girl and we

had a fling before we were both married."

Craig's eyebrows shot up at the confidence. Flanagan continued in a matter of fact voice. "Don't worry Craig, it's not a state secret. Melanie was a bit of a girl back then, so I was just one name on her list. It only lasted two weeks and there's been no hard feelings since, but being someone's lover teaches you things about them. The main one is that you can tell when they're lying."

He stared directly at Craig, holding his gaze. "Trust me, Marc, you want me in that room. She'll think that I'm there to protect her interests and I will be, but I'll tell you exactly when she lies and what about."

"You're sure she will, sir? Lie, I mean."

"Aren't you? ACC Trainor has got to the top in a man's world. She's very talented, don't get me wrong, but that wasn't enough in the bad old days. Do you think she got there on merit alone?"

"Why then? Contacts?" Craig already knew the answer, Hugh Trainor had told him when they'd met, but he wanted to see what Flanagan said. His next words surprised him.

"I know some people thought Melanie slept her way to the top, but that wasn't all of it. She got there because she could lie, lie with the best of them. She lied about her lovers and she lied about her achievements, even when she didn't need to. It might have taken her longer to get to the top if she hadn't, but she would have got there all the same. She just got so used to lying that she forgot how to tell the truth. She'll lie through her teeth to you, Marc. Unless I'm there."

Craig nodded, it made sense. An honest woman would have been desperate to help them solve her daughter's murder. She'd have told them anything there was to tell. He didn't doubt that Melanie Trainor loved Lissy and yet she'd stayed well away from the investigation for days, not through grief but in case she let something slip that might damage her career. Secrecy and lies had become second nature to her. Craig went to ask another question, struggling with how to phrase it. He needn't have worried. Flanagan had already read his mind.

"Don't worry, Marc. I won't say anything to interrupt your interview. I'll just watch and tell you afterwards what I thought. Think of me as a human polygraph."

"Thanks, sir. In that case, I'd be glad to have your help. In fact, I think the whole session might be better held here, at your invitation, if that's OK?"

Flanagan nodded. "Very wise. She's not going to refuse a meeting with me and by the time she sees you, it will be too late and too impolitic for her to run away."

He tapped on his computer screen and pulled up a diary. "How does tomorrow morning at ten o'clock suit?"

"Great. I'll be here at five past to give you time to meet and greet her."

"Good. I'll brief my secretary to show you in." He smiled. "How's Nicky Morris by the way? Bloody good P.A. I have to admit I was thinking of poaching her from you at one point."

Craig smiled and Flanagan saw the challenge in his eyes. You can try...sir. They laughed simultaneously then rose and Flanagan extended his hand to shake. He showed Craig out, knowing he was already thinking of how to frame his questions for the next day. They had to be sharp enough to give Melanie Trainor no wriggle room and force her to either talk or clam up. Knowing that if she did the latter she was admitting she knew something that could have caused her daughter's death, and that refusing to help was going to jeopardise her career. The one thing she really loved.

Chapter Twenty-Six

6 p.m. Belfast.

Liam gulped down his mug of tea and patted his stomach, satisfied. Hotel food was all very well but no-one could make an Irish stew better than Danni. He watched her as she moved around the kitchen unpacking the groceries without making a sound, her petite frame and delicate ways a stark contrast to his six-feet-six of noise. He crossed the room until he was standing behind her then leaned down and circled her waist with his arms.

Danni Cullen knew exactly what her husband wanted and she wasn't playing his game. She had a toddler to collect from nursery and a baby who needed changed. She loosened his hands finger by finger then handed him two carrier-bags full of food.

"Make yourself useful, Liam. Put the cold things in the fridge and the rest in the cupboards please. And in the right place this time."

She turned to leave the room.

"Aw, Danni. I haven't seen you for days. Where's your romance?"

"Upstairs crying because he needs his nappy changed." She smiled at him coyly. "Unless you'd like to change him, that is?"

Liam turned back hastily towards the fridge and she shook her head.

"No. I didn't think so. Well, I'm telling you now, D.C.I. Cullen, if you want any more babies you're going through nine months of being fat and you're changing every dirty nappy that there is."

Liam grinned, knowing that meant they would be practicing later that night. He closed the fridge door and deposited the last of the tins in the cupboard then turned towards the small back room that he liked to call his own. Study was too grand a name for it, it was basically a cubby hole with a door, but it was good place to hide when the hoovering needed done, citing 'work' as his excuse.

He actually was working this time. Craig had asked him about Catholic officers back in the day and whether a member of Mulvenna's family could have been one and changed his name. It was possible. Security checks existed back then but they weren't as rigorous as they were now. Unless they'd known of the link few people would ever have thought to look.

He lifted a shoe-box down from a shelf and pulled off the lid. It was full of small notebooks, standard issue to every cop even now, although hand-held computers were fast taking their place. He sighed heavily, gazing at the fifty books inside, crammed in tight as a drum. A second box grinned down at him from a higher shelf. This was going to take him all night. Visions of his romantic evening were starting to fade when he glimpsed something that gave him hope. His old GAA kit was lying in the corner, long since abandoned in favour of the couch and remote control. It gave him an idea.

A lot of Catholic officers would have taken part in the sport, even back in the day. It would give him a list of young men's names by year. Davy could eliminate them first then he'd start looking for the rest. If he was lucky he'd find Mulvenna's relative amongst the teams. He didn't want to think about the hours he'd spend flicking through his notebooks if he failed.

He pulled out a pile of fixture programmes and tried to put faces to the names as he compiled a likely list. He phoned them through to the C.C.U. for Davy to check against the Mulvenna link and sauntered back into the living room for an evening of

TV.

***

At seven o'clock Liam's mobile rang. Craig. He started talking without any preamble.

"I met the Chief Constable this afternoon. We're getting Melanie Trainor in tomorrow morning."

Liam made a half-hearted offer, hoping it would be refused. "Do you want me there?"

Craig heard his ploy and smiled. "Where are you?"

Liam tossed up whether to lie or not and decided to tell the truth. "At home sorting through my back files. I'm trying to find a Catholic officer who might have hidden his connections with Mulvenna back in '83."

"And?"

"I made a first list from the GAA teams back then. Davy's running the checks now. If there's nothing there then I'll try a few other sports and start working my way through my old notebooks."

It was a neat approach and Craig said so. Liam repeated his question about the Trainor interview.

"Sorry. I didn't answer you. No, I don't need you there, thanks. Flanagan's offered to be my wingman. He's not going to speak, just watch her reactions for lies."

Liam whistled, impressed. It wasn't often that the top brass offered operational support, even if it was going to be silent. Craig had stopped talking and Liam could tell from the silence that he was waiting for a reply to something.

"Sorry, boss. I missed your question."

"I said, how would you like to stay in Belfast tomorrow to pick up on the GAA stuff and whatever Annette and Jake have managed to find? Call in on John as well if you would. Andy and I can handle everything back up north."

"Excellent stuff. I'll do that. I've had enough sleep."

"I doubt that Danni has. OK, look, I'll be at Headquarters tomorrow morning, let's meet at the lab about twelve for lunch to catch up, then I'll head back up North. I'll warn John we're coming."

"Grand. Do that. He can get the kettle on."

***

Annette looked at the list in her hand and struck through another name. They'd interviewed every male relative Jonno Mulvenna had and they all had alibis. Her heart sank. Three of them had agreed to the D.N.A. test and the others had dug their heels in, saying she didn't have grounds to ask. They were right. She'd take what she could get but she didn't hold out much hope of any of them matching the hair at their murder scene. She glanced at Jake expecting to see a fed-up expression on his face, but instead he was wearing a puzzled frown.

"Five pence for your thoughts."

"That's inflation."

He fell silent again and Annette prodded him in the side with her pen

"What's the frown in aid of? A wasted afternoon?"

He shook his head slowly. "No, not that. Did you ever feel something nagging at you but every time you tried to find it, it slipped away?"

"Every morning when I try to remember where I left my keys."

He smiled and she noticed how young he looked. He was close in age to Davy, but Jake had an air of authority that made him seem older somehow.

"No, it's not something I've forgotten, it's something I don't know yet. It's like one of those magic eye photos that you can't quite see." He shook his head as if he was trying to clear it. "Ignore me, I'm talking rubbish." He glanced at the list in her hand. "What's next, boss?"

She smiled at the unfamiliar tag. She'd been the team's junior forever. It was nice to have someone to give her, her rank for a change.

"Let's get them D.N.A. tested tomorrow and see if anything comes from that." She glanced at the clock. "But for now, let's go home."

***

Craig lay on the couch and flicked on his TV, staring at the screen but not seeing it at all. He stared at it for hours until the dim winter light outside deepened to black and his watch said 'go to bed'. But there was no point going to bed, just to lie undressed in a different room instead of lying here. He wasn't going to sleep wherever he was. His mind was too busy.

He tried to work out what was making it churn and finally settled on three things. The case, Julia, and a growing feeling that something was going on in his team that everyone knew about except Liam and him. He pushed the last one away and marked it for attention another day then turned back to numbers one and two.

Andy had ruled out all of Wasson's rape victims after '83 and any of their families who had a motive for revenge for Wasson being set free. It was a blind alley. No-one except James O'Carolan fitted the mould and he'd been working with Lissy to re-open the case. He definitely wanted her alive. Declan Wasson's rapes weren't the motive for Lissy Trainor's death.

That left the boyfriend Conor Ryland and her stalker friend, Mary-Ann. No again; they'd both been ruled out by Liam's nose for a perp or an alibi. So that brought him back to Doe. Jonno Mulvenna. Somewhere in Lissy Trainor's death there was a link with Mulvenna, he was sure of it. She'd been buried in the sand in exactly the same way Veronica Jarvis had, a woman whose murder Mulvenna had been sent down for in 1983. Wrongly in his opinion; it was a frame, but they couldn't ignore the link.

Then there was the hair under Lissy's nail, the D.N.A. was a familial match for Mulvenna and now they knew it was a man. And finally the thirty something man Jenna Farrelly had seen, her sketch of him a match for Mulvenna, looking almost thirty years younger than his age. A younger relative of some sort, but they were still trying to find out who.

If it was a relative of Mulvenna, why kill Lissy? The only thing that sprang to mind was that her mother had put him away for twenty years. A grudge? If it was a grudge it wasn't one Mulvenna held, he was sure of that, but someone had definitely wanted to punish Melanie Trainor. Had she framed Mulvenna in '83, and if she had then why had she done it? Yes, people high up had wanted Wasson freed and she might have been acting on their wishes, but why choose Jonno Mulvenna to fill the gap? Who had fingered him and why? Mulvenna seemed a random choice, two years after he'd last been active.

Choosing Mulvenna felt personal and Craig's mind wandered back to someone wanting to silence him about an affair; gay or straight. He shook his head immediately as if there was someone there to see the gesture. No. Locking Mulvenna up wouldn't have silenced him, only his own discretion had done that. He'd been locked away for some other reason, to get him offside, to keep something quiet, and someone in his family had been pissed enough about it to kill Lissy Trainor thirty years after the fact.

Craig rubbed his eyes hard then wandered to the fridge to pull out another beer, knowing he'd all but exhausted every train of thought. Lissy Trainor had been killed to punish her mother for her part in framing Mulvenna thirty years before. Now he had to find out why Melanie Trainor had done it and who was avenging Mulvenna now. That was the direction his questions would take tomorrow morning but he didn't hold out much hope of her answering.

He sat down heavily on the couch and rested his head against its back, turning his thoughts to his other dilemma;

Julia. Half of him wished that he'd gone on to Limavady, had the inevitable tearful scene and then ended up in bed. At least he wouldn't be sitting alone tonight. Except that he would still be sitting alone eventually. Next weekend, and every other weekend and weekday after that, unless one of them transferred.

He'd been here before. A loving relationship pulled apart by two careers, neither of them giving an inch. They were only jobs so why couldn't any of them let go? Camille with her acting, him with his murder squad, Julia with her role in the North-West. What made them all cling on so hard? Was it money? Status? Power? Or the fear that without their roles and titles they were really no-one at all.

He shook his head. He didn't know the answer but he knew the impossible decisions that lay ahead. He'd been naïve with Camille, believing that their feelings could weather the distance when she'd first started working in the States. He'd been wrong. The realities of life had broken them up.

He smiled to himself in the dark. Maybe it was his Italian half that made him believe that love could conquer all. Romeo, Romeo, and a balcony in Verona. But it didn't. Life always intervened. Elderly parents who needed his proximity and care, a team he loved working with, and the chance to put killers away and protect people. He was good at it and he'd get even better, given half a chance. Would he get that sitting in an office in Limavady, working on burglaries or some other crimes? Or would he turn into another Terry Harrison, more worried about politics and protecting his back than anything else?

An image of Julia filled his mind. Her soft blue eyes and cherubic smile widening whenever she saw him walking her way. Her red curls flowed down her back, slim and pale when they were making love. He smiled to himself at the thought of her grumpy little moods, so fierce and defensive when they'd first met, but softer now and more playful. Lasting only a minute or two and then becoming giggles that pushed her frown away. He loved her. Perhaps that was why he'd proposed to her on the phone, the words rushing out before he'd had a chance to think. Did he want to get married right now? No, not really, but he would if it solved their dilemma. But she hadn't said yes. She'd got angry instead.

As he thought of it he realised that he was hurt. Hurt by her anger and suspicion of his motives, and even more hurt that she rejected his proposal. He'd only asked one woman to marry him before; Camille. She'd said yes and they embraced each other and their secret for months in their little flat, until life had intervened. He remembered her face when he'd asked. Her smile had spread and reached her eyes, making them dance and sparkle until she'd cried. But Julia…

He shrugged off his hurt, refusing to let it cloud the love that had prompted him to ask. He loved Julia. Suddenly another feeling slipped into the mix and he recognised it from the moment before he'd proposed. It was desperation, and it was ugly. Not desperation to get married, God no, not that. He was like most men, postponing the inevitable as long as he could. Marriage was forever, the final step; it could wait a while in his book. This desperation had been different; the desperate desire to solve a problem, but more than that. Desperation born of fear. Fear of reliving the pain he'd felt when he'd split from Camille. That was what he'd felt today and that was why he'd proposed. And it was no basis to marry anyone on, no matter how much you loved them.

He drained his bottle of beer and potted it in the bin, then went to have a shower. Maybe it would clear his head and maybe it would help him sleep, but it wouldn't answer his questions, he was damn sure of that.

Chapter Twenty-Seven

Thursday 10.30 a.m.

Craig sat discretely behind a partition in Sean Flanagan's outer office, waiting to be called. The Chief Constable had greeted him forty minutes earlier, done up in his finest, shiny buttons and all, then he'd re-entered his office to await Melanie Trainor's arrival. Craig's only concession to interviewing a senior officer was the Hugo Boss tie he hadn't worn for two months. In his book Melanie Trainor was no less special than any other grieving parent, but definitely no more. He knew she would attempt to use her rank in whatever way she could and he wasn't going to give her any encouragement.

He glanced at his watch. She was thirty minutes late. Passive aggressive behaviour if ever he'd seen it. Sean Flanagan was staring at his watch as well. He didn't pull rank often and he preferred democracy to hierarchy any day, but the ACC was really pushing it. Donna, Flanagan's P.A. knocked his door and entered on his 'yes', looking harassed. Craig watched her from his vantage point. She'd looked harassed when he'd been there the day before as well. It must be hard for both her and the Chief to deal with every day.

Flanagan asked her to wait and strode out of his office, beckoning Craig to join them inside. Melanie Trainor had lost her right to private time with him. Now she would be interviewed like anyone else. Craig took a seat at the desk and they turned towards the P.A., waiting for her to speak. She was a small woman, somewhere in middle-age, but it was hard to put a number of her years. Her face was creased in a frown and her hands fluttered nervously across her face as she spoke.

"Assistant Chief Constable Trainor is downstairs, sir. Shall I ask her to come up?"

"Not yet, Donna. Bring her up in ten minutes then give her a coffee and a seat. I'll buzz when we're ready for her. Can you cancel my eleven o'clock meeting please and we may need to have a working lunch."

She fluttered out and Flanagan turned to Craig. "It will do Melanie no harm to wait a while. Two can play at her game. Forget the nice introduction we discussed yesterday, Marc, go straight into it. I'll only intervene if I really think I should."

Craig nodded. They'd covered his thoughts from the night before when he'd arrived. Lissy Trainor had been killed to punish her mother for her part in framing Jonno Mulvenna in 1983. They knew it had been done to cover Declan Wasson, now they needed the answers to two questions, although Craig didn't hold out a hope in hell of even getting one. Why had Melanie Trainor chosen Mulvenna to frame? And who was hell-bent on avenging him now? He reminded himself she was grieving mother and she'd done a lot of good work throughout the years. That was why they were here instead of in an interview room. But it was the only concession Craig was prepared to make.

Fifteen minutes later Flanagan pressed the intercom signalling that they were ready and Melanie Trainor entered, dressed in her number ones. Donna hopped from foot to foot behind her gathering orders for drinks. The two men stood and the Chief waved Trainor to a seat across the desk then released Donna from the room like a bird freed from its cage.

Flanagan didn't mention the time. Instead he smiled kindly at the mother across the desk and launched into his speech, offering his condolences again and saying how sorry he was that they'd had to invite her in. Trainor sat with her hands demurely folded and her eyes locked on her boss' face, completely ignoring Craig. It was as if he didn't matter in her world. He wasn't put out; he *didn't* matter, except that he was the one that she would answer to, although she didn't know it yet.

Donna entered and left and Flanagan poured drinks for them all. Trainor's demeanour grew tenser with every sip, until finally she put down her cup and locked her hands together, every muscle taut and ready to snap. The CC spoke first.

"You know Superintendent Craig of course."

He indicated Craig, inviting her eyes to shift that way. They remained locked straight ahead, refusing to acknowledge Craig was in the room. Craig could feel her shame. He was her inferior in every way that she thought mattered, but she was going to have to answer his questions or be embarrassed in front of her boss.

"Superintendent Craig would like to ask you a few questions regarding your daughter's death and I'm satisfied it's essential that he does so." Flanagan's tone shifted from soft condolence to 'this is what you will do' and the ACC's hands whitened. She forced her head slowly towards Craig. Her anger was unmistakable but he couldn't divine its exact cause.

Craig straightened the pile of notes in front of him in a way that gave them weight. They were only rough notes and forensic results but she wasn't to know that. If she had secrets she would be afraid that they knew them, and that they were hidden in the pile.

"Good morning, ACC Trainor. Before I start I'm going to bring you up to date with where we are on your daughter's very sad death."

He outlined their searches and the questions they'd asked so far, watching her face carefully when he mentioned Declan Wasson and MI5. She didn't flinch, only her increased blink rate saying when he'd hit a nerve. He covered the interviews with rape victims and their interviews of Lissy's friends, then he reached the statement from Jenna Farrelly. As he described her sighting of the thirty year old version of Mulvenna Melanie

Trainor's hands twitched and gave her away. He was getting close.

He covered her daughter's contacts with James O'Carolan and her intended re-opening of the Jarvis case and watched as her eyebrows shot up in surprise. She hadn't known! She hadn't known that Lissy was working with James O'Carolan to have Mulvenna's conviction overthrown. It ruled out her killing her daughter to keep her quiet, although she hadn't been high on his list of suspects anyway.

His final card was the D.N.A. bearing a family link to Mulvenna. He watched as her eyes widened wildly when he mentioned it. Before she'd recovered he rounded up on the lines that he and the Chief had agreed.

"We believe that your daughter was killed to punish you for the conviction of Jonno Mulvenna in 1983 for a crime he didn't commit. We believe that you framed Mulvenna to protect your informant, Declan Wasson, and for a more personal reason that we don't yet know, although we will. We also believe that you're deliberately withholding information that can lead us to your daughter's murderer."

They both saw her leg jerk and her knee start to shake. She placed a hand on her knee to still it, giving herself away.

"So I really only have two questions, ACC Trainor. Why did you choose John Mulvenna to frame? And who would be determined to avenge him now?"

Melanie Trainor stilled her shaking leg and pulled her eyes away from Craig's face, fixing them on the floor. She said nothing so Craig asked the questions again, separately and together, rephrasing them in different ways. When he'd asked them for the last time she opened her mouth to speak.

"I have no knowledge that would enable me to answer your questions. May I go now, Chief Constable?"

Flanagan stared straight at her, his tone much less friendly than before. "Look at me when you speak, ACC Trainor."

She pulled her large brown eyes towards him and Craig

thought they held the glint of un-shed tears. She repeated her request and Flanagan shook his head.

"Assistant Chief Constable Trainor. By refusing to cooperate with our enquiries you leave me no option but to suspend you from duty."

Trainor nodded and rose sharply. "Will that be all, sir?"

Flanagan's face flushed with anger and his voice took on a harsh edge.

"For now, ACC Trainor, but Superintendent Craig will see you again tomorrow morning and this time it will be in an interview room at High Street Station." He paused and shook his head. "You're a very foolish woman, Melanie. You could be throwing away your career here, not to mention preventing us from finding the man who killed your child. If you're protecting someone…"

Trainor cut across him. "Thank you, sir. I understand. I'll present myself at High Street tomorrow morning at nine a.m." She gave him a sharp salute then turned and left the room. Flanagan sat back heavily and turned to Craig.

"Well, God knows what we're to make of that. We got nothing at all."

Craig shook his head. "On the contrary, sir. We got a lot. Enough to know that we're on the right track. Didn't you see her reactions when I mentioned Wasson and Mulvenna's frame-up? And the D.N.A.? We're spot-on there. But she knew nothing about James O'Carolan working with Lissy to re-open the '83 case. She didn't harm her daughter. I'd lay money on that."

"You got a lot from her saying nothing, Marc."

"Only her mouth said nothing, sir. Her body language was screaming at us. The most useful thing was her reaction to Liam's witness."

"How so?"

"When I mentioned that a young man looking like Mulvenna had been seen talking to Lissy, her hands twitched.

She knows who he is. But for some reason she doesn't want us to know."

Flanagan rubbed his chin thoughtfully then smiled at the younger man, knowing that the meeting hadn't been wasted after all. "So she was Wasson's handler back in '83?"

"I think so. It would fit with what Guthrie at MI5 hinted at; he said Mulvenna's frame was local business. Very local."

"She wanted Wasson exonerated so she could keep using him as an informant. That much I understand. But why choose Mulvenna to take his place?"

"Perhaps it was personal, or perhaps she was doing a favour for someone in the police who wanted Mulvenna out of the way." Craig stared intently at Flanagan. "I could speculate on who and why until I'm old and grey, sir, but unless someone's prepared to talk to us it's only speculation. It would fit with Mulvenna having a lover who wanted him kept quiet, male or female."

Flanagan shook his head. "He could still have talked in prison. If they'd wanted to guarantee his silence a bullet to the head would have been more effective. They just wanted him offside and for some reason Mulvenna agreed to keep quiet."

"Because he really loved them?"

"Yes, maybe. Although they obviously didn't love him half as much. Or…"

"Or what? If…"

Flanagan interrupted him. "If I dig around, I'm more likely to find answers. Leave it with me."

It sounded like an order; one that Craig had no intention of obeying. Flanagan stood up and extended his hand.

"Get yourself and D.C.I. Cullen geared up to interview the ACC properly tomorrow. The gloves are off now, Marc, so treat her like a suspect until you get the truth."

***

The man had been watching her for almost two hours. From the moment she'd emerged through the door of Headquarters, her face tired and drawn, as if what had happened inside had been an awful ordeal. He'd watched as she'd pulled open her Mercedes' door and thrown her hat angrily on the back seat, loosening her starched collar as she climbed in. She'd driven herself there, her usual bodyguard nowhere to be seen. He'd stared at her as she rested her head against the sporty steering wheel, the whole car a bright red testament to how well she'd done in life. In her career maybe, but how about as a mother, Mrs Trainor?

She'd sat there thinking for ages, a single tear trickling down her cheek. One week bereaved and only one tear. And who was it for? Her daughter or herself? Finally she'd pulled out of the car-park and followed the M2 from Belfast, up the Coleraine Road towards her home on the cliffs. She drove high above the beach until eventually she pulled into a private road and stopped outside her large detached house.

The man gazed at the white-stuccoed frontage three storeys high staring down onto the silent street, then he smiled up at Lissy's room. He'd been in there many times. It was small and warm like she had been and it spoke of a secure and privileged life. Lucky girl.

Now she was safe for good, beyond her mother's lack of love. Far away from the harm her indifference could do. Perhaps Lissy hadn't been damaged yet but it had only been a matter of time. He wasn't sorry that he'd killed her. He knew she was better off, even if no-one else agreed.

Melanie Trainor entered her expensive home, oblivious to the looks and feelings she was drawing from across the street. She walked down the carpeted hallway and closed the study door behind her, to sit alone and think. Her husband's car was in the driveway so the man waited an hour for him to leave, then he crossed the quiet cul-de-sac and stepped into the world that should have been his.

12.30 p.m.

"What's up, Doc?"

John Winter glanced up from his microscope to see the man who'd announced himself two minutes earlier, in a chorus of banged doors and heavy footsteps approaching the lab. Liam stopped and gazed around him, always fascinated by John's choice of décor; the Montmartre of Toulouse-Lautrec crossed with the movie set from Moulin Rouge. He never gave up hoping that Nicole Kidman would leap out from a corner. Instead Craig's tanned face appeared. He beckoned him in.

"Hi, boss. How long have you been here?"

"Since the time we agreed."

It was said with a wry grin. Liam looked more closely and saw the fatigue behind the smile.

"Rough morning?"

John put up his hand to still the exchange. "For God's sake don't ask him until I've had something to eat. I've already had thirty minutes of it."

He handed Liam a sandwich and a cup then waved him towards the coffee machine to help himself.

"Right, I won't ask then. How's the D.N.A. testing going on Mulvenna's relatives, Doc?"

"All done this morning on the ones that agreed. Of course, you know the fact they agreed makes it very unlikely they'll be a match."

Craig nodded and they sipped their coffee in silence until Liam broke the quiet. "Did anyone ask Mulvenna if he'd ever donated sperm?"

Craig glanced at him, wrinkling up his face. "Only you could ask that while we're having lunch."

Liam shrugged and they fell silent until the food was eaten. When the wrappers were potted in the nearest bin Craig answered him.

"Andy asked him after he'd calmed down."

"And?"

"Nope. He wasn't a starving student like John and me."

Liam nodded sagely. "I never met a starving terrorist yet." He paused and they knew the hunger strikes had popped into his mind. His expression said 'Oops'.

"That rules out Mulvenna having a son then."

John interjected. "Not at all, Liam. He may have fathered one without realising, from a woman he slept with."

"Or he may know he fathered one and not want to tell us. If there is a son if would fit the D.N.A. and the man your witness saw, Liam."

Liam frowned. "Aye it would, but then why wouldn't Mulvenna tell us and get himself off the hook?"

Craig shrugged. "Wouldn't you lie to protect your kids?"

Liam thought of his two small children and nodded. If one of them grew up and killed someone he would happily go to prison in their stead. Craig read his mind.

"And you'd do time for them, yes? But why?"

"What do you mean why? They're my kids, that's why."

Craig kept on pushing.

"Yes, but *why?* To protect them? Or because you felt responsible for what they'd done?"

Liam looked flustered for a moment then his eyes widened in realisation.

"Because if they grew up to be criminals it must be my fault. Something I did or didn't do."

Craig nodded firmly. "Exactly. Now apply that to Mulvenna."

"If Mulvenna knows he has a kid who turned out to be a killer he'll think it's because of him. It's his fault."

John and Craig nodded, then John threw a spanner in the works. "Of course, that's assuming he actually has a kid and knows anything about it. He might not, on both counts."

Liam shook his head. "I don't think he does. Know, I mean. I watched his face when you showed him the sketch, boss. There was no recognition at all. Andy saw nothing either. If he had a son he knew about he'd have given it away somehow. I don't think he's covering up for him out of fatherly concern. I think he doesn't know."

Craig squinted in thought. "OK. Either he has a son and doesn't know, or we're way off base. Let's say he has a son. Mulvenna mightn't know about him but the mother sure as hell does."

John jumped in. "Well he must have been born before Mulvenna went down in '83, or since he came out in '98. That would make him either thirty-something or in his teens."

Craig shook his head. "Thirty fits with Liam's witness and you're nearly right. He didn't have to be born before Mulvenna was sent away, he just had to have been conceived."

"That would explain why Mulvenna knows nothing about him."

"What if that's *why* he was stitched up, boss? You said that they mightn't have framed Mulvenna to keep him quiet, but to get him out of the way. If they didn't want him to know about the pregnancy that would've worked."

Craig leaned forward, warming to the theme. It was all speculation so far but it felt right.

"OK, so we're looking for a woman that Mulvenna had an affair with who didn't want him to know about the child. Someone who had connections powerful enough to arrange for Mulvenna to be sent away. Someone who he loved enough not to incriminate."

They gawped at each other, all having the same thought. John said it first.

"Melanie Trainor? Having an affair with a known terrorist?"

"No way, boss. She was too aware of her career even back then. You said as much."

Craig thought for a moment. It wasn't outside the bounds of

possibility but there were other fish to fry.

"A woman in the police, no matter how ambitious, wouldn't have had the clout back then to frame someone, and Trainor was only an Inspector then. Let's park that one. Although I'm not dismissing it, it fits on several counts. But let's look further. Jake and I think Mulvenna's straight, so let's say he was having an affair with a woman who got pregnant and she didn't want him to know. Let's say she had a powerful husband, someone in a position to get Mulvenna out of the way. Now the son's found out what happened to his real father and he's taking revenge on anyone he thinks might have been involved in having Mulvenna sent to prison."

John leaned back in his chair, steepling his fingers in thought. After a minute he leaped up and started writing on the white board, outlining the options that they'd said out loud. He added in another thought.

"Who, of the officers that were senior back in '83 has a thirty year old son? It shouldn't be hard to find out."

"Mulvenna was arrested in July '83 so if she was pregnant it's odds on she was only starting to show by the time he was sent down in the August."

Craig nodded and grabbed the desk phone, tasking Davy to check male births in early to mid-1984. They were still throwing ideas around when he called back.

"There w...were twenty-nine male births that fitted in Northern Ireland during that time. It was a big year for girls. There's only one name that lists the father's occupation as civil servant or government worker, a euphemism often used by the police. But you're not going to believe it, s...sir."

"Who, Davy?"

"It's the Chief Constable. Mr Flanagan."

Craig fell into stunned silence and the others stared at him, wondering what Davy had just said. Craig was questioning his judgment of everything when Davy broke the silence.

"S...Sir, I did another check and the Chief Constable's son

died in 1986 of drowning. He fell into a garden pond."

Craig nodded, half-relieved and half-sad. His judgement of Flanagan hadn't been wrong; he was good man. He'd often wondered what his background sadness was and now he knew. There was no way Kathleen Flanagan had had an affair with Jonno Mulvenna thirty years ago. She was the sort of girl who'd worn white gloves and gone to church, not the type to sleep around behind her husband's back. Flanagan didn't have a living son who was killing to wreak revenge. He gave Davy another search to run and waited on the line, bringing the others up to date.

"Phew, that was a near miss, boss. That would have made an episode of Eastenders look tame. 'Chief Constable's son in revenge killing spree horror' The Chronicle would have had a field day."

Davy didn't keep them waiting long. "You w...ere right, boss. There are four baby boys here with no father listed and mother's occupation down as civil servant or government worker. Two of them were put up for adoption a week after the birth."

"What were the mother's names, Davy?"

"Mary Wright and Mary Donnelly. But they're probably false. Do you want me to dig deeper?"

"Please. One of them could have been an officer's wife who hid the birth and gave a false name."

John interjected. "Or Melanie Trainor, Marc."

"Davy, did you hear that?"

"Yes. Are you s...serious, boss?"

"Deadly. Add Melanie Trainor into the mix then do every check you can think of. As quick as you can, please."

"OK. Did Jake talk to you, s...sir?"

Craig frowned and scrolled through his missed calls. "No. What did he want?"

"I think it was something to do with the charcoal from Mulvenna's gallery s...show. I'll tell him to give you a call."

Craig cut the line and turned towards the board, borrowing John's marker and adding Mary Wright, Mary Donnelly and Adoption to the list. The case was going to close itself, and soon. He didn't know just how soon.

***

Julia dragged the brush through her hair and pulled it back into a knot, then she turned her attention back to the files on her desk. She lifted the top one and turned over the cover, starting to read but not seeing a word. Her mind was on Marc and their last conversation. He'd asked her to marry him, and she'd got angry.

She shook her head at her own stupidity, but even as she did it she knew she would react the same way again. He hadn't proposed out of an overwhelming desire to marry her, he'd proposed to solve a problem and that was no way to start married life. It didn't mean that he didn't love her but it did mean that his answer to their dilemma was a fait accompli. If we're married we'll have to make it work. Or, we're married so you have to give Julia a transfer. Or, more likely, we're married so let's have a family, Julia, that way you can give up work and your career will take a back seat. You can move to Belfast and take a few years out to stay at home with the kids. Problem solved.

She shook her head again, this time in anger. Anger at the geography that kept them apart. Anger at Terry Harrison, for being an unreasonable bastard who was jealous of Marc and wanted to make him pay for being a better detective than him. Anger at a society that still said a man's job mattered more, especially when there might be children on the way.

Angry, angry, angry. But most of all she was angry at herself for what she knew she was going to do.

***

It hadn't been hard for the man to enter the house by the patio and slip into the kitchen without being heard. After all, it wasn't the first time he'd done it. There were all those nights when he'd waited until it was dark and watched the husband turn off the hall light, signalling to the world that it was too late to call. Too late to drop by for a drink or a conversation. Too late for anything but sleep.

He'd stood in that hall a dozen times and walked from room to room. Lifting books to read and pictures to peruse, before ascending the stairs to watch them in their sleep.

He'd watched them all, trying to work out what would hurt her most. How to make her feel the pain he'd felt all his life. Lissy had been the natural choice. An only child, a golden girl. Taking her away would cause the worst pain and put a knife through Melanie Trainor's heart. So he had.

It hadn't been hard. A note left in Lissy's bag as she'd slept, saying that he'd left it one day when he'd seen her at the law library. Its contents piquing her curiosity sufficiently to meet. Somewhere public at first so that she would feel safe, and what better place to meet than the promenade she'd walked since she could toddle? It had made him smile to see people walk by them; just a handsome young couple having a chat. No idea what they were seeing at all.

Lissy had been nice. A sweet girl in a slightly old-fashioned way. She had caring eyes, large and brown like his own. He'd made up a story that he was a journalist writing a piece on Human Rights, after that it had been easy to meet her again that evening, and then the next. Until the Sunday night they'd met and he'd suggested a quieter place to have a drink and talk. Where he had the notes for his article within easy reach.

He'd made it quick, putting her into a pain-free sleep then off to his special place where he felt safe. He kept her there for two days, caring for her like she was family. Until the time came when he had to kill her and bury her in sand so that they couldn't miss the link. They'd seen the link all right but they hadn't followed it to the source, the one he was pointing the arrow at. They were too slow, with procedure and evidence cluttering up their thoughts. It was too long to wait. He had to act.

The man walked towards the study knowing that she would be there, working at something irrelevant again. Hiding from the important things in life. Her husband had gone for good now. He'd watched him pack the suitcases in the boot. Off to a more loving woman to spend his life unconcerned by what people thought. Good for him; he was innocent of everything that she'd done.

He stared at her uniform hanging-up in the hall, smoothed and pristine, ready for another day. Her career mattered so much to her now and it had mattered so much back then. More than Lissy. More than her child.

He slipped open the study door unheard and walked towards the high-backed leather chair that she sat in every day. He stared at the nape of her neck then pressed the syringe down hard, watching as she slumped. Then he carried her across the patio to his waiting van, ready for the moment he'd been planning for years.

Chapter Twenty-Eight

Friday 8.30 a.m.

Jake scrolled through the microfiche archives at Belfast's Chronicle newspaper and high-lighted each frame that matched his needs. He printed them off in A4 then had a closer look. There were plenty of images, but none that matched the angle and clarity he was looking for. He rifled through the sheets, growing more irritated with each one until he stopped at a print near the back. He pulled it out and stared hard. It was from 1980 and it was almost right. But was it enough? It would have to do.

***

"There's no such person as Mary W…Wright, boss, or Mary Donnelly. At least none that fit with a pregnancy back in 1984."

Craig raked his hair then stared down at Davy. "They gave false names." He thought for a moment then had a fresh idea. "Contact the solicitors and see what we need to get the adoption records unsealed for the two new-born boys on the list."

Liam shook his head sceptically. "They'll ask for a warrant, boss. We'll need a friendly Judge and they're still not happy with us for putting Judge Dawson away for the Ackerman murder."

"Ask Judge Standish, Liam. He said Dawson brought the legal profession into disrepute."

Liam guffawed. "Is that even possible?"

Craig grinned and motioned Davy on.

"I've checked all the senior officers' wives at the time and it w…was a bit of a dead end. Either they had baby boys quite openly that everyone was happy about, or they had little girls. S…Some had families that were already grown up. These two cases seem like our best bet."

Just then Jake ran onto the floor. Nicky followed more sedately, raising her eyebrows in surprise.

"Eager to get to work, Jake?"

Liam grinned. "Here, stop that, son. You'll have the boss expecting us all to be that keen."

Jake ignored them both and rushed over to Davy's desk, grasping a folder in his hand. He gave Craig a quick nod then cut to the chase.

"Davy. Do you have that sketch from Mulvenna's gallery?"

Davy stared at him blankly, then reached into his top drawer and pulled it out. Jake grabbed it and rushed to his desk with everyone staring curiously after him. Craig smiled; he remembered being that eager once, before cynicism and the years had slowed him down. He turned back to Davy.

"Davy, try something for me, would you? Melanie Trainor's maiden name was Ross, find out what her mother's was please."

They watched as Davy's hands flew across the keys then he pressed print and Craig lifted a sheet. He nodded to himself and passed it to Liam. His hunch had been right.

Annette walked onto the floor, just in time to be hit by Jake's "Good God! Come and look."

Craig and Liam strode over to see what he had, staring first at his desk and then at the sketch in his hand. The Chronicle's microfiche print-out was nearly an exact match for the sketch Jonno Mulvenna had done. They were both of Melanie Trainor!

Jake looked up expecting to see shock on their faces, but instead Craig smiled and handed him the sheet in his hand. It held Melanie Trainor's mother's maiden name; Wright. Mary Wright was Melanie Trainor. She'd used her mother's name and kept her first initial the same.

Craig lifted a chair and sat down, motioning the others to do the same. He glanced at the clock. Melanie Trainor was due for interview at High Street at nine o'clock. She could wait.

"OK. We need to check a few more things to confirm it but my money's on Mary Wright being Melanie Trainor. Mary Wright had a baby in February 1984. That would fit with her conceiving in May 1983. Jonno Mulvenna was arrested in July '83. July was long enough for her to realise she was pregnant but still early enough to conceal her condition from him. She gave birth to a baby boy who she put up for adoption immediately after birth."

Nicky pursed her lips disapprovingly as he continued.

"Melanie Trainor would have been in her mid-twenties then and unmarried. She didn't marry Hugh Trainor until late 1988. So she was having an illegitimate child."

"Hell of a stigma back in '84."

Nicky shot Liam a hostile look and was about to launch into a diatribe about responsibility but Craig halted her with a raised hand.

"Even more of one if you're a young female police officer in a chauvinistic time."

Jake interjected eagerly. "And the father was Jonno Mulvenna."

Nicky and Annette's gawped at him and Liam snorted sceptically. "Do you really think Trainor gave the boy up because she was worried about being pregnant, boss? More likely she was worried what her career would go down the pan if anyone found out it was Mulvenna's son."

Craig nodded ruefully. "I was giving her the benefit of the doubt." He paused for a moment, thinking. "OK. The sketch in the gallery wasn't of Lissy as we thought, but of her mother. It must have been done in the seventies or eighties and she's changed a bit since then."

"Amazing what thirty years will do."

"And getting all buttoned up."

Annette glared at Liam then looked at her sensible shoes, making a note to buy higher heels.

"So she and Mulvenna had an affair and she got pregnant. Do you really think Mulvenna didn't know, sir?"

Craig shook his head. "I don't think that he'd any idea then, and he doesn't know now. It would explain a lot of things. Melanie Trainor has brown eyes."

"Hence the witness seeing a young man who looked like Mulvenna but has brown eyes instead of blue."

"Yes. And it explains the related D.N.A.."

Annette's interrupted indignantly "You're not saying he killed Lissy? His own sister?"

Craig nodded sadly. "That's exactly what I'm saying, Annette. Maybe that's why there was no rape. I think he blames his mother and maybe Mulvenna too, for having him adopted. Killing Lissy was a sure way to hurt Melanie Trainor."

"Do you think he left the hair on Lissy deliberately, s…sir?"

Craig turned to Davy and smiled. "Perhaps. Maybe he was trying to point us to who he was."

"The beach burial was a big enough clue."

"Did he w…want to get caught?"

"No, not that. Liam, do you want to tell everyone why he wanted us to know who he was?"

"He wanted everyone to start looking at the Jarvis case again and see that his father was framed. If he'd worked out Mulvenna was his Dad and identified Trainor as his Mum he would've wanted to ruin her, for abandoning him to God only knows what sort of life. Even if she hadn't wanted to raise him herself his father might have done if he'd known. But she stole that chance from him as well."

Annette leaned forward, looking puzzled. "Maybe I'm being thick here, but I'm lost. I get that he resented Melanie Trainor for giving him up for adoption and took revenge on her by killing Lissy. But even if he had realised Jonno Mulvenna was his Dad, why think he was framed for Veronica Jarvis' murder? Mulvenna was a known terrorist and it wasn't the first time that he'd killed."

Craig smiled. She was right. How would he have realised that Mulvenna was his father? And if he had done then why think he wasn't guilty of Jarvis' death? Nicky gave them the answer.

She spoke so quietly that they had to strain to hear her husky voice. Everyone turned towards her. Her face was solemn.

"There's only one reason a child's search for their birth parents becomes an obsession and that's if they're really unhappy where they are. He must have been abused."

Craig could tell from the look on her face that this was close to home. Her voice broke as she went on. "My sister and I were fostered after my Dad died. My Mum had a breakdown from the grief and ended up in psychiatric care. It was only for six months but I can tell you that in those six months I'd convinced myself that it wasn't our real Dad who'd died. Our real Dad became everyone from a film star to a prince, anyone I saw on TV, and he was going to come and rescue us any day soon."

Craig interjected gently. "Because you were so unhappy in foster care, Nick?"

She nodded, not trusting her voice. Craig smiled at her then took back the floor.

"OK. If Melanie Trainor's son was being mistreated by his adoptive parents, then he might have been desperate to find out who his real parents were. When he did, and let's be honest, the resemblance to Mulvenna wouldn't have gone on unnoticed in Northern Ireland back then for long, maybe he couldn't let himself believe that Mulvenna had killed a woman. It didn't go along with the image he had of him as a freedom fighter."

"What if he *was* right, boss? Mulvenna always told us he didn't do it."

"So he let himself be framed?"

Liam nodded.

"OK. I agree, Liam, but why? Do you really think it was pure altruism on Mulvenna's part? That he thought he deserved to do time for all his bombings so he let himself be put away? He knew how he'd be treated inside for killing a Veronica Jarvis, even if people believed she was an informer."

Annette interrupted, watching Nicky out of the side of her eye, concerned.

"How about if he loved Melanie Trainor, sir? Really loved her, and knew it was going to ruin her life if people found out about their affair? He knew how much her career meant to her so when she betrayed him he loved her enough to go down for a crime he hadn't done."

Craig nodded. "She wasn't framing him because of the affair, but because of the baby. She'd found out she was pregnant and she couldn't have hidden it from Mulvenna for long. Once he'd known he had a child he would never have let go of her, or let himself be sent to prison to protect her. He would have wanted to bring up the child himself and then everything would all have come out. The Jarvis case presented Melanie Trainor/ Ross with the opportunity to kill two birds with one stone. Protect Wasson and any future information he could give her to further her career, and get rid of Mulvenna before he found out about the pregnancy."

Liam let out a low whistle. "What a piece of work. She cared more about her career than about the man she loved, or her child. My God, I'm not surprised the boy wanted to hurt her. He should have killed her instead of Lissy."

The room fell silent for a moment until a ticking clock made Craig realise the time. They had an interview to hold. He stood to go then nodded at Jake and Davy.

"Good work, both of you. Look, Liam and I are going to interview the ACC at High Street now Jake, why don't you come along to watch." He pointed to the papers on his desk. "Bring your print-outs, they'll be useful when she starts to deny everything."

As they were heading for the door Nicky stood in Craig's way. He smiled at her kindly.

"We'll talk when I get back, Nicky."

She shook her head and he looked bemused.

"Haven't you forgotten something, sir?"

He searched for an answer then realised. "Jonno Mulvenna."

She nodded. "He has a right to know he has a son, doesn't he?"

Craig smiled down at her. Yes, he did. He turned back to Davy and Annette.

"Nicky, work with Davy here to get the adoption records unsealed. I'll ask Melanie Trainor for a D.N.A. sample but she'll probably refuse, so Annette, get a warrant for her blood. We've already got Mulvenna's. We should confirm the hair belongs to their son within twenty-four hours."

He turned back to Nicky. "When we're sure he's Mulvenna's son, and only when we're sure, Nicky, I'll go and tell him myself." He gave her a wry smile. "No hints until then, Mrs Morris, OK?"

She nodded grudgingly then they left for one of the most challenging interviews of their careers.

***

It had been too easy. The man had cleared the private road easily and driven below the speed limit for thirty minutes with her in the boot. Finally he'd crossed the Bann and pulled into the small clearing in Downhill Forest, inland from Castlerock. He could have killed her then and there but he'd waited for too long not to have his questions answered. He needed to see her face and watch her try to lie. Or worse, to attempt to defend what she'd done. There was no defence, and no punishment would fit now except her death.

He remembered the day he'd discovered who his real mother

was. He'd always known that he was adopted; the Fosters had taken pleasure in telling him how lucky he was every single day. How they could have chosen any little boy, but instead they'd picked him. To abuse.

He couldn't remember a day when he hadn't been beaten by Nigel Foster, a small man in every single way. He'd hit him with a strap or stick or whatever had come to hand, then he'd thrown him into his room for another night with nothing to eat. It had made him hard and determined that no-one would hurt him once he was big enough to fight back.

That day had come when he was fourteen and then he'd beaten his 'father' to a pulp, only stopping when his bitch of a wife had thrown herself at his feet, begging him to stop. He remembered gazing down at her, her fat cheeks reddening as she cried. It had made him laugh. He hated her as well, but she hadn't been cruel, just stupid and lazy and too weak to defend him the way she should. As frightened of her brutal husband as he had been.

He'd left then, all grown up, but not before he'd dragged out the name of the woman who'd abandoned him at birth. Mary. It had taken him years to find her, years in which he'd worked in dead-end jobs, until he'd found out who his father was. It didn't take long for people to start pointing at him in the street. He hadn't known why at first, until he saw a programme on the prisoner release and there he was, smiling out of the screen, his doppelgänger. He was tall and dark, just like the man he was the spitting image of; Jonno Mulvenna, king of the terrorist scum. That made him the prince.

He'd laughed then, imagining the shock on the Foster's faces when they realised their church-going lives would never be the same again. They'd adopted a leading republican's son. Ha ha. He returned a few times to gloat, Nigel Foster too afraid to hit him now. But what of his real mother, why had she given him up? Maybe she was underage and her parents made her have him adopted? He'd watched enough movies to know that's what happened back then.

When he finally found out that she'd been twenty-five he was angrier than he'd ever felt. She could have kept him if she'd wanted to. He wanted to smash the social worker's face but he smashed-up their office instead, grabbing his file and walking away before the police arrived. He'd been determined to find her and it had taken him years. Years of working to put himself through school, primed to say, 'look how well I've done, despite you, you bitch'.

He'd hit one dead end after another until finally he'd found the only two women who matched. Mary Wright and Mary Donnelly. Neither of them existed anywhere. It was a stroke of genius to search under date of birth. One visit to the Register of Births and Deaths had worked it out. Then he'd bought the bookshop near her house and waited. Danny Foster was no-one's fool. No, he wasn't and the woman lying at his feet was about to find that out.

***

11 a.m.

They glanced at the clock in turn. First Jake, with the impatience of youth, then Liam and Craig. No-one said a word but they were all thinking the same thing. Melanie Trainor was late, late beyond passive aggression this time. Senior officers didn't just ignore the Chief Constable's demands and dander in two hours after the time, yawning that they'd overslept or the dog had eaten their homework. This was deliberate defiance and what had so far been kept low-key out of deference to her grief and rank was about to escalate.

Craig picked up his phone and nodded Liam and Jake to do the same

"Jake, phone her office and make sure she hasn't just turned up there, ignoring her suspension. Liam, give Andy a call and ask him to nip round to the house and knock on her door. Just him, I want this kept quiet for as long as we can."

He went to dial a number and Liam raised an eyebrow curiously. Craig answered his look.

"I'm ringing her husband. Not that I don't trust you to be subtle, Liam, but…"

Liam made a face and turned to see the start of a grin on Jake's face. He squinted at him in warning and they broke into different corners to make the calls.

Craig walked past Jack Harris, the long-time sergeant at High Street, and pushed through the back door into the cool morning air. Jack smiled. He got his weekly quota of excitement from Craig's team using his station as 'interview central' for their murders.

Craig pressed dial and the call was answered quickly. Hugh Trainor came on the line with a welcoming tone. As welcoming as you could be to the man investigating your daughter's death.

"Good morning, Superintendent. Have you made some progress on the case?"

It was an innocent question and just what a father would want to know but it took Craig aback. So much had happened since they'd spoken last and none of it was repeatable to this man. He fudged his reply expertly.

"Things are moving, Mr Trainor."

Hugh Trainor interjected before Craig had time to twist more words.

"Good, good. What can I do to help?"

His openness and tone said he knew nothing about his wife's interview the day before, or her suspension. It could mean several things but one question was top of Craig's list.

"Could you tell me when you last spoke to your wife, please?"

There was silence for a moment and Craig resisted the temptation to leap into the gap. He wanted the truth from Trainor and he knew he'd get it if he was patient. He guessed why the politician was hesitating and he was right.

"I'm sorry, Mr Craig but I haven't spoken to Melanie for several days."

"You didn't see her last night?"

"No. I called at the house and her car was in the drive, but we didn't speak." He paused long enough for Craig to finish the sentence in his head. "I've moved in with Darlene. I...it didn't seem right to continue the lie, now that Lissy's gone. It felt as if I was lying to her, somehow."

"I understand." And he did. Lissy's happiness was the only reason Trainor had stayed with the ACC, now he could be happy elsewhere.

Trainor's tone became anxious. "Is there something wrong, Superintendent? Is Melanie OK?"

Craig made placating noises and ended the call as quickly as he could, pushing open the back door. He joined Jack in the staff room. Liam and Jake were already there.

"Well?"

Liam took the cue. "Andy's on his way there. He'll call me back when he arrives." He nodded at Jake.

"The ACC's not at work, sir. They said they haven't seen her since eight o'clock yesterday morning."

Before she'd come down to Belfast for the meeting with Flanagan. The hairs on Craig's neck stood up and he told them quickly of his conversation with the MLA.

"Man. It didn't take him long to move out, did it? Makes you wonder how long the marriage had been dead."

"Years." Craig glanced at his watch. Eleven-twenty. He'd give Andy twenty minutes to call back then he'd have to ramp things up. He'd already accepted they weren't getting their interview with the ACC that morning, now he was wondering if they'd get to speak to her again at all.

Just then Jack approached with a tray of tea.

Liam rubbed his hands. "Good man. Here, I hope you've got some decent biscuits this time. That last bunch were pathetic."

Jack halted mid-step and was about to say something rude when Liam's phone rang. He raised his hand. "Hold that thought, Jack." He pressed a key, answering the call. "D.C.I. Cullen."

The others watched as he nodded for a moment then he clicked his phone shut and turned to Craig.

"That was Andy. The ACC's wasn't answering so he walked round to the back. The patio door was open and the place was a mess, there was stuff smashed all over the place."

"As if someone did it deliberately."

Liam looked at Craig curiously. "Aye. How did you know?"

Craig was already on his feet and heading for the door. "She's been taken. Liam, get back onto Andy and tell him to get an all-points bulletin out for the man in Jenna Farrelly's sketch. And tell him to get a sample of Melanie Trainor's D.N.A. from the house for John to match; a hair or toothbrush should do. Jake, push Annette and Davy on the adoption records. We need the names of the adoptive parents. Now. I need to tell Mulvenna about the boy. If the ACC's son's taken her then there might be only one chance of saving her life. We need Jonno Mulvenna to reason with the boy."

***

Davy gazed at the records in front of him and then at Annette. The file looked old, and it was. Thirty years old. Its grey-coloured cover was curled at the edges and its yellowing official decals were peeling off. He turned over the top page and stared at the typewritten text beneath. The pre-word processor words were irregular; some of them jumping off the line below. Their unsophisticated presentation seemed to increase the pathos of the words even more.

'Male infant. Healthy.'

It seemed so sad. A brand new life summarised in one phrase. Not 'Baby Jack, welcomed by his loving family' or 'To

Geoff, a son Ian, much longed for.' Just sterile words that said exactly what he was; a healthy infant male.

He avoided Annette's eyes, afraid that their sadness would increase his own, and read. The mother's name was Mary Wright and she was a twenty-five-year-old civil servant. Not a helpless teenager living on the streets, but an adult woman with her own home. What could have prompted her to give up her child?

Perhaps she was afraid of going it alone, or the stigma of single-motherhood had made her feel ashamed? He stopped mid-excuse, knowing that neither of them applied in this case, and finally met Annette's eyes. He was shocked by the anger he read there and heard in her voice when she spoke.

"She gave him away because she was worried about her career! Her precious bloody career."

"W…we don't know that for sure, Annette. She might have been afraid. You've all said it; being a single Mum in the eighties wasn't an easy ride. Add to that she was in the police and he had a terrorist for a Dad."

"She bloody well should have thought of that before she slept with him! It wasn't the baby's fault. There's no excuse, Davy. God knows what happened to that child."

She jabbed her finger at the file. "How long was it before he was adopted? He might have been in a care home for years."

Davy turned the page and shook his head. "No, it w… wasn't. He was adopted at six months old by a Mr and Mrs Foster. A farmer and his wife from near Limavady. They couldn't have any children of their own."

Annette stopped jabbing. "Well, that's something at least." She turned towards the door, barking an order at him as she did. "Find the Fosters and get them brought in downstairs. I want to know everything there is to know about their son. I'll get the D.N.A. warrant and be back in an hour. I want them here then."

***

Melanie Trainor's fog lifted gradually, brief moments of clarity replaced by sleep again, until finally clarity became the norm and she opened her eyes. She expected to see her bedroom with the curtains that needed replaced, and the small TV on the chest of drawers switching on automatically to the morning news. They weren't there. Instead she saw a wooden-slatted wall. She closed her eyes and shook her head then looked again. There was no mistake. Instead of the bedroom she'd slept in for twenty years she was lying in some sort of shed.

She pulled herself to a kneeling pose and pressed her face against the slats, peering through them at the light. The sun was descending in the sky and filtering through dense spruce trees of varying heights. It was afternoon. And she was in a forest! How the hell had she got there? The last thing she remembered was sitting in her study at home, sometime after she'd left the CC's office on Thursday morning. The answer came to her quickly; she'd been kidnapped. Who would be idiot enough to kidnap a member of the police? Lots of people, but they would call it daring, not dumb.

She turned her head to search the floor and a sharp pain shot through her neck. She put her hand up quickly and it came back with dried blood, telling her how she'd got there. She'd been injected with something. It still didn't tell her where she was or who had brought her there.

A crunching noise outside the shed froze her in mid-thought. She held her breath as the sound of dried leaves cracking underfoot heralded someone's approach. Did she trust that they were a stranger and scream for help, or risk antagonising her captor more? She screamed at the top of her voice and heard the steps halt. The noise they had made was replaced by a man's sarcastic voice.

"Forget it, Melanie. No-one will hear. Or should I call you Mary?"

She sucked in her breath and prickles of fear ran down her spine. Mary had been her name for six weeks in 1984 but never since. Just long enough to give birth and arrange the adoption, then Mary Wright had disappeared.

A mixture of fear and excitement ran through her as images long forgotten filled her mind. Her lover's smile, soft and longing; the last time she'd ever felt overwhelming joy, before she'd made a choice to betray him for the life she had. A tiny hand grasping hers as she'd held her son and then handed him to a stranger so she could return to her career.

Her heart leapt unexpectedly and she longed to see the man's face. She pressed her lips against the slats and spoke in a softer tone than she'd used for years.

"Are you my son? Are you my boy? Please, please tell me."

Danny Foster stopped walking, frozen by her unexpected words. Confusion flooded through him, scattering his cold logic in its path. He had his plan and he knew what he had to do, feelings for the woman who'd abandoned him had no place now. And yet...

He pulled back the door of the shed urgently, peering into the darkness inside. His eyes adjusted slowly until he saw her face and she saw his. He watched her mouth fall open and tears smear the dirt on her cheeks as they held each other's gaze in silence for too long. Melanie Trainor spoke first, her words tumbling over each other, colliding to make no sense. Only one word was clear. "Sorry." Sorry, sorry, sorry. She said it a hundred times then more, until he could stand it no longer and he shouted. "Shut up!"

Her mouth closed then and she stared at him with sheer joy in her eyes. He looked like Jonno, exactly like her only love. The man she hadn't been brave enough to be with or perhaps a different kind of brave woman who had wanted to be a warrior like the rest. But why hadn't she kept her child? She'd asked herself that a million times, searching for him and begging to have him back. But no-one would talk, a sealed adoption was final. 'For the best'. Really? For whom?

She stared at the young man and he stared back, his brown eyes all hers. In every other way he was his father's son. He had his thick dark hair and his soft full lips. Ah, Jonno. Danny Foster stared at his mother, trying to shore up the fence round his heart that it had taken him thirty years to build. He placed the planks upright one by one only to find them falling again at her smile.

He shook his head hard and turned his back, striding into the cold autumn air to think. He stared at the sky through the trees, begging the God he didn't believe in to tell him what to do. He couldn't care about her. Wouldn't. She'd left him alone at the mercy of the Fosters. She was a bitch and she deserved to die. He railed against the world and her and God for what felt like hours, screaming so hard that he thought his lungs would burst.

Melanie Trainor listened to his cries inside the shed, not caring whether she lived or died. She'd been numb for years, unable to show love to anyone after she'd betrayed them both. She'd prayed to see her son again and now she had. She could die content. Finally Danny Foster pulled out the gloves that signalled the end of her life and slipped them on before her lying words could change his mind.

***

"Andy's got cars out looking and the C.S.I.s are at the house."

Craig shook his head in irritation. "Don't waste men on forensics. Time enough for that if she turns up dead. Get everyone out on the ground." He turned towards Nicky. "Where's Annette?"

Davy answered him. "S...She went to get the D.N.A. warrant and said she'd be back in an hour."

He glanced at the clock. That had been two hours ago. Craig

wrinkled his forehead and shot Davy a look he couldn't quite read. It didn't take that long to get a warrant. There was something going on in the squad besides the case. He'd get to the bottom of it if it killed him, but it would have to wait. Davy broke his stare and started reporting on the adoption file.

"The baby was adopted by a farming couple up near Limavady. They didn't have children of their own and they were in their forties w...when they took the boy. Annette asked for them to be brought in downstairs. A car picked them up an hour ago. They should be here in ten minutes."

"Good thinking, lad. Maybe they'll be able to give us something on their son."

Craig shook his head, distracted. He wasn't disagreeing with Liam but whatever the couple could give them wouldn't alter what they knew. Melanie Trainor and Jonno Mulvenna had a son who'd been given up at birth. Trainor had framed Mulvenna to get him out of the way and the boy hated her for it, possibly even hated them both, it would depend whether he thought Mulvenna had known about him or not.

Craig wheeled round and left the floor without a word. Liam shrugged his shoulders at Nicky and followed, catching up with him at the lift.

"Mulvenna?"

"Mulvenna. If anyone can get through to the boy it will be him."

"I thought you wanted to make sure with D.N.A. before you told him he might have a son?"

Craig shook his head. "No time." Events had overtaken them and they had to move fast. Melanie Trainor might already be dead but if she wasn't then Mulvenna was her only chance. He glanced at Liam knowing that he got the irony of the situation as well. The terrorist who'd killed so many police officers saving one of them. A lover saving the woman who'd betrayed him.

"Give me five minutes with Mulvenna then release the boy's sketch to the media. We need to catch the evening news.

Someone must have seen him."

They exited the lift on the garage floor.

"Will do. I'll stay here and help Annette with the parents and keep Andy up to date. You fine with Mulvenna by yourself?"

"Jake's still at High Street, I'll meet him there. See if you can get some idea where she might have been taken from the Fosters. It will be somewhere near the Trainor's house. Somewhere quiet."

They stared at each other for a moment and then nodded, knowing it was the end game in more than one way.

Chapter Twenty-Nine

Danny Foster gazed down at his mother, flexing his fingers in the tight latex gloves. He was going to kill her, there was no doubt about that, but he needed to know first. What did he need to know? So many things, but the main one was why?

Melanie Trainor stared at the ground as he asked her the question repeatedly. Why? Yes, why, Melanie? Was it because you were ashamed of Jonno?

He wasn't exactly a young girl's dream of what she'd marry growing up. All those mornings at Sunday School, praying to a Protestant God, only to fall in love with a boy from the other side. She smiled to herself and her son watched her lips curl, wondering how she could smile this close to death. His fury grew. How could she smile when he been so unhappy all his life because of her choice? Then he glimpsed her eyes and saw that she was recalling another time.

Why, Melanie? She shook her head. It hadn't been Jonno's religion, if anything that added to the romance; love across the divide. If only he'd been a nice ordinary Catholic boy and not a terrorist, killing her colleagues as if he had some sort of right. Was that why she'd betrayed him? It would have been understandable if it were. No. Tell the truth, Melanie, it wasn't done for honour, or loyalty to a higher cause. It was done for your career. A job, a salary and a car. Respect in a small village called Northern Ireland 1983, where everyone knew everyone and you had to marry the right boy, sod how happy you were.

A job and she'd betrayed her love. A job and she'd given up her child, married a good man and made his life hell. A job and she'd lost her daughter. She stared at the young man in front of her, knowing he was going to kill her. Hating him and loving him with one breath. Answering him with her bewildered stare in a way no words could ever have done. He read the book behind her eyes and asked another thing.

"Did my father know?"

The question hung between them and she saw desperate hope cross his face. If she told him the truth he would hate her even more and her life would be at an end, but...He was her son, he had to know the truth.

"He didn't know. He doesn't even know he has a child. I framed him for Veronica Jarvis' murder to get him out of the way before my pregnancy showed."

She paused, waiting for his first blow. Or joy, his next word. A question or a tirade, she would take whatever she could get, anything to hear his voice. But there was nothing. Only a silence so heavy that she had to fight to breathe. She risked some other words and waited for him to react. The silence deepened further and she said them again as if she could somehow make him hear.

"He was the love of my life. He still is."

He stepped towards her and she closed her eyes, waiting to feel his hands around her neck, tightening and wringing until her life was gone and he'd achieved some peace. The sound of the door being locked and his steps moving away from the shed took a while to filter through. She opened her eyes slowly and stared round the empty space, realising she was out of danger for a while. But there was no relief. Her ambition had made her turn her back on everything that she'd loved thirty years before, and it had ruined both her children's lives. She closed her eyes again, trying to shut out the guilt and let the tears flow.

***

Mulvenna glared at them resentfully and Craig and Jake

stared back. But only for a second. They had a life to save.

"I'm going to get straight to the point, Mr Mulvenna. I can't be one hundred percent sure until we match the D.N.A., but I'm as sure as I can be. You have a son and he's about thirty years old."

Mulvenna stared at him incredulously and then shook his head. "You're wrong. I would have known. I wasn't promiscuous and the last woman I dated before I went to jail was in New York."

Craig gave him a sceptical look then spoke in a tone to match. "That's not true, and if you're trying to protect Melanie Trainor, then don't. We know all about your relationship. More than you do."

Mulvenna looked shocked then he laughed. "I doubt it somehow."

Craig continued unrelentingly. "She was running Declan Wasson as an informant and when he raped and killed Ronni Jarvis the powers that be decided he was too valuable to lock up. Melanie Trainor chose you instead."

He leaned forward as Jake looked on and learned. "Didn't it ever occur to you that you were a strange choice of patsy? You'd been in the States on and off since '81. You were out of the game."

Mulvenna nodded. He'd lost his appetite for killing and volunteered to go abroad. The only thing that had brought him back had been Melanie.

"I was still a wanted man. No-one was going to cry about me being sent down."

"And you just accepted it without a word, knowing how you'd be treated in prison. Were you really that tired of life? Or was it because you were protecting someone you loved?"

"If you know about me and Melanie then you already know the answer to that. She needed a patsy and I was close at hand. It was the least I could do for jeopardising her career. She'd worked too hard to throw it away on a loser like me."

"But you loved her."

Mulvenna nodded. "And I could show that by getting the hell out of her life and keeping quiet."

Craig shook his head. "Her career wasn't the only reason she wanted you off-side."

Mulvenna shot him a questioning look.

"She was pregnant with your son and she didn't want you to know. She gave him up for adoption a week after he was born."

They watched as shock and disbelief rushed across Mulvenna's face. It changed swiftly to anger and he sprang to his feet. Jake leaped up too, ready to move. Craig waved him back down and listened as Mulvenna called him a liar and a bastard until he was tired, then he slumped back in his chair and Craig saw realisation dawn. The room was silent for a moment then Craig started to speak. He quickly outlined their suspicions about Lissy's death, the sketch of the man seen talking to her on the front and the D.N.A. from the hair found in her hand. He ended with the biggest shock of all.

"He's kidnapped ACC Trainor. She was taken sometime last night. We believe he's going to kill her for having him adopted. We need your help."

Mulvenna stayed mute as competing thoughts deepened the lines on his face. Craig could almost hear them from where he sat. How could she? What is he like? He's turned out to be a killer, is that my fault? What do I care if she dies, she lied to me? And more. Craig urged him out of his thoughts.

"Her time is limited. Either she's dead or they're talking, and if they talk he may find out that you didn't know and get even angrier with his Mum. You're our one hope of stopping him."

"How can I stop him? He'll be ashamed. A mother who gave him away and a father who was a terrorist. At least if he didn't know who his father was, he could imagine a better man."

Craig brushed his self-pitying aside.

"You've served your time and you're an artist now. There's a future for you; and for him, if we can stop him now. Are you going to help us? I need to know now."

Mulvenna hesitated then nodded once and Craig headed for the door, signalling Jake to un-cuff him and bring him along. He needed a conversation with the Chief Constable then they were going on TV. He just prayed that Annette had got something useful from the Fosters or they'd be hunting nationwide.

***

The elderly woman sat in the C.C.U.'s relative's room hunched on the edge of the black leather sofa, clutching her shabby leather handbag in her hands. She was around seventy, older than Annette had thought. A glance at the adoption file told her why. Adele Foster, forty-two-years-old, wife of Nigel. Unable to have children of their own, they'd finally approached the church elders for their help. They ran a small adoption society for their congregation, supplying babies to God-fearing couples whose options were running out. Six months after joining it was 'To Adele and Nigel, a baby son' and rejoicing all around.

Annette scrutinised the woman in front of her, taking in the tired tweed coat buttoned up to the neck and her sensible shoes. She looked like she had a matching approach to life. It must have been a barrel of laughs for the kid. She tried to picture his loneliness. A solitary child making its own fun on the farm, in between chores and prayers. And beatings no doubt. She added them mentally one by one, picturing the hard-handed farmer, beating the fear of God into his son for his own good, ignoring the frisson of pleasure he got with every stroke.

He was dead now, but not soon enough to prevent the stain of fear and submission that indelibly smeared his wife's face, even after his death. She pictured her weak attempts to temper his father's ire when the boy inevitably did something wrong. He was a child and children aren't privy to the harsh standards their parents judge them by. They play and laugh until it's beaten out of them.

Annette pushed the tea tray across the table until it touched the woman's knees, rousing her from her trance. She dragged her eyes up slowly to meet Annette's, letting her glimpse a semblance of regret before she brushed it away, afraid to betray the husband who was dead. Annette read her instantly and altered her pose from one of sympathy to an interview. This woman would concede nothing about the blame she held for the tragedy unfolding miles away. She wore her guilt like a metal cilice, tightening it with every blink. She was a hostile witness now and that made her fair game.

***

Craig was driving blind, pointing the car north on the A26 towards the Atlantic coast and hoping the phone would go any minute and Annette would give them something to put in their G.P.S. Finally she called.

"The mother says Danny used to go orienteering with his school in Downhill Forest. There was a small hut there that he used to run to when he was upset."

That would have been pretty often if her instinct about his childhood was right.

"It's somewhere off the Ulster Way, sir. She doesn't know any more than that."

"Good work, Annette, get Andy to head there now and we'll meet him. And tell him he'll need Armed Response." He paused then added more quietly. "They called him Danny?"

"Yes. After Daniel in the Bible."

Craig watched Mulvenna's expression change from the shock he'd been wearing for the past half hour to a softer surprise. The son he hadn't known existed had a name. Danny. Craig was about to cut the call when Annette had another thought.

"What if he's found out about Mulvenna not knowing, sir?

He'll either have killed the ACC already and left to find him, or he'll go looking for him then head back later to finish her off."

Craig thought for a moment. She was right. He said so then pulled the car over to the verge, working out the options. Andy could lay siege to the hut with the ARU. Either Danny Foster was inside with the ACC, in which case it became a hostage negotiation and they still had time to get there with Mulvenna to try to talk him down. Or he'd already left and they'd find the ACC alone, alive or dead, leaving Mulvenna's son out hunting for his Dad. Where would he hunt him? Annette waited in silence until finally Craig spoke.

"Stake out Mulvenna's house on the Mussenden Road, Annette. You lead on that and take an ARU. They're not to shoot unless it's absolutely necessary. Get Liam for me, please."

Two seconds later, Liam's bass was echoing around the car. "Boss?"

"Liam. Andy's going to Downhill Forest to find the ACC and Annette's staking out Mulvenna's house in case the boy goes there. I'll wait here until Andy says she's alive or dead. If the boy's not there then we'll meet you at the art gallery on the Lisburn Road. The odds are it will be the second place he'll look for Mulvenna. The exhibition's been advertised all over N.I."

The line clicked off and they sat back to wait. Craig's gut told him Melanie Trainor was still alive. Not because she deserved to be, that was for sure, but because if the boy had had his father's ignorance confirmed then he had bigger fish to fry.

Chapter Thirty

Andy circled the small hut silently, motioning the black-suited armed response team to spread out and form a perimeter twenty metres back. When he was satisfied they were in place he lifted the megaphone to his mouth and gave the warning they were obliged to give. He'd always thought it was stupid; telling a perp you were there and losing the element of surprise, but rules were rules. The wood's icy quiet was broken only by the groan of the trees overhead, thrust roughly back and forth by the rising north wind.

He gave the warning again, then signalled a single officer to move stealthily towards the building's rear, working the odds that their target would watch the front. The slim figure slipped through the trees and pressed himself against the hut's wooden wall. He pointed his Heckler-Koch downwards and pressed his eyes bravely to the wooden slats, knowing that an armed assailant would shoot if he saw their whites. He peered into the darkness searching for signs of a man with a gun but only a huddled shape on the floor came into focus in the gloom.

Andy held his breath as the wind lifted, transforming the forest's groan to a high-pitched whine that still didn't drown out his thumping heart. For a few seconds nothing moved then the officer turned and raised his thumb, giving the signal it was safe to approach. The cordon shrank cautiously towards the hut until finally Andy stood by the door waiting while it was checked for a booby trap, then it was opened slowly and they counted off one by one.

"Perimeter safe, check. Armed target, no. Hostage secured,

check."

It was almost surreal and he had to smile. Play-station games had nothing on this. He strode through the door and saw the huddled figure of Melanie Trainor inside. She was lying on the hut's grubby floor, dishevelled and crying and clutching a blanket around her. He motioned the others to stay outside; she wouldn't thank them for seeing her weak. He was wrong. As he hunkered down in front of her she grasped his hand, much more like a victim than the woman they all feared so much. Her words surprised him with their desperation.

"Don't let them kill him. Please, please, they mustn't shoot him. It's my fault, I'm to blame. I'm not pressing charges. I came willingly, that's what I'll say. He's not to be harmed, please. Promise me, promise me."

She gripped Andy's hand tighter and a look of fear spread over her face. "He's gone to find Jonno. I don't know what he'll do. Find Jonno Mulvenna, protect him. Please protect him." She wrung his hand so hard that his fingers turned white. Her voice was wild. "Promise me, promise me. You have to swear you'll protect them both."

Andy stared at her in disbelief. Danny Foster had killed her daughter and kidnapped her and Mulvenna was a known terrorist, and she was begging him to save them both. He saw the look in her eyes and nodded, freeing his hand gently and walking to the door. One minute later he was connected to Craig.

"The ACC's OK. Not making much sense, but OK. She's begging us to protect the man who kidnapped her, and Jonno Mulvenna of all people. She says he's looking for him. Any idea why?"

Craig put the phone on speaker and drove the car over the central reservation into a U-turn. He accelerated down the A26 towards Belfast yelling into the dash.

"The boy's her son, Andy. Jonno Mulvenna's the father."

"What?"

"Long story. I'll fill you in later. Ask her if she has any idea where he was heading?"

There was silence for a moment as Melanie Trainor murmured in the background, then Andy answered no. Craig nodded Jake to bring him up to date and slipped through the traffic like he'd been pursuit driving all his life.

"The boss is heading for the art gallery on the Lisburn Road. We're meeting Liam there. Annette's covering Mulvenna's house on Mussenden with an ARU."

"She says they're not to shoot him, Jake. And she's still the ACC."

Craig interjected. "Tell her we'll do our best, but she's suspended, Andy. We take our orders from the Chief Constable. Give him a call and bring him up to date, please, then get her to a hospital."

He motioned Jake to cut the call. Twenty minutes later they were approaching the Lisburn Road. The ACC had said her son had left about fifty minutes before and it was at least an hour from the forest to Belfast. It had only taken them twenty minutes to retrace their steps, with any luck they'd get there first. As they neared the gallery Craig knew Melanie Trainor had got her times wrong.

Liam was standing by a patrol car parked on the other side of the road, leaning his elbow on its roof. He was muttering into a radio mike and frowning. Craig parked in Cranmore Park and approached on foot, motioning Jake and Mulvenna to stay in the car.

"What have you got, Liam?"

He gestured tiredly across the street. "Mulvenna's lad has taken a girl hostage in the gallery and he's demanding to see him. He's carrying a machine pistol. Looks like a Steyr. I've called armed response back from Mulvenna's house."

Craig squinted across the street into the low-lying winter sun. Through the glass-fronted façade of the small gallery he saw a girl he guessed was Sonya Murray, the receptionist Jake said he'd spoken to two days before. She was pressed against the front window staring wildly at them through the glass, her body rigid with fear. Leaning against the gallery's back wall, deep in the shadows, was a tall dark shape. Craig could make out a gun. Liam had been right. It was a Steyr Tactical Machine Pistol. Lethal. Danny Foster wasn't messing about. He gave Liam an update.

"The ACC's desperate for him not to be hurt, blames herself for everything."

"Aye, well, so she bloody should. The poor bastard's so fucked up he'd killed his own sister to get revenge. That's at Trainor's door."

"He killed Lissy, not the ACC, Liam. Let's not forget that. Anyway we can debate who's guilty when we've sorted this out." Craig rubbed the back of his neck, thinking. "OK. Has he made any demands?"

"Not a one. He hasn't said a dicky bird. Just pointed the gun at the girl once and made her stand at the front, that's all."

"He's telling us what he'll do. OK."

Craig slipped his Glock from its holster and placed it on the car roof, then he took off his jacket and rolled up his shirt sleeves. Liam knew what he was planning and shook his head hard.

"No bloody way, boss. I'm not letting you cross that road to get shot."

Craig turned to his friend with a wry smile. "I've no intention of getting shot, believe me, not until you pay me back for all the beers I've bought. But if I can bring him in peacefully then that's what I'm going to do. Trust me on this one."

Before Liam could answer Craig had raised his arms and walked across the narrow road, stopping at the window in front of the girl. He smiled reassuringly at her through the glass then he spoke. His voice was clear and strong, stronger than he felt.

"Danny, I'm Marc Craig. I'm not armed. I'm here to find out what you need to end this peacefully."

He was answered by complete silence. No-one in the street moved and there wasn't a sound except for the radios echoing through the cold November air. Liam signalled everyone to turn them down and stared at Craig's lean back. He had a random thought that his arms would get sore then he shook it away as Craig started talking again.

"OK, Danny. Then let me tell you what I think you want. You want to see your father, Jonno Mulvenna."

The gun barrel twitched at the back of the shop and Craig knew that he'd hit a nerve. He pushed on, risking his life on a hunch. Annette had described Adele Foster's tight-lipped coldness and abject refusal to answer questions about her husband or son. If Annette had read her lack of words and body language right, there'd been no love lost between them. One glance at the well-worn bible protruding from the woman's handbag and the large silver cross around her neck said the couple had ruled the boy by the strict word of God, Old Testament style. It was only a short step from there to beatings and abuse. Craig could hear Annette's words in his ear.

"It's only my opinion, sir. I can't be sure."

Annette's people-reading skills were better than anyone else's he knew and he prayed she was right this time. He was about to risk lives on it.

"You've had a very rough time, Danny. We know the truth of your childhood. No-one should have to suffer all that. It wasn't your fault, you were a child. Melanie Trainor isn't pressing charges for kidnap and she wants us to tell you that she was wrong. It's all her fault for giving you away." He swallowed hard then repeated what Trainor had just told Andy. "She regretted her decision and tried to get you back many times, but she was told the adoption was final." The gun twitched again but Craig pressed on. "Your father didn't know you existed until an hour ago when I told him, Danny. He didn't even know she was pregnant. He wants to meet you. I've got him here with me. In the car."

Nothing moved inside the gallery and for a moment Craig thought Foster hadn't heard then a broken, deep voice came through the glass. It sounded tortured and Craig could only imagine what the boy had been through. If Annette's instincts were anything to go by he'd been abused and beaten for years. He could hear every stroke of it in the pain of his next words.

"She didn't want me, so why should I believe that he will?"

Tears pricked at Craig's eyes as he heard years of ruined childhood in the phrase. But there was no time for sympathy. Only honesty could end this; sympathy could come later. Craig's voice softened slightly and he gazed protectively into the young girl's eyes. They were wide and green and he could see her legs trembling from where he stood. He wanted to reach through the glass and steady her but all he had were his voice and brain.

"Because he's here now, Danny, and he wants to meet you. Will you at least talk to him?"

After a minute the dark shape nodded. It was progress.

"OK. I'm going to turn round now and signal that I want him brought here, beside me. OK?"

He was answered by a grunt and he turned slowly, nodding Jake to bring Mulvenna from the car. Mulvenna took off his leather jacket mimicking Craig and walked hurriedly across the street to stand by his side. He peered through the glass and then spoke to his son for the first time in his life.

"Danny? I'm your father, John Mulvenna."

Craig watched as Mulvenna spoke coolly to the young man. Danny Foster could shoot all of them in the time it took for them to turn and run but Mulvenna didn't show a single nerve. His voice was steady as he recounted how much he'd loved Melanie Trainor but their relationship had been marred by the times they lived in.

"Try not to blame your mother, son. She was young and she made mistakes."

Harsh words cut across him and Craig saw the pistol jerk.

"She gave me away and she lied to you, for a poxy job! A job, for God's sake." His hurt was visceral. "I should have had two parents who loved me and a home, instead I got the Fosters. They beat me every day and said it was God's will. It was all her fault." Tears clogged his voice and Craig thought he see them glistening on the dark figure's cheeks. "She did this to me, and you. Her. That bitch. For a fucking job."

Mulvenna interrupted firmly, as if he'd been a father all his life, soothing his son with his tone and words. His next words shocked Craig, and then he knew it was what he had to do.

"Let me come in, son, and see you. I want to talk to you face to face. Just me, I promise."

They both heard the sobs that the words provoked. They were the sobs of a child not a man. A young boy, beaten and unloved and exhausted from struggling alone.

"I killed her, Dad. She was nice to me and I killed her."

"Lissy?"

The shape nodded and went on. "I had to make the bitch feel the pain she'd caused. I had to do something that would make her see." He sobbed so harshly that Craig could hear it tearing at his throat. "I didn't want to hurt Lissy, but I had to make her see."

"All right, son. We can talk about all of that. Now let me come in and let the girl go. Please. She's frightened and she's done you no harm."

Mulvenna glanced at Craig and he saw serenity in the new father's eyes that said this was right, then Mulvenna swung the glass door open and stepped inside. A moment later the girl stumbled out of the gallery and into Craig's arms. He signalled Jake to guide her across the street and held his position as he watched. Danny Foster and his father moved to the back of the gallery and sat on the floor against the back wall, hidden behind high canvases shielding them from view. Craig could hear them starting to talk. He walked back to Liam to stand post, ready to wait for as long as it took.

***

It was hours before Jonno Mulvenna stepped onto the street, beckoning Craig over with an order for food. He walked back into the gallery with his parcel as the day dimmed into evening and the blue lights of the squad cars flashed into high relief. It added to the prosperous road's pre-Christmas air and Craig could make out late-night shoppers beyond the cordon going about their business just like on any other day. It was bizarre, but then so was what was happening in the gallery fifty metres away.

Finally at ten o'clock the glass door re-opened and Jonno Mulvenna beckoned Craig across the street. Craig went to remove his jacket again but Mulvenna shook his head, signalling that everything was OK. When he reached the door Mulvenna beckoned him in, his glance saying it was safe. At the back of the small white gallery Danny Foster was sitting on the marbled floor, his head resting in his arms like a child. The Steyr was lying ten feet away, disabled, its magazine sitting on a chair.

"The gun's no threat. I stripped it down."

Craig stared at him, knowing that he'd done it many times before.

"Danny and I have had our first chat and he knows that we'll have a lot more." He smiled at his son and the young man shot a weak smile back. "I'm coming with him to the station and I'll not be leaving him ever again. He knows that too." He smiled at the boy again. "Don't you, son?"

Foster nodded uncertainly and Craig saw a flash of doubt in his eyes. It didn't matter. Time would prove that he had a father now, one who would never mistreat him or leave.

"He knows what he did to Lissy Trainor was very wrong and he'll have to pay for it." Mulvenna helped his son to his feet and for the first time Craig saw the two men side by side. The resemblance was astonishing.

Mulvenna grinned. "It would hard to say he wasn't mine, wouldn't it?"

The pride in his voice was so obvious that even Foster smiled. Craig pulled a pair of handcuffs from his pocket and Mulvenna nodded his son to turn round while he slipped them on. Craig lifted the gun and nodded him ahead. The siege had ended without anyone being killed.

Liam loped across the street to join them and grabbed Foster's arm, catching Craig's warning glance not to be rough. He walked Mulvenna to the car and they headed to High Street for the long night ahead.

***

Five hours later they had Danny Foster's account of Lissy Trainor's death and her mother's abduction and they left Jonno Mulvenna to talk to his son. Foster would be charged with murder even if they didn't progress Melanie Trainor's kidnapping charge. His solicitor would argue diminished responsibility due to his years of abuse. It might fly, but either way he was looking at time locked-up. The sins of his parents were being visited on him. Both sets.

Adele Foster would carry the can for child neglect and abuse, her husband far beyond their reach. Melanie Trainor would lose her job for what she'd done in 1983. She might do a stretch for framing Mulvenna, if he was prepared to complain, but her longest stretch would be a future without either of the children that she'd brought into the world. Maybe her son would forgive her, if Mulvenna had his way he probably would, but Craig wasn't holding his breath. It was a result all round, if not a happy one.

It was six a.m. by the time Craig fell into bed, teeth brushed but still fully clothed. His dreams were fitful and disturbed, with a distinctly female theme. By the time he woke up in the morning he knew what he had to do.

Chapter Thirty-One

Saturday 8 a.m.

"Annette, can I see you in my office first thing, please?"

Annette stared at the handset as if it was going to bite her, then swallowed and answered 'yes' in a subdued voice. She knew what it was about; she could hear it in Craig's tone. He wasn't stupid. He'd worked out that something was being kept from him days ago, but he hadn't known what. Only a monumental effort from all of them had managed to keep it that way.

"I'll be there, sir. Everyone's coming in to tie up loose ends. Nine o'clock?"

"Nine o'clock's fine. Good bye."

No 'see you there', no joke or laugh. She was in deep shit. Mind you, it didn't help that his relationship with Julia McNulty was taking a dive. She knew the boss loved her, but she for one wouldn't be sorry to see the back of Madam Julia. She took offence at the smallest thing. Touchy was the nice word for it, Liam had a few more.

She fixed her scarf and lifted her bag then smiled down at the sleeping dog. Life must be easy if you had loving owners who fed you and took you for walks. She was coming back as a Jack Russell next time round. She pulled the front door quietly behind her and climbed into the car, then drove to the C.C.U. as slowly as she could without actually blocking the road. Postponing the inevitable explosion at nine o'clock.

***

Craig stood in the shower letting the water run over his face, dreading the conversations he needed to have that weekend. He was almost cross-eyed with tiredness. They'd been interviewing Danny Foster until five in the morning and he'd tossed and turned for the rest of the night. He needed a difficult Saturday like a hole in the head.

He stepped out of the shower and grabbed a towel, just as his mobile rang. Lucia. She was never awake at this hour on a Saturday! There must be something wrong with his folks. He seized the phone urgently.

"Lucia, what's wrong? Is Dad OK?"

Lucia had her speech all prepared but her brother's anxious voice left her lost for words. In the seconds it took her to recover he'd said "I'm on my way" and cut the call. Lucia gave the handset a puzzled look, then pressed dial again. This time she was ready.

"Marc, there's nothing wrong with Mum and Dad. So just sit down and listen."

Craig was stunned into silence by her authoritative tone. The fact he was so tired he was almost a zombie didn't help. He listened blearily as Lucia recounted the events in her life over the last few weeks, leading him to the day she'd phoned Annette.

"What did you phone Annette for? Why not me?"

She cut him off firmly. "Because you would have over-reacted when you heard what it was about."

"What? I wouldn't have over-reacted. I never over-react!"

"Just like you're not doing now, I suppose?"

Craig blustered his way through a few protestations then shut-up. Lucia wasn't bossy often but when she was it was usually important. He sat on the bed letting the warm air dry him and listened as she told him what had happened that week, leading up to the arrest of Ross Devlin and the case being taken over by sex-crimes. When she finished he said nothing as the other events that week slotted into place.

That was why Annette had been evasive. And Davy, Nicky and Jake had been in on it as well! In fact the only people who'd known nothing had been Liam, John and him. Lucia waited in silence and held her breath, wondering when the explosion was going to come. Instead Craig laughed. It wasn't an amused laugh, more one of surprise.

"You managed to keep me completely in the dark."

"Yes. But it was for your own sake, Marc. You had a murder to solve, and..."

Craig rubbed his wet hair with a towel and stood up, starting to get dressed. "And you thought I would lose it and kill the guy."

It was a statement of fact.

"Well, wouldn't you have? And you'd have told Mum and Dad and they need that worry like a hole in the head."

He laughed again. "You're right on both counts." His voice softened. "Are you really OK, pet? Did he hurt you?"

Lucia laughed. "Not as much as I hurt him." She launched into the story of how she'd knocked Ross Devlin down with so much glee Craig almost fell sorry for the man. Almost.

"Where is he now?"

"Oh, no. I'm not telling you that. You'll go round there are start something."

His voice rose. "Bloody right I will. Tell me Lucia. I'll find out anyway."

"No. I won't. And I'm just as stubborn as you are, Marc. I'll tell Liam and he can make sure you don't do anything stupid. And don't you dare give any of your team a hard time about this. Annette wanted to tell you. She only gave in when I promised her I would move home, which I did. I've been waking up to 'Take That' all week."

She started laughing and Craig caved in, knowing that by the time he got to Liam she would have told him everything and sworn him to help. He signed off saying he'd call into the shop that afternoon and prepared to thank his team for saving him from himself. Then he dialled another number and arranged the rest of his weekend.

2.30 p.m.

Annette had got congratulations instead of the bollocking she'd been braced for, and Craig had taken them all for lunch at The James. He and Liam had disappeared for an hour after lunch and when they'd come back Craig had a face like thunder. They'd gone to see Ross Devlin and Liam had stopped him doing what he'd wanted to do; punch Devlin hard. He'd get over it when he saw him locked up.

Everyone slipped-off home for what was left of the weekend leaving Liam tidying up the loose ends on the GAA lists. The idea that Mulvenna had had a relative in the force had been a long shot at best, and it had been wrong. It didn't matter. They had their killer and John's forensics would match the spores from Lissy's body to Downhill Forest, sewing things up tight. By the way Craig closed his office door Liam knew he had other problems in his life.

Craig lifted the business card from his pocket and turned it over in his hand, reading the name to himself. Dr Katy Stevens: Endocrinologist. St Mary's Healthcare Trust. The Trust's number was on the front and her mobile was scribbled on the back. He stared at it for a minute then opened his top drawer and placed it inside. He couldn't be her friend and he'd be lying to them both if he said he could. Perhaps he'd call her someday, but not yet.

He swivelled his chair towards the window and gazed out at the dark November sky. A cruise ship was weighing anchor in Belfast Harbour, ready to head across the Irish Sea to other climes. He thought of the North Atlantic Ocean with its wild waves and cold white foam, washing over Lissy Turner. It was a lonely image. Her death had served no-one. Then he thought of Lucia and smiled, remembering her account of how hard she'd hit Devlin. She hadn't hit him hard enough in his opinion. He'd be out in a few years to do the same again to someone. But not his sister.

He was about to leave when Liam knocked hard on the door.

"Come in."

Liam thumped into the room and grabbed a chair.

"Hell of a week, eh?"

Craig smiled. "You wouldn't want it every week, that's for sure." He glanced at his watch. "You should go home, Liam."

"I will, just as soon as you tell me you're not heading back to High Street to deck Ross Devlin."

Craig laughed ruefully. "I think Jack would stop me if I tried."

"I don't. I think he'd close the door behind you and turn off the lights. Swear that you won't, boss."

Craig hesitated for a moment then thought of his promise to visit Lucia at the shop, and nodded. "I swear I won't go near Devlin, although I can't promise not to cheer at his trial."

Liam sniffed, satisfied, and rested his hands on his paunch. "That'll do for me." He glanced at the clock. "Any plans for the rest of the day?"

"I said I'd call in to see Lucia, then I'm heading up to Limavady, seeing as Annette managed to get us off the rota for the weekend."

Liam stared at him wisely, knowing it wouldn't be a happy trip. Craig could see him searching for some words of wisdom and waited to hear what came out.

"When a relationship's right it isn't this hard, boss."

He stood up and nodded goodbye then closed the door behind him, leaving Craig thinking about the truth of his words.

THE END

Fantastic Books
Great Authors

Meet our authors and discover our exciting range:

- Gripping Thrillers
- Cosy Mysteries
- Romantic Chick-Lit
- Fascinating Historicals
- Exciting Fantasy
- Young Adult and Children's Adventures

Visit us at:
www.crookedcatbooks.com

Join us on facebook:
www.facebook.com/crookedcatpublishing

CPSIA information can be obtained at www.ICGtesting.com
Printed in the USA
BVOW05s1242080714

358479BV00001B/10/P